IT
WAS
CALLED
A HOME

IT
WAS
CALLED
A HOME

A Novel

Brian Nisun

atmosphere press

For

Mom, Dad, and Kev

"You go from dream to dream inside me. You have passage to my last shabby corner, and there, among the debris, you've found life."

— Thomas Pynchon, *Gravity's Rainbow*

1

The cold air, the dank staleness of the cellar, gunpowder, the victim's blood, rich in iron, the intruder's blood, spilled ceremonially of his own accord, the disturbing difference between the two, and petrol leaking through the cracks above, drip by drip by drip...how it all blended together to create an aromatic stench straight from hell. He splashed the canned petrol around like a kid playing in the deluge brought on by a busted fire hydrant on a hot summer day. There was a rhythm to his move-ments, a dance, no mistake about it...how unsettlingly carefree his feet were and how they carried him to and fro from one corner of a room that used to be a sanctuary of life and safety to the other with a burning intention to destroy it all. Wonder where Mikhail Bakunin would find the silver lining in this mess. He laughed all the while. It was a sick laugh, a poisoned laugh, yet it carried a childlike element that was so full of life...like he had it all figured out.

"Please," Karl Müller had said softly, only moments earlier, with dire mercy and a desperate want to rise from his knees that burned agonizingly with pain, to hold Ruth—his wife, love of his life—tightly and keep her safe. Her fearful sobs stabbed violent jolts of agony into his heart that were far worse than the physical torment his knees endured. "Let us—"

And like a flash of lightning, Private Jenson Reynolds—who appeared to be gazing off into nothingness, lost not only in his own maddening and scattered thoughts but also within the stable webbings of a spider's home in the corner, where ceiling meets wall, transfixed by the black beauty toiling away at a fly, understanding loneliness—had turned his attention back to Mr. Müller, pistol in hand, pointed between the old man's eyes, and, before he could get another syllable out, pulled the trigger.

Ruth Müller screamed in terror, her love's warm blood painted across her face. Jenson turned to Ruth and stopped her screaming with a bullet to match. Sergeant Zachariah Noah, the professional, had his gun pointed at Jenson, who once again moved with impossible speed, like a blur, and shot Sgt. Noah through the heart. The ever-pious man of honor clutched his chest as if that would help or save him somehow, then fell to one knee, then flat onto the old wooden floor, his eyes, still open, peering through a crack between two panels, gazing directly down into the cellar. This was the last image his waking consciousness would see and he only had time to process what it made him feel: disappointed, the grand old bitch itself, as if he failed his last mission by not being the one who killed them.

Jenson tossed the can of petrol aside: it hit the wall with a forceful *thud* and smashed directly into the framed artwork that hung proudly on the wall—*Called a Home* by Dr. Kyo Koike—and brought the picture to the soaking floor with a melancholy crash and a small, invisible shower of glass that touched no light. Pvt. Jenson Reynolds lit a match and admired how it immediately began to eat away at everything the flame came in contact with as soon as it came to life, ready to consume all, its only mission...all too human.

Flames burning a juxtaposed, holy white crawled along the

memories embedded in the house—all the laughs that reverberated off of the walls, all the tears that had, like the petrol that quickly burned, soaked up into the floor, every single *ich liebe dich* that hung in the air and in the spaces in between, how instantaneously they can be taken away, as if they could only exist in the material aspect of it all until you find them again within—and began to cover the bodies of Sgt. Zachariah Noah and Karl and Ruth Müller like a blanket. Their blood still flowed from the bullet holes as their flesh began to melt off their bones. Staff Sergeant Booker ("Book") LeDu would've likely reported this, what he would call a "crime," to their Major by now, not that it mattered to old Jenson much: his mission was done...he didn't know who was in charge anymore or which voice gave the order first, but it was all in agreement, and his new mission was to leave this place and go home, to a place that was not only on a map but in his blood and fully a part of who he is, a place he was never supposed to leave, a place that time altogether forgot about, something foreign...what lucky ones call home, like no place there is.

The road would be long and cold, which he was used to. Walking, one foot in front of the other one, the entire way. There wasn't much to pack; he knew what he needed: his gun and his copy of Shakespeare's tragedies that were more like a bible to him, something to make him feel more at home when he was away, whenever he had time to read. The others in the 422nd Military Police Brigade always poked fun at him for reading what they called "plays" and "poems" and for how he, as they put it, "pretended like he was a part of it." Corporal Indiana Pope once asked Jenson what it was like living in the past, Jenson responded by asking what it was like living in the future, which confused Cpl. Pope so he forced himself to ask the question again, like maybe he wanted a certain answer from Jenson, as if he had a good joke all lined up in his head, but Jenson responded, emotionally and candidly, with: "It's...horrible. Each day I get further and further from tomorrow, where there's hope, and closer and closer to yesterday, where the pain is still real and exists."

To no one's surprise, none who may or may not have been listening—which none likely were: cards, books, and a tall bottle, the cousin of death, all felt like better options to them rather than listen to that Cat talk that crazy shit—did not attempt to find reasons in the words that hung eerily too long in the air like a foreboding ghost waiting for something new to haunt.

2

During those brief moments of horrific injustice, SSG Booker LuDu stood about ten feet behind Jenson and held his pistol, but did not point it, just gripped it tightly, frozen with anxiety. Nothing moved save for his own lungs that he felt barely worked at all, as if trying to hide himself in plain sight with ghostly silence or attempting to hold onto those last few precious breaths that one takes for granted.

"Fuck," Book whispered, voice a little shaky, almost inaudible, his body completely numb with shock, only a stabbing feeling in the bottoms of his feet like they had fallen asleep.

Jenson snapped around as if he had just remembered his Staff Sergeant was still there. Book put one hand up slowly as the other made a slow move to holster the pistol. A genuine smile of wonder and bewilderment slid across Jenson's face like butter across burnt toast.

"You were always a good man, Book."

"Didn't have to be like this."

"Why do you think spiders are always alone?"

"W-what do you mean?"

"When they're born there are hundreds of them, right?

Hundreds of little babies. Look at this one," Jenson looked back at the spiderweb in the corner, pointed to it, approached it, "alone in its web. You never see two making a web together. It used to make me wonder why they choose to go their separate ways. I think I understand now."

"Listen," Book said carefully. "Jenson, man, we can fix this."

"Fix what? You're implying something is...broken? No. Go, Book. I'll let you. I've to burn the house, the children are hiding somewhere, I can't spend all day here, I have to get home soon. I'll let you go before I'm no longer me."

"What're you talking about?"

"You're my commanding officer so I can't tell you what to do, I can only suggest that you leave. Now."

"W-what?" Book didn't even know what he was questioning anymore.

"Run!" Jenson said in a voice that was not entirely his.

And as told, Book fled. He wasn't embarrassed or ashamed. Didn't care that he didn't do anything to stop the horror that Jenson—who was low on the proverbial 422nd Military Police Brigade totem pole—had created. Didn't care that he just gave him an order, that he let him live. Didn't even think about the kids. Forgot all about the cellar information. That they might've been down there, according to the late Sgt. Noah. He attempted to create a reality where they were never really there. The hope was, in creating this reality, that if he were to think of them one day, that's where his mind would land: it would settle onto a place of peace, far from guilt or regret. He would train himself to never question the improbable achievement of this Zen-like state of mind, for he was already fully aware of this awareness that has become so real that there was nothing left to do but to live and let be.

Meanwhile, the place they had called a home began to cave in completely just as they navigated through the smoke that had sunk to the cellar and lingered there like a ghost that is always around to haunt you but this ghost finds its way into your throat and wants to reside in your lungs. So by the time Laura ("Bambi") Müller and her younger brother Joseph escaped the cellar, tried to breathe in fresh air, and were forced to first hack up as much of that ghost as they could before their lungs worked properly again, Cade Nyström arrived, frantic and filled with worry. He ran to Bambi, who was still on her hands and knees, and knelt beside her. Her face was stained with tears and Cade could tell that they were not tears from hacking up a lung, but tears of an intense and undesirable heartbreak the likes of which he did not know existed until he saw her face and his heart broke for her but not with the level of pain she endured. He looked to Joseph, who had been scream-crying the whole time, then to the house. The smoke and flames crawled towards the clear blue sky and with them traveled the souls of Karl and Ruth Müller.

There was nothing that could be done except to get the children away from the heat of death. Cade helped them up, guided them to his truck—as a doctor would with a patient after a traumatic event that had left them in shock and slightly smoke-blind—away from the place they called home, the place that was once full of life and love and cherished memories and was now all but reduced to ash and pain that they would carry with them forever. The slight image of the man called Jenson Reyolds permanently burned into Bambi's mind's eye as well as his voice, what they each heard clearly, that would become something like a second voice in both of their consciousnesses and play on a loop, that laugh especially...so twisted and maniacal, like nails slowly scraping across a chalkboard.

By the time Cade had stopped the truck snow had begun to fall from stone grey clouds that formed or moved in from out of nowhere—one minute it was clear blue skies and sunshine, the next it was bleak, wet snow from an ominous and somber ocean that hung from above. No one had spoken a word. What was there to say that could even attempt to make a sliver of light of the situation?

Neither Bambi nor Joseph questioned why they were taken to Pete's Last Stool, as they didn't even realize where they were, as if both had blacked out during the ride. They shared the same thoughts, like their consciousnesses were not separate at all but were one and the same, a collective consciousness, which focused on a dark, brooding void of unnatural violent motivation.

Unbeknownst to them, another car was on its way to meet them at Pete's, and passed but did not see—the driver's mind was focused on the people in the car with him, his children, and those they were on their way to see—SSG LeDu, whose pair of panicked, stomping boots marched him frantically up the dirt road to the only Tuscan villa in the state of Washington. Last night's snow still clung to bits of the earth like it was not yet ready to let go and welcomed the newly falling snow. Book saw that the front door was open. They rightfully left in a hurry, he figured. He ran in with a fool's hope that the scene he just left would be the worst of it. The air was rich with blood and he felt like he had just run in a complete circle that he couldn't escape. He called out a simple "Hello?" and was surprised, at first, to hear his own voice and jumped a little, but there was no answer. He moved as quietly as he could. He was not sure what he expected to find or what he was expected to do when he found something, which was:

The Poletti Family dinner table, littered with open bottles of wine and half-eaten food—cold lamb racks and prosciutto along with an incredible variety of cheeses and jams and a few pickled items as well, such as mushrooms and onions. In one chair, with his head on the table, Private First Class Jeremiah Castle drunkenly passed out and across from him, also passed out with his head back and nose pointed to the ceiling, Captain Alan MacPhail, snoring softly and drooling disgustingly. But what shocked Book the most was Major George Wynne, with an empty bottle of Merlot tightly gripped by the neck in his hand, an unconsciously dangerous way to hold a drink, facedown on the ground in a puddle of blood and piss with his left leg snapped in half, bloody, white bone clearly visible through his flesh and uniform. Book puked instantly on the floor—watery vomit with bits of half-digested oatmeal—and sprinted out of the house, hopped in the military jeep, and drove the hell out of there, back to the 422nd Military Police Brigade barracks, where he began to frantically pack his shit. The only one still there was Pvt. Roland Joyce, who insubordinately questioned what the fuck his commander was doing. Book never liked the racist prick—all racists fuck off—and didn't feel the need to say anything to him, after all the shit he just saw, so he clocked him in his windpipe, a shot that set him on his ass and left him gasping for air. Just as Book was about to turn the key, ready to leave this life behind, Sgt. Westley Underhill pulled up with Cpl. Indiana Pope, Pvt. Clarke Hume, and Pvt. Lamar ("Red") Atwater, who all piled out of the vehicle as soon as the tires slowed down. Book didn't get out of his jeep. Sgt. Underhill walked over to him while Pvt. Hume stood scared stiff with his gun ready and Cpl. Pope kicked rocks before realizing Pvt. Red Atwater had run for the barracks and running to join.

"S'goin' on, Book? We saw smoke coming from the German's place and by the time we left the Swede's and got there, it was toast. Everyone was gone. Hell, thought you might've been in there."

"Nah, man," Book whispered, hands gripping the wheel tighter...he wouldn't consider Sgt. Underhill a friend, but he always did right by him, and for that he respected the Cat and told him everything as fast as he could, knowing Westley would not understand all of it right away and would need a few minutes to think about it, and then would likely go and clean up the Major directly after. Book, though, did not need more death on his mind today. He said his farewell and drove away, onward to a new life that he would be proud to call a home, that would be filled forever with peace—but had to slam on the breaks before he could begin that journey as he saw what could be none other than two ghosts walk into a bar, and felt utterly compelled to follow them in.

3

Pete's Last Stool was known locally as the farmer's dive bar in the agricultural area of Walla Walla, where any and all who worked in the industry were welcome. There were, of course, the unspoken rules on who was allowed in on certain days (harvesters, farmhands, and production teams on Tuesdays and Wednesdays, winemakers and owners on Mondays, Thursdays, and Fridays, all welcome on Saturdays, and closed on Sundays [in regards to the separation of winemakers and their crew: it was not by choice of either listed party, but instead declared and enforced by the owner, Peter Phoebe, as he possessed the radical philosophy that, if campaigned correctly, would generate local and long-term international buzz that winemakers were to be perceived as some sort of elusive and exclusive artists, like he had personal and private hopes that he would be welcomed into their inner circle instead of just watching from afar]). Though it was considered a "dive" bar—a title given by the regular citizens of Walla Walla, for they were on the outside unable to even look in, so they created imaginary tales about how awful the place must be on the inside, how dark and small and cramped, with sticky floors, horrible and burnt or undercooked food, slow service, watered-down mixed drinks (mixed drinks in general were hardly ever made, but when ordered, strong as hell), yet still they went back to their habits of buying the wine that the artists inside Pete's Last Stool made for them, essentially paying for them to have a good time in there—it was the furthest thing from that. It was small, yet spacious and comfortable. The walls were lined with fine art, original pieces that museums across the planet would pay abnormal amounts of money to display—original prints from members of the Seattle Camera Club, Dr. Kyo Koike's *Along White River*, *Autumn Mist* and *Flowers of Frost*, Frank Asakichi Kunishige's *Butterfly*, *Despair*, *The Reflection,* and many of his *Untitled* pieces...history covered nearly every inch of the walls, Renaissance pieces that were all but forgotten from artists whose names were overshadowed throughout time. Everyone who came in had a personal favorite.

Victoria VanVleet, owner and head winemaker of V. Vintners, sat alone at the end of the bar, jotting down her thoughts quickly in her thick notebook whilst sipping on a glass of Conner Family Winery Merlot as she did almost every Thursday morning, though the beverage was often likely to change based upon what she wanted for breakfast, today being wagyu flank steak, cooked medium-rare, sprinkled with orange zest, wild grilled leek placed atop peppered egg whites. It wasn't even ten o'clock.

Victoria had begun this ambitious weekly breakfast tradition three months ago out of broken-heartedness and exhaustion from lamenting at the same four walls of her bedroom when she became sole owner and winemaker of V. Vintners. Before that, as the assistant winemaker and feeling— and assuming that others felt it too—that she was only in that position and even allowed into Pete's Last Stool because her parents, the late Violet and Vlade VanVleet, were the owners of V. Vintners—Vlade the head winemaker who studied and worked five harvests in Southern Rhône, Châteauneuf-du-

Pape, and the rest of his life before Walla Walla in his homeland of Stellenbosch (they actually grew, in Walla Walla, two different types of Syrah: five acres from Rhône [two acres from the North and three from the South] and five acres from their old home in S.A.) before moving to Walla Walla with his six-year-old daughter, where he met and fell in love with Violet O'Shea—first generation American from an Irish father and a French-Canadian mother who settled in the Pacific Northwest to get away from the madness on the east coast, to find peace out there, to buy into that American Lie—and together, after marriage, they started a winery that would be the first in the state to offer free, on-site tastings in their facility, it was a mixed feeling in the wine world, this tasting room, and they all watched closely to see how it would do and if they all would have to follow suit. V. Vintners were the first to plant Syrah in Walla Walla, joining the few other wineries nearby as breaking grounds for planting the varietals they loved from foreign, faraway lands, of course grafting the old European vines onto phylloxera (*Daktulosphaira vitifoliae*) resistant American rootstock. Their Syrah and Viognier were already the stuff of legend, having only been in operation since 1937, and their Grenache, Syrah, Mourvèdre (GSM) blend was blowing people away as the American palette hadn't been exposed to this wonderful juice. What a time to be alive in Walla Walla. Until...

It was a week after her thirty-first birthday when she received the news that her parents had been brutally murdered while on holiday in Yakima. It was more of a business trip, as her father was always thinking of ways to improve their business. They inquired about the soil there and were seriously considering buying a plot of land to plant new vineyards to see how Walla Walla Valley and Yakima Valley wines would compare throughout the years when, on their last night there, intruders broke into their motel room and stabbed them twenty-two times each, leaving one bullet each between the eyes, both bodies sodomized after the fact. No one had ever seen a scene like it before—unprovoked, unnecessary carnage. How Victoria survived the guilt of being alive was, to her, a miracle. She focused fully on the business her parents had started, which, surprisingly, took her mind off of them. Though anytime she looked in a mirror, a flood of emotional memories washed over her like a tsunami; her strawberry blonde hair that her mother gave her and her emerald eyes that matched her father's. The things that make us who we are, individuals, pieced together by those who created us, never really leave us.

As she took turns chewing and sipping and writing and adjusting her large, wire-framed glasses—the likes of which, to some people, looked like a design from the future—she would occasionally look around at the artwork, mainly her favorite piece, on the wall to the right: *Landscape in Moonlight* by Ma Yuan, a delicate scroll, ink and light colors on silk, so delicate (how exactly did Pete get this stuff?), the ancient work depicting a man toasting to the moon, surrounded by rocks and trees and earth. Nature always stuck with her, made her feel as though she understood something deeper, as if it was all connected, that people should thank the moon more often. As she surveyed the painting, a man she had never seen before, and certainly never in Pete's Last Stool as everyone knew everyone, sat down next to her—which really pissed her off as every seat at the bar was free. She kept her eyes on her notebook and pretended not to notice him, though she could feel his eyes, and pictured them in her mind's eye: small and beady, dark and lifeless, looking over her shoulder, observing what she was writing.

"I'll've a pint, Sam," the stranger said to the bartender, Joe, without looking at him. "If you've some of that Nyström stuff, that is?"

Joe, without batting an eye, poured the midnight-colored brew and placed it in front of the stranger.

The entire exchange made Victoria uncomfortable. The fact that Joe, usually a man with too much to say, was eerily quiet was off-putting. The stranger pulled out a cigarette and lit it, which pissed her off even more. She thought about moving to another seat at the bar, given that she refused to sit at a table alone, but the thought quickly went away as pride trumped all. If anyone should move, she told herself, it ought to be this fucker.

"Care for one?" the stranger suddenly asked.

It caught her off guard and she froze for only a second, but played it cool, never looked up. "No thanks," she said. "I don't smoke."

"Don't even know what it is though?"

"I've seen a cigarette before."

"How about a Marijuana cigarette?"

"Still not interested, thanks," she said, still refusing to look at the stranger.

"Why's that?"

"Don't need it."

"Really?"

Fuck it. She finally looked up, filled with a boiling annoyance. He had a face that masked his age—he could've been her age or thirty years older. His eyes were small, beady, dark, and lifeless like she imagined. His jaw was sharp and looked like it was probably made of glass, he had a thick silver mustache, no eyebrows, and atop his head sat an outdated top hat with no signs of hair poking from beneath. The only expression on his face was that of genuine puzzlement.

"I'm fine, really."

"Not interested in opening," he tapped the middle of his forehead, the spot where the bullets had passed through her parents' craniums, where the third eye rests, "the Ajna?"

"I don't know what you're talking about."

"Oh?"

"Now if you don't mind..."

"More for me then, eh?" He sparked the joint with a nickel-plated Zippo lighter.

She couldn't help herself. "Why do you do that?"

"Sorry? Do what?"

"The way you talk."

He stared at her blankly.

"Meaning, it sounds like you question everything."

"Why wouldn't I question everything? You don't?"

The direct, matter-of-fact way he sharply yet kindly delivered this statement took her aback. Like it was second nature to simply question everything, never fully believing in one thing or the other, always searching and fully pursuing his own truth.

"I—"

"Should start?"

Blessed be who walked in next, and who else but Emilia Poletti, another local winemaker, and Victoria VanVleet's best friend? She walked over like the true angel she was to unknowingly save her friend from this uncomfortable encounter. She stood there with a glowing smile on her face and waited for the man—whom she, too, had never seen before—to move. He felt her presence, a zealous aura, the likes of which he had never seen before, and turned to look at her.

"Sorry," he said with a strange, warm sadness that flowed passionately from those five letters, as part of him knew and accepted that he would be sorry for the rest of his life, the other part questioning why it was his job to be sorry for everything anyway. He placed an ox-blood-colored card next to Victoria. "In case you change your mind?" He took his beer and went down to the other end of the bar.

Emilia sat down and ordered a glass of Müller Estate Riesling, Pete's Last Stool being about the only place in the state—the world, actually—where you can order a glass of the stuff. Karl Müller provided a few cases every now and then of both the Riesling and Blaufränkisch, something everyone at

Pete's Last Stool was thankful for—other than being *at* the Müller Estate. Neither of them acknowledged the card.

"How goes it?" Emilia asked, as warm as her smile, still carrying her homeland of Tuscany in her accent.

"It goes," Victoria responded. "Surprised to see you here today."

"Oh," Emilia said, not as warm this time, like she was putting on an act for her friend in order not to worry her. "I like our breakfast routines."

"You haven't ordered food yet."

"I will."

"What're you feeling today?"

"Well, to go with the Riesling, this vintage is one of their driest, point-two residual sugar, I believe? So maybe the ruddy duck, a wedge of lemon, lathered in bacon grease—"

"No, I mean, what are you *feeling*? Like, inside. States and your homeland are at war now. Officially."

"Oh. Right. That..."

"Everything okay at home?"

"The kids don't really understand it, the bombing, I mean...we haven't had time to talk about actually being at war now...don't really know how to...and this new order? From FDR? Michelangelo and I, and our parents, we're all...frightened."

"Understandably so. If you need anything, whatever it may be, I'm always here for you."

"Means the world, Vic, really. Thank you. I think I'll have that duck, Joe, whenever you get a moment."

Ruggles Thibodeaux, winemaker for The Peoples Winery, and 'Flip Peoples, owner of The Peoples Winery, walked into Pete's Last Stool and sat down at a table, carrying a recognizable weight of melancholy with them that was quite out of character for both men. Ruggles, of New York origin, with parents native to Bordeaux, had moved to Walla Walla when he was twenty after Prohibition had ended. He had considered a move to his parents' homeland, which they had visited frequently throughout his life, but, with the state of the world and all—still feeling the scars from WWI and bearing fresh new wounds—he thought better of it. His father, Marco, had suggested Walla Walla, as he heard from Ruggles' cousin, Jérôme d'Holbach, that he was currently on his way there with his father to start a winery of their own, as the climate was ideal for Bordeaux and Rhône varietals. Jérôme's father, Armand, wrote to them before they departed, saying that his wife, Noèle, had passed away from a horrible flu that claimed her in three days. She had caught it the day she finished packing. They departed for New York on a ship four days later and planned to fly to Washington with hopes of seeing family before then. Marco and Méline (Ruggles' mother) thought this was a perfect opportunity for Ruggles, who always expressed interest in going overseas—whether to France or Italy or even across the planet to New Zealand or Australia—to work harvest and pursue a career in winemaking. They waited a month with no word, no unannounced pop-in. They figured, ultimately, that Armand and Jérôme found a flight to Washington and couldn't afford to delay, and were still getting set up there, busy as bees. So Ruggles took off, alone, to meet them. And he would never forget the proud look of genuine happiness in his parents' eyes as he hugged them and departed. It wouldn't be the last time they would see each other, as they would, over time, visit him in Walla Walla, the first time not being until 1936, three years after he left. Though, when he arrived initially—electing to hitchhike all the way there to see the country's true face without the disease-ridden mask of people—he did not find his family at all. The property they were planning to buy was soon to be bought by a Mr. Phillip Peoples. Ruggles wrote to his parents, praying they had heard something. Two days later, he received a letter back (he still doesn't understand how it traveled so fast) with the dreadful news that his uncle and cousin had died aboard the ship from the same deadly flu that took his aunt. The d'Holbach line was erased in a mere eight days. God decided to work overtime. The deadly, never-before-seen flu on a mad killing spree, about half the passengers on the ship died as well and were not allowed to dock for four months, quarantined on the water with little supplies ferried over by brave souls who would throw them over the railings. And there Ruggles was, not knowing a soul in this growing state, with more people with the same ideas as him and his family arriving every day to take advantage of the newly-growing industry—French people, German people, Italians, Hungarians, Spaniards, hell, even Swedes. Fuck it, he decided. He asked Mr. Phillip Peoples for work the day he bought sixty acres of the land after sleeping on the streets for five days. Phillip Peoples, known as 'Flip, looked upon this sad man, who clearly hadn't been sleeping or eating well, nor bathing...how he could own so much land, while all this lad owned was his soul and whatever he crammed into his bag? And so, 'Flip decided to take a chance on him after Ruggles told a little white lie that he studied winemaking in Bordeaux, mainly on the right bank in Saint-Émilion and a bit in Pomerol (he'd visited many estates there and tried their divine wine, but never had the opportunity to study there). 'Flip, a man who enjoyed wine (mainly getting fucked up on it, not quite having the palette to distinguish great wine from okay wine), believed every word of it. By the time of the first harvest at The Peoples Winery in '38, they focused only on three wines at the time, Cabernet Sauvignon, Merlot, and an oaked Chardonnay, which were, to Ruggles' palette, all shit, but 'Flip found them to be fantastic and knew they were on the right track to being one of the best producers in the state. Ruggles slowly improved his craft over time, learning on the job through trial and error and reading ancient texts on the philosophy of winemaking, mainly from the French. It also helped that 'Flip had what he called "fuck you money," meaning anytime Ruggles suggested or asked for new equipment he would usually get it. The two became close friends despite being separated by sixteen years in age, Ruggles twenty-nine at the time and 'Flip a cool forty-five. 'Flip, the lovable, clueless bastard, never knew what to think of Ruggles as—a son? He was seven years older than his only daughter, Sara, whom Ruggles had been fucking occasionally without 'Flip knowing. It was nothing serious, something he didn't see going anywhere as he could never bring himself to love her the way she wanted or deserved. He'd also fucked 'Flip's wife, Amanda Peoples, once, whilst both intoxicated off the '39 blend of Merlot and Cabernet Sauv. Sara and 'Flip never found out—it was just some shit Ruggles lived with and he tried to find ways to forget and forgive himself, like drinking or mediating, classic remedies, like this all was a big deal. Perhaps 'Flip thought of him as a brother? A friend? Or, simply, an employee? In his own way, he sort of combined them all into one.

The faces of The Peoples Winery sat down at a table. 'Flip's chair squeaked as if in pain when he sat; he'd packed on a good deal of weight since he started the winery—drinking for free will do that to you—and had also gone bald, though was in complete denial of that. Ruggles, on the other hand, had gotten back into the shape he was before he left New York, back when he was a fly-half for the local rugby club and former all-state pitcher for his high school baseball team. The two looked like they normally would never speak to each other—'Flip was a well-respected man and successful business owner as his winery was producing solid blends and single verticals. Though, if you didn't know him, he looked like a sad sack of bones who spent most nights alone, begging whores to take his money—and even they would be reluctant—and might even bother you from afar as he had trouble controlling the sound of his voice: always seemed to be shouting though never out of anger. Meanwhile, Ruggles, a newly-respected winemaker who had found his path thanks to 'Flip, looked like a flannel-wearing meathead who may or may not have known how to read and may or may not have slept on the streets.

Don't judge a book by its cover. Fuck that. Don't judge people.

They didn't acknowledge or even notice Emilia or Victoria sitting in front of them at the bar, though they were friends in the industry whom they were quite fond of. Ruggles himself was madly in love with Victoria but felt like a fucking fool, every day, for fucking other women when his heart had belonged to her from the moment he met her in 1934 when he had taken a tour with 'Flip of V. Vintners' property and saw her bottling some Syrah. His heart had pert-near jumped out of his damn chest. They were close friends now, though he never made a move, fearful of rejection, a fool...left her wondering why she was still waiting for him.

Victoria had watched them walk in with a smile on her face—as she did every time Ruggles walked in the room. That was the kind of effect he had on people; he just lit things up. She, of course, didn't know about him and Sara, nor Mrs. Peoples, secrets Ruggles was trying to bury and break off completely so he could follow his heart for the second time in his life. Victoria's smile faded, however, when she saw the somber look upon their faces. 'Flip called for a bottle of the V. Vintners GSM, still not realizing the owner and winemaker sat just seven feet away. Joe brought the bottle over, popped it for them, and splashed 'Flip, who found it acceptable. Ruggles and 'Flip clinked glasses and poured a splash onto the floor, honoring those who weren't there to appreciate it with them.

"Appreciate the support, boys," Victoria said as she raised a glass to them.

"Oh," Ruggles said, surprised to finally see her. "Hey, Vic." He raised his glass. "Cheers."

"Emilia?" 'Flip practically yelled in his usual manner of speaking.

"Cheers, 'Flip," she said warmly after swallowing the first

bite of her duck.

"But we thought you were—"

"When did you get here?" Ruggles quickly asked.

"Twenty minutes ago. Why?"

Ruggles and 'Flip looked at each other then took their wine, Ruggles grabbing the bottle, and moved to the bar, 'Flip to the left of Emilia and Ruggles to the right of Victoria, his heart fluttering a bit but sinking when he looked at Emilia. "There was...some—"

"Trucks!" 'Flip interrupted, spittle flying across the bar (the other three were too polite to say anything or show their disgust). "Army trucks!"

"What are you talking about?" Emilia quickly responded.

"At your house! And at the Müller's!"

"Nyström's, too," Ruggles said, then took a sip like the wine would make the intolerable feeling of dread magically melt away.

As if by natural reflex or some powerful gravitational pull, Victoria placed her hand on top of Ruggles' and looked deeply into his eyes, a muddled forest green that tried to hide fear from her from the world.

"Why were they there?" she asked, knowing the answer but hoping it wasn't true.

"I'm not sure..." Ruggles said, not having the heart to say it then. He took another sip, longer this time, not taking the time to appreciate the nose.

"We're at war now!" 'Flip hollered, his face turning red. "They likely think that immigrants are enemies of the state! That damned Order! Can't believe I voted for that bigot!"

"Well, that's just—" Emilia's voice cracked like a shattered vase, "—simply not true..."

"Of course not! Simply ridiculous!"

"I must go—" Emilia went to get up, but Victoria held her back, lightly, with little restraint.

"No, Em," said Victoria, her voice on the precipice of

cracking, filled with fear not only for the safety of her dear friend's family but for all the immigrant families across this broken country who would now surely experience the same thing if they happened to be born on what America deemed the wrong plot of land. "It would be safer, for you, here."

"That is my family! My children are there! What is happening? Why are they there?" Emilia was hysterical, tears running down her face.

"They could just be asking questions! We mustn't assume the worst!"

Victoria placed her left hand on Emilia's back, her right still locked on Ruggles. "It will be okay. Everything—"

"You don't know that!" Emilia cried.

"Emilia," Ruggles began softly, "Just breathe for a minute, don't let your mind run wild. How about this: finish your meal, our wine, and we'll all go over there together. Okay?"

Victoria looked at him and seriously wondered if that was a good idea or if he was out of his fucking mind. Ruggles, as if reading her thoughts, simply shrugged, and then thought what an inappropriate time it was to want to kiss Victoria VanVleet for the first time.

"Okay..." Emilia finally said.

"Gah!" 'Flip said, throwing a slug of wine down his throat. "Americans are so hostile and fearful! And for what reason? We're all products of immigrants! Every single one of us! Ruggles! You're French! Just happened to be raised here! When did you move?"

"Came to America when I was six."

"Six! Victoria! You're a product of South Africa, correct?"

"Yeah, came to this country when I was six as well, actually."

"I didn't know that," said Ruggles, falling deeper and deeper in love at the worst possible time.

"Plenty of time to get to know each other better later! And our dear Emilia Poletti! Straight from one of the most beautiful countries on god's planet! Italy! The rolling hills of Tuscany! Yet all her beautiful children were born here! Just as American as I am! Why, I can't help but wonder *why* these damned fools care so deeply about flags and words on a map! Saying you're only good if you came from here, here or there! It makes no sense! Borders?! They're *invisible lines* that are drawn in the dirt! Whose idea was it, I wonder! To separate humanity! To keep the human species apart instead of bringing them together! Force hatred upon us instead of teaching us how to love thy neighbor!"

"Business," Victoria suggested.

"A terrible business it is! This world! I imagine that once, it may have been perfect!"

4

Bambi, Joseph, and Cade could hear the lively, boisterous, or—as he would have you say—lovingly enthusiastic roar of the voice that belonged, of course, to 'Flip Peoples before they walked in. Once inside, there was the matter of the "Are you two okay?" fiasco, which they did not bother to answer and likely did not even hear. It was all static to them, dead radio. They were followed by Michelangelo Poletti with his and Emilia's children—Noemi, Teodoro, Vito, and Ciro—who all ran instantly to their mother and embraced her with a group hug, followed lastly by Cade Nyström and his parents, Edith and Mathias. They all sat together at a table in Pete's Last Stool like one big broken family, the only ones there aside from Joe the bartender. It was, for one reason or another, the safest place any of them could think of.

Bambi Müller and her brother Joseph sat silently with tired, blank expressions pasted upon their faces, listening to those around them drunkenly rabble like some nervous mob that was too anxious and distraught and shocked to properly conduct themselves in an orderly fashion and instead attempted to speak all at once, which accomplished nothing, and their silence allowed them to carry on as they did not realize that they held the power to settle them all down if only they just spoke. They sat wordlessly, with that shared thought gnawing away at them, and wondered when all of it would end.

A fast, cool breeze blew forcefully through them and collectively chilled their bones, like Zephyr had unleashed some warning upon the mortal world, like some ghosts who had come to comfort them but forgot that their touch was cursed forever to chill the recipient and that they had lost the warmth they once had and would forever pine for. The chill, which silenced the rabble in an ominous way—where'd that come from, anyway?—made Bambi think of a time when she was eight, fifteen years ago, when her parents, still very much alive then, of course, had taken her and Joseph on a holiday to the coast of Oregon. They had spent a day at the beach, close to the spot where the Siuslaw River ended and the Pacific Ocean began, a point she stared at back then for hours and was certain existed, was right there after all, and held just below the surface a warm light that she was not yet ready for, but was unaware of the fact that each time she came to this place in her memory, as she did now, she mistakenly picked a new spot in the water where the river met the ocean, where the light was—though she wasn't to blame, as in the water one spot is never really the same again. The chill set deep in her bones and she allowed her thoughts to fully eat away at her mind in a metaphysic and cannibalistic sort of way: *This can't be fucking happening...is this happening?* with a dash of *Was any of it even fucking real?* and seasoned with *Am I going fucking crazy?* While Joseph's thoughts shared the same intensity, this was the first shift in a change from collective thoughts back to a single one, which admittingly was not that different and was not a question but a statement, like he was in the early stage of a dramatic shift toward a thought process that determines who you are as a human being, where he unconsciously and forcibly began to carve a mazelike blueprint that, at the center, told him: *I am fucking crazy.*

The silence lingered over the group long enough that they were able to see the light in the idea of one speaker at a time. 'Flip Peoples stood up but was politely and silently reasoned to sit back down by Ruggles Thibodeaux, who whispered something to him, maybe that he had something he wanted to say, but in the end, knew it was for the best to have a softer voice even if 'Flip's thunderous voice did carry with it the weight of living and with it years of experience. It was best to handle what came next with words that were to be delivered remorsefully and delicately. Ruggles, began, of course, with his sincere condolences but could not look their way and see for himself the pain that radiated from them and became their aura, and vowed that not only those there but the entire city of Walla Walla and the state of Washington, even, would bring those responsible to justice and have them answer the call of punishment for their unspeakable crimes, to which 'Flip Peoples was unable to contain himself and bellowed out:

"Yes! We must trust the government now! They will do right by us! They will help!"

An anger-fuel spark lit inside of Bambi and Joseph.

"'The government?'" Bambi asked bitterly.

"Of course!"

"The man who killed our parents worked for the government."

"I—"

"His name is Private Jenson Renyolds. We heard someone say it. I heard his voice...and I...I saw...him, his filthy smile...he—"

"Laura—" Cade started, gently, in a counseling way.

"Did you know that the Vernons are dead? Did *anyone* here know?"

"What?" Ruggles Thibodeaux gasped in shock. "How? When?"

"They were murdered months ago," Michelangelo Poletti

said after a few moments when it was clear Bambi did not want to speak of death. "The men who came to our homes questioned us in connection with the murders."

"What the hell? Why?"

"They seemed to think," Michelangelo tried his best to explain, "that one of us did it for their land."

"That's preposterous!" 'Flip Peoples screamed. "I know that no one here would harm a fly! Let alone kill Ward and Macy!"

"Convenient that they found out about now," Victoria noted.

"None of it sits right with me," Ruggles muttered.

"Who can we go to?" Edith Nyström cried in concern. "What can we do?"

The rabble resumed—everyone suddenly found a bright idea on how to fix their fractured world and shouted their two cents and then some, even though they really did not realize what needed fixing and that, in reality, it could never properly be fixed unless some ancient secret was unearthed that showed how to mend a broken—or shattered—heart while also changing the entire mental dynamic of a xenophobic society.

Victoria VanVleet, who had been jotting down notes in her notebook during the rabble, stood up after Ruggles was able to regain the quiet by repeatedly tapping a knife against an empty wine bottle.

"First," she began, "we need to focus on what is most important, and that is helping Laura and Joseph. We can start by setting up a fund in their name, we will take and expect donations from all here and in the Walla Walla wine and agricultural community. Ward and Macy Vernon were quiet folks who kept to themselves and it's a shame that they've gone this long without a proper burial, so we shall see to that. Karl and Ruth Müller...well, I'm sure everyone here will say just about the same—they were outstanding human beings filled with kindness." A real sadness filled her voice as she remembered her own parents, and how she had something more in common with the Müller's now. "I'm tremendously sorry for your loss. If anyone has anything they'd like to say—" She quickly slumped back into her chair, Ruggles grabbing her hand and holding it tight.

During the speech, Bambi and Joseph could only think how no amount of money or condolences would ever truly make anything right ever again. There would always be that feeling of genuine despair. Money can't bring dead people back to life. Prayers can't, either. Yet there they sat—silently, like they forgot how to speak and were forced to listen to everyone tell them how sorry they were and how they promised to donate to help them and how they would pray for their parents' souls, as their brains suddenly did not want to block this bullshit out for them. No, it wanted to retain it all, as is human nature. None of it made any sense. They were trapped in a very real nightmare that they could not wake up from and they were only at the start.

Cade Nyström felt, for some reason, that it was his turn to stand and say something, though without a clue what that something was as it all sounded the same at this point and Bambi and Joseph were probably tired of hearing it. He had even less of an idea as to what else he could do, why he should feel any pressure at all to make a sliver of this situation somewhat better—but when he looked at Bambi and saw that torment radiating painfully off of her being, all he wanted was to cut himself open and pull his own heart out, to give it to her, to say, "Here, take mine, it belongs to you anyways." It was foolish, impossible, and some words he did not register began to crawl their way out of his throat and, just as he began he was silenced along with the rest of them, that absolute quiet interrupted by the sudden and unmistakable cry of the door slowly creaking open.

5

Who should walk in but SSG Booker LeDu, who had every eye glued to him and realized, almost instantly, that he had half a mind to turn the fuck around. But something made him take a step forward, an action that caused Joseph to let out a shriek that would be appropriately suited to that of a poltergeist if they still had voices to speak.

"Be cool..." Book attempted to reason.

"What—" Bambi spat, "—are you doing here?"

"Be cool. I come in peace."

Joseph was still screaming.

"'Peace?'" Michaelangelo questioned. "You? You're monsters!"

"Ain't me. Cool him," Book said, which was hard for him to get out.

Joseph stopped screaming then, his voice nearly raw. He began quietly sobbing for a few minutes, then stared at Book with a burning hate that did not seem natural to him at all but was a feeling he did not fight but let grow on him. He looked like he could throw up at any second.

"You want to find the Cat responsible for..." Book struggled to say.

"Say it," Bambi said.

"For...hell..."

"Say what you have to say," she said coldy.

"The guy who did it—"

"Private Jenson Reynolds."

"—y-yeah...him. I'm sorry, really, I am...I should've done something. It happened so fast..."

"Save it," Bambi said. "Please."

"He's from a place in Wyoming. A small place, I guess, that time forgot about, he'd say, at least."

"Why does his home matter to us?"

"He said something about going home soon."

Book explained to them what Jenson had told him, what Bambi and Joseph hadn't heard earlier as they dealt with the shock and trauma of witnessing their parent's murder.

"Ten Sleep?" Cade said when Book finished. "Where the hell is that?"

"If you want it bad enough, you'll find it."

"Who else?" Joseph asked, his first words in God knew how long.

"Whatchu mean?" Book shot back.

"Who was in charge? Who gave the order?"

"Major Wynne?"

"Where can we find him?"

"He didn't have anything to do with it."

"Bullshit," Michaelangelo spat. "He was at our house, drinking our means of income."

"He didn't order anyone to kill anyone, is what I mean."

"He ordered for you all to break into our homes, though," Emilia noted. "Right?"

"We were tasked to conduct investigations into the murders of Mr. and Mrs. Vernon."

"They haven't been seen for months!" 'Flip Peoples said, anxious to get his voice back into the mix. "Why did it take so long?!"

"It is convenient," Bambi said, "that you found those bodies right when your president gave that order. Like you needed the excuse?"

"Look," Book pleaded. "I had nothing to do with that shit, I'm just trying to help, if I can."

"You had a chance to help."

"I...I know."

Ruggles Thibodeaux stood up. "I think it's best if you take this opportunity to leave."

"I'm sorry."

"Now."

Book turned to leave. There was a justified fear that came with turning his back on a group of angry white folks. It was only a few steps to the door but it felt like miles.

"What was his first name?" a voice asked, causing him to freeze. "Major Wynne's?"

"George," Book told them without turning around. He wasn't sure who asked, hadn't been there long enough to match the voices to the faces, but it was a man's. He knew if he turned around he'd just see those sad, blank, and hateful glares that would stab into him once again, and all he wanted to do was be on the road. "Last I saw him he was passed out at that villa...with his leg snapped in half. If he ain't there anymore then he's likely somewhere where the grapes grow well."

"Why wouldn't he still be there?" someone asked.

"Some people are still loyal to this bullshit." He wasn't sure why he said it, but it just came out. He waited another half a breath before he left them for good.

There was a heavy silence that lingered, that no one was anxious to be the first to lift, yet none of them wanted to dwell in it any longer than necessary. Each one, at some point, tried to see what someone else was doing but their eyes would quickly drop when they saw someone look their way while they were looking their way, and it went on and on and on around the table until:

"So, who's going to get this guy?" Ruggles asked, breaking the silence like glass towers that suicide onto stone, falling from heights unimaginable.

"He must be brought to justice!" 'Flip hollered.

"Government won't do shit," Joseph lamented, his head down.

"Reckon Cade and I should go," Ruggles suggested. "Bring him back if we can or put him down."

"What're we?" Cade asked. "Cowboys?"

"After today it sure as fuck does feel like the wild west."

"What gives you the right?" Joseph questioned.

"Huh?"

"You had no part in this."

"We're the logical ones to send, you know this."

"It worries me," Edith Nyström confessed.

"It's a far ways," Mathias agreed. "The trip alone would be dangerous, let alone the animal you'd be hunting..."

"No," Bambi said. "I'll go."

"Don't be ridiculous," Cade objected.

"Don't you insult me. I am capable of more than any of you think and I will see this done myself if I have to."

"Laura—"

"He took *everything* from me."

"I'm going with you," Joseph said, a backbone finally in his voice.

"You're serious," Ruggles realized aloud.

"It'll be the four of us then," Cade said.

"No," Bambi told the room. "It will just be the two of us. Me and my brother."

"Laura," Victoria VanVleet started cautiously, but her words were lost as rabble consumed the table:

"Don't be foolish," Emilia Poletti said,

"You'll need protection," Ruggles Thibodeaux interjected,

"We're here to help," Cade Nyström promised,

"Get you and your brother some sense," Edith Nyström said with concern, and:

"We're all in this together!" 'Flip Peoples assured them all.

"No!" Joseph yelled to quiet them all.

"This is," Bambi started, "something Joseph and I must do alone. We're the ones who lost the most. This is our war."

"You don't have to fight it alone," Cade said to her like they were alone there together.

"This time we do."

"When did you two figure that?" Ruggles asked.

"When we watched our parents die in front of our eyes," she explained.

That settled that. They packed what little they had into their late father's truck. Emilia and Michaneglo lent them two horses, just in case, that would spend the first part of the journey in a cage on wheels—also lent to them—which Michelangelo attached to the truck bed.

The goodbyes were quick and somewhat awkward: Joseph stood with his chin touching his chest, eyes on the ground while everyone wished them luck, and Cade snuck a kiss on Bambi's cheek which didn't make her smile then but would later as it did mean something: a memory she could reflect on when the night was at its darkest and she felt most alone, her fingers would lightly touch her cheek where his lips had gently rested and would instantly feel that warmness he meant to deliver and it would flow through and it would help a bit, but it would never save her. None of them had the energy anymore to stop them, knowing they wouldn't listen. None of it seemed real. Their minds would drift to other matters to which they would be forced to attend after they faded from their view. It wasn't their fault—they were only human. At the Poletti household (where Major Wynne and Co. were nowhere to be found), they had a deep cleaning to attend to, hoping that the blood hadn't soaked in too deep, and Victoria and Ruggles would watch the Müller crops, a way to preserve their legacy, while everyone would help salvage what they could from the ashes for whenever—if ever—they came back.

6

Five months earlier, near the end of September, it was harvest season, in the year of their lord 1941, when the air was still caked hotly throughout the vineyard—breathing it in was difficult, like it wanted to choke in throats—and hung lazily, unmoving, being, as it were, a nauseating annoyance that caused not only a dull headache but uncomfortable sweating on the small of the back, the armpits, and the brow only thirty minutes after the traditional morning wash-up. It was still three hours before noon. Karl Müller's calloused hand ran through his damp hair. His hard yet weary eyes gazed out at the crops (strained, actually, as his vision was getting poorer and poorer with each passing day) —they'd been coming along well. The days were unbearably hot, though in the coming months it would all change, the air bound to turn crisp as October neared, bringing with it the time of year most families in Walla Walla were most excited for: The Peak. Peak harvest season, when, in utopian years, ripeness reigned and the grapes, juicy and swollen, practically begged to be taken off the vines. Yet still, that morning, a silent prayer was offered up for the biblical drought to continue for just a few more days. Everything performs better after struggling for a bit.

There were eight rows of grapes and, off to the right side, making do with the limited space they owned, a small garden that grew beets, carrots, cucumbers, onions, potatoes, and tomatoes, all mostly tended to by Ruth. They secretly hoped that their nearest neighbors, the ever-pious Vernons—an older couple who lived quietly a mile away and whose religious devotion forbade them from utilizing their ideal soil and farming conditions to capitalize on the growing wine industry—would die off or, more humanely, sell them a small bit of land or fucking move, so they could grow apple trees. Karl noticed that one of the three rows of Blaufränkisch was infected with grey mold, a loss of around twenty vines. He spat and watched as his own DNA cut through the warm summer air and fell fatly onto the dry soil, only to be drunk up as quickly as it fell, for the earth was thirsty, more so than ever.

Bumblebees buzzed to and fro, knowing vinifera grapevines were self-pollinating, electing to collect the small sugars off his livelihood. For once, he didn't mind the tiny thieves. Still, he kindly brushed his hand and shooed them away, as if acting on human instinct.

With the help of his cane, he slowly hobbled across his small farm. He always felt that he was too young to be using a cane at a healthy—aside from the knee—forty-six. For the longest time, he had put off the idea of using a cane for support, thinking it would be belittling, embarrassing, and would make him look older than he was (which it did). But what was really belittling and embarrassing was having his love, sweet and tender Ruth, help him off the floor because he had fallen over, his leg having given out under the weight. This had happened more than once. He had shattered his left leg completely in The First Great War, tearing every ligament in the knee along with it. By some miracle, the doctors who had operated on him were able to save the leg. They were all surprised as it had gone nearly two days just wrapped up with gauze and held in place by two pieces of wet plywood. The smell of the rot that had started to set in the day he was finally taken off the front line and given over to the doctors was something that would always stick with him—a phantom scent that would haunt him until his final days, filling the air with that foul stench when there was nothing else around. The odor was so strong; it was really the only thing he could remember as passed in and out of consciousness due to shock. Even in that unconscious dark, the stench followed him. A sickening rot that he knew wanted to devour every cell in his body. The doctors had warned him that he should get his leg looked at every six months (or was it every three months?) just in case, which he did not. Thankfully, no infections found their way back to him. But now, the years of hard labor had physically worn it down. Bone had begun to run against bone. The ligaments—what was left of them—had strained thin, held loosely together by scar tissue that couldn't form fast enough given the state of things, ready to snap. He needed to take the weight off of it. So last Christmas his son, Joseph, had given him a hand-carved wooden cane. It had taken the lad all summer and right up till the day before Christmas Eve to perfect it. The wood was of a silver maple tree; they grew in abundance in and around the city, so Joseph figured the city could sacrifice one for the benefit of his father's health. He had painted it black and at the top of the round handle had carved a message:

Für bessere Straßen zu folgen.
For better roads to follow.

It was written in both their native tongue and English as he found this land's language, oddly enough, to be one of the prettiest he had ever heard. Go figure. Now and then, Karl would find himself rubbing the letters with his thumb, the seamless transition from smooth wood to the slight indentation of the lettering, admiring the detail that his own blood put into it. How often did he do that?

Growing beautifully near the Blaufränkisch was his second (and most precious) crop: five rows of Riesling. At the time, he was the only grower of the varietal in all of Washington. He picked one ripe grape off its vine and plopped it into his mouth, the juice exploding as soon as his teeth broke through its soft skin. A near-perfect ripeness—beautiful acidity. Another week and they would be ready for harvest...he felt tired just thinking about it. None of the Riesling vines, he noticed, had taken on an Edelfäule—that noble rot—yet, completely ruling out any possibility of a late harvest or, even rarer, that elusive dream: an ice wine, this vintage. He turned and slowly limped his way back to the house.

There were twenty-one wineries including the Müller Estate (the name that other nearby vintners dubbed their "winery," which was the smallest, but one of the most respected), none of which had any great success as of yet and many posing themselves seriously for the future, for their children's children to inherit. Of the twenty-one, only seven were established pre-Prohibition. The rest were founded during Prohibition, including the Müllers' who had settled in '22 and planted their first vines in secret, of course. The neighboring Polettis were quite ambitious, growing not only Cabernet Sauvignon and Merlot but also Sangiovese and Pinot Grigio, all brought from Italy. Their ambition, everyone knew, would pay off beautifully soon enough. They only sold bottles of their Cabernet, Merlot, and P.G., as their Sangiovese was still adjusting to the new climate. Karl thought he heard, down at Pete's Last Stool, that Michelangelo Poletti was planning on making a trip back to the old country once the world settled down a bit, and bring back the finest vines he could get. Many were anxious and curious as to what he wanted to bring back, what he desired to grow—Nero d'Avola? Dolcetto? Nebbiolo? How bloody long would they have to wait, anyway? It takes *how long* for vines to grow? Oy vey. Hey, settle down. There'll still be drinking to do. We're all in this together.

The limited amount of wine that the Müllers made was stored away in their underground cellar (most of the Riesling as it can age for ages) or consumed at the family dinner table. A few bottles were given away to neighbors and friends and other winemakers (and Pete's) if they could spare them. Their first few harvests during the mid to late '20s were trial and error, frustrating and disappointing. Now they were getting it right. A drop of their wine was never sold for profit; it was— not necessarily by choice—never their intention of making a serious business venture out of it.

Karl wanted to think of himself as an honest man, a follower of the law, a man his family could be proud of, which is why it pained him from time to time when he would look at his crop, usually with a feeling of pleasant enjoyment, and out of nowhere the sickening, dark thought of the very real moment of inception which would lead to the only lie he and Ruth ever told their children, the lie they had to tell, for the truth was that the vines were stolen. How could they raise their children to be honest and good if they looked at them as thieves? It was the only crime they ever committed—though he still thought of war as an outrageous and immoral crime that he should never be forgiven for, but told himself that he understood, sadly, why it was a necessity—and from time to time they would still find ways to justify the crime committed so long ago. He sometimes looked at how the vines stood rooted in the dry soil, trunks twisted and gnarled, leaves fully green, and thought how they never made a single cent off of them, how all the risk was not worth the reward, financially speaking—though the reward was in just doing it, making people happy, Ruth would remind him of that, because it's hard looking on the bright side sometimes—and these thoughts had only been birthed within the past decade as they learned that living in America was all about having money, not necessarily making art, though that, of course, was the general population of the failed state they'd learned to love and call home, for in their community art reigned higher than that of material wealth. Who gives a fuck how much money you have if you have no one around to love? They found themselves, sometimes, struggling silently, with the confounding pressure of anxiety likely stemming from a mix of utter guilt and humiliation at the realization that they ever could have stooped so low, and fear for one day having their label (still yet to be made; every Müller Estate bottle had one of the children's handprint on it, white paint, nothing else) recognized by the party they stolen from, the *real* labels they dreamt about together, talked about over empty bottles, drunk between just the two of them, for hours into the night that silently bled into the red rising sun—but that was back when they were young and felt as though they could go through with it. Because of this, he'd been dreaming of his cousin Hermann Fux—the lonely bastard they had stolen the vines from. They were shocked to find Blaufränkisch then, only five rows, as it seemed such a rare delicacy at the time, the general drinking population erring on the side of clean, crisp, and acidic or lush, soft, and sweet white wines. They took two whole vines of it, and two from the Riesling as well, and would later successfully clone them. Hermann Fux's estate was old: a stone fortification made originally to house the servants of Hadmar I of Kuenring, which sat right beneath the Burgruine itself, but now housed Hermann Fux, and to preserve the Riesling, Blaufränkisch, and Grüner Veltliner that he so proudly grew, thanks largely in part to a young Lenz Moser's incredible vine training system, Hochkultur, to elevate the grapes from often-forgotten varietals to a truly sought-after one. Karl had only been there once before, with his parents, when he was five or so, at the turn of the century in 1900. His father, Jakob, took him and his mother, Oda, one sunny summer afternoon to visit family that, at that time, young Karl did not know existed. It was a near-perfect day: cool, fresh winds blew in from the sky-blue waters of the Danube, dancing through all the children's hair before going off to dance throughout the night with the clusters that grew so boldly on the ideal slopes, the canes swaying ever so slightly, as far as the wiring from the canopy would allow, which was never much. He didn't remember a great deal from being there, aside from running through the endless rows of century-old vines—his first real encounter with wine—with Hermann, and, of course, the fight between Jakob and Oda's older brother, Urs Fux. The fight was tattooed in his memory, as it was the first time in his life he ever saw his father physically and emotionally upset and that it was all his father could talk about on the drive home, arms shaking with frustration as he white-knuckled the steering wheel. The argument was about the new bill that Admiral von Tirpitz had proposed, which the Reichstag passed easily, that would double the German Navy's fleet over the next twenty years. Urs loudly and passionately boasted that it was a brilliant move for the Empire, as it would make them the second-strongest naval power on the planet. Jakob—with what Urs thought was ignorance, melancholy, bleak remorse, and longing to inject compassion, physically, into another—disagreed entirely, reasons being, in his mind, that the bill would only cause more tension between the Empire and the Kingdom in the battle for supreme, untied power. That was the base of what Karl could remember; what insults were likely said were lost in the milky twilight of young consciousness, words he was not yet ready to hear. The one thing he always remembered is how long it took them to get to Dürnstein, Niederösterreich; both times, as child and adult, the four-wheeled journey seemed to last a lifetime—the only thing which he truly, fondly remembered not minding at all. The sunset looked like an oil painting over the clear, calm river, making you wonder if Albert Bierstadt ever visited this place, and if not, where the hell are all those secret paradises trying to compete with this one, then?

Karl had dreamt of that night twice over the last seven days: when they walked among Hermann Fux's rows of vines, a sting of melancholy filling him as the wind did its ancient dance with the fruit, this time the air lacking that of laughter, of love, of warmth as the cold started to set in like it knew what was happening that night, the only light that of the ancient stars and the ever-ageless moon...they were easily able to steal and store the vines as Hermann was not home that night. When his mind was at a halt, it often found its way to Hermann and wondered if the dear old gallant cousin was alive or not, and where was he that night? Off burning books, most likely. Karl wondered if he ever noticed or cared—Hermann never tended to the vines himself anymore, but paid a crew of immigrants (Swiss, Czech, Italians, and a few who preferred not to pledge allegiance to any flag) to cultivate the vineyard—what they stole, and if so, did he know it was his dear cousin, Karl, his father's sister's son?

Another catalyst, he knew, for all this mental fatigue, was because the time was coming soon to abandon the fears that forbade them from capitalizing on the industry. Soon they would have to sell their wine, to abandon the forced, original philosophy of never becoming a business, and to take the risk, for they would not be able to survive—or worse, be able to afford their land in a few years—even if the children began working. It would not be enough. Ruth was a family photographer at a studio in the city and Karl was a teller at the bank, and it was still not enough, especially when their passions led them to their backyard (though, for Ruth, she was deeply passionate and fond of her career). It was something to be even more proud of, though: to spend all those hours away from your dreams and still be superb, phenomenal. It was understandable, then, why some people found it insulting and pompous when they would go to the market looking for a fabled bottle of the Müller Estate kind only to be disappointed when they found out the truth; that what they sought was a delicacy they would never have the chance to taste, save for in the memories of those who live in the rumors that were passed around like the last cigarette: everybody wanting a bit more: some filled to the brim with a mass of jealousy, demanding precise details of the elixir (whether it be to fact-check them [not that many outside the wine community ever got to try any, anyway] or to try and memorize every precise detail about the wine so they might be viewed as, in certain circles, a representation of rarity and interest, like the very beverage they put on a pedestal, was never really found out): What was the acidy like? Goes great with fish? Oh, Belgian endive, you say? Mouthfeel, mind you, is an important and sometimes unnoticed category that I, frankly, appreciate over anything; tell me, does it rival that of the '32? My cousin, who's had it, says it's the best Riesling in the world. Now, how do you pronounce that red they make again?

7

Ward and Macy Vernon sat at their dinner table, posed like they were *At Eternity's Gate*—lifting their tired skulls only to drink their twin amaretto and orange juice cocktails, the pulp swirling around their warm glasses, sticking in between their teeth with every sip. The juice itself was bought fresh two days ago when they last braved the outside world and had been hand-squeezed in front of their eyes, not that either of them cared or even knew that the precious fruit had traveled all the way from the tropics of Florida just to give them their dose of vitamin C, to be their chaser—the manic depressives just needed some juice.

Unbeknownst to them, both silently wished that they had done more with their lives so they could have at least afforded an icebox to chill their drinks. Room temperature beverages were something they had become used to but never truly enjoyed. Such is life. Still, they sat and sipped away and stared anxiously at the revolver that sat in the middle of the table. Fully loaded.

"When," Ward said, clearing his throat, "do you think we lost ourselves?"

"I'm not sure," Macy said truthfully.

"It worries me, sometimes."

"I know."

"Sleep has been hard to find lately."

"Yes, it has been."

They looked into each other's eyes, dry of tears from depression so hungry that it ate away at the brain's ability to remember how to cry. Ward's hand trembled madly, like he lost all control, and as he brought his glass to his lips he spilled some of the drink on his white shirt and their old wooden table, which drunk it up fully—thank you very much—as soon as it splashed, drying quickly and warping again like the twisted memories of the lives they had grown to loathe.

"I don't think I ever truly knew who I was," he admitted. "I'm but a stranger to myself."

"We were so lost in the lives we thought were appropriate to live that we forgot what it meant to be alive."

"We didn't even know how to pretend to live those lives."

"No."

"Bit late now."

"Yes. I'm sorry we couldn't find happiness here, in this life."

"There's no blame. It's as you said: we were lost."

Outside the sun was beginning to set; the last of the dying light slipped through their thin curtains and stretched across the table—a skinny ray of warmth that barely covered the revolver like a spare blanket, just enough to be appreciated. It shimmered there for half a second, maybe more, casting a different light entirely, a once-nonexistent thing that was being birthed and dying all within the same moment before their eyes.

Ward looked down and saw a grainy black line across the top of his left foot. Grainy—no—the line was moving. A line of ants marched over him, following orders, blacker than that unknown eternal midnight that the Vernons pined for. He looked to see where they were coming from: the kitchen.

Where, then, were they going? He turned his head to the right, following the small army's trail down the hall, where they were hardly visible anymore, blending in with the shadows, to a destination unknown but that could be only one of three places: the bathroom, the guest room (never once used), or their bedroom.

"What is it, Ward?"

He ran a hand through his thin black hair then scratched his peppered beard. He looked at her, with that still-fiery red hair that now carried a few streaks of silver and those pale blue eyes that held eons of hidden sadness, and she at him, with his chestnut browns that she loved once, long ago, and that wished to go blind after seeing a lifetime's worth of horrors. Both looked a decade and a half older than their fifty years, tired and worn thin with melancholy. They never understood why that was (nor was it something they ever questioned—it was like a cloud that hung over them, blotting out the sun, which was something they thought they recognized, youth, but perhaps didn't trust their memory enough to pursue it with care), for they never did anything strenuous or labor-intensive enough to cause such grotesque and rapid aging—not only of the flesh and bones but of the mind and soul, too.

"Nothing, dear," he said. "Nothing at all."

Wood exploded, caused by an almost tectonic forceful kick, sending fragments of the door flying across the room. Initially, the sound jolted Ward and Macy, and caused Macy to turn in her chair to see the front door—the weak barrier between them and the outside world—was no longer there. Two dark figures entered, both gripping something tightly in their right hands. Macy rose out of her chair, not as fast as she would have liked, and then remembered to grab the gun on the table. Words that she would never speak were caught in her throat and remained there. The first man raised his right arm, revealing a gun firmly gripped in his hand, and fired a single shot. The bullet traveled straight through Macy's forehead, out the back, then through the window behind her, which, surprisingly, did not shatter completely. She managed to raise her arm and fire one shot just as the bullet connected with her skull and her consciousness painlessly faded into the unknown, her arm falling like a rag doll's and her aim diverting from the direction of the intruders to that of her husband. The bullet that was saved for his brain struck his left shoulder and stayed there. He screamed out in pain and terror. The pain was hot and intensely palpable. Their blood stained the walls. Macy's lifeless body slumped back into her chair, head lolled to the left, blood flowing to pool onto the floor, deep black with bits of pink and grey matter floating around like sinking ships and to which a few ants lost their lives, swallowed completely and drowned alone in this giant's DNA, in what to them must have been a horrific crimson tsunami, which caused an insanely major catastrophic inconvenience. Ward stared at his dead wife and for one strange moment thought: *Well, this is what we wanted, right?*

Picture, if you can, a statue or sculpture that suddenly projectile vomits, like an explosive spray of water rushing free from a hose. That what Ward looked like when he—still as a stone sculpture—puked all over the table. It was the kind of vomit that was both runny and chunky, with bits of his still-digesting dinner (a small steak, a little too well done, and mashed red potatoes with watery gravy) and drink all mixed to create a disgusting display of rejected human waste that, somehow, lacked a sense of living color and was just a sort of forgettable grey. This time, the wood refused to soak it up. Their drinks stood idle on the table like lonely towers longing to be closer to one another and he saw, as the very last ray of light retreated into darkness, condensation on the glasses. It was the strangest thing in the world to him: glasses sweating at room temperature...what've they got to worry about?

The two men were on him. The one with the gun pulled

him from the chair as if he were a child. The other man wielded a large knife, which he used to cut up the length of Ward's boring clothes. Before he could blink a single eye, the man with the knife had begun to dissect his insides like he was some sort of lab experiment.

They hardly made any sound, one exchange of fast words in a language unknown to him—and horrible to his ears, like someone chewing sloppily right next to one ear, and in the other ear, piercing, knife-like squeals—and then silence aside from their heavy breathing, which sounded like neanderthal-like grunts. They were both quick, disgusting animals. He looked into both eyes. A mistake. Dark and filled with rage and hate, and yet they carried an eerie calmness as if they knew no harm would ever come to them. Their pale skin was reminiscent of a corpse's, à la Macy Vernon. Their greasy, dark hair fell long, brushed his lips, snaked into his mouth, onto the tip of his tongue. They must have been twins. Ghostly, silent twins.

He didn't know how long it lasted, what organs they ripped out of him, or which one slit his throat—he was just glad that it was over, that they would be left alone. They ransacked the house and he listened for as long as he still lived as they searched through his and Macy's possessions, knowing they wouldn't find anything of great value. The blood that spilled out of him was warm. A euphoric surge of realization that nearly took all the physical pain away rushed through him: all the regrets, the mistakes, the pain, the sadness, the loss, the heartbreak—it would all be gone. It would be over. They'd be together again.

Any second now.

8

No one knows how to save the world, or who's responsible for doing so, or how one would even go about doing a job so impossible...Where do you start? With people? Yourself? The environment? The government? We'll never be able to collectively agree. There really is no answer. A butterfly flaps its wings on the coast of the Tyrrhenian Sea and a hurricane decimates Florida. A person sneezes in Japan and a tornado rips through Kansas. A family refuses to sell a pig and the good old U.S. of A. allegedly finds a way to enter the fray. You can't stop the inevitable.

Emilia Poletti was the winemaker at Poletti Cellars, a master in viticulture and chemistry, while her husband, Michelangelo, was a renowned farmer. Both were known and respected statewide for their brilliant, natural, organic wines. They stayed true to their Tuscan roots but had that Washington touch the Americans could get behind. It always astounded people when they first heard the story of the Polettis; how Emilia was the first successful woman winemaker in the country; how it didn't hurt their sales at all, but rather *increased* them—tremendously.

Since they married at eighteen in Walla Walla, they began

farming and making wine, at first just for family consumption, for their parents (Giuseppe and Gisella Poletti, and Alfonso and Agnese Rossini, who had been close friends and neighbors in Tuscany and planned to wed Emilia and Michelangelo once they came of age, though there was never a reason to "plan" it at all, for the two were in love with each other from when they first met, their first dialogue with each other being around the age of four or five, before they were ever introduced to the concept of true love, a silent voice in the back of their consciousnesses speaking the idea into existence, down the road trying to remember the day when they each knew they would recall the same moment and how instantaneous it was, like they shared the same soul, made from the same stardust, were always meant to be, inevitable), who moved them to Washington in 1920 to buy into that "American Dream" they had heard so much about. They chose Walla Walla specifically because they heard through the grapevine that the soil and climate were similar to that from back home. It wasn't entirely true, but they made do.

As a wedding present, their parents collectively constructed a villa for them (completed in 1921, when the winemaking officially began—their parents lived less than a mile away, next door to each other in small, humble homes), only asking in return for grandchildren they could all spoil— and wine, of course. Whispered rumors began to circle the town, the one that started it unclear, but every time they came back around, those quiet words of wonder, not necessarily ill-fated but with a hint of jealousy, the story grew and morphed into something grander, when in actuality it began with a simple question: Where did that money come from? You'd never get the same answer twice, like you could somehow come to learn from someone who learned from their consciously aware cousin who overheard some winemakers who should not be named that the Rossinis were the ones with deep pockets and were part of something called—foreign to the viticulturists of Walla Walla—the Gambino Crime Family. Be that as it may, it was never proven nor denied nor asked directly. Everyone came to love the families and the wine, yet the rumors never really died.

They didn't sell a single bottle until 1934 after Prohibition had ended and, being one of the first to take advantage of the new market, they saw unimaginable success right away. It was never about profits so much as it was about sharing their art with those who wanted to enjoy it—it seemed to be an unspoken philosophy throughout Walla Walla that passionate artists who gave a fuck about their craft were all more than willing to support one another.

In 1923, in their third year of marriage, Emilia and Michelangelo welcomed their first child, Noemi, who would one day become the first openly gay woman on the moon. Two years later, their second arrived—Teodoro, two clubbed feet and all. Two years later they had their third, Vito—blind as a bat and to eventually use a sort of hybrid-echolocation call to get around when alone and independent. Two years later their fourth one, Ciro—whose vocal cords were overdeveloped, and allowed him to speak his first words at four months and hold full conversations at six months—arrived. And that was enough of that. Even all the grandparents agreed. So by 1929, they had a happy family, were secretly making wine, and had an income from what Michelangelo farmed and sold (tomatoes, avocados, and cucumbers along with a few sheep and goats [and one special pig] that helped fertilize the soil, produced milk and cheese, and won local prizes in town during the Livestock Festival where animals were shown off and judged and where the Poletti's pig, Soave, earned first place three years in a row ['37, '38, '39], a Walla Walla record that still stands).

There was a curious case at the Livestock Festival when old Soave completed his three-peat, an encounter that would rather not be remembered by any of the Polettis, a memory suppressed deep within their subconscious, perhaps too disturbing for them to relive regularly. The Poletti's had just taken a family photo with Soave—a bright gold medal hung snug around the hog's girthy neck, if you could call it that (then he'd pretty much be all neck, no?), a photo that still hung, framed, in their home, all smiles, even Soave—when they were approached by two men whom Michelangelo nor Emilia had ever met or seen before. They were both dressed in black suits and grey trench coats. The one who introduced himself as Hálfdan Kříž had a right eye made out of a mirror—so when you looked at him you were looking at yourself—a jagged pink scar running down his right cheek, and was completely bald. The other man, one Güvenç Zafar, holding a large satchel in his left hand, had a thick, black beard, a row of solid gold teeth (the top row), and a tattoo of the Turkish crescent moon and star on the middle of his forehead. They both smoked cigarettes that reeked of the poor labor that was used to harvest the tobacco. Their accents, both different, were thick and raspy from years of chain-smoking.

"We've come to offer our congratulations," Hálfdan Kříž told them. "What a glorious achievement for your family."

"Allah has blessed you," Güvenç Zafar told them. "This beautiful beast was chosen by Allah himself."

"Sorry?" Michelangelo was completely dumbfounded. "Who?"

"That pig," Hálfdan Kříž blew smoke into everyone's face and pointed at Soave, "has a higher purpose."

"What?"

"He's meant to save the world. We want to buy him off you."

"Oh...he's not for sale," Emilia explained.

They both glared at her as if insulted either by the news itself or by the fact that she was the one to deliver it or perhaps both.

"Any currency you wish," Güvenç Zafar said. He opened

the satchel and revealed stacks upon stacks of money—thousands and thousands of dollars in American, Italian, English, Australian, and a few they didn't recognize...how did he hold that whole bag with one hand?

"Very kind...but like my wife said, Soave isn't for sale."

"You don't seem to understand, we need him. Didn't you hear Hálfdan? Soave is meant to save the world."

"How so?"

"Are you familiar with animal sacrifices?"

"You want to kill him?" Horror rushed to mask their children's faces.

"No," Hálfdan put out his cigarette and lit another one. "We want to save the world."

"It is the only way." Güvenç preached.

"It is the only way." Hálfdan echoed.

"I-I've had enough of this. Emilia, kids, let's go. Good day, gentlemen. Sorry to disappoint you."

The Polettis walked away from the two strangers, not looking back even when Güvenç Zafar called out: "The blood of the world will be on the hands of the Poletti family!"

Little did they know how long these two strange-looking strangers would linger around them, how loyal they were to the strange orders, how they would watch them from afar and, sometimes, when they were able to stop for a chat, offer more money to Michelangelo, each time the price higher and higher, numbers that Michenagelo did not know existed, more stacks of bills somehow crammed into that bag...all for one fucking pig. And to each and every generous, yet intimidating offer, the answer would remain the same: "He's not for sale." It was a conscious routine they played, sprinkled with a bit of anxiety on both sides, never knowing if one day they might have had enough rejection and decided to resort to brute force—until, of course, a few months later, when the world went fully into that raging fire, pouring more fuel onto it...it was then that the Polettis saw the last of the pig-fond strangers.

But until then, Emilia sat down with Michenagelo and seriously picked his brain on the matter. Since the first visit from Hálfdan Kříž and Güvenç Zafar in 1939, the conversation took place at least once a month. Emilia changed her initial stance and argued *for* taking the money—not only would it help them financially, beyond their dreams, but would also get those men out of their lives for good. She became tired and unsatisfied with Michenagelo's answers, as he never really provided any good ones:

"Doesn't feel right...something off about it."

"Soave is family, I cannot give away family."

"It's only money, we have money."

"They will grow tired and leave us alone soon."

H. Kříž and G. Zafar were always a "safe" distance away—though, in all honesty, "safe" is a poor word, for who could ever fathom or define the idea of "safe" when two dangerous-looking men are stalking your family?—but close enough to be seen, puffing away on cigarettes that smelled different and fouler each time (foreign petrol, human shit, misremembered heartbreaks, rotten fruit, etc.), and watching. They never gave a straight answer to the question of "Why?"—which was shouted, usually from afar and usually from Emilia as she became progressively fed up with it. Whenever she and or the family were outside gardening, tending to the vines, feeding stock, or coming home from the store, there they fucking were and it just ate away that they just fucking watched...and they would always give the same answer they were instructed to give: "That pig has a higher purpose," for they were loyal as ever to their employer and his orders, which were to sacrifice Soave and then consume him. They said it would save the world. There was no reason to think any differently. It was almost somewhat of a relief when the War broke at the start of September because the moment it did the strange strangers vanished from their lives. Though, unbeknownst to the Poletti family, they were nearby, a mile or so away, in a small home that they lived in during the duration of their failed mission.

HEAVEN WAS A PLACE ON EARTH WITH YOU

The note laid flat in the middle of the small wooden table, a crease down the middle not touching any letters. The table was made of dead cedar, round and rough, and sat up against a cold stone wall, right below a small, square window that looked out at the grand Walla Walla scenery: crops and some vineyards that, to them, never looked like much. A bottle of Cypriot Zivania stood like a soldier of death next to the letter. Two shot glasses sat next to the bottle next to the letter...along with a loaded revolver. Güvenç Zafar looked from the bottle to the letter, back to the bottle, and back to the letter again. Then to the revolver.

The letter on the table read:

Termination approved.
You will be taken care of on the other side.
Cheers.

Hálfdan Kříž sat across from Güvenç Zafar and read another note that he held in his hand, his face perplexed, annoyed. "Don't get it," he said as he set the letter down. "Why's he writing a fucking tech sheet on the bottle he sends with our fucking death certificate?"

Güvenç Zafar watched as veins pulsed and throbbed on Hálfdan Kříž's red neck. He was aroused—sexually. His penis began to bulge at the seam of his pants. He flexed his calves and told himself it was the idea of violence that got him like this, an old lie he came up with to suppress the urges he refused to recognize. But maybe...was now the time? Here at the end of the line, with nothing else to lose and everything to prove. Why the fuck not? Why—

"We supposed to drink it all?" Hálfdan Kříž asked as he opened the bottle and poured two shots, to which Güvenç shrugged.

"Cheers." They raised their glasses in a toast. "To fuck all." Down the hatch. Two more, please. Obliged. Another toast: "To Soave Poletti, eh?"

It was harsh stuff for Güvenç Zafar, who had grown up on the much sweeter raki of his homeland that was usually had as an after-dinner nightcap. He was more inclined to herbal substances such as Marijuana and Kanna which he had been put on to by an Australian man he met in South Africa about five years prior who went by the name of Toon Berglund. Kanna, a "natural ecstasy," could be made into teas, chewed, or smoked, the latter which Güvenç preferred. For Hálfdan Kříž, who grew up drinking brennivín and țuică—*literally* grew up with them, if the stories he was known for telling were to be believed: how, if he was drunk among others, he would catch a whiff of competition in the air and challenge any and all to a drinking game: shot for shot, how he could out-drink anyone, having trained his whole life by "having three bottles of țuică a day by the time I was thirteen. By eighteen I was having a full bottle of Black Death to myself every day." ("And you're proud of that?" a voice once called out, belonging to who else but old Bořivoj Fülöp, the tall, blond-haired, blue-eyed Nihilist, as he dubbed himself, and nemesis of Hálfdan Kříž—a feud that had been born three years ago when Bořivoj Fülöp was *performing* in the of the heart of Bucharest on the boardwalk of the Dâmbovița River different aphorisms from Friedrich Nietzsche's *Human, All Too Human* by means of spoken word and interpretive dance, which he would refer to later that night as "Shakespearean," which, to those who liked to call people out on their shit, would come off as a bit paradoxical. Normally Hálfdan Kříž would walk on without paying a fucking street performer any mind, but on that day was with his wife-to-be, Žofie Zieliński, who was struck frozen when she heard the words of the dead philosopher emerged from the lips of the living wannabe. She left Hálfdan for Bořivoj that instant [as did many men and women during that summer when Bořivoj performed daily, sometimes from sunrise to sunset, no breaks, soiling himself in front of everyone for the sake of his art, as everyone was uniquely affected by the words: some became hypnotized, some killed themselves, some fell in love...the majority, of course, did not give a shit], and Bořivoj did not care what damage was caused in this decision while Hálfdan was broken as ever a man could be, his soul leaking from the cracks in his form and there was nothing he could do, ever the helpless. It was the last he ever saw of her, but not of Bořivoj. When last year Bořivoj Fülöp yelled out: "And you're proud of that?" it was like a switch going on in his head and with it a voice screaming: "Violence, motherfucker!" followed by Hálfdan plumbing Bořivoj's pretty face in front of a dozen or so people, howling all the while: "I loved her, you bastard! Where is she?!" to which Bořivoj was able to reply, through blood and broken teeth, ever so meekly: "Who?" which then sent Hálfdan further into a violent red rage. He blew a gasket so to speak, to where he pushed both of his thumbs down into Bořivoj's soft blue eyes and kept applying more pressure, ignoring Bořivoj's screams and pleas of mercy, ignoring the horror that emulated from the mouths of those who watched, ignoring the warm blood that oozed onto his thumbs and slithered under his nails...before he finished it he whispered her name: "Žofie Zieliński..." but it was masked by all the commotion and violence and screams [he genuinely pictured that line coming out dramatic and romantic like he was in a popular motion picture where he would have a spotlight on him and just saying her name would make her appear again and the crowd would go crazy and they would love the way they were in love] to where it's unsure if "Žofie Zieliński" was the last thing that Bořivoj Fülöp heard or if he was too honed in on the sounds of his own screams).

Güvenç picked up the letter Hálfdan had set down and felt the warmth from those callused fingertips through the paper—was he just being foolish again? ah hell. "It's his thing," he said. "He loves sending 'tasting notes' or 'historical articles' on whatever alcohol he sends." Hálfdan waved him off.

"Do all his bottles come with this order, though?" Hálfdan wondered.

"I cannot say," Güvenç confessed. "Though I received from him a bottle of Daiginjō-Shu saké for my birthday last year. Attached to it was a job to assassinate Tälgat Oz-Protz, who served as an ambassador of sorts for—oh who am I kidding, he was a damn *spy* for the Soviets. Had twenty-four hours to do him in."

"Oy vey," Hálfdan sympathized. "On your birthday, eh?"

"Yeah."

"You did it?"

"Of course. Had no choice."

"How was the saké?"

"Divine."

A small moment of silence found its way between them and caused them to sit dumbly and think about what they were doing: just following orders, right? And the booze was worth it? Well, maybe dying isn't all that bad...everyone's doing it, anyway.

The tech sheet read:

Attached to your termination notice is a farewell present for you to share. A bottle of Cypriot, from Cyprus, Zivania, which is a pomace brandy, which is a distilled liquor from leftover pomace from winemaking, pomace being the actual solid remains from grapes after a pressing. Seeing no skin-contact and made up of two (2) different grapes, both native to Cyprus, a 50/50 split: one white, Xynisteri, and one red, Mavro. This is an ancient drink, aged, meant as a welcoming treat for new guests.

Enjoy. xx

V－－－－

A third shot. The letter and table reunited. Both men raised their glasses again. "To...hell—" Hálfdan searched for the words, "—the end of the world." They threw them back. Another shot poured, courtesy of Güvenç this time. His glass raised first. There was a moment of hesitation from Hálfdan which Güvenç didn't really think about until later as he was too excited to deliver his toast, but when he would think about it, moments before the end, he would think about, in that brief moment, not the morbid look of wanting-it-all-to-be-over-and-done-with painted on Hálfdan's somber face, but him looking exactly like—shit you not—Théodore Chassériau's *Young Monk* (if H. K. had hair), which is a look that blindly distracted Güvenç from the whole morbid look that was painted underneath.

"To you," Güvenç said, not waiting for both glasses to be raised in the proper ceremonial toasting position, an act known in unspoken lore as a sinister foul and a curse of bad luck. He threw the shot back.

"Eh?" Hálfdan said.

"Oh, fuck it." Güvenç leaped across the table, fat hands clasping Hálfdan's smooth cheeks. He forced their lips together in a wet kiss that drew blood from lips unknown that sat in the mouths of both men. It was better than he could have ever imagined. Sweet fucking christ. He wondered if Hálfdan loved it, too.

Suddenly Hálfdan forced himself away, pushing Güvenç off of him and causing him to fall off his chair and onto the ground, and grabbed the revolver. The shot rang out before Güvenç hit the ground. He didn't feel a thing. His body laid still. He raised his head after a while, after the tears had filled his eyes and spilled over and ran down his face to his ears, then sat up and saw the pool of blood around Hálfdan's corpse. He crawled over to his expired interest. The revolver still tightly gripped in Hálfdan's hand, the fatal wound in the back of his head, smoke still escaping from his mouth like the ghosts we can't remember to forget, eyes still open...tears dotted his face as Güvenç loomed over him. He traced that deep, long pink scar on Hálfdan's face with his finger then kissed him softly, tasted blood and smoke. He laid his head gently upon Hálfdan's broad chest.

"Want to tell you a story," he whispered, which is how he began all the stories he thought worth telling, which wasn't often, this being the third and final one he would tell to his late partner. He was more inclined to have people *ask* to hear a story—was the kind of guy who would ask you how your day was just so you'd have to reciprocate and ask about his. The first story he told was when they first arrived in Walla Walla: a bottle of alcohol on the same table, split between them, and a letter from the same author but with information on the Poletti family and details of their mission, which Hálfdan was initially frustrated with— "...actually have to *buy* the fucking pig? Can't steal it, can't kill anyone. Unreal." To which Güvenç cooly laughed and said: "Want to tell you a story," and began to tell a story of how, before he was in this line of work—a decade or more ago—their employer, Vidal de la Fuente—said without naming him aloud, of course—had his hand in the entertainment industry as a private and independent film financer, is how they first met as Güvenç revealed for the first time that he was once an aspiring actor, believed that meeting Vidal was what he needed to elevate his way to stardom, tired of being an extra in the background. The reason for his belief in Vidal was that when they met on the set of *The Gold Rush* (1925), he saw the honesty and trustworthiness in his eyes, how he promised big things for him, how he told Güvenç that he "had that look," the first time he ever heard that. He told himself that it was like something in their brains connected and told them they had to stick together (Vidal saw and knew instantly—but never told him—that he did not have what it took to be a top-dollar actor, or a bottom dollar even, but upon diving deeper he found many things that would make a good soldier: bilingual, easily manipulated, sexually fluid, borderline Nihilist, etc.). A couple of years later Vidal had delivered for him a supporting role in a King Vidor picture (a project Vidal knew was going to fail, just needed that final push, one last failure to lure Güvenç, the dreamer, into a new life). The film-to-be was a sequel to *Stella Dallas* (1937), *Stella Dalla: Part II*, which no one understood the concept of. "A '*sequel?*'" King questioned like he did not understand the word. "'*Sequel?*' There's nothing left to tell." A shrug of the shoulders as if to say oh well, *c'est la vie*. "Maybe the daughter grew up," was all Vidal said, knowing that King would never have that idea. He left him a check anyway, which King used later to fund *Northwest Passage* (1940), then apologized to Güvenç, saying: "This was likely the last shot for you as the studio wanted you for the part but King doesn't want to do it and the studio doesn't want to do it without King, understand?" which, of course, he did not understand. It was a heavy blow, but Vidal was able to cure him with help from a steady dose of heroin after they left Hollywoodland and began his initiation into the Underworld. Suddenly Hálfdan asked, drunk (Finnish vodka was the bottle on the table then) and trying to suppress a laugh: "What the fuck has this got to do with the pig?" which brought Güvenç back from his memory. He thought about the question for a moment before saying: "Shit...I had something. Maybe it was...just follow orders as they are. Yeah. He means well for us."

The second story he told a fortnight ago, while they sat at the table. He smoked a pipe and sipped on a glass of single malt scotch, observing Hálfdan reading the *Walla Walla Union-Bulletin* where he spied on the front page an event taking place at city hall that night, "Pacifists United," featuring speakers that made him read over the names three times: feminist and pacifist icon Rosika Schwimmer, Australian cricket legend Warwick Armstrong, and mathematician-turned-poet Isabel Maddison. It stunned him. So many famous strangers, with no real connection to each other, having only pacifism in common, that and their old age and the freedom and privilege that came with retirement which allowed them to dedicate more time and energy and money to passions and causes like the greatly misunderstood Pacifists United.

"Why do you think they're having it here?" Güvenç asked aloud, to find that Hálfdan wasn't even interested in the story, though that didn't stop him from continuing to question why here, why Walla Walla, out of all the places on the planet Pacifists United could be held. It was like Walla Walla was the center of the universe, or maybe he was, everything revolving around him, which forced Güvenç to say: "Want to tell you a story," a tale that was largely and boldly filled with claims stating that the very same Rosika Schwimmer who was to speak at the upcoming Pacifists United was his great-aunt or some such which is why he was so deeply moved by the odds of her being in Walla Walla. "I thought she was still out in New York," he said, claiming she would be rightfully disappointed in him if she found out what he was doing in Walla Walla or any of what he'd done in the past.

"So, I take it you don't want to go, then," Hálfdan remarked at the end of the story, or at least what he thought was the end—it was pretty vague as Güvenç kept repeating how sad how disappointed she would be in him and how he didn't even remember the last time he saw his stateless great-aunt, over and over again, the words coming out quieter and quieter until he paused to take a sip of scotch, when Hálfdan made his remark, thus ending the second story as there was no reply made, just another sip of scotch and back to silently reading the local American newspaper.

"—about the first time we met," said Güvenç of the third and final story. "You probably don't really remember it, I wasn't really me then. It wasn't last year when we started working together...it was four years ago, we were in Geneva, each on separate missions. You were there protecting some politician I was undercover trying to expose an illegal sex ring within the League of Nations...your politician was a part of that ring. Allegedly.

"I was undercover with a sex gang called The Circus who was at hire for high ranking politicians, celebrities, basically anyone who could afford us. For certain rates we—they were yours. The gang began in Ballarat, Victoria, Australia but once it grew in quiet popularity relocated to Paris, where I was deployed and joined, before relocating one last time to Geneva and was run by ("The Lion King") Bo McAtee, a mad, sex-crazed Aussie who kept lions and tigers as pets and insisted we all have animal nicknames. I was undercover with them, before meeting you, for nine months as ("The Horse") Kelsay Kogelman...I was the bearded lady known as The Horse who hailed from Manchester, England...my accent was terrible. On the day we met, you were there, standing guard outside a room where your politician, a Dutchman I believe, was being sucked off by ("The Alligator") Jean Zarly, the lovely beauty from Luxembourg...you were unbothered by it all. I was going into a room with ("The Snake") Cormac Woodcock—the famed sex worker from London who had a 'python for a cock,' which I can attest to—and four large Nigerian diplomats when we walked by you...and...and..." A part of him seriously began to think about the legalities of necrophilia in America, then wondered why legalities mattered if he was going to finish the job soon anyway. It felt like his mind was swimming in a hurricane, no land in sight, knowing fully fucking well that everything was not fine, thanks anyway though, and before he knew what in the bloody hell was happening he was undoing the dead man's belt, looking up at his chin, waiting for those eyes to look back down at him, maybe give him a nod of approval...but that would ruin the idea of committing this specific crime. His hand wrapped around the fat flesh. That's when he came back to—it was like he had blacked out for a moment and his body, driven blind with horniness, acted on impulse—and his first thought was of what his mother would think if she found out he fondled a *dead* man. It was bad enough when she found out he liked living cock, back in the dying days of the Ottoman Empire where such a lifestyle could find you in prison—which it almost did for Güvenç until he ran from home and lived on the street for several years and raised himself, not seeing his parents again until earlier this year when they deemed him successful enough (he told them he was "security for foreign diplomats," not entirely untrue) and he was able to buy back their "love." He instantly gagged at the thought, puke sticking in his throat, warm and sour, a truly gross feeling which for some reason caused him to grip Hálfdan's dead penis harder, which made him gag again, a small amount of vomit squeaking through his sealed lips and spraying onto the corpse and his own beard. This at long last forced Güvenç to release the flesh and replace it with the revolver. He put the gun in his mouth, the same gun that Hálfdan just had in his mouth, the thought of which made Güvenç quake and wrap his lips around the barrel, tasting iron and Hálfdan, then stopped as he began to tremble with sobs and tears started to run free again. He was never a man to view crying as a sort of weakness, knew when and when not to show his own emotions when it came to matters of business and who he was surrounded by, more or less a case of his personal interest in the way humans portrayed their emotions, centered on certain situations like he was studying them, collecting data—and this was the result you got. He laid there and found himself, for some fucking reason, searching for a heartbeat. Nothing.

What remained was the corpse of a man who followed

orders and the shell of a man who was mentally shutting down as a way of protecting himself due to a combination of mass stress overload, traumatic shock, crippling anxiety, severe depression, self-loathing, a sense of lost identity, hopelessness, and meaninglessness, a broken heart, and a need to follow orders. He was not ashamed. So incredibly exhausted from thinking and feeling this way and being in this position, Güvenç put the revolver back into his mouth and pulled the trigger quickly without a chance for his consciousness to second guess itself again.

Meanwhile, in the days that followed, while Emilia and Michelangelo began to notice that the strange pig-obsessed strangers were not around anymore, they did the human thing and found a new paranoia to obsess over (though neither would admit it, but would silently wonder what if they did sell old Soave...). This one, given the circumstances of their homeland being on the wrong side of history and under the label Axis, which in itself sounded evil, was understandable: it finally felt, for the first time since their initial arrival, unsafe to be an immigrant in the United States of America...upon which it was fucking built on the backs of.

9

At the Müller family dinner table, the conversation was always nonexistent.

Meals were always consumed in silence, conversation saved for after, the only sounds the clinks and clanks of forks and knives against plates, of the chewing and grinding of food between teeth, of the sipping of wine that they always had opened. It was their unique way of showing their utmost appreciation for the meal before them. Tonight it was smoked chicken breasts with mushrooms, chopped onions, and lemon juice; fresh from the garden and the two birds Joseph and his father had killed that afternoon. It was rare that they killed their chickens, as they preferred other meats such as beef or pork and relied on them for their eggs. Joseph had also become somewhat attached to them, saw them as pets rather than just a thing that produced another thing they desired; they all had a higher purpose than that, to him, yet Karl—for one reason or another not entirely explained to Ruth or Bambi or Joesph even—felt that it was important to know just how the juxtaposed peaceful slaughtering of a chicken was done for a special occasion, which it was. Joseph refused to eat it, but it was Bambi's twenty-third birthday, and this was her favorite meal. This was only the fifth time in her life that she tasted it. Some years she forgot to ask, some years she was denied and promised a meal far better (which was delivered with love) of steamed and stuffed cabbage and smoked pork shoulder, and on her twelfth birthday, the chickens had all died that morning, without any sign of struggle or foul play or violence of any kind, just there, dead as could be. It took years for them to restore their coop, and still, eleven years later, it was not filled: they had lost thirty-seven chickens, and before dinner tonight they had twenty-four. With the meal, they enjoyed a bottle of their '37 vintage Riesling. The wine was more full-bodied and paired brilliantly with the chicken, a beautiful thing that always slipped their minds given how little chicken they consumed.

After dinner, they all stood in a row, unintentionally shortest to tallest (Ruth, Bambi, Karl, and Joseph "by a few hairs"), and went through the process of scrubbing, soaking, and drying the dishes, and then putting them away, passing them down the line one by one by one by one. All done in silence. After that, they sat in the den together. Routines can be important. Sometimes. Karl put a log in the iron-stove fireplace in the corner of the room that warmed their home. He sat in his old armchair and filled his pipe with tobacco, lit, puffed—it was almost like a religious ritual in a way, how every movement and motion was, unbeknownst to him, exactly the same every time. Bambi and Joseph sat on the couch, Ruth in her rocking chair that had only a thin feather cushion for her bottom that she loved—she refused to sit anywhere else. The Müller children reached underneath the cushions on the couch and each pulled out a small chalkboard and a perfect, somehow unbroken piece of five-inch white chalk. They looked at their mother and then their father, who nodded. They pressed their chalk against their black-boards and wrote in silence for no more than sixty seconds. Joseph held up his board. It read: SELF? Ruth looked at the board, forced herself to blink, then looked at Karl, who stirred uncomfortably in his chair. Bambi spied the disappointment on Joseph's face out of the corner of her eye. She wondered what exactly he meant by what he wrote. Did he want to talk about himself? What possible mishaps or adventures could Joseph be getting into that he so desperately wanted to share? They were not a family that talked about themselves often, for they knew everything there was to know about one another...or so they thought. When appropriate, they discussed a majority of topics, as they would tonight, such as politics, religions, or philosophy, which is what Bambi hoped Joseph wanted to talk about: the idea of having a self. Finding yourself in a world so uncertain. All parents forget what it was like to be their children's age; it is entirely possible that once your consciousness reaches a certain age, if it ages the same way as our physical forms, it will no longer be capable of fully relating to and sympathizing with that of a younger generation's mind, just as their children cannot understand the fears and anxieties that come with growing up until they realize they are doing it and can't stop (even though, technically speaking, everyone *can* stop—growing up, living— but that's a whole other thing that people don't like to talk about: choosing when or how you die), for that is the only thing in life that they really have yet to experience: life itself. No, parents don't fully understand the reasons their only son lies awake at two in the morning, trying to muffle his sobs so as to not disturb the house, forcing himself to not be more of a burden than he thinks he already is. It's a melancholy that you're born with, a deep sadness that you can feel physically flowing through your bloodstream, bogging you down as if your whole life you've been walking through quicksand, and you've only just noticed, and fuck, you're up to you're chest now, and it seems so easy to just let it consume you, eat you alive, and your eyes burn from crying so much, you can't see, and it doesn't look like there's anyone around to throw you a lifeline, so why ask for one? It's uncomfortable and difficult to come to terms with the fact that you require help, not realizing when you are drowning that it doesn't actually hurt anyone nor does it burden anyone to ask for help. But, in the moment, the young sometimes do not understand what their elders feel, how they think, what they have learned from their lifetime of experiences—just as they don't understand that, even when you grow up and have responsibilities of your own—a house, a career, a family whom you love dearly—you can still lay awake at night, as you did all those years ago, and be consumed savagely by your thoughts. But for the life of us, we can't understand, and nor can they: they had their time, what could they possibly be worried about now? They've so much life yet to live, what could they possibly worry about? And, if all that is true, why isn't it easier to talk about?

The idea of presenting a topic of discussion did not strike Bambi until her father asked, "Well, which one?" She looked at him with a puzzled expression, which caused him to flash a frown of disappointment, then a glance down at her chalkboard, which sat flat in her lap, the thin white letters screaming at her: WAR?

"Now, Laura," Mother began, "your father and I discussed the Great War with you two not two weeks ago."

"You were both drunk," she said, still looking at her chalkboard, not remembering tracing the perfect lines.

"Hmm," Father groaned as he puffed smoke.

"And I don't wish to discuss your war or your father's war." Bambi looked at her mother. "We have yet to talk about this current war."

An uncomfortable silence hung over them, denser than that of the pipe smoke that floated about without care or regard to the dialogue that struggled to survive below it.

"What about it?" Father asked.

"How do you feel about it?" Bambi asked.

"War is never good, süßes Mädchen."

She rolled her eyes at that. How she loathed the little nicknames he still used—aside from Bambi, of course, which, she felt, was just as much her real name as Laura was at this point in her life; she liked it better, too—as if she were still a child and not the grown adult she was trying to be. Though it was difficult, her being twenty-three when her mother had already had two years of experience as a mother when she was twenty-three and it being so human to constantly compare yourself to someone else. Marriage was a topic they would try to drop subtly (but fail horribly). Bambi branched away from her parent's traditional foundation of ideals and logic and possessed a more open mind, not entirely sold on the concept of marriage, due in part that she never had a relationship last more than three months. The two she had were private and without her parent's knowledge, the first when she was thirteen with Davin Tennyson which lasted a total of nineteen days and was birthed by Davin being dared by his friend Liam Hodges to plant a big, fat, wet kiss on the German girl in class, and it was the only kiss they shared. Nineteen days later, Davin came to school and told Bambi he was breaking up with her for Sammy Tittensor...Bambi was unaware she and Davin had even been dating—wasn't big into labels, even at that age. She was more aware of the second relationship with Dusty Beverly, a cellar rat at The Peoples Winery, who only got the job because because his parents knew 'Flip, and dumped Bambi two months after they had offically started dating— around the time you really begin to fall and start feeling those butterflies in your stomach and, if you really want it, most of your consciousness is occupied by that person, just their presence, how you start to appreciate things more when they are around, this is what it was like for Bambi and it is better that it ended, not necessarily in the way that it did, but for the fact that they were dependent on one another for happiness— after he finally fucked her, after she let him, wanted it bad enough, even lying and telling him that he was her first time, and pushed that lie a little further by throwing in some fine acting—moans and heavy breathing—she imagined he needed that self-esteem boost, but fuck if she had known that piece of shit was just going to hit and run she likely would have been more up front with him. But, yeah, she would love to fall in love one day and start a family of her own, but she was afraid that the opportunities for the life she longed for was passing her by in places she had never been, living lives she couldn't fathom while she was stuck on that small plot of land, destined—expected—to take over simply because she was firstborn. Now, it seems, with each passing sunrise and sunset, the idea of holding on to such dreams that she kept locked away in the private confines of her soul was more painful and difficult than to just let them die and pass into memory and create room for new dreams, easier dreams, simpler dreams, settling. Though, if you keep your heart and mind open enough to the possibilities, it, what you've always wanted, can come from anywhere...even when you're not looking for it.

"I don't feel good about it," Mr. Müller confessed, staring at his feet. "Only a matter of time before this country gets involved."

"Will I have to fight?" Joseph asked.

"Of course not!" Mrs. Müller gasped in horror.

"But I was born here."

"Would you want to?" His father asked.

"I...don't know."

"War is not something that one should be proud to be a part of."

"Yes, father."

"I wish I never had to fight...and of course, if you for some reason made a choice to become an instrument of war—for that's all you are, an instrument in Their grand, violent orchestra—you'd be killing lads who might be no different from you."

"And I'd be fighting against our homeland."

Mr. Müller locked eyes with his son. Unable to hold his father's harsh glare, Joseph dropped his eyes and looked at his mother, whose gaze was just as harsh.

"Das ist nicht unsere Hemiat," Mr. Müller said.

"I—"

"Das ist nicht unsere Hemiat!"

Silence flooded the room, save for the small crackles and pops of the fire, the last cries from wood older than all of them combined.

Bravely, Bambi lifted her head and surveyed the room, saw that the walls still stood, the anger and frustration seeming to have subsided from the room. Her eyes drifted past her mother until her gaze locked on a picture hanging to the right. It was a black and white photograph of a small wooden cabin floating on a lake; a broken dock lay distance from the shore; low, thin clouds hung over the dark mountains, almost masking them completely, created a ghostly backdrop; trees on the bank to the left, naked, bearing no leaves, drooping a bit, one branch reaching out to the old cabin, a tiny hand that longed to touch the buoyant home, let it know it was not alone.

"You've never asked about that photo, have you?" her mother asked.

"No," she said as she shook her head.

"What do you think of it?"

"I always thought it looked sad."

"It is."

"What's it called?"

"*Called a Home.*"

"It's called *Called a Home?*"

"Yes. Does that make it more or less sad?"

The question caught her off guard. "I'm not sure..." She avoided it, naturally, a thing she had gotten good at. "Where did you get it?"

"From the photographer, our friend, Dr. Koike. It was

taken in 1925, I believe."

"You have a friend who's a doctor *and* a photographer?" Joseph asked.

"Yes, we obviously don't see much of them that much these days, given they're in Seattle."

"'Them?'"

"That would be," Father said, "Dr. Kyo Koike, Mr. Iwao Mastsushita, and Frank Asakichi Kunishige. Founders of the Seattle Camera Club."

"Don't forget Hiro, dear."

"Ah, young Hiro Hachimura, not technically a Founder, but one of the world's most gifted photo-graphers."

"Can't believe we haven't heard of this before," Joseph said, bored.

"Do you have any of his pictures?" Bambi asked, now fully interested.

"Hiro's? Only a few. It's almost a risk hanging them...Hiro was a strange artist, brilliant...but also very critical of himself. He only ever made one single copy of his shots. Any of his art that was put on display at one of their galleries was the only print in the world. Many people would make copies, or try to, but if he found out he would politely ask that you return it to him, then he would tear it up in front of you. Having copies are important not only to the consumer but to the artist as well, it lives as a physical memory that they can always go back to. Hiro didn't believe in that, I suppose. Once it was done he wanted nothing to do with it. He followed a—what did he call it? A wabi-sabi philosophy...that everything is finite."

"I've been thinking of them recently," Ruth confessed, "given the state of the world."

"Ja, I find myself thinking of them, too. I'm nervous for them...nervous for all of us."

"Because of the war," Bambi said sharply, coming full circle.

A heavy silence filled the room and weighed on their

minds, blocking their thoughts momentarily, focusing only on the worst-case scenarios, their anxieties all equally turned on high—consumed by them. Before she spoke again, Bambi saw out of the corner of her eye tears swelling in her brother's own, and she found herself imagining how hard it must be to fight this unbeatable and unspeakable sickness in front of them, the comfort of crying in front of your own parents. "Tell us about them," she said, saving them all from that ugly silence they found themselves trapped in far too often. "About the Seattle Camera Club."

Their parents looked at one another, faint smiles of nostalgia appearing on their tired faces. A happy distraction.

"My love," Mr. Müller said to his wife, "would you be so kind?"

"I would love to," she replied warmly.

GOD'S WORK AND HUMAN'S

It was 1924, and your father and I took a weekend holiday to Seattle—I think it was May? Yes. You were six then, Joseph had just turned two. We never saw the city before, really, only when we first landed in this country, we didn't stay long, of course, not long enough to appreciate it. Not to get into the whole trip itself. So we went and we came across this self-funded art exhibition that was going on that weekend only. It was fate.

We wondered if it was a paradise. Some of the most gorgeous photography I've ever seen, still, to this day. I could've spent all day there. And I remember the look on your father's face, so joyous—not because of the art before us, but because he was so happy to see *me* so happy. Always putting my happiness—anyone's, really—before his own. Such selflessness. Oh, I'm getting a little carried away.

(Karl, in the corner, puffed on his pipe so the smoke

concealed his blushing face. "No, no. Go on, dear. It's a nice story to hear.")

There weren't that many people there if I recall correctly. Well, not as many as there *should* have been. It was a free art show, after all. They asked for donations, that was it. And it was good to see people chip in. Everyone saw them for what they were: artists. They didn't care if they weren't from here or if they were women. It was an open community, and I desperately wanted us to be a part of it. It just made sense, for us—natural, organic, purposeful.

We were lucky and fortunate enough to meet them all, yet Hiro stuck out particularly, for he was so unique, and, in a way, I think your father thought of him as a little brother of sorts.

(He again puffed heavy smoke. "Hiro is a good man...hope he's able to come round again soon.")

Or, dear, we take the kids to the city. Anyway, we spent almost the whole day with such beautiful and creative people and learned so much from them that we still stay in contact today; they are dear and close friends. We write. What was really compelling was the uniqueness of Hiro's wabi-sabi philosophy that your father mentioned. It was something we were unfamiliar with. How he believes the art of photography to be singular, that the moment he captured is just that: a single moment, which to those lucky enough to view it is in between the space of beginning and end but to the artist, to Hiro, he witnessed it all in its entirety and totality. He gave us his work for nothing. Priceless photos, single copies. They were indeed some of the kindest souls we met in this country. There's a photo of your father that Dr. Kyo took that I'll have to show you both, it's my favorite of him. It's of him like he is now, a little younger, though, just sitting and smoking a pipe, handsome as ever. Oh, ha-ha, sorry, dear, I could go on for days about that photo, but I know you're blushing heavily behind all that smoke, so I won't. One of you just remind me to show you it, okay?

It is a shame that it's been so long since we saw them. We'll change that. Soon. Oh, they're such wonderful people. Oh, dear, why haven't we told them about them sooner?

("Thought we did.")

DOVES OF THE MISSION

It started, for me, at least (Hiro Hachimura began), by the burning desire to capture a moment in time. Forever. Not just portraits, but tangible things in nature that would be going about their business whether or not you were pointing a camera at them. Trees yawning ever so greatly in the brisk Pacific breeze, a flock of ducks, ten or so, floating along in a vast lake, staying relatively close to the shore, as if they knew something was lurking under the surface deeper out there, yet still unbothered by that and the warning signs of impending rain: a dark and ominous black cloud of rolling thunder bellowing in, beginning to cover the sun, leaving, for a near nonexistent moment, a god-like sliver of light shining, almost piously, onto the peak of Mount Shuksan. All these moments in time...gone in an instant. Now they only exist by the grace of my memory, which, I was told, can be quite unreliable, another reason why I wanted to get into photography. I was told that people will subconsciously begin to alter their memories, or simply forget them altogether. Everything I just told you—who's to say, aside from me, that they all really happened as I explained them? They all seem real and possible enough, but did I get every detail correct? If at the time I had a camera, I would be able to prove it to you. And sometimes I think, painfully, that those shots would have been some of my life's work. I've been back to the same spot I had this calling many times since we started the Club, yet the scenes have never been reproduced. Nor will they be. That's the beauty of it.

I am a product of Agenosho, Oshima-gun, Yamaguchi-ken, Japan, same as one of our founders and my mentā, Frank Kunishige who introduced me, not only to the legendary Dr. Kyo Koike and Iwao Matsushita—the first man to establish the Japanese language course at the University of Washington—but to a new philosophy, wabi-sabi, and how to perceive art, how finite the world is, even if you're able to capture it in an 8-millimeter film box it will only be there for so long before it, too, will fade away.

I used the word "product" because that is what we all are, products of our environments. Before Frank left for photography school in Illinois, one of the only club members to be properly trained and educated on art, we would run around the city snapping pictures of all the ghosts we were chasing. I know you can see them in the works that hang in the city here. They were different back there. Separate but the same. A full moon on a cloudy night. We liked the idea of capturing the mysteries of life, the impossibilities of it. I, of course, took a step farther by creating only one copy of each art piece, a method Frank only questioned once, then came to respect, but I don't think he ever fully understood: my philosophy on this art form and how it pertains and practically mirrors our grasp on the idea of our mortality, that the photos act as a sort of portal to a choice of multiple dimensions where time is infinite or debunked all together, where everything is still and unmoving, a moment so perfectly captured that it will live forever, or so we wish to think—and that's why it's the fastest-growing art form, anyone can do it, and everyone wants to. Everyone wants to physically hold their memories, everyone wants to stay young forever...even if it's only within the borders of film. In a way, I wanted people to understand the finite gravity of the situation, the idea everyone wants to avoid and never face: our mortality: one life: one copy: forever was just a lie created to fulfill a false sense of purpose.

10

Bambi found herself the first one awake, a rarity, as her father was almost always the first to rise, often even before the sun had risen to warm them. So to stand alone in the kitchen and stare at the empty chair that her father would usually occupy—with a mug of coffee, black, and the morning papers, a piece of buttered toast, his pipe; those small peaceful routines before work—was terribly eerie. All she could think to do was scream, which seemed so silly. It was only an empty chair after all, but at this hour of the day, it felt like much more than that.

"Morning, Bam," Joseph said in a sleepy haze, walking into the kitchen.

"What are you doing up so early?" Bambi asked, still rooted to the same spot, heart pumping at a slightly faster pace from the unintentional fright Joseph's entrance had caused.

"What? Am I not allowed to be up right now?"

"You're never up this early, is all."

"There's a first time for everything." He took a glass from a cabinet, went to the icebox, and took out a cool jar of milk. "Where's ma and da at?" he asked as he poured himself a glass.

"I'm not sure." That eerie feeling crept back into her bones and she choked down a scream. "Still sleeping, I guess."

"First time for everything."

Bambi saw a shift in his posture then, like his primal DNA woke up and sent unconscious messages through the body that alerted his human realization that he might need to be the man of the house now, a thing the mind and body did subtly, just in case something actually happened, a sort of way it prepared itself for the absolute worst, to expect the unexpected. He finished his milk and stared out at the window, at the sunrise—something he rarely saw—and took his time to admire it. The soft vibrancy of colors he had never seen blended so well together, melted effortlessly, and stretched out for miles: bloody maze and ripe tangerine, midnight lavender and milky ultraviolet, burnt butterscotch and watery coffee, like an aged Riesling.

"Hell," he finally said after he had his fill of the natural splendor. "I'll go feed the chickens."

A violent cough boomed through the house like a sudden explosion, multiple attempts to clear the throat, a build-up of phlegm—reassuring sounds they were happy to hear. Into the kitchen walked their father, who had never before looked so tired. Even so, he managed a smile when he saw both of them.

"Guten morgen," he said to them as he sat in the chair that had frightened Bambi with its emptiness.

"Feeling okay?" she asked, still statue-like in the same spot.

"Ja. Kaffee?"

"I was going to go feed the chickens," Joseph said.

"I can't make it as well as your mother."

"Where is she?"

"She is still sleeping, Bambi. Why do you sound so worried?"

"Not worried," she lied, though honestly, she wasn't one-hundred percent sure why exactly she *was* worried to begin with, something that could have been located early on but drifted away out of consciousness, not too far away, but far enough to where she knew it wouldn't come back anytime soon. Something in the air. In the bones. "Just never knew you two slept in this late."

"Ja, gut," he yawned as he stretched. "Zum erstenmal mal für alles."

"That's what I said," Joseph said.

"It'll be a later start to the day now."

"That's okay. You don't need to worry about these things. It's not often, but sometimes you need days like this, to sleep in and slow down a bit."

"Why?"

"It's a nice change of pace. It's dangerous staying in the same routine, you'll lose track of the days very easily."

"Really?" Joseph asked as he sat down at the table, prompting Bambi to realize she was tired of standing and sat down as well.

"Oh yes," Karl said, pulling his pipe and tobacco out from his worn leather-carrying pouch that he always wore and beginning to pack it full. "Not that this routine is bad, but it's nice to sleep in sometimes. Back before I met your mother—well, actually, we *had* met, but this was before we were 'going together'—I must have been eighteen then, working my life away as a bricklayer and a janitor at the university I was enrolled at, I was drowning in stress and repeating the same cycle that I actually started *dreaming* about the same routine I was stuck in." Lit, puff, puff. "To the point where I didn't know what was a dream and what was reality. That was a dangerous routine."

"Geez, da, really?"

"Oh yes, my son. If it wasn't for your mother, who knows? I might still be stuck in that same routine."

"Don't get it."

"What's that, Bambi?"

"What'd ma do?"

"She's a wonderful woman, you know. She showed me who I really am, my potential, all that. It was always in me, just like it's in you, she just helped me tap into that."

"So you're both happy then?"

"Of course, why wouldn't we be?"

"Just the state of the world is all."

"There are no regrets here."

"Will it get much worse?"

"I'm not sure."

"But the other night—"

"I let my emotions get the better of me. There's rightful cause to worry, of course, comes with being alive. But don't let it consume you."

"Right."

"We will be okay. Come now, something more lighthearted, while we wait for your mother's famous kaffee. Did anyone have any interesting dreams?"

"Oh ja," Joseph said almost too quickly.

"Care to share, son?"

Joseph went on as best he could to verbally paint a vivid picture of his dream. It started with him clad head-to-toe in medieval armor at Tvrđava Klis—he did not contemplate the meaning or importance of the location, having been there once with the family when he was seven, in 1929, the territory's last days as the Kingdoms of Serbs, Croats, and Slovenes, and the beginning days of Littoral Banovina and the Kingdom of Yugoslavia. The walls of the ancient fortress looked a lot taller back then, easily touching the sky and whatever lay past it, but in the dream the walls seemed smaller; he could see people on the top of them, walking around. Everything seemed flat in a way, one-dimensional. He was to stand guard outside a room that held a princess who was to be married to some prince who wasn't featured in the dream at all. Somehow, without any information given during the dream, he knew of countless rumors and gossips and tales of the princess's beauty like it was something of the gods. He could not fight the urge to break into the room (Bambi and her father exchanged a curious glance) to see if the legends were true. What he found inside was a bedroom empty of everything that would make it unique and personal save for a bed, with a frame made from old wood that was once burned but for reasons unknown saved and given a second chance, and the bed itself of grass and dirt, hay and feathers, with no blanket or furs, just a body laying on top of the rectangular mound of earth surrounded by the sad wooden frame. He stood at her bedside and looked at her: she was dressed in a snow-white gown, holding a flower with hands as white as the dress, fingers as thin as bones, fingernails long fallen off. Her hair was on fire, a crown made of bones from species unknown resting atop her bloody skull, and her face was not there at all...just a pale, blank void, cold and unbecoming. He could hear her voice whispering in his head—which was when Joseph woke up and Bambi had woken up too, having heard him crying.

"I wish it were ma," is what he said. Like he wanted to spin it as a hero-story of sorts, where maybe he frees her or opens the door on the wedding day and he's the officiator, and his old man was the price.

"Interesting..." Karl said between puffs. A long, drawn-out silence followed, one that forced them all to sit and be weighed down a bit but mainly to think about that dream, because there was just something about meaning and interpretation. "You've any dreams, Bambi?"

"No," she lied.

"Really? Nothing?"

"Nothing."

"No, no. You must try to remember. I am old and can no longer dream, or remember them. You're young. Your memory is sharp."

She smiled and appreciated the compliment but really

didn't want to talk about her dream(s) and couldn't think of anything off the top of her head because everything was upside-down that day and she hadn't had her kaffee yet, so no, she didn't feel as sharp as her father made her out to be. Mother Ruth walked in just then—like she could sense in the psychosphere that Bambi needed to get out of a jam, not anything major, bit of an inconvenience, though—to make kaffee and breakfast so she would not have to talk about the odd dreams she could not explain. The day had been saved.

"Hello, my loves," Ruth said with a sleepy smile. "Sorry for sleeping in. I'll get breakfast ready."

"How was it?" Joseph asked.

"What's that, J?"

"Sleeping in?"

"It was lovely."

"No need to be sorry then."

Everything began to slowly creep back to normal and Bambi breathed a sigh of relief as if she had been holding her breath the whole time. She looked at her younger brother, who had gotten another glass of milk during the narration of his dream and sipped at it leisurely.

"What're you doing today?" he asked Bambi.

"I'm not sure yet."

"No plans?"

"Not yet. Why do you ask?"

"Just curious. Thought you said something about seeing Cade tonight."

"Oh, how has he been?" Ruth asked.

Bambi shook her head at Joseph. "He's been well."

"That reminds me," Karl said as Ruth set a fresh cup of black kaffee in front of him. "Danke liebes. If you do see him, let him know that I've been meaning to get a hold of his folks."

"Swapping with them?"

"Yes. Stouts sound nice, now with the weather changing so rapidly."

"I'll let him know."

"Danke."

Ruth had finished her creation of breakfast that consisted of speckpfannkuchen—thin pancakes with diced bacon—a dozen weißwurst, and some pumpernickel with butter. She set the plates down in front of them, looked at Karl, then Bambi, then Joseph, then herself in a pocket-sized mirror, after which all of them thanked her and she sat down. Thus marked the end of the conversations as silence fell upon them and the only sounds came from forks and knives and teeth. And that is how things were, how they went.

Bambi would go to sleep that night and find herself in a vivid dream, the same one as the previous night and the night before that, where the colors of the falling leaves were rustic, an overcast of steel grey clouds and the petrichor that seemed to rise directly from the ground below the first signs of evidence that it had rained recently, a rain that took away from the vibrancy that one would usually find in these woods. The wet leaves sank deeper into the soggy soil as her boots marched over them with every inevitable step. This was their life: a never-ending cycle of growing, drinking up the light, shaking helplessly in the cold, falling with their brothers and sisters to the roots below, only to be crushed, to be quickly eroded away so they may live once again. Aesthetically it was breathtaking, and, in a melancholic sort of way, it was tired, dulled out, as if these woods were somehow letting her know that their time for the year was drawing to a close and she just happened to catch the last bow. Just in time, the wind whispered softly as it carried a gentle dance through her hair to the music of the universe, the sounds of nature, how lush it all was then, how quickly it all wanted to die. The fading colors paid little mind to her as she walked alone. She couldn't remember why she was there, or what she was supposed to be doing. For some strange reason, this did not bother her in the slightest. There was a deep fondness for the stillness and the quiet that grew rapidly in and around her, a warm appreciation that flowed mirthfully through her bloodstream, made her feel as if she was always supposed to be here. The path she walked on was worn from years of other travelers, as all paths were, but held no signs of fresh or recent activity, except when she looked back and saw her own footprints. She stopped suddenly, as though she were forced to a halt by some invisible guard. The temperature dropped ten degrees. Her breath became visible before her eyes. She looked to her right: a wire fence, six feet tall, shaping a six-foot-wide box with four wooden posts. Held hostage inside the cage were six empty milk crates—one broken completely, all swollen fat from the recent rain—and a lone zebra. The exotic animal stared at her, a bored and tired expression on his long face. This was the first time (third time, technically) she had ever seen such a creature, in this world or the other. Leaves continued to fall in and around the wire-fenced cage, the temperature climbing back to comfortable. In the distance behind the animal, in a clearing where no trees met the great sky, Bambi spotted a parachute: yellow and orange, with a body dangling from its harness, guiding itself for a safe landing. She rushed to follow.

The deeper into the woods she went, the more the environment around her changed. The trees themselves morphed into pine and Douglas firs, lush, green, and towering, a thin layer of fog descending like a curtain at the end of the final act, the earth below becoming a mirror of the sky. She lost sight of the parachuter entirely. A great rush of noise flooded the woods suddenly. It came from above. She covered her ears and looked up, hesitant at first, fearing the worst. There, upon the heavens that looked a lot like hell itself, depressingly bleak, she saw nothing.

By the time she looked back down at what lay in front of her, she found the path that led to an unknown destination blocked by what was responsible for the noise. The Lockheed Model 10 Electra had its engine off, its pilot standing silently next to the great machine. There were no markings of any kind on the plane or the pilot's uniform. The face and head of the aviator were covered. The yellow and orange parachute hung like a coat on a tree nearby.

"I've been lost," the pilot confessed, pulling their scarf down to reveal their mouth, lips chapped, dry of moisture that sat selfishly on the tongue. "For quite some time now." Their voice was soft, confident, feminine, patient, and loveable. "Where is this?"

"I'm sorry," Bambi said. "I'm afraid I don't know."

"I used to be afraid of not knowing, too." The pilot looked at the world around them. "I wonder how long it's been."

"Since...?"

The pilot looked back at Bambi, eyes shielded behind dark goggles, which caused her to wonder what color hid behind them: did they match these new trees that she finally noticed, a deep green that beckoned strongly for more life? Were they a resemblance of the forest from before, which was fleeing from her mind now, tired, like her memory of it, and always casting down that which is light? Perhaps they were like the ground below the fog: dark and filled with hidden knowledge from long ago? Or the sky above: a melancholic grey? Or like the brighter days that did not yet exist here, today: a livelier, slightly paler blue?

"Since I've been afraid."

"But you're lost...doesn't that scare you?"

"We're all lost, in our own ways. What is it that you don't understand?"

"You fell."

"Oh, right."

With the blink of an eye, the pilot and their aircraft vanished completely without a sound. She waited a moment as if thinking they'd come back but knowing that there was nothing else to do. So Bambi walked on, down the lonely path whose only occupant was, once again, her and all the ghosts that never left this place, that could call it a home...she could feel them watching her from behind the great trees. Silent and empty, forgotten and replaced. They knew not how they could call what they had, what they experienced hitherto, a life. They watched enviously as what-could-be walked on by, what they once had, what they did not appreciate then, now forever trapped in the in-between.

The path continued to bleed ahead, the great trees that surrounded her seeming to move in closer—some stood tall and proud, others slouched and leaned from eons and eons of less-than-immaculate weather, all of them longing for lands that they didn't know existed...something better than whatever this was...they knew it was out there. They told her this. The path diverted to the right while also continuing straight and disappearing into the dark. A warm light illuminated the bend to the right, and she followed it. There, sitting in a meditative position by a small fire, was a young woman, featureless, waiting to be sculpted like a mold of clay. She turned her blank face towards Bambi and slowly a smile she wished to see began to appear; she smiled—not only with her mouth, parting her lips to reveal her teeth, which were beautiful and straight—but with her newfound eyes, which brought about a peaceful sensation of calm and warmth that the fire itself could never provide no matter how long it burned. The pale blue windows of Bambi's soul fell deep into the cool river of her irises. She was happy there. Still smiling, she grabbed a stick that lay nearby and began drawing something in the dirt between their feet. She stared at her, her attention on the ground, the smile never fading, which filled her with the idea that happiness *could* last. It was her first realization; she didn't know what to make of that. She put the stick down and looked at her. She looked at what she had been drawing in the dirt. The lines were clean:

$$\left[\frac{-\hbar^2}{2m}\nabla^2 + V(\mathbf{r})\right]\Psi(\mathbf{r}) = E\Psi(\mathbf{r})$$

Her eyes lifted from the ground and cut into her softly, like a lover's would, and he continued to smile so innocently, her eyes pleading for her to understand—she couldn't find a voice for her. She did not understand at all. The equation made no sense to her, but when she looked at it again she did find it to be beautiful, in a simple way; how so much complexity, puzzlement, and importance could be tucked away in such a small assortment of horizontal, vertical, and curved lines.

"I'm not sure I fully understand."

"No?" she said in a voice that wasn't spoken aloud but rather in her head, a voice that sounded like her own.

"Am I supposed to?"

"Maybe not...we don't fully depend on time 'here.'"

"'Here?'"

"You know: 'here,' or 'there,' it's all the same, really. All influenced by arbitrary means which we want to believe has true meaning and value, like time: the greatest construct we were tricked into obeying."

"What does this have to do with me? With anything?"

"You're alive, aren't you? A part of this world?"

"'This world?'" she asked, gazing around at the trees, which had morphed into something sickly and foreign, near dead. "I'm not sure if I want to be."

There came a chilling, bloody howl that traveled thick and heavy with the wind and froze her bones. Something dark.

Like a crack of lighting, she bolted upright, found herself sitting still as stone in her bed, the only movement from the pumping of her lungs that filled with oxygen as if they had forgotten to do their job while she was asleep, from her chest rising and falling rapidly, from her mouth that hung agape, inhaling, exhaling, sipping on the air. That world of mystical

woods and kind strangers—folklore, she told herself silently—
was pure illusory: her subconscious constructed a world that
she could use as an escape from the very real reality she
returned to. What a silly thing to want—when she went to bed
every night knowing that dreams were finite, knowing she
could not live in them forever, and yet there she was, still
trying to.

The roaring silence was deafening but interrupted almost
as soon as it was acknowledged by soft cries from Joseph's
room next door. His nightly routine. It must have been around
three in the morning then, the time of night where silence
reigns supreme, the time when the whole house is fast asleep
and he's at peace to pour his emotions out softly into his
feather pillow, his face pressed firmly against it to drown his
wails a bit, still fearful that he would wake someone one night.
He'd woken Bambi, a light sleeper, many times, but she did
not blame him tonight. She doubted that their parents ever
heard him, heavier sleepers with hearing that was slowly
fleeting with each passing day. It was always an annoyance to
her—which is why she never checked on him, as it was always
late into the night, her body so physically exhausted but her
mind running with rage at the melancholy that flowed
through her brother's veins and disrupted her sleep—but
tonight she felt as though she ought to check on him. That is,
until a voice in her mind pinned her to the bed, told her that
she deserved some sleep, it was late, if he wanted to talk about
his melancholy he would come to you, there's always the
morning, you worry too much, dear, and wasn't that a nice
dream you were having, like to go back, eh? With a simple,
voiceless response filled with belief that it was, in fact, a rather
nice dream: Yes, please...and thank you.

11

Two small cast iron pots—one filled with Poletti Merlot (1940), the other with V. Vintners Syrah (1940)—gently simmered over a fire that burned low and hot over under the watchful eye of Edith Nyström who, from time to time, would stir the liquids with a wooden ladle, have a taste, then, if she found it necessary, add just a bit more spice, a pinch of sugar, a handful of raisins and diced almonds. She reached down and grabbed air.

"Mathias," she called patiently.

"Yes?" his voice echoed from the other room.

"I need the brandy, just another drop or two."

Mathias Nyström walked in with an old brown bottle. "Sorry, dear."

Edith smiled and kindly snatched the bottle from his monolithic hands. "How'd you swipe that without me noticing?"

"You're dedicated to the work. I'm guessing the glögg is nearly ready?"

"Nearly. Just a few more minutes."

"Perfect." He kissed the top of her head and began to walk away.

"Is Cade still bottling?"

"He'll be done soon."

"I think it might be time to hire some help. You two can only do so much, and demand is growing."

"I know, Ed, I know. These Americans, it would seem, never had a good beer before. In the New Year, we'll find reliable people."

"Cade will appreciate that."

"Yes," Mathias mused, smiling. "He still loves it though, even with how busy it's been. Our boy hasn't complained once."

"We've done well. Now go, please stop distracting me."

They shared a laugh—voices filled with the same love they had found within each other thirty years ago, light and carefree, never a need to worry. They'd been in Walla Walla for fifteen years and missed their homeland of Sweden but found real happiness—real peace of mind—in America, a surprising home. They never lost their accents, still spoke their native tongue in the house together, and had only begun brewing their own traditional Swedish-style beers five years ago (the laws back home prevented brewers from producing beers over 5% ABV, the Nyström's began after Prohibition which had become a fading, drunken memory. Mathias experimented mostly with Stouts and Sours, with ABVs ranging from 5%-10%, the latter no one at the time thought was possible for a beer). Their success, which took them all by surprise, was talked about through the Pacific Northwest and was a crucial catalyst in the inception of the craft beer industry.

Before he left, Mathias breathed in the aromas of the simmering pots deeply. It filled him with a childlike joy—this is what the holidays were all about to him: warm glögg and time with family. He walked past the small table that held their mail—mostly letters from folk begging them to ship a case of their delicious brew—when one envelope caught his eye with the return address from Tórshavn, Føroyar in the top right corner. He grabbed it, palms already damp with sweat—opening mail always gave him the most curious case of anxiety, fearful that, for some reason, Uncle Sam would create a bullshit excuse to get rid of immigrants—and nearly dropped it when he saw it was from his cousin and League of Nations Member, Mårten-Ludvig Stenberg. He couldn't remember the last time they spoke. Not that they had a falling out, but communication around the world was difficult these days—he heard about a war going on out there.

Mathias ripped the letter open and began scanning it. His heart sank, at first for his cousin, who, in the first half of the letter described being a "prisoner" on Føroyar—Members were sent there in secret as a "last resort," with no way to leave until it was "all over"—how alone he was on the Island, with no real friends or family to talk to aside from one fellow countryman he had only just met, though he did write the better half of a paragraph detailing that he would consider this man a friend now and regretted saying in the beginning that there was no one to talk to, it's more a matter of who you can trust now, you see. How painful his cousin's confessions sounded. Then he got to the end, to the part that would affect him, his family, and his new homeland. Every Member was writing the same message to their loved ones: that very soon the U.S. would be entering the war most violently. There was a paragraph that went well over his head, with what Mårten-Ludvig started by saying was, possibly, "incriminating evidence that the League was able to obtain against the U.S.," something about Japan and oil. What that meant for the world—for this tiny slice of heaven they made for themselves—he wasn't sure, but the feeling in his gut was a dark and negative sludge, like a demon swimming through his bowels. He needed a drink, something a lot stronger than cheery old glögg.

12

Bleak greyness covered every inch of the sky like an infinite gravestone hovering above the city, filling every mind with even more dread and worry, a feeling that the world really was coming to an end. There was no sign of rain. Only grey.

A brisk gust of wind shook them as they exited the Tórshavn Cathedra, yet they found it strangely warm, comfortable. Mårten-Ludvig Stenberg followed Kasper Lindquist down the street, past the harborside buildings painted different colors: red, white, yellow, blue, black, white, green. Though the colors were far from vibrant, they almost blended in with their environment, as if the architecture of the buildings planned it with that natural landscape. Nearly every roof in Føroyar was covered with the same brown and green grass, further fueling the legend that the house did, in fact, grow right out of the ground. The first two buildings—the red one (remembered later on by its lucky neighbors as a faded cardinal shade) and the white one—were now mere piles of rubble and bricks and broken memories, all credit to the air raid two nights previous from the Luftwaffe, their first raid in well over a month. Mårten-Ludvig felt a tug at his heart when he saw the debris like it was a ball of yarn wound tightly and someone was trying to pull and pull till they got to the center, only to find nothing there. How strange...things once filled with so much life now served as a reminder of the many faces death can wear. No one heard the planes—the winged carriers of death that flew at such high altitudes and so late at night that their noise was practically inaudible to even the younger ears, dropping bombs that you only heard if you were lucky enough to be outside of the blast zone, the orders being to kill the enemy below which turned out to be anyone living and breathing, children included—only the deafening *boom*. Some foolishly thought it was an earthquake at first, somehow forgetting that the world had been at war for the past two years, somehow forgetting that their small home of Føroyar, which they once thought was practically invisible to the outside world—aside from the Danish, of course—now had new occupants thanks to Operation Valentine: the British. The natives had gotten used to them; they were kind enough, having occupied the Islands a year ago and "protecting" them from any German invasions, just not German air raids. He heard that they were still looking in all those piles of ruined brick for the bodies of the innocent lives that were lost, and so far had only found one: a child, no more than seven.

The two Swedish men sat on a wooden bench at the end of the dock; the wood was wet from the spray of the ocean, but neither of them cared. Kasper Lindquist was carving something on the bench with his right hand using a small pocket knife, not looking at what he was carving, his old eyes fixed on the world in front of him. Mårten-Ludvig tried to see what he was doing but couldn't, and noticed that the old goat stopped when he peered over. It was then he silently remarked to the voice in his head just how awfully dry Kasper's hands were: yellowed and cracked fingernails, even in this place with air so rich with moisture. His eyes went to the top of his countrymen's head and a surge of friendly envy whirled through his bloodstream as he stared at the thick, full head of hair, whiter than a fresh December snowfall in Lycksele, swaying slowly with the pull of the wind. It had been ten years since he first started losing hair, and a full three since he went completely bald. Oh, the simple joys he missed that Kasper, the oldest League Member on Føroyar, didn't do at all: running your hand through the thick locks, pulling it a bit, hard enough to know it's still there, maybe how your lover used to in the bedroom—remember that?

They stared silently out at the dark, choppy waters and wondered how many souls Poseidon had trapped down in the Locker; at the Royal Navy cruisers that floated still as buoyant statues, unfazed by any forceful push from the North Atlantic; at the gullies that cried from high above and came down to hover low above the water, looking for an easy meal. Kasper had gone back to blindly carving. It was something of a tradition for them to come to the harbor after every meeting at the Cathedral, which took place at noon on the first and last Tuesday of every month, after which they philosophized on the discussions that took place in the meeting. All twenty-one League of Nations members who lived on the archipelago met in secret, fearful of German spies that were rumored to have infiltrated the small, autonomous country. Mårten-Ludvig and Kasper were the only representatives from Sweden, the rest of their colleagues taking care of other matters in Stockholm or Geneva, depending on their value and importance to the League. They were sent to Føroyar (along with two representatives from Argentina, four from Denmark, two from Finland, three from The Netherlands, two from New Zealand, three from Norway, and three from Switzerland) when the war started as a precaution: in case all hope was lost, they would ensure their nation(s) carried on their duties in the League. In hindsight, Føroyar turned out to be less than ideal for the League Members as ever since the British occupation non-military people were no longer allowed on or off the

Islands. They were forced to stay until the war was over, communicating with the outside world through letters, one of which Mårten-Ludvig would be penning to his cousin, Mathias, out in Washington, later tonight, in which he would express the fears that he and fellow League Members discussed only ten minutes ago: the United States entering the War. This letter and the information he would put in it was a risk, but he was aware that every other League Member would likely be doing the same, secretly writing to loved ones, wherever they may be, telling of secrets that could very well cost them their careers and years in prison. Even so, it was done. Their private ways of saying, "Fuck their war."

They didn't speak at all while they sat this time. Between the two of them, they unconsciously understood that there was no need, not right now anyway—that they were here for tradition's sake. They were both exhausted: the thought of not only being a prisoner but fearing that when you close your eyes at night they may never open again was taking its toll. The price of being alive.

The old man finally rose, finished with his secret art, bones tired of the chilled sea air. "Viche Pitia?" he said softly.

Mårten-Ludvig stood, taller than his companion, still looking out at those metal statues carrying the want to create death, but with a vigor in him sparked by those two magic words: "You're saying you've got some?"

"Oh, yes, quite a few bottles."

He looked at Kasper, studied those old, dark eyes, noted how tired they were yet how they still carried a tinkle of youthful innocence, or the faintest memory of it; how they were filled with old tales that wanted to be drunkenly spilled for another soul to inherit if only their windows were left open.

"When the hell were you going to tell me?"

"Now, my friend. Today."

It was understood. Might as well get proper fucked, then,

end of the world coming and all. He heard a whisper of a party tonight, though not likely he or Kasper or any League Member would be invited given it was a Limey Officer throwing the mad ball. Oh, just think of all those beauties they passed on the streets every day, the kind faces who always offered a warm smile, no matter the weather, how, without a doubt, they would all be there, given that all the women loved the English.

His eye caught the carving Kasper left as they began their walk back: a massive erection, alone, ready to burst. How Mårten-Ludvig underestimated the horny old goat—seventy-three years young and one thing constantly on his mind, even amid true chaos: sex; fucking; wanting somebody to pull on his hair a bit. No wonder it was only a whisper they heard about a party.

13

Two Kiwis walked into a Tórshavn pub with a real, proper need to quench their thirst and suppress the maddening anxieties that they felt crawl up their spines and through their brains like an army of ants, only to be eye-fucked, in the most unpleasant of ways, by nearly every British officer stationed on the tiny Island. An awkward silence lingered for no more than five seconds, though it felt more like five lifetimes to the Kiwis. Before anyone could speak, Geoffrey Braxton—the elder Kiwi whose idea it was to digress to Føroyar's oldest pub—took his accomplice, Malcolm Levy-Willis, by his jacket collar and together parted the Sea of Limey Officers and ponied up to an empty spot at the bar, as if it had been reserved for them all along. They sat with their shoulders hunched and their heads down, the universal sign that they meant no harm, only sought happiness in a cold glass like the rest of the lot.

Conversations resumed. The representative of New Zealand breathed a sigh of relief and realized that this was the only time that they wished they, like their fellow League Members, were *both* bilingual. English ears picked up all forms of gossip without a thought. Though they were no different, all the Islands were buzzing with news of a party tonight and it seemed like they and other fellow League Members were the only souls not invited. Avoided like the plague. Better they drowned those sorrows quickly.

Upon ordering two pints of the swill the rest of the place was drowning in, they clinked glasses—cheers, mate—and downed half each. Bitter, stale, boring, and not as cold as either of them liked. A sour look morphed onto Geoffrey's face. "Would rather have some of that Landsdowne. '03, preferably..."

Malcolm rolled his eyes, spoke into his beer, "Storytime..."

"Pardon?"

"Nothing," he said, licking away the foam that nuzzled into his thick mustache.

"You doubt I've had the '03 Landsdowne, then?"

"Doubting you've had any Landsdowne, Geoff, let alone the fabled '03."

"Oh, don't go on like you know anything about it, you prat."

"Hey now—"

"Just cause the vineyard itself has halted all production, does not mean the bottles that are already stored away cease to be."

"How did you procure one?"

"My father was the assistant winemaker."

"Didn't realize I was in for such a treat."

"Honestly, Malcolm, being honest here. My family was quite close to the late William and Hermance Beetham. My father started from the bottom, harvesting, working long days in the baking sun to bring home little pay. But I never heard him complain. Nor my mother, whose main duty was to teach Madam Beetham English. As a bonus my mother learned a bit of French from her—and I must say, it's a bit of a shame you don't know the language—but I digress. By '88, the year our Lord took William home, my father had worked his way up. I was still just a boy then. It was the year the first-ever Pinot

Noir grapes were planted in our country, and, mate, it breaks my heart knowing that William never had the chance to try it, never got to know what art he grew there. I was with Romeo Bragato when he tried that inaugural vintage; this was 1901 then. We, of course, tried it throughout, barrel samples, bottles upon bottles. We loved it. But it was our only exposure to it, so what did we know? By then I'm still young, but old enough to really have a true appreciation for the world that I was growing up in. So, when my father tells me that renowned oenologist and viticulturist Romeo Bragato is coming to our vineyard to try New Zealand's first and, still, only Pinot Noir, you must understand, this was a very big deal. As you *should* know, he loved it."

"But of course."

"But of course, of course. Now, 1903, specifically, holds a dear place in my heart. It was the last vintage my father worked on, *his* masterpiece, for once. He died of a heart attack...during bottling. Only sampled it a few times...said it was the finest art he ever consumed...'Liquid Velvet.'"

"Wow."

"He was also the first non-white winemaker in New Zealand, possibly the world for all we know...gone too soon."

Malcolm stared at Geoffrey with a look of pure confusion.

"Something wrong, Malcolm?"

"'Non-white?'"

"Ah. Yes. Well, my father was Māori, and my mother, still living, is a waYao from Nyasaland. She escaped Africa with her family when she was thirteen. Found a home in NZ. Met my father. Adopted me...and..."

"I am sorry to hear about your father, Geoffrey."

"Ah." Geoffrey pushed away tears. "It was a long time ago. Come on—" *Clink.* "—another round then."

Two fresh pours of the piss-gold pints were placed in front of them. Geoffrey took a sip and noticed that he was enjoying it more than the first; maybe the first had already worked its way through his bloodstream, maybe he was getting old then, almost sixty now, ah, hell. He looked over at Malcolm, who hadn't touched his new pint yet, was seemingly lost in a memory, staring blankly forward, a smile creeping dangerously onto his face, a bad thing around these parts— hope, that is. Geoffrey suddenly slouched forward, sweating hard, leaking from every pore...he stared vilely at the pint as if it were a neck he'd like to wrap his hands around and throttle.

"Geez, Geoff, I know you're craving that family juice but no need to get upset now." Malcolm couldn't even fake a laugh. Something wasn't right.

Geoffrey looked from the pint to Malcolm: eyes bloodshot, neck bright red, veins pulsating violently, foam running out of the corners of his mouth. He placed a firm hand on Malcolm's right shoulder. It looked as though he may fall over at any moment, and the physical link between bodies was all that kept him stable. Malcolm grabbed his countryman's forearm.

"Killed myself," Geoffrey pointed with his left hand at the pint that stood on guard, tall and proud, sweat just starting to trickle down its side. He nodded his head back as if he was trying to point someone out, but Malcolm couldn't tell who he was gesturing towards, with too many people there, all looking the same, and he's dying. Fuck, shit, wait. *And he's dying.*

"Doctor!" Malcolm hollered. "Is there a doctor here?! I need a doctor!"

A crowd gathered around them. Anonymous hands without faces helped lower Geoffrey to the floor, and Malcolm used his jacket as a makeshift pillow.

"I am a doctor," a woman said as she stepped forward; slow English indicated that she was still learning.

"You?" He scanned the crowd. "No one else?"

"Don't bloody insult her, mate," an Officer called out.

A small rabble started, insults from faceless trolls thrown

his way.

"I'm sorry...what is your name, miss?"

"Dr. Eir Dahl."

"Dr. Dahl, can you help him? I..." How embarrassing, lost in her native blues while a man lay dying on his jacket. "I think he's been poisoned."

A hushed murmur filled the silence that tried to slip in— English gossip. Smoke filled the room, blending with the murmurs, senses upon senses, everyone lit up cigarettes in unison as if there was some kind of cue. He found it odd that all of them should be so concerned with the outcome of this, not likely anyone truly hoping for death, but it seemed that none had the intelligence or even the common decency—or common fucking sense—to realize that they were actually increasing his chances of enjoying his fill of divine bottles with his old man and the Beetham's at the Pearly Gates by filling his weak, struggling lungs with their toxic smoke.

She bent down close to him. "Ljós," she said sternly, extending her hand blindly. Three Officers, quick to react and learned in a bit of føroyskt mál, offered up their own Zippos. Dr. Dahl grabbed one, a nickel-plated lighter with the Three Lions etched on both sides.

"Open his mouth," she said to Malcolm.

The light illuminated his wet cave. It was shallow: tongue and tonsils had swelled considerably, uvula nowhere to be found—closing time. The red walls of his mouth filled up with blood with each passing heartbeat, which became slower and slower until all blood flow stopped completely.

Malcolm stared dumbly at the fresh corpse that he may have considered a friend at some point during their careers together, but it was all too soon. Sadness didn't grip him fully, only brushed by him like a stranger on a busy sidewalk, and for that, he supposed, he was thankful. Death started to fill the room. The smell of it. Dr. Dahl pulled him to his feet, walked him out of the crowd. She held his face, eyes locked upon his.

"I am sorry."

"Me too."

"They will find who did this."

"I hope so."

There was what she thought was pure terror in his eyes. She thought this must have been the first time he really encountered death, perhaps a lucky one with parents still living, grandparents alive and well enough to be great-grandparents, aunts and uncles all accounted for, cousins on the straight and narrow, brothers and sisters striving to be just as great as he...all alive, all strangers to the foreign tragedy of death that now lay a few feet away. What strength. What glory to behold. To be there at the end for someone. To be so close to death, to see it at work and say: "Is that all?"

"Are you alright?"

"Yes. Yes, thank you, Doctor. You did all you could...whoever did this knew what they were doing. He was beyond saving."

A young Officer whose name tag read Church, walked up with Malcolm's jacket, which was now horribly wrinkled and likely smelled like Geoffrey—and likely would forever and ever and always—and stood by awkwardly, even after Malcolm had taken it, as if he was waiting on Dr. Dahl.

"If someone could bring him to the Cathedral..."

"Consider it done, sir," Officer Church assured.

"I'll be up there in an hour or so..."

They nodded and watched silently as the Kiwi who spoke like his words were not his own—ghostly, like his physical form was just a vessel for phantom commands that seemed to flow right through him—walked out of the Tórshavn pub and into that familiar greyness. Past anxieties that feasted constantly on his consciousness were joined and, without invitation, began to dine with fresh worries.

When he got back to his appointed home, a wild thought occurred to him that he'd half a mind to kill poor Geoffrey ten times over if it got him a dance with that Doctor at that party tonight. He decided that he best have a quick think about Dr. Eir Dahl before he informed his fellow Members. Fantasy ran amok: that soft pale hand of hers wrapped around his throat, his own lucky Zippo in her other, her thumb flicking it on and searing the hairs off his ass, his right hand twisting her bare nipple, a smirk of genuine euphoria pasted across her face. The image of Mary appeared before him then. Eighteen years of faithful marriage and here he was, standing alone over a toilet with the fabricated memory of a young doctor he'd only just met, and the very real apparition of his wife's face watching him with pure disgust, loathing, and utter shame to have ever called herself Mrs. Levy-Willis. How the hell did she know? It vexed him—so much so that he went completely soft, like a balloon that was slowly depleted of air, embarrassing. He zipped up, blue and filled with more than just shameful guilt, and went on to delay the calls to the fellow League Members a second time as he decided to pen a letter to his wife. After he sat down and brought words to life, it did occur to him that he had not received a letter from his wife in over two weeks. Was he the only one? Were there others amongst him, alone, left to wonder whether their lovers—who, by all accounts, may not consider themselves to be their lovers anymore and moved on—half a world away, still held them in hearts? Had the Brits finally stopped all forms of communication? Or, worse, had the outside world fallen into that deep and evil darkness that would soon consume them, too?

14

A cool breeze gently blew through the garden. French lilacs, pink and white and yellow dahlias, violet-vined hollyhocks—all strangers to this place but finding peace with the soil that welcomed them all to this perfect land. A warm ray of sunlight bled through the window, melted across the still bodies that eloped vigorously, inhaling and exhaling as one as if they shared the same breath, saving the air, put on display for the thousands of quiet little dust mites that watched them so curiously. Sweat from below evaporated, consumed by those spying creatures. Would they, those tiny spies, ever go unnoticed once, if ever, noticed?

It was a shameful pleasure for Mary Levy-Willis, whose teeth were seductively sunk into the young man's broad shoulder, and he whose nails dug into his employer's flesh and left red trails of ecstasy across the white canvas of her back, but she enjoyed it still, if not presently then later, privately, the memory of it. He was fifteen years younger than she, a gardener that Mary and Malcolm had both agreed to hire, the one responsible for the luscious garden—renowned around Wellington—that Malcolm almost always took credit for— unless Mary was around to give credit where credit was due—

whenever brought up in conversation, which it often was as it was a thing of beauty.

At first, André Dejardins had only wanted to fuck Mrs. Levy-Willis as a way of getting back at Malcolm for not only taking credit for his life's work but for paying him less than what he would pay a white gardener, but the private relationship had grown into something far more beautiful than either of them expected. It offered an exuberant rush of ecstasy whenever they were alone in the bedroom together, a rush neither of them had experienced before. She still locked the door, always, even now, when Malcolm was half a world away...but a part of him was still there in the unread letters he had penned for her: they laid nearby on her bedside table, a stack that quietly grew over time, a bed for the dust that eventually grew tired of floating around them.

He usually found himself in dreamland afterward and bounced between the same handful of recurring dreams: in one he beat Malcolm to death with his bare hands, with some help from a few gardening tools, then buried him in the garden, causing some demonic plant to sprout almost instantly and haunt him from afar. In another he not only killed Malcolm but then went on to *eat* him: he started, usually, by slitting his throat, then breaking nearly every bone in his body, which made it easier to flay him completely, reducing him to a broken, bloody-pink sack of grotesque meat, after which he was impaled with a long metal spear and slow-roasted, like a pig, over a large fire. The third dream was of fucking Mary in front of Malcolm, the bastard tied up in the corner with his eyelids taped back, or sometimes cut off, so he was forced to watch it all, though whenever he fell into this dream he was never quite sure if Malcolm was enjoying it or not. The last and newest dream was one he had half a mind to act on: to plant new seeds in that forbidden garden of Mr. Levy-Willis: help grow a new life, a welcome-home surprise if Malcolm were to ever return, instead of pulling out and painting her body like a canvas. He thought once would be enough, but the sex turned out to be a powerful drug (for both of them), something they both constantly craved; a burning desire; a want; a need. He thought once that he would actually tell the Sir what he'd done and quit on the spot, bid them both *adieu*, and sing his way towards the sunset—proud and happy, in search of other gardens that required his care—a song of his own creation:

> Je suis un avec les arbres,
> L'herbe, ces fleurs,
> les abeilles occupies.
> Tu vivras dans un tableau
> Au moment où je suis avec vous.
> Pas besoin de me remercier,
> Parce que je ne peux pas
> t'emmener à Eden,
> Mais je peux te faire
> la prochaine meilleure chose.

The song was never sung aloud, only in his mind. The tune coincided with a pining for his homeland of Chablis where any day he wished he could walk about the town and enjoy the finest Grand Cru made from the finest of Chardonnay. Les Preuses was his preferred bottle, vintage didn't matter, maybe some brie to go with that, too. What he had to drink down here was the complete opposite of Les Preuses: Sauvignon Blanc from Otago, from vines that were seventy-five years old, planted in 1865 thanks to one Jean Desire Feraud and the Otago gold rush.

He didn't think of himself as a coward for leaving his old homeland—he was never that hard on himself, always the rare optimist—just a young man who saw an opportunity to get away from hell. After the war broke out, everyone with some sense began to flee. Many went to South America, some stayed in Europe, but a few quietly went to "The Last Paradise on Earth"—a place still alive and breathing, evolving most peacefully, going shamelessly unnoticed by we who are far too "busy" to stop for a minute and appreciate what's out there waiting, hidden a world away under untouched stars, with land so green, air so pure, and water so clear you'd swear they were lying, or you dreaming—New Zealand.

He was only twenty-two but had been tending to gardens since he could walk, having learned from his mother and his father who were gardeners and harvesters in vineyards in Chablis, working for anyone who needed the help. André's parents, Tionge and Makena Dejardins, left Côte d'Ivoire after Tionge had successfully fulfilled his duty and fought for the French in World War I, somehow not becoming one of some 150,000 casualties of fellow Côte d'Ivoireians who lost their lives fighting a war they wanted no part in to begin. For their heroic efforts, the French government gave an acre of land to a thousand individual men and their families upon completion of three years of active military duty while still stationed in France. Tionge applied immediately and was quickly accepted. Somehow—maybe a mix up with paperwork or a true and honest stroke of luck—the government blessed him with a small plot of land in the heart of Chablis, where he was the first non-native, non-white landowner, though able to speak the language and understand their story, and the community was quick to accept them. He sent all the money he made back home until Makena could afford to make the trip over and finally reunite with her love. A year later, they welcomed their first and only child, André.

He lived in peace up until that word was foreign to every tongue, if anything he realized how thankful he was that his parents passed before the War itself broke out so they would not have to experience another bloody conflict in their lifetime, that they passed in a time where peace and love were still believable...a thing he lost all hope in when he saw fires ravage the country he grew up in...that was until he came to the last holy paradise on earth. The kind of place anyone would be able to find fine enough to die in, which he would do one day when he was old but not the son he would raise alone one day whose mother he would never meet for she was unable to bear the shame of her family knowing her unfaithfulness, as that boy would leave that place when his father died and with it find a new place of his own, just like his old man did, but with a different passion in the vicinity of the same field.

André quickly found that many of the beautiful people of this land believed in certain philosophies with which he was wildly unfamiliar concerning the world, how it all began, and how it all would end. The Māori truths, "legends/myths" as some would have them called, are not only to be told through generations to detail their people's rich history, but to share knowledge of the universe entirely. Mary Levy-Willis, whose father and grandparents were Māori, grew up listening to truths—she told them to André sometimes, after they were done fucking, during that special moment of pillow talk when one is on the verge of sweet, blissful sleep and the other is whispering sweet nothings—that would not only, in her mind, define and shape her personal philosophy of the world and how to exist within it, seeing it more as a part of her rather than apart from her, but a haunting outline for the story of humanity that paralleled reality itself.

(Ka mate, ka ora. [Eternity times eternity plus infinity until it was all created as a whole collective consciousness.] Ā, upane, ka upane. Ā, upane, ka upane, whiti te ra.)

How, back before the beginning, it all looked the same in the dark. Until: the Sun, from the utter black abyss of darkness, shined forth Light, illuminated the world, and with it the realization that all things can end—that yes, it is always night, but we can stop it with some light if we choose to be consumed by it—

Let your valor rise,
Let your valor rage.
We'll ward off these haunting hands
While protecting our wives and children.
For thee,
I defy the lightning bolts of hell
While my enemies stand therein
    confusion.
O god—to think I would tremble,
To a pack of wolves seeing fear,
Or running away,
Because they would surely fall
In the pit of shame
As food for the hounds
Who chow down in delight.

—or love, for love is the most intense and intimate battlefield
there is, or so they want us to believe. It cannot be simulated
nor described to someone who has no previous correlation
with the sacred emotion. And that is our curse: to feel and
experience. Spending lifetimes fighting for something that we
do not fully understand, like that was the only purpose, what
we were created for, and to question the idea of free will and
with that idea the creation of human nature and all that comes
with it: lust, violence, greed, empathy, apathy, faith, bullshit.
Every-thing all at once. Again and again. What began was the
beginning of the end...because no one will notice the cracks in
something till it's fully broken in front of them.

15

A light dust of snow covered the sidewalks. Anytime a strong gust of wind blew just right it would kick up some snow and twirl it around, dance with it, and create a tiny snow tornado for no one at all unless you happen to be out there, waiting for it, and caught a glimpse. It was cold but not unbearable. The mitten-covered hand of Lilibeth Pepperwood was wrapped around the leather-gloved hand of her boyfriend, Baxter Black, and together they walked happily down the quiet streets of Walla Walla. They weren't the only ones: a few couples and some groups of friends were out, but not many. Most of the shops and restaurants were closed for the night, a few bars still open—Whiskey Dick's being to the go-to spot for the college kids, like them, which is where most of the people were headed if not home. Lilibeth and Baxter, however, had no destination in mind—it just felt good to walk and feel the cold air fill their lungs, to be outside and not crowded in a loud, dimly lit bar where you can't hear each other speak. Not ideal.

Lilibeth and Baxter had met on campus at Walla Walla College last year in the English class they shared. He was six-foot-three and part Amish—kept that traditional beard and all—while she was just about five-foot with intoxicating, emerald-green eyes and a voice sweet and soft like cream. They were both in their final year of school and were excited for it to be over. She was going to finish with a B.A. in psychology and a minor in education while he was studying to be a Theology major with a minor in Biblical languages. They had not yet discussed what they were going to do after graduation; they both had their plans, and they both knew they did—Lilbeth wanted to get a teaching job somewhere preferably *out* of Walla Walla while Baxter wanted to work for a ministry preferably *in* Walla Walla and build a church for the college—but neither was mentally or emotionally ready for the conversation yet, or so they tried to convince themselves, as they both felt that it was a "big deal" and both unknowingly shared the sinking feeling that if they brought it up it would bring with it the end of their relationship. Neither was one-hundred percent sure how, like neither of them would be willing to compromise for the other—after all this time was there still a lack of trust between them?—for the past month foolishly locking onto that worst-case scenario idea and, unable to let it go, let it fester and feed, tip-toeing around it because that was best they could do.

Their walk was done entirely in silence which they enjoyed, comfortable with one another to the point where they no longer shared that awkward silence, both unable to pinpoint the exact moment in time it had happened, one of the more natural things about them. The silence ended when they came across their friends, T.H. Locke and Serenity ("Goldie") Rivers—the latter who, growing up, was a toe-headed kid who insisted that everyone call her Goldie, which eventually and finally stuck as she one day completely stopped responding to Serenity and only communicated if referred to as Goldie. That was eight years ago but she was still the same way even though her hair had darkened over the years into a more dirty-blonde on the verge of brunette, with not much gold to see anymore. Everything fades away eventually. If you were to call her Serenity, even by accident, she would shut down completely, and likely walk away. She once threw a drink into the face of her ex-boyfriend, Dixon Wragge, during a house party off-campus. They had been there not ten minutes when they got their first drinks and Dixon had introduced her to a fraternity brother and called her Serenity by mistake. He didn't even get the full name out of his mouth when her drink—a very strong, gin-based punch—splashed all over his face. She ended up leaving with the fraternity brother to which he had failed to properly introduce her, who was now her current boyfriend, T.H. Locke—who stood there in a full suit and tan camel-hair overcoat with his curly hair ruffled by the wind, Jewish pride radiating off of him. He was a man who could one day be a great, trustworthy-looking politician—if there is such a thing—or a mob boss who would kill your whole family if you looked at him the wrong way—and who knew better than to call her Serenity and had done well the past two years.

"Where're you two off to?" Goldie Rivers asked, bubbly as ever.

"Just out for a walk," Lilibeth Pepperwood said with a smile.

"Nice night for it."

"Indeed. How've you been, Goldie?"

"Oh, real swell. You know I broke my leg, right? Just got the cast off."

"What? How?"

"And how've you been, old boy?" T.H. Locke inquired of Baxter Black while their girls carried on with their conversation.

"Oh," Baxter started, "same old same old, really. Nothing too exciting to report."

"No news is good news, eh?"

"Yes. And how've you been?"

"Never better, old boy. Getting ready to shove off to Seattle after graduation."

"Oh?"

"Job lined up. Law firm."

"Ah."

"Safdie, Heid, Isaac, Tatelman."

"Pardon?"

"That's the law firm." T.H handed him a card that read:

SAFDIE, HEID, ISAAC, TATELMAN.
ESQ.

(There was a phone number and address on the back of the card, but Baxter never saw it as he never flipped it over—was too focused on the names.)

"Biggest and best in the Pacific Northwest."

"Wow, that's something...how come they're not in alphabetical order?"

"What?"

"The names."

"Why would they be? The order represents power. It...ah, you wouldn't understand."

"And that's," Goldie continued to Lilibeth, "why I will *never* wear road skates again."

"Golly," Lilibeth responded genuinely. "I really can't imagine. Where'd you get them anyway?"

"T.H.'s great-uncle Wally used to work for a British company that designed them. They weren't even from this century. Can you believe it?"

"Gosh, it really is something, Goldie. May I ask why you were naked, though?"

"Oh," Goldie gave a mirthless chuckle. "T.H. and I do prefer to be completely pure and nude when alone. We'd do it all the time if we had true freedom. But we understand the public is not ready and wouldn't accept this lifestyle."

"Freedom isn't free," T.H. added.

"Y-you...prefer to be naked? All the time?"

"Of course," Goldie said, somewhat surprised by the question. "You don't?"

"I—"

"Oh, it's so freeing, Lilibeth. Really you ought to try it. You and Baxter both, really. It's so freeing."

"You just...do the same things you normally do at home...but naked."

"Correct."

"Golly."

Goldie and T.H. mentioned that they were headed to Whiskey Dick's and insisted that Lilibeth and Baxter join, giving the old shtick:

"At least just come out for one round."

"It's been so long since we've seen each other."

"Not sure when I'll see you again."

So they agreed, not actually feeling forced at all, just going along with the flow, perhaps with the predetermined intention to stay for one drink, two max.

To no one's surprise Whiskey Dick's was full, though not horribly full like Lilibeth and Baxter previously envisioned. They could at least hear themselves and were able to find a table for the four of them right away as two couples were leaving as they arrived, to which Goldie said it was meant to be and they all were inclined to agree. The bar itself was technically a basement of some shitty apartment complex and you had to go down a flight of stairs to get in. The ceiling was low, the floors were always sticky, there was a constant fog of cigarette and Marijuana smoke that covered the place like a milk-grey curtain, and the mixed drinks were dangerously strong, but the beer was perfectly chilled whether a bottle, can, or draft. The owner, ("Whiskey") Dick Blythe, was a loving owner who wanted to see people enjoy themselves in his bar—

a Walla Walla native and legendary hooker for the Walla Walla Rugby Club back in the early '30's, where he would bring pints of bootlegged whiskey to every match to be consumed afterward, sometimes before, thus the nickname—he was just over fifty, a true silver fox, and not like those other bar owners who resented and loathed human beings for being in their establishment like they were heathens, who hated being there and were only in it for the money, who thought it'd be easy...no, Whiskey Dick loved everything about the bar ownership life, all the trials and tribulations, and wouldn't have it any other way.

At the table, Goldie started off and ordered a Singapore Sling (gin, cherry brandy, fresh lemon juice, and soda water) with a couple of rocks, Lilibeth a Bourbon Lancer with a lemon wedge, T.H. a Rob Roy, and Baxter politely asked for a Shirley Temple, which he did get, but old T.H. insisted on him also having a real drink and ordered Baxter an American '77 which was the Whiskey Dick's take on a French '75 (replacing gin with bourbon, simple syrup with dry vermouth, and Champagne with an American pilsner—no fruit, ever). T.H. said he would pay for it, of course. Their server was Joandra Kingsley, a few years older than them, near twenty-five but a Walla Walla legend—or infamous soul depending on how you looked at it. She was a single mother of four with a fifth on the way, all with different fathers, a known fact that made pious men like Baxter shake his head and never look her in the eyes, while to others like Lilibeth and Goldie she was something of a feminist-hero and rebel-icon as she never let the fact of her age, her children, or who they may have come from shame her in any way. She wore her heart on her sleeve and was even promoted to assistant bar manager and given a raise after her third child, Joline, because she went right up to Whiskey Dick on her first shift back, two weeks after the birth, and told him that she could no longer survive on what she was making and if he did not pay her what she deserved then she would walk.

A legend was then born.

All around them was an animated scene of people a lot like them: young and ironically happy and unaware of how bad the world really was outside their Walla Walla bubble—or if they *were* aware they were not as educated as they should be to speak on it well enough. Nearly all of them consumed cold beer with violent thirst, some enjoying a bit of death in the afternoon, a few uncomfortable black velvets at a table in the center of it all, which made some wonder if they ought to feel a bit guilty for having such a good time while folks might be mourning nearby. A couple of geniuses enjoyed some hangman's blood—gin, whiskey, rum, port, brandy, and a dash of porter at Whiskey Dick's, the smooth and hangoverless go-to that if you know about you know about—while a select few had some adios motherfuckers and one chaotic soul casually sipped on a glass of three wise men—a concoction of Nikka Single Malt Whisky, Shichirō Rye Whiskey, and Two James Bourbon.

Not long after their drinks were set down on the table, who should walk by but Bambi Müller and Cade Nyström on their way out. None of them really knew each other well—T.H. and Cade had gotten to know each other when Cade asked advice on legal copyrights for his parent's beer a few months back, and Bambi was a Müller so she was at least known of—still, Bambi smiled at Lilibeth when their eyes connected in passing and Lilibeth smiled back. Common courtesy. Cade and Bambi left the building, out into the cold dark of the night. Baxter looked away in disgust and shook his head.

"Damn foreigners. They've no right, no damn right thinking that they can mingle amongst us."

The statement took everyone by surprise. Lilibeth was caught completely off guard, Goldie genuinely did not care after a few seconds passed, and T.H. Locke and his ancient blood took serious offense.

"You said you were building a church for the college, eh?"

T.H. asked, quite matter-of-factly, a bit of a bite to the question.

"After graduation. It's a work in process."

"'A work in process.'"

"Yes."

"Aren't we all."

They ordered another round. T.H. elected not to pick up another for Baxter, figuring he was a big boy and could order his own if he liked. He did not. He sat there and chewed on ice and did not add to the conversation anymore, which would cause them all to wonder later, when the night was truly over, why the only two cents someone would put in for the night would be something so fucking stupid and hateful.

"Well—" Baxter cut in loudly, his next spoken words about one hour later, while the three of them were in the middle of a conversation centered around the silent film era—Goldie was particularly fond of this era of art, as was Lilibeth, who loved Victor Fleming but was more impartial to his more recent speaking pictures like *The Wizard of Oz* (1939) and *Gone with the Wind* (1939), which to her were already classics, while Goldie's favorite film was *The Arizona Express* (1924) and she would die on the hill of Tom Buckingham being a "genius who left this world too soon ... ahead of his time," and always seemed to speak of the late Tom Buckingham with an emotional tenderness that always piqued T.H.'s interest (who was more of a Lex Ingram man himself with *The Garden of Allah* (1927) as his favorite), and how she nearly choked up every time like she still wasn't over Tommy B's death (which happened when she was around thirteen and offically no longer Serenity)—and only a quarter way done with their drinks, "—really think we should get going soon."

"We're not even done with these drinks yet," Lilibeth explained. "Bax. What's the rush?"

"Yeah," T.H. said. "B-Man. What's the rush?"

"Church tomorrow morning. It's Sunday tomorrow."

"Ah," Goldie and T.H. said at the same time.

"Yes. Need to be fully rested whilst praising the Lord."

"That right?"

"Oh yes."

"Huh."

"Right, then." Baxter rose from his seat (like one does in church when you're asked to rise again after you've weirdly knelt for the hundredth fucking time for the hundredth fucking prayer, all in unison, very cult-like, and it's only been fifteen minutes? for fuck sake mate, o lord, bad knees over here). "It was a pleasure seeing you two. Lilibeth, ready?"

"No."

"Beg pardon?"

"I'm going to finish my drink, Baxter. Maybe have another one, you're welcome to stay. But I want to talk some more with my friends I haven't seen in a while, okay?"

Was it the drinks talking, or the realization that the conversation about Her and Him—their relationship—needed to be brought up? Either way, for the best...

"Lili—"

"She isn't asking for permission," Goldie told him.

"I—"

"Alright there, B-Man?"

Sweat slowly rolled from Baxter's brow as six eyes total stared hard at him.

"Well...I hope to see you at church tomorrow, Lilibeth. Goodnight."

"Goodnight, Baxter."

He left quietly with his head down and his shoulder hunched up a bit, like he was trying to hide his face, and at the same time the world went back to its regular volume of background noise and chatter and glasses being dropped—you know, human things, none of them noticing that the sound had even gone away during that brief dialog. And why would they? Their roles called for them to be in the moment, to focus on their business and what they deemed and convinced themselves was important. Blame it on the alcohol. Fine. It very well could have been the reason that they dove back into the topic of nudism and how free and less stressed Goldie and T.H. felt since they started practicing it at home, and they actually *convinced* Lilibeth, after round three, to come back to their place so they could show her what the nudist culture was like firsthand.

But none of them, nor anyone in Whiskey Dick's that night, could even fathom the thought of angels of death—hundreds of them—that would change the landscape of their life in this country...how those hellbent angels would all fall from the sky like shooting stars that no one wished upon...thousands of miles away...how they would crash violently into those unaware Americans...it wasn't real. Yet. Wouldn't be for another nine hours or so.

16

The ancient stone walls of the Cathedral provided no warmth, breath nearly visible—a ghost from the past trying to reach out as if it wanted to assure you that it was still there—mixing idly with tobacco smoke that was exhaled frequently as all nerves were set on high. The only sounds that echoed softly off the walls were those of minor coughs, chattering teeth, and anxious whispers, all in different languages.

Nineteen men sat in the old wooden pews, each next to their respective countrymen. At the podium stood Malcolm Levy-Willis, alone. He looked at his fellow League Members and wondered which one killed Geoffrey Braxton—which one was a Nazi spy. His head was swimming in dangerous waters, though not with shock or sadness or confusion or anger but with drunk nostalgia, as he found himself slipping into the few memories that he had of Geoff and wondered how many more could've been created...this, of course, was the cause of the three room-temperature beers he had chugged just after he had finished his letter to his wife and after the necessary calls to those who were seated in front of him, the moment when the realization hit hard and all but forced him to go into the late Geoff's stash of Speight's Ales, New Zealand's finest—the dead man had so much, at least twenty cases worth that obviously could not fit in the small icebox which already contained half a case, but for some reason, Malcolm still elected to consume a the room-temperature brews, perhaps a subconscious way of punishing himself.

"I've called this emergency meeting," Malcolm said, silencing the room, "between we League of Nations Members, who have been delegated here to Føroyar, because of the sudden assassination of my fellow countryman, Geoffrey Braxton."

There was an intense murmur between everyone, as if they didn't know already, as if they hadn't seen Malcolm throw dirt into the open grave on their way in. It annoyed Malcolm that he could not understand any of them, their foreign whispers.

"I do not know why," he said, which silenced them again, "someone would choose to kill Geoff...not knowing how they poisoned his pint without us noticing disturbs me. Gentlemen, what I bore witness to today leads me ultimately to believe that someone in this room killed him."

All but two Members stood up in anger and defense, insulted by the accusation; one who remained seated was Kasper Lindquist, who had dozed off a bit from the vodka earlier and whose old bones wouldn't have even allowed him to stand had he been awake; the other was Vidal de la Fuente of Argentina, a quiet, mysterious man with shadowy eyes and an ageless face. His countryman, Máximo Ureña, stood next to him, animated and shouting. Malcolm looked at Vidal, who looked back, dark eyes fixing his way into his soul. It chilled him. They had all heard strange rumors about the man. The one that stuck out to Malcolm as he drifted deeper into the black wells that stared back at him was the origin of his name and how his ageless features were just that: ageless. The story goes that he was one of two hundred men aboard one of three ships that Ponce de León left Puerto Rico within the year of their lord 1513, in search of the Fountain of Youth, and he was one of the few whose lips tasted that thought-to-be-mythical elixir, which granted him immortality. How many lives he lived throughout the centuries, how many identities he held, how many loves he found, and lost, and found, and lost, and...depending on the storyteller, it ranged from the thousands to infinity. The tales he heard were in gossip from other League Members when they decided to speak English with him and Geoff, who had heard these stories from the British (when were they talking with the British? they always wondered), who had heard it from certain women Vidal had slept with, though no one could ever find the true source of origin, the original teller of tales, though ground zero, he supposed—when he actually stopped and thought about it— was sitting only fifteen feet away.

"Gentlemen," Malcolm said, finding his voice. "Gentlemen! Please, calm yourselves!"

One by one they all reluctantly sat back down, accepting the fact that some attempt at order should be acknowledged.

"What if it was a soldier?" Lukas Lykke, of Denmark, asked with warm sincerity in his voice. "There were...many there, no?"

Small whispers of what Malcolm could only guess were hopeful agreements. The idea of doing business for this long and living with a possible Nazi assassin was horrific to all of them.

"Well, I—"

"They don't like us," François Reuter, of Switzerland, pointed out. "They want us to go away from here, but won't let us leave."

"So they're killing us one by one!" cried the youngest of the three Norwegians, Asbjørn Ruud.

Another eruption of languages, this time surely filled with disagreements, Tower of Babel reborn. Malcolm couldn't help but marvel at how they all sounded, and wonder what old

Geoff would think of the scene.

The dark eyes of Vidal de la Fuente locked onto Malcolm again, though this time the ageless wonder was standing, tall and with perfect posture, as if about to make an announcement. Words caught in Malcolm's throat, and for half a second he imagined this is what Geoff must've felt at first: nothing out of the ordinary, a slight tickle, something he could cough out.

Vidal's towering presence silenced them all as he slowly walked down the aisle, his fellow countryman looking on, unsure if he should follow. He was dressed in all black—shirt and tie, even—leather gloves lined with ocelot fur, a walking stick in his left hand that, unknown to anyone, concealed a blade in its shaft, and in his right hand a rather large briefcase that, by the way he was carrying it, appeared to be lighter than air. Behind the podium that Malcolm stood at was a long table that would usually hold the body and blood of old J.C., Vidal walked right past Malcolm and set the briefcase down softly on it, with grace. He quietly opened the case and removed four bottles of wine, two whites and two reds (the two whites were the same wine as were the reds for he knew he would need this much if everyone would get a taste and he had an old saying: if you have one you have none), and an elegant decanter. He lifted the flat section upon which the bottles laid, revealing another layer—wine glasses, Bordeaux style, enough for everyone, which made them wonder if that case was some kind of black hole or bottomless pit that continued to unimaginable treasures. He placed them gracefully on the altar and removed the flat to show ten more glasses. The man had prepared well for this meeting.

Malcolm let out a soft chuckle as if he was expecting something far more sinister. He, of course, was the only one to find any humor in this, his dry, dull laugh bouncing off of every cold stone in the ancient building, an echo that would never die. No one noticed. It was like he didn't exist anymore, just that he more or less had become invisible, transparent, faded from this reality into another which his colleagues could not perceive, yet he still saw them, or what he assumed were like permanent burn marks in the fabric of time that would slowly fade away like he did when his consciousness was ready to accept that.

"Did you question the bartender?" Vidal asked, quietly enough for Malcolm's ears only.

"He...had a heart attack shortly after the incident."

"What a shame. Someone, fetch us some water," Vidal said. His voice was soft, but it seemed to cut the air like a knife.

Everyone looked at one another for longer than Vidal would have liked when, finally, brave Mårten-Ludvig stood and silently walked out of the Cathedral.

While they waited for the water of life, Vidal opened one bottle of red, held the cork to his nose for half a second, and then poured it in the decanter. Every eye was watching. He opened a white, poured a small splash—an ounce—into a glass, and offered it to Malcolm, a surprising gesture that brought him back to the real world.

"Malagousia," Vidal said.

"Not familiar with that varietal," Malcolm admitted.

"It's Greek. Comparable to a French Viognier."

"My god, that nose. Oh. My word, this is beautiful."

"Yes, I know."

"Stop!" Kjell Gundersen, of Norway, screeched. He stood pale and shaking like a thin branch being ravished by harsh winds. "Please! Put it away!"

Everyone looked at him curiously and with concern. They looked to his countrymen, Asbjørn Ruud and Ingvar Håkon, whose looks of stone were cracking under the weight of embarrassment. Ingvar, the eldest, stood set a hand on Kjell's shoulder, which made the man jump nearly out of his suit.

"Få dem til å stoppe!" Kjell pleaded.

"Berolig deg selv, vær så snill," Ingvar said sternly, as a

father would to a child who had been misbehaving and who may or may not even be his own flesh and blood. Reluctantly, the manic Norwegian sat down and looked at the cold stone floor, fighting back tears and the intense urge to throw up. Ingvar stroked his beard and looked at the altar, at Malcolm and Vidal. "Apologizes. Kjell here suffers from dipsophobia. Please don't hold this against him."

There was an exchange of side-eyed glances followed immediately by an eruption of laughter, save for Vidal, who stood swirling his wine.

Mårten-Ludvig returned with a pail of cold water, lost in the commotion. He set it on the table. The laughter faded, the last echoes dying slowly as if wanting to make the memory last somehow, to live a little bit longer than intended.

"What a shame," Vidal said when silence returned. "For we—and I hope it's quite alright if I speak on everyone's behalf when I say this—are all dipsomaniacs."

Silence again, all of them not knowing if this was some sort of test from an alleged immortal.

"No? I brought glasses for everyone. Step up if you care to share with us. What we need to discuss will sound better with this running through your veins. Here, Brother Måtren-Ludvig, since you were kind enough to retrieve water for us, have some. And yes, there is enough for everyone. More, even, now that we understand Brother Kjell better."

Philippe Liebernez, the eldest of the three Swiss, approached first. "More of a red man myself. Mind if I start with that?"

"Of course I mind, Brother Philippe." (It astounded everyone how the man was able to remember everyone's name, the proper pronunciations, and they were sure there were more personal details about them that he retained as well.) Vidal's words were never harsh, but they carried a certain edge to them that cut every man deeply—even when the words were not directly addressed towards them—in the area where the soul would be located if it were a tangible artifact. "This is Xinomavro, think of it as the Barolo of Greece. We must allow it to breathe."

One by one they lined up for a healthy splash of that delicious and ancient Malagousia, which, Vidal explained, was nearly extinct, but was confident someone would find it again and bring it back to its rightful place as one of Greece's top white varietals. He told them this with an unexplainable twinkle in his eye as if light was both passing through and being created within the windows of his soul. The Dutchman, Jurgen Van Der Hout, a nonbeliever of Vidal's mysterious past, asked between sips how he managed to get such a rare bottle and one so incredibly old, so well preserved. There was a chance Vidal smirked, though no one could confirm, and he looked at him and said, "You already know this answer, but come now, there are far more important questions to ask."

"Like who killed Geoff?" Malcolm politely inquired.

"Yes."

"You agree then?"

Vidal looked at Malcolm now, studied him, almost came to admire his thinning brown hair; his baby-fat face with a mustache that looked like it was glued on; his dark eyes that, in any situation, were filled with dread—and waited, playing with his thick mustache, a habit after all these years he never really realized.

"Had to be..." Malcolm unbuttoned the top of his shirt (why did it get so goddamn hot all of a sudden?). "Well, someone here?"

"Let's not forget," Máximo chimed in, more to Vidal, voice a bit hushed but strategically loud enough for others to hear. "Project Clockwork and how this all ties together."

"Of course, thank you, Brother Máximo."

The Members swirled their juice and stared in bewilderment, wondering what the fuck Project Clockwork was.

"The answer to your question, Brother Malcolm, is not necessarily a straightforward one."

"How's that?"

"Simply put, the answer is both yes and no."

As Malcolm forcefully pulled his gaze from Vidal's, a nigh impossible thing since his eyes cast a sort of spell, faces flushed red from confusion, with anger that they were possibly being accused, and in part from the alcohol swimming through their bloodstreams.

"I...*we* don't understand."

"That, Brother Malcolm, is because I've yet to explain. Aristotle taught us that temperance is *literally* a virtue, did he not?"

"Ik wed dat hij hem ook kende," Bernard Jonker whispered to the two other Dutchmen.

"No, Brother Bernard," Vidal said, not looking his way, "I did not personally know Aristotle."

"Kuinka monta kieltä hän puhuu?" Valtteri Markkanen asked his Finnish colleague, Eljas Takala, in a rather nervous tone in between puffs of smoke, the only two still lighting up cigarettes at this time.

"Many languages, Brother Valtteri, and please put that Nortti out, you two are ruining the wine. I've cigars, Cubans, for when the red is ready."

"I say," Werner Eriksen, of Denmark—a true lightweight, already tipsy off the one glass—spoke up. "Who put you in charge anyway?"

Vidal looked at him, then his Danish companions.

"Uh-uh," Mikkel Skovgaard stammered, making a great impression, no doubt.

"Forgive him," Leif Dalgaard blurted. "Can't handle his drink."

"Clearly, Brother Leif," Vidal said with that sharp edge. "Clearly."

Old Kasper sat peacefully in the first pew, listening to bits of the discourse here and there as he nursed his glass and occasionally took sips from his flask that, of course, contained Viche Pitia. He did not care if it ruined his palette and took away from truly experiencing the wine, nor did Vidal care, it seemed, as he was somehow fully aware of every situation around him. Let the old man have his fun. Mårten-Ludvig backed away from the awkward commotion and sat next to Kasper, who immediately offered him the flask. He thanked him silently and took a long, healthy swig.

"You know what this Project Clockwork business is then, Kasper?" Mårten-Ludvig asked upon handing the flask back to the old man.

"No. Not entirely. I've heard rumors, as I'm sure many here may have as well. If any of what I heard is true, it sounds like...an impossible thing. Something...I truly, especially for my age, cannot understand...I hope this man may bring light to it."

"And the rumors you heard, they could possibly connect with the death of the Kiwi? Was he a part of it?"

Kasper looked at his colleague, his friend—his eyes were foggier than Mårten-Ludvig remembered like he had started to go blind within the passing hours, as if the light from within the windows of his soul had begun to dim, replaced with a certain fear he hoped to never understand: "My friend, I don't know...but truly, with all my heart, I hope not...my old colleague, before you, Åsa Wuopio, had somehow heard about it and became obsessed with it, to the point where I'm sure it was the only thought on her mind...then one day...she was gone...no word, no trace, no explanation...that was about two years ago now...I still think about her everyday...and if she went there."

"Went where? What is it, Kasper?"

Kasper took his time, choosing his next words carefully and, even though only a few spoke their native language, spoke in an almost inaudible whisper. "Tror du att vi är ensamma, Mårten-Ludvig?"

"What?" Mårten-Ludvig motioned to the lot around them. "We're clearly not...?"

"Yes...the universe is a rather big place indeed."

"Time for the red," Vidal called.

"What's the water for, then?" Eugène St. Pierre, another Swiss delegate, asked.

"Cleaning the glass a bit, couldn't bring enough for each bottle, forgive me, but try to dry it out well. And don't drink it right away. Let it breathe still, let it learn the glass."

Samples of the Xinomavro were passed out by Vidal's impossibly steady hand. They all silently admired the complex nose: tobacco, anise, leather, spice, ripe plum, black currant, and raspberry, all swirling together, powerful enough to give some of the bastards who could still get it up an embarrassing erection. The first sip matched the palette note for note like a velvet wave washing down their throat, and tannins that could rip a less experienced drinker's face clean off was neigh ecstasy—so much like the drug itself that the eldest of the three Dutchmen, Sylvester Klassen, was observed with a tremendous tremor in his right leg, had fully completed orgasm from the beauty of the wine, had never experienced a beverage so fine in his life, had turned away from the group as if in deep thought with the wine but a few had already spotted the dark, wet blotch on his grey trousers that stuck to his thigh, not that anyone could blame him—was that good.

"Are any of you gentlemen—" Vidal began, ignoring the sexual arousal the juice had produced, "—aware of what the largest desert in the world is?" He twisted his wrist effortlessly, the red liquid spinning with such velocity that the dark, inky red was but a thin red blur falling from the mouth of the bottle, cutting through the air and into the bottom of the glass.

"The Sahara, of course," young Asbjøn Ruud said with confidence. Ingvar Håkon patted him on the shoulder as if he'd won some prize. Kjell Gundersen, of course, wished he dared to do the same but instead was cowering, still, in the pew behind the two Swedes as it was all he could do as he waited desperately until the alcohol was depleted.

"One would think so, Brother Asbjøn. But alas, it is Antarctica."

Asbjøn flushed red with embarrassment and threw the rest of his wine down his throat. Like he disappointed his country by getting the answer wrong, like he was back in school and all the kids were going to make fun of him for it, and the only thing that could protect him now was more alcohol to blot out the noise, to blur his vision so he was blind to their hatred towards him. But it was never really that deep.

"Yes," Vidal went on. "The frozen tundra down south is the largest desert in the world, nearly always forgotten about, with good reason too, no? Who would want to venture then, when nothing grows there, nothing survives? This, my Brothers, is where Project Clockwork comes in. You see, Brother Máximo and I have been able to obtain precious information before we were sent here as many Europeans—Nazis included—fled to South America when this madness broke out."

"And you're just now sharing it with us?" Jurgen Van Der Hout blurted.

"We didn't think it was necessarily credible, nor important, Brother Jurgen. That was, until Brother Geoffrey was assassinated. We've no doubt now that our League of Nations group here, created as a fall back if the world falls into darkness, has been infiltrated by the enemy."

"How can you be so sure?" Eljas Takala asked. "Maybe it *was* just a British soldier who killed Geoff."

"We're sure that some Brits are not what they seem. How many and who, though, is much harder to determine. There are more of them than us, obviously, so we must keep the status quo, act as if everything is normal, don't blatantly accuse them."

"What's this got to do with Antarctica?" Malcolm inquired.

"Getting there, sorry, the wine has carried us away. Project Clockwork, we found out, is an operation developed by the top Nazi scientists, who claim to have found the *center* of Antarctica itself, made possible by secret and ancient tunnels that led them there. Who or what designed them, we're not sure, but they are testing, within these tunnels, a new kind of weaponry. Flying ships that move at impossible speeds, *teleportation*, one case, we were told, meetings with other beings...possibly those who created the tunnels, and who now live in the center of the ice, hidden from the world, plotting, knowing no one would ever disturb them there."

Everyone was dumbstruck; the wine didn't help at all. What they were being told had to be impossible. Mårten-Ludvig himself did not believe it, and then he thought of what Kasper had said, looked at his old friend, and saw that fear on his face, deep in his foggy eyes, and instantly believed it all. Every word. One after another they all voiced their disbelief, silently at first then louder and angrier.

"Can't be true."

"Makes no sense."

"Who would want to live in ice?"

"How do you know this again?"

"Lies! All lies!"

"Who's to say you're not the Nazi?"

They all froze, turned, and looked at the man who spoke the words, the accuser: Kjell Gundersen. He sat upright, still pale with fear from the booze that flowed through their veins and in the air. His heart was in his throat.

"It's an honest question, is all..."

"Come here, Brother Kjell. The wine won't hurt you."

Timidly, after what seemed like an eternity, Kjell rose from the pew, the wood whining and creaking from the relief of the weight of his body. He stood in front of Vidal de la Fuente and tried his absolute best not to shake but failed miserably. His deepest fear surrounded him, bringing him back to his youth when his father would drink until blind and beat the living fuck out of his mother, him, and his three brothers, just because it was a Wednesday and it was something to do.

Vidal placed a warm hand on his shoulder. "My friend," he said calmly. "Accusations like this are very dangerous; it's how we lose ourselves into madness and distrust. We cannot accuse anyone until we are one hundred percent sure of it. I know I am not the enemy, and that is all I know, truly. I know, therefore I am not. Understand that we will find the man. Perhaps not tonight, but he will be found. Soon."

"I...I'm sorry." Kjell broke down and began to cry.

Vidal wrapped his arms around him and held him tight. "As am I."

Instantly, before anyone could realize it, Vidal dunked Kjell's head into the wooden pail of water and held him there as he thrashed and kicked. They all looked on in terror. Frozen, as if he cast some sort of spell over him—which he may have—as he looked at his fellow Members and stared them all in the eyes, one by one by one. No one could move, not even Kjell's countrymen who desperately wanted to save him. They just stood there, mouths agape, a dumbfounded look set upon their faces as if Vidal would suddenly see and realize the horror in their eyes, recognize his mistake, and let Kjell breathe again. It didn't take that long. His body went limp and Vidal allowed his corpse to slump dead to the floor. The trance was broken. The two Norwegians ran to him and tried, with sad desperation, to wake him...to no avail. He was gone.

"Why?" Ingvar Håkon cried.

"Was he..." Mikkel Skovgaard, the stammering Finn, spoke from the back of the group, sounded almost convinced, "the enemy?"

"What?" Vidal said. "Oh, unlikely. Not sure. Like I said, we won't find out until a proper investigation is done."

"What the hell is wrong with you?" Asbørn yelled.

"I cannot trust a man who denies the wine I offer him, all pasts aside. There was something off with that one. His eyes held demons...demons I've no interest in being involved with any longer."

They were all shocked and sickened with disbelief of what this man had done and of the words he spoke...like none of it mattered. How unflinching he was, as if life itself—Kjell's, at least—was never sacred to begin with. And now they had to continue to live with him, do business with him...with a fresh thought that sprouted in everyone's mind that if he wasn't already the enemy hidden amongst them, then there were two murderers they all had to worry about.

"Now," Vidal spoke, his voice slicing through the silence, the soft yet harsh echo bouncing impossibly, it seemed, off of every old stone in the building...something about this stonework..."I think we should adjourn this meeting, pick up again tomorrow." No one dared object. "After all, I heard something about a party going on tonight?"

17

Before Operation Valentine, Dr. Eir Dahl felt like she blended in with everyone else. A character in the background of a play that was bigger than herself. People were kind to her, she fell in love—once—but when the British arrived it was like she was something really, truly special and that, for the longest time, was something she could not understand.

She had only left home once: when she attended Aarhus University and obtained her doctorate in medicine and a bachelor's degree in philosophy, the youngest woman to do so. Though, upon returning home to Føroyar, it was as if nothing changed, for it hadn't. There was no grand celebration, no old friends coming out of the woodworks to congratulate her on her historic achieve-ment, the mayor of Tórshavn not there to welcome her back at the docks—no, none of it as she had foolishly imagined during long nights alone in her foreign bed when anything was possible. Nothing changed. Everyone still went about toiling away with lives they weren't happy or sad with but were just used to, forgetting, altogether, to dream as she did.

Her family, of course, couldn't have been more proud of her. They threw her a *small* party when she returned home—

aunts and uncles and cousins from Denmark whom she barely remembered from her adolescence, and some who clearly hardly remembered her, all attending and barely speaking to her after the routine, "What an amazing achievement," and "You've grown up so much," which made it all the more awkward and obvious that none of them remembered each other, like they were bad actors hired for the occasion and couldn't deliver a proper performance. It was the furthest thing from grand. Or meaningful. By the end of the night, having told the same story to numerous faces, all pretending they cared, she wished that it was just her parents and her younger brother, and realized she didn't need a crowd to feel validated (if you could call thirteen people a crowd).

Then came the foreigners who kindly invaded their peaceful Islands for their "protection." And since then, she never blended in. It was as if every lad who stepped off the boat was fawning over her, a few actually asking for her hand in marriage at first sight. It annoyed her at first, sickened her, all of them wanting the same thing. Her views changed when her close childhood friend told her, after a few drinks, how *she* should be taking advantage of these silly boys and their newfound lust, and how she was doing just that; how they'd buy her nice things with what little money they had; how she rarely paid for a drink anymore; how she could fuck anyone she wanted, then never speak to them again because she suddenly forgot their stupid language.

"It's your body, Eir," she explained in a hushed tone in their native føroyskt mál, as if someone in the small pub was listening. "The world could end tomorrow. Some of these fools are *really* packing, if you get my meaning. Have some fun. You don't have to fall in love as they do. And who could blame them, honestly? They've never seen goddesses like us before."

Dr. Eir could not help but laugh, blush, and feel some butterflies fly around in her.

"Finish that drink. I know you haven't fucked since you've

been home. We're going to change that."

"You're serious?" she asked with a small laugh. She never had sex with someone she didn't know, but was growing fully enticed by the idea...she could always blame it on the alcohol.

"I don't joke when it comes to this. Our bodies are temples. We get to decide who worships us. Best part is, if you're unhappy with who you picked, there's plenty more willing to step up. Tonight, every night, we fuck."

With a graceful determination, she slammed the rest of her Veðrur—a pilsner from one of the oldest breweries in Føroyar, Föroya Bjór—whipped the foam from her red lips, and looked hard at Dr. Eir, who was still nursing her brew—Jóla Bryggj, a winter lager—and wondered what was taking her so goddamn long.

"What?" Dr. Eir finally said.

"We're leaving."

"To go where? There's alcohol here. And cock?"

"Very good observation, my sexy little doctor, but there's a party going on tonight, British Officers are throwing it at the Three-Headed Sheep."

"Ah, well...why are these gents lingering here?" She gestured discreetly, with a simple nod of her head, as if waving her golden hair about, towards the sad-looking soldiers, five of them, not quite sitting together, spread out at the bar, socially distanced but aware of those around, maybe each waiting for someone special or working up the courage to make a move, killing time by slowly drowning in those delicious beers. The names of which they could never pronounce properly.

"Them? Who knows, or cares? Perhaps they don't want to have fun, or they're only here *because we're here.*"

As if on cue, the lonely five turned their heads in the direction of the only two women in the dank, dim pub, a place that was once vibrantly lit with live music of local artists, where they didn't have to worry about what language they spoke, for all were friends then, a place they usually always felt comfortable, until *they* came along and the natives altogether stopped going out. Yet here they were. They really were goddesses. Women possess the means to be the most powerful entity on the planet. Understand this. And like a shot of adrenalin, Dr. Eir did. She realized. She understood what her friend had been preaching and burst out laughing at the sad fools gawking at her, knowing they would never taste the pleasure she had to offer, knowing she was better than them. Suddenly, always, they—she and her—were God.

She finished her drink, finally, to her friend's satisfaction.

"To the party, then?"

"Obviously."

They walked arm in arm out of the place they had grown up drinking in, and in the strangest way it was like leaving behind a chapter in their life they would be happy to never remember, for now—at least tonight—it was tainted with sad souls who looked viciously at their perfect forms—arguably the best asses on any of the Islands, Dr. Eir dressed in black, her friend in red, hypnotizing everyone, even the old barkeep who had been pouring the same beers for thirteen years and never batted an eye like that, faithful to his wife and all, but fuck, he could not help himself, his eyes betrayed him, and who the hell could blame him. The girls knew all those eyes were upon them—how they wondered what they had underneath, but knew at the same time that they would never actually know and knowing, too, that they would go back to their lonely cots and have a wank off some dirty, imaginative fantasy about those goddesses they had caught a long glimpse of—yet still, they did not give a fuck and laughed on the way out, where they felt, truly, finally, like the Queens they are, and hoped that one day, soon, all women would wake up and feel this way as well. As you should, Queens.

Upon entering the Three-Headed Sheep, the party was already raging. Half-naked people danced and poured drinks down the bodies of one another before licking it off, men and women alike. They thought they'd recognize someone there, but all the faces were the same: foreign. Maybe the booze—having had three pints at the pub before—had affected them, or the booze that these folks were consuming had some manic effect, the likes of which caused the strange horror-show of faces before them, like it physically altered their DNA by the second and only they could recognize it for they had yet to drink what they were pouring here.

They were almost immediately offered the odd concoction when they found two seats at the bar, as if reserved for them, which, to them, made sense, that almost everyone there was drinking a mixture of absinthe and Kahlua, lit on fire then quickly snuffed out to give it a nice, smoky, aromatic kick. The liquors were smuggled in by the Brits who found out how to make the deadly drink from a few Russian girls, who, most likely, were smuggled in as well, as it was, for some reason, a popular drink over there. Side effects, it seemed, caused your fucking face to melt off and slurred your speech. Other than that, the partygoers found it to be quite good and just what they needed.

A thin, ghostly layer of smoke gently covered every visible inch of the establishment. No one covered their mouths—they wanted to fully inhale the aroma of it all. The smoke itself was a mixture of the fire from the drinks, thick cigars, and from a few who took to smoking substances completely foreign to the Islands: Marijuana, heroin, methamphetamine, crack cocaine, angel dust...just sitting there for twenty minutes would give you a second-hand high. Mass amounts of sage also burned. Directly to their four o'clock sat an older South American gent with an ageless face filled with knowledge and wisdom and eyes that held secrets and horrors that few could ever live through. A young, red-haired girl played with his dark mustache, her pink tongue licking the ends of his curls, his face illuminated by low-burning candles, his right hand dancing with the burning sage over a deck of cards, larger than poker cards. Tarot cards, the curious girls finally realized, some cracked and worn rough, made of leather. After a few go-rounds with the burning bush, the man placed the sage in a large ashtray and began to shuffle the deck, speaking softly, yet somehow loud enough for the girls to hear, as if by design...like it was for them. Across from him was a soldier— an Officer by the looks of the patches and medals on his handcrafted wool suit, tailored precisely for the exact proportions of his body, by a face he never once wondered about, by hands he would never shake, what painstaking work went into not just his uniform but every single unique uniform for every single unique body that harbored every single unique soul in the entire Royal Army, never once contemplated how many threads that surmised to, how many fingers may have bled from constant dull stabbings from the needle that they were all too used to, those nameless heroes that go unnoticed, songs unsung, giving you everything you need, asking nothing in return, for a while not understanding how you could forget them, they were always right there, forever aware of your impenetrable unawareness to the world outside of your perspective. Women kissed their necks, fondled them underneath the table, the men somehow bore faces that did not register emotions near to the state of visible awareness or the ecstasy-state of mind that comes when receiving world-class felatio from soft, wet mouths and hands to match or even, though likely impossible, the disappointed look of being the one stuck with too much teeth—no, nothing then, not a flicker of acknowledgment towards the world around them, all sense of business and consecration centered on the table and the cards now before him, three cards, facedown.

Themen each took a sip of wine, dark purple and inky, and the ageless man refilled their glasses—the bottle, he explained, was extremely rare: "Penfold's Shiraz, *very* early vintage, 1852." Much to the Officer's surprise, "Doesn't taste, or even *look*, no more than ten years!" Much to the man's surprise, "You know wine, eh?" Much to the Officer's slighted honor, "Just cause we can't grow 'em back home doesn't mean we don't drink 'em. I grew up on bloody Bordeaux, *Vidal*." Much to Vidal's delight, "If you don't want to believe me, that is fine, though I do have a document proving its authenticity, as I try to do with my rarer bottles. I got it from Dr. Christopher and Mary Penfold when I visited their Estate some years back. This is living proof of what good cellaring can do. Wine is alive, like us, it doesn't want to die." Much to the Officer's eye roll as he stroked his thick, rustic orange mustache, "How many years back that'd have to be? Late 1850's, I'm guessin'?" Much to Vidal's recollection, "Sounds about right. I'll show you after your reading. Where are you coming from?" Vidal started at the right, flipped one card over: Five of Cups. "Hmm. What are you heading towards?" The middle card flipped: The Tower. The Officer was visibly disheartened, showing for the first time a real sensitive emotion. "And, what are you becoming?" He flipped the final card: Death. The Officer sat, mouth open, blood drained from his face, heart in his throat, while Vidal swirled his wine that had turned a rustic red. He stuck his nose in the glass, "Oof. It's oxidizing quickly," then took a sip. He looked at the Officer with a sly smirk, "Problem, Captain Bloodworth?"

Captain Bloodworth stood up and pointed a shaking finger that was supposed to be threatening. "You're a bastard, Vidal de la Fuente, a cold, cold bastard," he cried, his voice unmistakably filled with fear, and then turned away and disappeared into the smoke and bodies.

Vidal sat back, gathered up the cards, and began shuffling them, wondering why people asked for readings then become angry at the results, like they were afraid of the truth, like they thought they could fight the future, like they believe they have—or had—a choice at all.

A man named Máximo Ureña approached Vidal, sat where

the distraught Captain had been sitting, and whispered something to his countryman, news that caused Vidal's face to slouch into a state of anguish. Then, just as quickly, he put himself back together, changing a mask for a different scene, a different character. They quietly discussed the situation: Vidal shook his head, put his finger to his lips, shook his head again. Suddenly, they rose. Vidal looked at the ancient bottle of Shiraz and contemplated taking it but felt that he had enough, and there were always more bottles to be had. They left the building, gone in the blink of an eye, vanishing into thin air.

The girls looked at each other and shrugged, returning their attention to their drinks and more important topics:

"For fuck's sake, it doesn't seem like any of these bastards will even be able to get it up by the end of the night. We probably would've had better luck back at the other spot."

"If you're looking to settle, sure." Dr. Eir and her friend had to shout just to hear each other.

"You're learning quickly, Doc. That's my girl. Never settle. Never let them shame you. You choose who you want. Not the other way around. Oh, and one other thing." She leaned in real close. "Stop going out alone, always go with a friend or two you can trust, like me. They will take advantage of your loneliness one day."

They observed their surroundings for a while, slowly sipped on their drinks, and saw, in the back of the bar, a bit of a sex party, which cause wet excitement to hit them at the same time.

"Perhaps we should have another drink," Dr. Eir observed.

"Perhaps so," said her friend, and she placed the order and turned her attention back to the fucking. "Does look like they're having fun."

"Are you already...? Oh!"

She was. For Dr. Eir's eyes only, as everyone else's had fallen out; though, the idea of putting on a show was quite enticing, empowering. She began playing with herself underneath the bar, her red dress lifted to her thighs, two fingers deep inside. Their new drinks were placed in front of them and they took a sip each. Two fingers out and into Dr. Eir's mouth who welcomed that dirty sweetness like she was hoping for it, waiting for it, ready for it.

"What do you think?"

"I prefer it over the drink."

"Good."

They were about to kiss when the return of Captain Bloodworth brought a sudden end to the night, a killing of the mood. He attempted to climb a table, slipped hard on some fluids—alcohol, semen, vomit? it remained undetermined—which brought the whole table down. A chair splintered on impact with the ground as if it had had enough of being sat upon and kicked over for so long that it finally settled for this dramatic suicide in front of everyone, unaware that the crowd itself was more invested in the Captain than the demise of an old chair. Even so, gone but not forgotten. The crowd was laughing at him. Captain Bloodworth struggled to stand as he had blown out his right ACL on the fall down. Underneath his thick uniform, the knee began to swell, doubling in size in a matter of seconds, unknown, of course, to anyone laughing at the poor lad. Yet he climbed another table, this time more slowly; it was all he could do to bury the pain coursing through him, and he threw his arm around an old wooden pillar that had supported the old ceiling since the building's inception in 1889 and now acted as a giant cane for the Captain as he looked out through the smoke, at all the high faces, at all the fucking and consumption.

"Everyone!" he yelled to deaf ears. "Everyone!" Louder this time. "The Japanese have bombed America!"

The noise began to die down, moans of pleasure receding, fucking ending altogether, the precipice of ecstasy pushed back.

"Pearl Harbor has been bombed!" It was quiet now. "I...America...will be entering the war." He straightened as best his bum leg would allow and gave the folks a salute. "As you were."

Some returned to their lives as they had been thirty seconds before the news, unbothered, while some were too soft to continue, some unable to deal with it all—too fucked to properly rationalize—a few broke down into tears, bought another round. Dr. Eir turned to her friend, the breathtaking woman in red, and wondered about her thoughts. Was it time to be afraid? If they could get America, they could get anyone, right? She looked at Dr. Eir, neither of them loving the vibe anymore, admiring her baby blue eyes.

"Well," she began, with hints of melancholy that rolled freely off her tongue, acutely noted by a simple drawing out of the first word and a prolonged pause that filled the space between them with a soft form of sadness that wasn't quite ready to ruin your makeup, still unsure why it was there in the first place, what situation it was actually meant for, and with eyes that didn't match her voice at all. "Fuck me."

18

Freezing rain struck exposed flesh like knives, like a murder of crows pecking violently at some newly-dead carcasses—what they always were—soaking through their wool uniforms and chilling their bones. The wet sloshed around everywhere and already a few men were sniffling and sneezing. The grey, dreary clouds completely blotted out the sun, as it had been all morning, and the air itself did not smell like a fine rain at all, no aroma to let you know—if all other senses failed—that a deluge was occurring; just sight and sound and the stinging feeling of the sharp drops. The overall morale of the men was low, all of them carrying the same sinking feeling that something god-awful was about to occur that would send them all over the world and into madness. It was written loudly over all of their young faces: eyes anxious and filled with melancholy, longing for their childhood homes, for their warm beds, their mother's soft caress on their infant cheeks. Only a few "Gravity Heads," as the "Cats" (dubbed by the G. Heads, short for "Pussies"—real creative, they thought) called them, whose egos were higher than the bombing air raids, genuinely excited for bloodshed, to be judge, jury, and executioner, for they believed that there was glory to be found in being a bringer of death, for they grew up in believing the old lie old that young Wilfred Owen warned them about: Dulce et decorum est pro patria mori.

Rumors spread through the barracks: tensions were increasing between the U.S. and the Axis. Some whispered that there was no way we would ever get involved (those boys were hoping their words would become true and breathed a sigh of relief every morning that they stayed out of the war, yet still a dark feeling that hung over them like their own personal storm cloud that would not allow them to fully believe their quiet talks of peace), others said that we were bound to enter the fray any day now and were just looking for the right excuse. No one knew what would happen; it wasn't likely that their outfit would be sent off to fight, but then again, these days, it seemed like anything was possible.

The voices that spoke darkly to Pvt. Jenson Reynolds bounced sporadically in his head, like he could feel them—not exactly in his mind, he would tell you—but rather physically: they bounced from one end of his thick skull to the other, as if someone had just hit a fresh break in billiards and there were no pockets in his consciousness, nowhere for the voices to go but everywhere. For the moment, they all told him the same thing: *Be still. Stand straight. Keep quiet.* So he did. He was one of thirteen men stationed at the 422nd Military Police Brigade outpost in Eureka, Washington; Jenson was one of three ordered to stand guard outside during the downpour. He looked at the two men who were forced out here with him, Pvt. Roland Joyce and Cpl. Indiana Pope, actors playing their roles, slouched and sniffling, tears surely lost in the rain, both likely wondering what they did to deserve this when all they ever wanted was to serve. None of the MPs here wanted to be MPs, but there they were, not knowing what exactly they were waiting for. The reason being why all thirteen men were, unwillingly, assigned to MP duties in a small ghost town was for their exemplary achievements during the mandatory IQ test, at puzzle and problem solving, and their horrible faults when it came to handling long-ranged weaponry—or any weapon, really, aside from their pistols.

They stood shivering and dreamt silently of a way to push time forward so that their shifts may end and they could climb into their warm beds. Jenson didn't dream. He only thought of the place he called a home and felt, again, literal cracks in his consciousness, as if it was his skull itself that was breaking, spiderwebbing throughout like a tenebrous wildfire, which allowed the dark to sneak in like smoke. He distracted himself, unwillingly, by allowing the voices to chaotically clash: they blended together, argued amongst one another about all that dark: how they didn't mind it, really, felt natural they told him it felt like home.

"*Fuck!*" a terrified voice shouted from inside. Jenson knew right away that it was Sgt. Westley Underhill, for all the voices that filled the bodies he'd grown accustomed to being around occupied his consciousness, too. Pvt. Joyce and Cpl. Pope, with outstanding reaction times, imme-diately rushed inside to see what happened. Jenson stood still, remembering his orders were to stand guard out here—that was his role now. He thought of what must have happened: the first thought was that Sgt. Underhill, the Cat that he was, must've been playing with his firearm, trying to impress, and shot his balls off, then it occurred to him that no shots were heard. The second thought was that Sgt. Underhill must have simply cut himself badly while shaving—his balls, of course, as he always made sure to remind his brothers-in-arms that he was the proud owner of the cleanest manscaped jewels in the barracks, claimed that taking care of the hair down there was vital, essential, to every man's health.

Jenson, unmoving, monitored the rainfall, hard and heavy, visibility limited to no more than five feet in front of him, listening to the music it created with every drop, then wondered why he was wondering about Sgt. Underhill's balls—or possibly the lack thereof—anyway.

Inside the tiny barracks, the men—save for SSG Book LeDu and Sgt. Zachariah Noah who, per usual, were both richly invested in a book—were gathered around a now-silent radio. Noah's great white beak of a nose was practically buried in the King's James Bible he always carried: Genesis, fitting, or perhaps not so fitting for the few who knew the dark secret he buried deep in the depths of his soul (he was not positive who of the 442nd knew what had happened): a few months back, after a night of cards and drinking some rare barrel-aged gin from Detroit—the first legal spirit made in that great city since Prohibition—Sgt. Noah, shitfaced for the first time since he and his younger brother, Ezekiel, stole their father's homemade moonshine, which of course got them fucked up not only from the booze but from their father who beat them raw with his studded belt, a lash for every year they lived which was fifteen then for Zachariah and twelve for Ezekiel who would grow up to become a raging alcoholic...Zachariah was drunker in the bunker than he was back then, and actually drunker than the rest which surprised them all: "Thought it was against your belief, Z, 'Thou shalt not get fucked up,'" Pvt. Lamar ("Red") Atwater chirped, which Sgt. Noah didn't acknowledge, was too busy concentrating on not puking in front of them. He proceeded to stumble into the room where old Jenson slept (they all had separate quarters), having skipped out on cards and dreaming sweet nothings while he cradled his book of Shakespeare tragedies. Sgt. Noah hovered close and watched the lad for a minute—how soft and innocent his breathing was, how low and quiet he whispered to himself in his sleep, in other voices—then, as if pre-meditated, ass-raped the boy, actually *threw up* on the back of Jenson's head, and had the audacity to cuddle him throughout the night. It had happened on another occasion two weeks ago, and for a third time four days ago, when Jenson swore that Sgt. Noah was *sober* that time and had just splashed some liquor on his neck to give off the scent like a cologne...Sgt. Noah, of course, never looked Jenson in the eyes since that first time and tried to avoid him during the day, yet always had the mental image of the back of his head at the front of his mind, while Book— when not talking about the Louis v. Conn fight and how Joe was the greatest heavyweight alive (true) and how Billy was ducking a rematch which was why he broke his hand on his father-in-law's face, old Greenfield Jimmy, just looking for a way out, an excuse, he would say—was a lover of fiction and kept the books he read *in bed* with him, nine books total, having just finished *The Hobbit, or There and Back Again* by J.R.R. Tolkien, he was now onto *Anthem* by Ayn Rand (Richard Wright's *Native Son* was up next), and, unknown to him at the time, was having a sort of intimate and private awakening within his own consciousness from this idea of "I," of breaking away from a unit, being his own person, and this just two days after hearing about that Conner Family down in Napa Valley, which to him, once he thought on it later, seemed like the answer to the question he'd been silently asking himself since he got here: *what the fuck are you doing with your life?*

The Conner Family, Book told his comrades—like it was his own tale and he was already a part of it—was living the true "American Dream," it just took a little time for them to get there. He had heard their story from some winemakers when he went down to Walla Walla to find a fucking drink, away from the G. Heads at Pete's Last Stool, who notoriously only allowed members of the industry inside but upon seeing Book serving the Nation, rocking three strips no less, they couldn't say no, which caused Captain Alan MacPhail, a racist fuck at the end of the tale, to call the only black man in the 422nd a goddamn liar, which prompted Book, always cool as ice, to smile and explain to the simple man that "They don't give a fuck about that black or white or brown shit out here, yeah, the strips helped, but if you're a good person they'll treat you like one."

The story went, he heard from these winemakers—who had nothing but praise for the family and the wine they made, their Cabernet Sauvignon revolutionary for the region—that they were the first black family they knew of to grow and sell wine in this country. One man, Garfield Womack, a winemaker for Dharma Cellars—owned by a free-thinking, pacifistic, wine-drunk wannabe Buddha known as Skip Bronson whose employees were willingly trapped in the same collective consciousness, as located on the right bank of Mill Creek in Walla Walla or as Skip dubbed it, "the Tight Bank"—was, for some unknown or unasked reason, something of a Conner Family historian. Garfield Womack was overweight and balding, his face always red as if the wine he consumed constantly flowed through him, and breathed heavily as he told Book that a slave ship from Ghana unloaded 150 stolen souls in Philadelphia to be sold against their will in 1864. One buyer, an Irishmen by the name of Murphy O'Connery, purchased forty-two and immediately put them on another ship for a long and unforgiving journey, this time to O'Connery's homeland of Ireland, specifically his hometown in Cork. It was the first and last time they ever saw the man who bought them, he never said a word to them, it goes, for when his business in Philadelphia had ended, a few days after the forty-two had set sail, his ship across the Pond was not so fortunate as it went down to Davy Jones's Locker six days out. When the forty-two landed on shore there were only thirty-five still alive, when they had reached Cork and the O'Connery home there were thirty-three. When they arrived, a sickly old man who worked as a groundskeeper escorted them inside while he hacked up a lung, blood spraying onto a dirty handkerchief he used to cover his mouth, and told the thirty-three to wait while he went to fetch the lady of the house. They all stood silently and looked up at the high ceilings, chandeliers, and casting lights they could never dream of before, at the framed paintings on the walls that were so richly detailed it was like they were looking at a portal to another world. One man even raised his hand as if to put his arm through the art and climb through into paradise until a woman next to him quickly pushed it down with a new paranoia she had never felt before, like someone was watching them...After standing still and silent for an entire hour, some literally pissing themselves, they agreed that they should have a look around—surely no one could have forgotten about them? After quickly finding every member of the household dead (the mother, six children [four boys, and two girls, ages from three to eighteen], and the old man who had just shown them in) a horrible sense of worry went through them. *Is this place cursed? Will we die next? What now?* A few ran away immediately, thinking anywhere would be better than here when old Murphy comes back. Those who stayed did it for the food and shelter free at hand, curses be damned. Throughout the days and weeks that passed, some formulated proper plans and left, others continued to stay and began to realize, after enough time had passed, that the owner of the house would not be coming back, and carved out a nice life for themselves, cunning and clever enough to trick their rather dumb neighbors into believing that Mrs. O'Connery had taken ill and her father (the old man) as well. Séamus Boyle, the neighbor who taught them how to take care of the O'Connery potato crop, unintentionally came up with the rumor on what happened to the children, when, upon talking with four of the eighteen who were still there, asked if the O'Connery children were sent to stay with their aunt and uncle in Dublin and when he didn't receive a no, he took it as fact, a nod of the head and said, "Lord, they must be in hard shape to ship all six up to Dublin. Even Colm, eh? The lad turned eighteen four months ago, could've stayed to help you all out. Ah, maybe s'for the best, though. Gotta look after the young ones, he does." What great blissful peace they were able to survive in at the hands of ignorance and unforeseen death. After a while people forgot who the original O'Connery's were, what they looked like—no, wait, they were here all along, these nice people, we are one and the same, they lived and loved just the same. For those who stayed, it lasted an eternity, but on the invisible cosmic timeline of the universe, it was less than a second. They lived and learned the languages and shared laughs and created lovely memories, until An Drochshaol came around in 1845 with the deadly blight that wiped out a million people, which caused the family that had been living in the O'Connery house—who knew no other life than this, who held stories from their ancestors, the same stories that were still alive in their hearts and were talked about but that way of life was foreign to all now, they were free and owners of their own destiny—to emigrate from this place they called a home. They were able to make their way over to the U.S.A., like everyone else, with the help of Erin Boyle, the great-great-granddaughter of Séamus, who forwent the farm life and instead found a life on the seas by starting her own fishing company. The ship took the unconventional path and landed in Georgia instead of New York and from there they made their way West, towards California. By then there was no more O'Connery family, as they elected to drop a few letters, blend in a bit, forge their own identity, and it was the Conner family that would find gold in the waters out in California during that great rush. James Conner, with his wife, Magnolia, and their seven children—three boys and four girls—were rich. They went to Napa Valley and bought land there, planting and growing what they knew until they were visited in 1862 by John Patchett, who had opened the first winery in Napa County back in '59. He implored James and Magnolia to start planting grapes, that were living on the ideal soil, that it would only get better, and that he was willing to help them with the process. Hesitant at first, not under-standing the willingness to help strangers succeed at something their neighbor also does, for practically no charge, didn't sound "American" to them. They had heard horror stories about the country and would have gone to Canada if words of the gold rush never found them. But the sudden realization of how they even knew how to farm at all, the shared ancestral memory of the exact moment shot through their DNA. In time they agreed to start small by growing just a few rows that Patchett sold them for a rate that could have been much higher, Cabernet Sauvig-non straight from Bordeaux to start. Since then the Con-ner Family Winery has been considered a well-respected Napa Valley producer, later growing and bottling Merlot and Sauvignon Blanc along with their famed Cab.

Word has been—aside from how good the juice is—is that they're hiring down there, was what Book heard two days ago. And now with the shit they just heard on the radio, this new horror to some, this new opportunity for glory to be found to others, is what he tried to ignore, the voice in his head growing louder and louder, screaming Rand's words to block out reality until the words in front of his eyes went blurry and the voice was consumed, drowned out by a tranquil hum that consumed him. Reality seeped in, and still, all was well.

Japan bombed Pearl Harbor.

Growing up in The Bronx exposed him firsthand to a lifetime's worth of violence before he was sixteen. Gangs fought over territory they all thought they had some sort of imaginative title over, crooked police kicked down doors and stole from the poor, easy as one-three-one-two. What kind of life is that? Filled day in and day out with hate, unable to show compassion to your fellow humans, unable to see that we are, all of us one. It made the escape to fictional worlds that much easier for him. Since those days, he never strayed from his path, never fell to the violence and hate around him, with goals of one day writing a work of fiction akin to those great works which he read daily. He had never wanted to join military service, had the belief that all life was sacred and wanted no part in taking one, but his father, a veteran, practically forced him to join some sort of branch (never heard of Wilfred Owen), like the LeDu name needed to stay in the military forever, even if it just got him through college. "Maybe you'll learn to love it," Russell told his son. But disappoint-ting your parents was second nature when it came to a love for the arts, which left Book to join an MP unit, the safest route he could find (the only one in the 422nd to *willingly* join), that eventually shipped him to Eureka, Washington. He figured the money would be good enough for a while until he found something better, never thought the world would get to this point, which is why he was unjustly deemed a Cat in the divided barracks. Fuck it—Book told himself as he closed his book and let reality pour in—they all think I'm a Cat anyway, they even think about shipping my ass overseas, catch me in Napa: working, drinking, reading, writing. Living.

All the men were silent and all of them were aware of the silence, each of them aware that they were all in possession of the same thought: *are we going overseas?*

Technically no, though they didn't know it then. Some, the Gravity Heads would go AWOL before it was all said and done and find their ways to the bloodshed. Until then, they all shared the moment of silence that wrapped them numbly in shock. PFC Jeremiah Castle pulled out his lucky flask—nickel-plated with an etching of an incredibly detailed medieval castle atop a kite shield (a family crest?) —after an appropriate amount of time had passed and poured a splash of its brown liquid onto the ground, a toast to souls he never knew. He looked at the ground, the whiskey pooling on the dirty concrete floor, the grey paint already chipping away. The drink satisfied no souls; was wasted, of course, they all knew, but none said a word. They played their roles.

Eventually and one by one, the men looked up from the wasted whiskey, which to all of them—save for Sgt. Noah, who was trying out a new role, sobriety—was like holy water, and stared at Major George Wynne, the G. Heads with hopeful eyes, a few Cats trying to hide their tears and act like men, all searching their commander's face for answers. They could see the words caught in the Major's throat, his mouth agape...he stared at his men like a fool with nothing to say, choked on thoughts. A man more fit to be a Sommelier than a Major—it's all about who you know, not everyone gets to live their own life—knew for a few weeks now that he had lost the respect of his men, or maybe never had it to begin with. What was there to say? He needed time to prepare something, words that he could string together that would make him sound better than this lot (which he believed in more than anything that he was). He was no good on the spot, but a bit better when one-on-one with his men, mainly the Cats.

Cpl. Sonny Monday—a tall, lanky lad from Littleton, Vermont, wrongfully accused of being a Cat, when, in reality, he was infected, possibly at the moment of his conception, with the neigh incurable state of mind that spread across the globe like wildfire, recently consumed Pvt. Clarke Hume, something Sonny could see in anyone's eye: Nihilism—took his pistol from his holster, realized there was no better opportunity than to give them all one last show, something else to talk about for a while. The gunshot was a bomb to their ears in those close quarters. Sonny Monday fell on the ground, face in the whiskey, brains pasted over the wall and on a few brothers-in-arms, too. At first, to Major Wynne, it was almost a happy occa-sion as this situation took residence, for the moment, over some moral speech about entering the War, which he would now have the time to pen masterfully and deliver to his lads in the morning. But that feeling of relief was short-lived as he now had to deal with that shit. The men, machines as ever, stood still as if all were normal. Even the Cats were unfazed, by which Major Wynne was surprised.

"Alright," the Major croaked. "Let's get him out of here."

"Sonny Monday," Jenson Reynolds said, to the surprise of

everyone as they had not realized he had entered the room, quiet as a mouse longing for the crumbs that fell to the floor as it watched you stuff your face, soaking wet like a forgotten dog, always lurking like some unwanted ghost, his voice carrying with it a strange accent they hadn't heard from him before, as if he wasn't fully in control of himself. "Killed on a Sunday."

19

Vidal and Máximo had returned from the party and felt as though the Cathedral was the only place in the world they belonged anymore...no one wanted to admit that they did not want to be alone. Vidal, as if in apology for abandoning the League for the party after the murder of Kjell Gundersen but not directly apologizing for the murder itself, of course, offered small pours to all the men of one of his rarest and most precious bottles of wine: a 1702 Tokaji Aszú 6 Puttonyos, which was the first blend of all six allowed grapes (Furmint, Hárslevelü, Sárga Muskotály [Muscat Blanc], Kövérszőlő, Zéta, Kabar), aged for twenty months in the finest Hungarian oak barrels, a wine, which during that time, Vidal explained, was the most popular and sought-after wine in the world. Extremely sweet, having a minimum of 150 g/L residual sugar, it was a delicacy reserved mainly for royalty. Vidal claimed that he happened upon a case of the stuff back in September 1705 outside the small town of Szécsény, where he had met—was a guest of, actually—Francis II Rákóczi (officially Franciscus II. Dei Gratia Sacri Romani Imperii & Transylvaniae princeps Rakoczi. Particum Regni Hungariae Dominus & Siculorum Comes, Regni Hungariae Pro Libertate

Confoederatorum Statuum necnon Munkacsiensis & Makoviczensis Dux, Perpetuus Comes de Saros; Dominus in Patak, Tokaj, Regécz, Ecsed, Somlyó, Lednicze, Szerencs, Ono) after he had been elected the vezérlő fejedelem of the Confederated Estate of the Kingdom of Hungary. In the midst of his War of Independence, he decided to throw a party and invited high royalty from all corners of the earth, because if the world was going to end of they might as well go out with a bang. Rákóczi had finished congratulating his newly-appointed Senate—because if the world *didn't* end people still desired titles—when he ran into Vidal de la Fuente, a man he swore he recognized from somewhere, but was unable to place his finger on the intangible memory and was unsure, ultimately, if it had been from a dream or another life altogether. Had he heard of him before? It was a powerful enough name that made its way deep into his consciousness. As he looked into Vidal's dark, smoky, and ever-changing eyes that revealed no secrets nor light, he felt, for the first time, completely undermined by another soul and he wasn't quite sure if that was the man's intention or not. Vidal thanked him in Rákóczi's native tongue. Without a thought, Rákóczi opened a bottle of the '02 Tokaji Aszú 6 Puttonyos and wondered why he invited this man, what secrets he held—it was some kind of spell cast over his consciousness, memories and thoughts clouded, a veil thrown over his window of perception. All of his senses seemed dimmer than usual, but, most strangely, he didn't mind it, and, of course, this was a realization he realized a day later, that the culprit of his lowered sense of awareness was none other than the cigar Vidal offered that he claimed would pair perfectly with the Tokaji, claimed that he hand-rolled himself using twenty-five percent of the finest Ecuadorian tobacco, and seventy-five percent of what he called—recovered from Rákóczi's personal writings— "C. sativa from Jamaica, slightly sweet to not only complement the wine but also marry quite joyfully with the spiciness of the tobacco," whose tetrahydrocannabinol, Vidal didn't mention, was the highest percentage he'd ever come across at that time, clocking in at twenty-two percent pure THC. Vidal, in exchange for some of what he called the greatest wine he ever consumed, pulled out an old deck of cards, leather-bound and maybe only a few decades old at most, shuffled them slowly, and lit some sage with care...

Aside from Máximo, Malcolm and old Kasper were the only ones to accept the rare drop. Vidal assumed everyone would forget about the terrible news for a minute, envisioning how thrilled they would be that he brought another ancient bottle with him, wondering what whispers they would pass amongst one another to add to his never-ending story, this being a perfect distraction and all, so he decided to pour them all a splash, whether they wanted it or not. He felt deep in his bones, for the first time in a long time, no sense in killing them all, under-standing completely that enough blood had been spilled, not just by him in this place, but by and in the universe as a whole. He sat with Máximo and began to reminisce.

"Do you remember Hálfdan Kříž and Güvenç Zafar?"

"They failed us," Máximo Ureña said matter-of-factly.

Vidal was silent, almost hurt by the statement. "They played their part well for a long time. There's still a possibility of finding replacements here."

"Majority is older than Hálfdan and Güvenç by almost a decade."

"They're all young to me."

"Will be hard to gain their trust after the incident with—"

"He was a pawn that had to go. Those we choose will come to understand."

"Why do you ask if I remember them? Hálfdan and Güvenç?"

"I was so sure of the pig..."

"You weren't wrong. They failed."

"Thought I knew human nature well enough that it would

succumb to fucking greed."

"There's still time to save this."

"It's far too late, my friend. There are too many souls here now...predictability is no longer alive...America will seek to destroy its enemy, the world, with a power this universe has never seen...they're going to put our small little lives on notice."

"They tried to warn us."

"If anything, we failed Them."

"What then?"

Loaded question. "There is no one I trust here but you, my Brother."

"But if we fall—"

"When."

"—who will inherit the intel?"

Vidal already knew who he had in mind but still took a few seconds to appear to contemplate it, to look more human. "Suecos."

"With your dying breath," Máximo said like a mantra. Vidal nodded. "And until then?"

"We must take them home."

He understood and left Vidal alone with the weight of that thought: death—like he was subtly forcing him to finally think about his actions. Which he did. And for the first time in an age, as he somberly sipped his wine, he felt tired. Awfully, awfully tired.

Only a few found sleep; many stayed up through the night, their minds infected with the incurable disease of paranoia that spread from brain cell to brain cell like cancer, invisible voices all internally screaming the same question: *What happens now?*

It was not Vidal or Máximo who told them the news but a young, high, half-naked soldier who blasted through the ancient doors: Japan had bombed Pearl Harbor. A few (the Swedes, Dutch, and Finns) thought it was oddly funny—a

British Officer came to warn them, them who despised the trapped League of Nations Members. How high the lad must've been to think they were important enough—finding it unlikely he was *ordered* to tell them the news—and how fast he must have run to beat Vidal and Máximo back. They all sat relatively close together in a few pews, countries be damned, and thought silently about where those other two could be.

When the Argentines did arrive, five minutes later, they were still rooted to the cold, holy floor and the old wood, shocked into stillness. Some eyes lingered on them a bit too long. The Swiss and Norwegians cried openly—the tears Ingvar and Asbjøn shed still reserved for the late Kjell who now laid on a pew, the stench of his death filling the air— without shame, thinking they were good as dead already.

Outside, snow began to quietly freefall from the black sky. Kasper, having inched himself away from the gossip between his countrymen, sat near a window and opened it a bit, allowing some of the cool night air inside as if it was all supposed to be in secret. He watched the snowfall. A wave of nostalgia flooded over him and took him back to his childhood, to one Christmas, back when he was eight or nine, 1877, maybe, when his family totted up to Storuman and stayed in a cabin for the holiday weekend, but got snowed in until January 3rd. Kasper recalled seeing the most beautiful work the universe—or God or whatever—had ever created. Lake Storuman was frozen over completely. His father, Matthijs, and his brother, their uncle, Niklas, sat like statues on small wooden stools, massive corn cob pipes protruding from their mouths as if they were designed that way, a part of them, with thin fishing poles whose lines disappeared into two separate holes in the ice. He and his older sister, Helga, ran, slipping over the ice, not worried about the idea of falling through. Nothing bad would ever happen to them. Somehow, they just knew.

Kasper watched the snow fall soundlessly and wished

desperately that the world would go back to how it was—that the suffering would end; that children would smile again and laugh and play in the snow; that unexpected acts of nature would turn into the grandest of experiences; that adults would right their wrongs and realize that we can't go on killing each other or living this way; that those responsible for senseless murders of innocent lives should be held accountable. We can't keep doing the same thing because the same thing isn't working—it has never worked. It's time to stop lying to ourselves. It's time to wake the fuck up.

He sipped his wine, adored it, and turned away from the memories to look at his brothers—how terrified they all looked as if the world was really going to end now that the yanks were involved. Everything was so uncertain. This tiny spot on the globe was important enough to be protected, to be destroyed. He felt, and knew the others did as well, that no place in the world felt safe anymore, that the unpredictability of all the madness would scorch the earth until there was nothing left to fight over save for the ashes. The bastards were really going to blow up the world this time, or at least have a proper go at it. Die trying. He saw it flash before his mind's eye like a swarm of locusts: a cloud of darkness and ash covering what was left of humanity, silenced after a blinding light that left behind only shadows glued to walls that could barely stand anymore as if their only purpose now was to support the still frame of the shadow that once followed a soul...for the walls themselves had no souls living in them anymore to support and protect from elements falling from the sky. He'd give anything for a different light, the ones they whispered about...from the watery depths of the unknown.

How they all longed—collectively as if all their consciousness were merged on the same mental field—to die quietly at home in their soft, warm beds with their arms wrapped around their loves, a reassuring whisper in their ear: "Everything will be alright."

"We have to leave," Jurgen Van Der Hout said, which shattered the silence, not realizing the thought was audible.

"Oh?" piped Eugène St. Pierre. "How the devil do we go about leaving, exactly?"

"Surely Vidal has a connection. A boat, perhaps?"

"Why should we trust him?" Asbjørn cried. "He murdered Kjell! Probably old Braxton, too! *He's* the spy!"

All eyes turned to Vidal, who sat in a pew alone, bringing the wine to his lips now and then. He took his time collecting his thoughts and navigating his consciousness to find the right words for each of them. But like a personal storm that loomed over and raged inside him, his thoughts and judgments were clouded for the first time since he met with Captain Dragutin ("Apis"/"King Killer") Dimitrijević and the Black Hand Society out in Sarajevo, Bosnia, and Herzegovina:

1914. Three years prior, Dimitrijević and the Black Hand Society formulated a plot to assassinate Austrian Emperor Franz Josef, which never came to fruition. He first met Vidal de la Fuente months after the Balkan Wars (1912-1913), where Dimitrijević received high praise for his military planning and tactics that led the Serbian Army to many important victories.

"Ah, the King Killer," Vidal said infamously as Apis, the Black Hand Society, and a few members of the Young Bosnia group entered a lively pub in Belgrade, Serbia and enjoyed a shot of rakia, in their native tongue for all to hear. The warmth was spreading through their chest and all were ready for more when Vidal's words cut through the air. They walked over—a Young Bosnia member, Gavrilo Princip, one of the youngest in the group, whose cold eyes seemed to age him as if he had already experienced horrors enough for one lifetime, ordered another round to be brought to them, this time requesting the special Očevu krv for all of them, a drink popular within the Black Hand Society, consumed when things were going to get bloody, a mixture of raw eggs whipped together then strained into a glass, a dash of hot sauce, crushed Bosnian black pepper, and two shots of rakia—and surrounded Vidal's lonely table that bore nothing save for a bottle of the extremely rare white grape, Juhfark, from the small region of Somló in Hungry, which sat on the slopes of an extinct volcano—one of his favorite white wines, though there was a legend that came with every bottle: if a woman consumed the rich, smoky, fruit-forward wine she would then conceive a male heir, something that has eluded Vidal all these long years, and yet all the countless women he'd shared that particular varietal with had either turned completely fertile or produced a stillborn...it vexed Vidal terribly.

"And you are?"

"A man who can help."

"We need no help, thank you."

"How'd your last outing go?"

"Ah, mustn't worry about that. We'll get him soon enough."

"Will you."

"You forget why you call me King Killer? It was I, Dragutin Dimitrijević, who started the revolution against King Alexander and Queen Draga."

In 1903, Apis organized The May Coup that led to the overthrow of the Serbian government and the assassina-tions of King Alexander Obrenović I and Queen Draginja ("Draga") Obrenović, put in motion when King Alexander proclaimed Queen Draga's brother, Nikodije, as heir presumptive to the throne.

"That was a decade ago, my friend."

There was a stillness in the room, a visible frustration that boiled inside of Apis, his comrades looking on in concern. He ordered another round.

"We just need time."

"For what? Time is always fleeting."

"The Emperor is expecting another attempt on his life, as he should, we must wait for his nerves to die down."

Vidal laughed.

"Stop that."

He didn't stop.

"I said stop that!" Apis pulled out his gun.

Click: a sound that everyone acknowledged universally as a gun ready to fire, which sort of froze the world. The server that carried the tray of Očevu krv stopped before he reached the table. Apis realized instantly it wasn't his gun and figured it must be a comrade behind him until he looked back and saw all his men empty-handed. Vidal had a dangerous smile on his face. He twirled his mustache with his left hand. His right was underneath the table, gripping his own pistol, cocked, fully loaded, and aimed perfectly at Apis's balls.

"May I sit?" Apis asked.

Vidal nodded. Apis holstered his gun but Vidal did not, his eyes focused on the six men behind their captain, unsure if they should fill this fucker with lead or wait for a proper command. There was a darkness about this man: his aura was all dark.

"I trust that you'll tell your goons," Vidal said. "To breathe a little bit. Have those drinks there. They're making me think they might do something...foolish...if they don't relax. Which *means* I might do something...not foolish, but..."

"Po lakoći," Apis commanded.

His men were reluctant at first, then, after some lengthy consideration—which fueled Apis's rage insur-mountably—consumed their drinks, ordered another round, and sat on old stools at the bar, making sure to face the table, to watch Vidal closely.

"Good listeners."

"Who are you?" Apis demanded.

"Vidal de la Fuente."

"That's impossible."

"And yet," he waved his hand in *volià* sort of way, "here I am."

"Is it true then?"

"Depends."

"On?"

"The nature and foundations of your personal belief system."

Apis opened his mouth, closed it, and was at a loss for words for the first time in his life.

"Archduke Franz Ferdinand will be your next target."

"The Emperor's nephew?"

"His Thronfolger. He will be in Sarajevo next month."

"How did you come by this information?"

Vidal merely glared at him.

"How can I trust you?"

"I haven't blown your balls off yet, have I?"

Vidal finished his glass, stood up, and finally holstered his weapon. "Only way to trust a person, I suppose, is to trust them." A third of the bottle on the table still contained that rare juice. "Please, enjoy the rest." He turned to leave.

"Wait!" Apis cried, embarrassed at how loud it came out. "Your cards. Do you have them? I want a reading."

"I think you already know what your future holds, Dragutin. It won't bring you anything."

"I want to see!"

"You will, soon enough. You will change the world."

Vidal never stopped nor looked back at him, but wondered if he would go through with it. It was the first and last time he ever saw Dragutin Dimitrijević.

"I'm not sure," Vidal confessed somberly to his fellow League of Nations Members. "How we can get off this rock." He finished his wine then stared with great melancholy at the glass, watching the tears slowly roll down the length of the china. "Maybe this is how it finally ends..."

"How what ends?" Mårten-Ludvig asked.

"The world."

"You're just being a bit dramatic," Malcolm said, his throat dry.

Surprised, everyone looked at the lone Kiwi who had a shy look of hope that clearly wanted to radiate free but was wisely held back as the majority erred more towards the belief that, somehow, Vidal knew what he was talking about and the world really was going to end. Under-standable though. Fucking Americans.

"Could always steal a boat," old Kasper chimed in.

"I say!" Bernard Jonker declared. "Stealing a boat from the limey lads will certainly end with us being shot."

"There are local fishermen who've boats that could carry us...for those who want to go."

"We can't steal from them! That's their livelihood!" said Eljas Takala.

"Why's it matter? World's ending anyway." Like that old melancholy-fueled nihilism was airborne and infected a few already on the Islands.

"The old man has a point," said Sylvester Klaasen, the second oldest there behind Kasper at a cool sixty-one. "It must be done. If the Nazis invade here, I fear they won't just shoot us, but slaughter us in unimaginable, demonic ways." He said it as if he had foreseen this twisted image before, a dream...if one could call something that fucked up a dream.

"I know a crew stationed here, rogue lads..." Vidal confessed. "They may be willing to take us all aboard for the right price..."

"Where would we go?" Mikkel Skovgaard asked, trying to hide the fear in his voice. "There's a dark shadow over all of Europe, and now American, too."

"And shadows move faster than water..." Vidal whispered, loud enough to chill everyone.

"We could," Máximo began, "go to our homeland."

"Argentina?" Lukas Lykke questioned as if he had just taken a bite of something sour. "Would *we* even be welcomed there?"

"Our people welcome most."

"President Ortiz does owe me a favor," Vidal said. "Many people there do, now that I think of it."

"And many of them hate the British, so we won't have to worry about them once we land."

"Why does your country hate the Brits?" Malcolm asked.

"Who here doesn't hate them?" Máximo asked rhetorically.

"Yes, we all have good reasons. But why do *they* hate *them*? How do they feel about the Nazis?"

"What do you think?" Vidal asked sharply.

"I think I'm asking important questions."

"You people always seem to think you're onto something."

"What the hell does that mean?"

The weighted silence lingered for seconds too long, enough time for thoughts to fester and feast like rats on trash in their minds, to sprout and take hold of them, anxieties and all. Eyes glanced between one another, to the floor to the ceiling to the men in question.

"Listen," Máximo said lightly. "Everyone is nervous. We go to Argentina, I say. It's the safest bet. Then we could even get a jump on them, hire a private military—"

"Some will have to go to Antarctica," Vidal cut in. "To answer for us."

"O-of course." Somehow, throughout all the terror and turmoil in the world, all that death and destruction, the mention of old Project Clockwork caused Máximo Ureña to grow visibly erect.

"Mind if I see you over here, for a moment?" Kasper quietly asked Mårten-Ludvig.

The two slid away unnoticed, down to the end of another pew, away from everyone else. Kasper finished his wine and now took long drags from his flask, which he offered to Mårten-Ludvig, who accepted kindly and took a healthy swig.

"It's him," Kasper said plainly with the clear sign that age had finally caught up in his voice.

"How's that?" The alcohol from throughout the night was now hitting Mårten-Ludvig and caused his head to swim a bit.

"The spy. *Spies*. Both of them."

"Meaning 'cause they murdered Kjell Gundersen."

"Shhhhh." Kasper looked over his shoulder, but no one was paying attention to them. They were all still debating on how they should get out of this place, Máximo still hard and going on about Project Clockwork with Vidal. "It's deeper than that."

"Murdering one—sorry, *two*—people sounds deep enough to me."

"It's a lot more than two, my friend."

"What? How do you know?"

"Heard them talking openly together when he gave us some of that delicious wine."

"How did no one else hear?"

"I don't think anyone else speaks Spanish."

"What the...what're you going on about? You speak...?"

A mouse scurried by them, grabbed their attention immediately, stopped, and looked at them curiously as if wanting to know what they had to say next. It was the cute kind of mouse, if such a thing exists—light charcoal grey, big black eyes, and ears too big for its body like it was designed to eavesdrop. Part of Kasper's drunken consciousness believed that Vidal himself had created the rodent to spy on them.

"Go away..." Kasper said, brushing a hand towards it. The mouse didn't move.

"Pay it no mind," Mårten-Ludvig told him.

"Ah. I just...don't feel comfortable here anymore."

"So you're with them? Think we should steal a boat and flee for Argentina?"

"No. Not Argentina. I'm sure the weather is lovely there, but we'd have better luck in the States."

"I think our government would want us to stay, or at least

go to a neutral territory."

"You believe Argentina is neutral?"

"They've not declared?"

"No, they've not, and they likely won't. But..."

"Out with it, dammit, Kasper."

The old man glared at his friend and countryman.

"Sorry."

He turned his attention to the two he accused of being spies.

"All I am saying, we who've heard of Project Clockwork only know bits and pieces. Fragments. It's like a ghost story, something that might have been created just for the purpose of scaring us. But after hearing them going into such great detail, and these murders. And how long they were away when we received the news, why wouldn't they come directly back when they heard it? No. It seems clear to me now that they're the spies. I recall Máximo telling me, a week or so ago, about the large German immigration that occurred in Argentina within the last twenty years."

"He told you that?"

"We were just getting to know each other. I didn't really think anything of it, just innocent people wanting to get out of a bad spot, or maybe that's how he put it?"

"Why did Vidal kill Geoffrey then? And Kjell, so openly?"

"Geoffrey Braxton, I believe, was onto something similar, and was taken out quietly. As for Kjell...I'm afraid that's just Vidal's nature. He's a psychopath. Just got carried away with it. Ages of killing, one more life is meaningless."

"Yes, sure, but to do it in front of all of us? Surely he must suspect that *we all* suspect the same thing now?"

"I'm sure he does. Which is why we should leave soon. Without them."

"Think he means to...get rid of us?"

"If not here and now, then on the boat. Bit easier to get rid of bodies in the ocean, I imagine."

The mouse still sat nearby, watching them, and looked to be listening intently, an actual twinkle in its eye that cried out to them, pleading to let it join their escape.

"Alright then," Kasper said to the mouse as if he understood on some cosmic animal-to-human wavelength that the mouse didn't want to die here. Spy or not, the creature deserved to see more than just this rock. He placed his dry, wrinkled, liver-spotted hand low. The mouse crawled up and was placed gently in his coat pocket. It peeked out, small paws on the fabric like it had done it before, and winked at Mårten-Ludvig as if it was always part of the plan or had won the game and really was Vidal's little spy. Whichever one—it didn't matter anymore.

"Should we tell anyone else?" Mårten-Ludvig asked, still looking at the mouse.

"I'd save them all if I could. We can try, I suppose. But we need to leave before the sun is up. With most of the Officers at that party *that we weren't invited to*, they'll be too high to send anyone after us. Not sure how long it'll take you to pack, but I'll be ready within the hour...if we can get out of this place first. Which we should do soon, that stench is becoming unbearable."

"That's death for you."

20

Trees sometimes fall in unnamed forests and may or may not make a sound. They say it depends on who is there—like a human has to confirm it because their being there makes it important, but surely some birds heard it, a deer or two, hungry wolves, raccoons maybe. But fuck if a human didn't hear it, if that which thought it was fucking God was not there and present at that moment, even though God is supposed to be omnipresent, then it did not happen, right? A bear will take a massive shit in that same forest, as one does for it is nature, but for some fucked-up reason it is debated whether or not such a natural act occurs because humans are so goddamn bored and do not truly believe in something unless it is right in front of us, even though we are a species that will openly deny facts even when they are right in the palms of our hands and read aloud, those with the loudest voices saying facts are fake and the news is a lie. Religion runs through the world like a plague and those who are pious enough to rise and bow and rise and bow will believe in what they cannot physically see, so think of the bear shitting that you cannot see and real tangible facts in the forms of newspapers in your hands and how they are one and the same and how each one might be called fake by the same person who in turn believes in God—yet the bear will eventually be seen by someone or something (other animals conscious and aware enough to spot a big bear and know what shit smells like). Facts are fucking facts and science and nature are real, even if we're not always there to see it, like God. And sometimes British soldiers get too drunk and fall asleep when they're not supposed to and therefore—as the saying went—would let shit slide, unintentional but nonetheless worthy of punishment, as in the midst of a fucking world war and all but try as they must the world will eventually digress the dichotomy between the tree, the bear, and the young drunks is always palpable...for if those Brits were passed out and unaware, not doing their jobs, unseeing, then did the League of Nations Members really steal a boat and escape into the cold, dark, rocky, watery abyss?

It was, then, a perfect opportunity for the Members to escape. The procurement of a ship that would carry all of them away from the prison they were trapped in proved easier than expected—Vidal never confessed what the price for their voyage was—and there were, of course, many doubts of Vidal de la Fuente's honesty, sure that he was just going to leave them all behind, but he pulled through and they boarded with eerie ease. He paid one nervous and possibly drunk Englishman whose lone responsibility was to watch the docks from which they were preparing to leave—quite handsomely it must be noted—a thick stack of English currency. The man smiled as he held the quid, more an expression of relief than a look of joy one would feel upon receiving tax-free money. All of the Members were aboard. Vidal thanked the Englishman, shook his hand, brought him in close, kissed him on the cheek, and whispered something for his ears only...then stabbed him in his heart with the short blade that hid in the lion-head handle of his walking stick, nearly touching the man's breast. The Englishman couldn't make a sound; it was over before he knew it. Once there was light. Vidal gently set him down, placed the quid in the dead man's pocket, shut his eyes, and laid two coins over his lids. Then it was dark.

Mårten-Ludvig Stenberg witnessed the scene. Vidal boarded, looked him in the eye and smiled, then walked past him, confident in the fact that he wouldn't need to pay the eternal ferryman to take two witnesses across the river Styx tonight. Mårten-Ludvig wished more than ever that Kasper had kept his word and been ready within the hour, but the old man had fallen asleep—and who could blame him with how much that had to drink? It was only natural. So now they were all but forced to ride with the alleged spies of the enemy or stay on the godforsaken rock they so desperately want to leave behind, unsure of when fate would show its hand again and offer them a free ride out.

The vessel itself—*Clout* was her name—was nothing more than a commercial fishing boat that flew no colors and was manned by a small crew whose captain was one Anton Wade and with him his loyal mates: Holt Endicott, Trent Gore, Atticus ("Grease") Holland, and Finn Jespersen. Vidal headed up some stairs and through a door, Máximo Ureña behind him like his shadow, finding Anton Wade himself along with Trent Gore and Finn Jespersen preparing to steer them to the endless black of the ocean. Mårten-Ludvig saw the inside for a second, maybe two, and all the maps and charts that covered the walls behind the men. Anton looked in that brief instant both young and old—a baby-faced forty-something with the only signs of age in the thinning of his salt-and-pepper hair and the dark bags under his eyes that spoke of many long nights with just him and a bottle and his thoughts. The other man, Trent Gore, stood next to him, a foot taller if not more, arms folded across his wide chest, looing bored or stoned—or possibly both—his face too small for his head, eyes too close together, nose too sharp and pointy for a man of his build, mouth just a pair of thin lips like he had to draw them on every morning. The man behind the wheel, Finn Jespersen, looked something like an experiment gone wrong: he suffered from a strange type of progeria that affected his face and hands and made him look fifty years older than he actually was. He was just as tall as Trent Gore, if not taller, well over six feet. But, just as quickly as Mårten-Ludvig calculated their images, the door shut and they were gone. On the other side, once safe from outside eyes, Anton Wade chugged half a pitcher of a strong Bloody Mary that contained garnishes of a smoked chub fish, a pickled pig's foot, dozens of artichoke hearts and diced pickled beets, green olives stuffed with blue cheese, five strips of greasy bacon drowning in the jalapeño-infused vodka, tomato juice, Worcestershire sauce, horseradish...he set the massive cocktail down, produced a cold bottle of a Cologne's finest Kölsch seemingly out of nowhere, and poured the cool, crisp liquid gold into the Bloody Mary. He gave it a little gravitational swirl, then took another healthy chug.

"Well," Vidal said as if he'd seen it before.

"If all are aboard, we'll take off," Anton said, wiping some Bloody Mary from his chin.

"How are the waters?"

"You know how they are, Pound's boys are everywhere."

"And Raeder's?"

"You really are a sick fuck."

"Why would you have us worryin' about both sides?" Trent Gore asked.

"Might be easier to go unnoticed that way."

"The hell makes you think that?"

"It'll be fucking chaos," Anton noted.

"Chaos is being yourself. I thrive in chaos. It's better this way."

"If the others find out that you sent word out to the fucking Nazis they'll—"

"What makes you think that my Brothers will find out, Mr. Wade? do you have some hidden agenda I am unaware of?"

"N-no, course not."

"And your men here? Mr. Gore? Mr. Jespersen? Can they be trusted?"

"Of course."

"Can they speak." None of them caught a question mark at the end.

Anton nodded to his men.

"Aye," Trent and Finn said, both with voices that erred on the side of dishonesty.

"Well then," Vidal said, faking satisfaction like an ex-lover. "Let's set sail, cast off, whatever the hell you call it."

"It's—"

"Just go."

Elsewhere on *Clout*, the other League of Nations Members were ushered to a door: "Down below!" as they would come to know it, as Holt Endicott called out. "All of yah, down below!" Holt stood next to the open door that led to the belly of the vessel. He was a tall man with long arms and short legs, a square jaw and a hooked nose, auburn hair with sideburns that split into two separate strips of hair, making an inverted *v* and technically four sideburns in total, and dark eyes that shifted here and there far too quickly. Once they reached the bottom of the stairs they were greeted by Grease Holland, who cooly smoked a cigarette and stood next to another open door with another set of stairs leading further down. His beard was shaggy and thick and was the only visible part of him as nearly his whole face was covered by cigarette smoke as it just hung around his head like a ghostly mask. Grease motioned his head towards the stairs and down they went like sheep. Grease and Holt, along with their crewmates, were armed with military-issued assault rifles. At the bottom of the second set of stairs, the Members found an empty room: everything from the walls to the low ceiling to the floor they stood on was old metal. There were three doors, all mechanically locked, and the floor had a few rubber mats tossed here and there as if to provide some sort of comfort, and that was as far as furniture went.

Dim lights glowed low and hot from porthole lights that cast a pathetic halo if one stood directly underneath it. Pools of black water dripped slowly down the walls as if they were living things and had worked up a sweat, maybe due to the sudden influx of bodies. The water snaked around the room like small rivers. Lastly, there was a haunting, acidic stench of piss, rust, and petrol that the men could practically taste on the tips of their tongues...but the place was, if anything, spacious enough to hold all of them. There was no way for them to tell how much time had passed, the only constant flow the sway of the ship as it chopped its way through the dark and heavy waves of the great Atlantic. An eternity or two could have flown by. A few had let their imaginations convince them that they were in hell's waiting room.

Malcolm Levy-Willis—after finding an ox-blood-colored business card on the ground for some obscure location known as The Garden—had hovered over to Mårten-Ludvig Stenberg and Kasper Lindquist, who were silently smoking cigarettes and listening to Valtteri Markkanen tell them and Eljas Takala a story about a time when he was younger: back in his home of Karvia, playing hockey with some friends on the frozen waters of Nurmijärvi. A neighborhood rival, Vilho Hämäläinen, had already netted five against his squad (score was 8 - 9 for Vilho's team) and the son of a bitch was trying for a double hat-trick when Valtteri decided to take matters into his own hands and delivered a hard—and unprecedented for their game—bodycheck, which knocked Vilho to the ice and the wind out of his lungs. In all honesty, Valtteri swore, that was supposed to be the end of it...but little did any of them know that his teammate, Jaakkima Laaksonen, had an idea of his own, to skate over Vilho's exposed neck, an act that proved to be surprisingly easy for him; before the blade touched flesh he lifted his skate up just enough, then brought it down on top of the naked throat as if taking a forceful step up a hill, then came back with the same foot, dragging it back and forth with each assertive glide of the blade across flesh and muscle, struggling a bit when it reached bone but taking to grinding away at that. Even when people were pulling him off he kept at it, and kicked Vilho's face and took the left eye out with the tip of one of his skates. Valtteri laughed hysterically while Eljas chuckled a bit, lit a cigarette, and shook his head like he was in on the joke...if there was one to be in on. Mårten-Ludvig and Kasper looked at Valtteri with horrified looks that went unnoticed. Malcolm stood awkwardly nearby, not understanding a lick of Finnish and not really even paying attention, mainly wishing, absolutely craving, more than anything, that he had a fucking cigarette.

They rocked back and forth, some able to find comfort, perhaps from a memory that they shouldn't have been able to retain—a time when they were just a baby, newly born, and their mothers would rock their cradles and sing some pretty song just for them, and this happened to them, in Denmark, in The Netherlands, in Switzerland, to all of them, as if all of their mothers were a part of some secret guild and given instructions on how to properly raise a child—whatever it was they did a fine job, thanks moms—and with it, sleep. The old Dutchman Sylvester Klaasen managed to find sleep whilst standing straight up against the wall, a trick—he would tell Kasper before the end— learned during his time serving in the Royal Netherlands Army. What purpose it served, he wasn't entirely sure...possibly had forgotten, had been a long time since he learned, and he had just gotten so used to it...

Everyone was awake when they heard the explosion that shook their metal tomb like a thousand peals of thunder. There was a momentary lull before the second explosion, and another before explosions began to absolutely fucking rattle them in rapid succession—BOOMBOOMBOOMBOOMBOOM— which caused a few cries of terror, open prayers, real tears, belief that this was the end of the world, and caused Denmark's finest, Lukas Lykke, to piss himself, and another

Dutchman, Jurgen Van Der Hout, to have a fatal heart attack which went unnoticed by the others until it was all but too late.

Malcolm Levy-Willis must have had an out-of-body experience, for he had never acted so quickly in his life; he was the first one to the stairs. The Finns, Valtteri Markkanen and Eljas Takala, followed next, then Mårten-Ludvig Stenberg with old Kasper Linquist along for the ride. The others wavered back and forth on what to do. Sylvester Klaasen and Bernard Jonker stayed behind once they discovered their countryman was dead next to them, initially thinking he was somehow still asleep. Lukas Lykke and his piss-stained pants stayed as well, as did Ingvar Håkon as they tried to confront their countryman Asbjørn Ruud—who, after the second explosion, bore the look of a mental cascade and would not be held back by anyone, a matter only they would have the misfortune of knowing and would take to their graves, and were left not with the feeling of abandonment, but of pure terror for what they allowed to be let loose.

The top of the stairs was unguarded. On the next level, they found Holt Endicott at his post with a crater where his face should be, blood oozing out like slime. Shouts echoed from everywhere in a blend of different languages. An ominous wind rushing in, not hushing the voices or echoes but overshadowing everything. When that ghostly wind faded to non-existence, in came the explosions. Massive firepower from all sides lit the dark sky to an impossibly bright white light of sinful piousness only made possible by the sinfully divine acts of terror that blindly fired into the blackness of the night. They scattered recklessly with full faith in thinking that any moment could be their last, and they'd leave this world with that being their final thought: that any moment could be their last because a missile could crash upon them, split them in half, and blow them up so there was nothing left to find but bits and chunks. Another bright flash, and Mårten-Ludvig found himself alone with old Kasper holding onto the end of his jacket, warming his heart a bit. He snapped back quick enough to catch sight of the stairs up which Vidal had disappeared when they first boarded. He figured if they never came down, then they must still be up there.

They pushed forward: saltwater sprayed them relentlessly as if they didn't have enough to deal with until they finally reached the stairs and climbed them like the slick mountains they were. They crashed inside. Lights flickered on and off to illuminate a horrific scene: Finn Jespersen dead on the wheel, his body, littered with bullet holes, hanging like a ragdoll. Anton Wade laid nearby, broken glass all around him and in his face, a pool of Bloody Mary and his blood forming around his head and neck and leaking through holes in his torso. In a chair, like he was attentive for class, sat Máximo Ureña with his head split open, pulled apart like an apple, brains spilled onto the floor, a look in one eye that still held some deep, dark secrets beyond this life, and in the other eye a look that told them to get the fuck out *now*. They didn't. Neither of them questioned why the room was riddled with death; there was too much to take in...then they heard the agonizing, poorly-masked moans from Vidal, who had crammed himself in a sort of miniature broom closet, a trail of blood flowing from under the door that temporarily hid him.

"Brothers," he said when they opened the door.

Mårten-Ludvig hauled him out of his cramped hiding spot and onto the dirty floor. Vidal stretched out and removed his hands from where they were clamped over his stomach, revealing a deep knife wound four inches across like whoever stabbed him dragged it across him, like they wanted him to spill his guts.

"What happened here?" Mårten-Ludvig asked.

"They didn't listen," Vidal explained. "If we just stayed on this course, it astronomically coincided with the Three Sisters, we would have been fine, safe. We deviated..."

"What *happened* dammit? Why are we in the middle of a damn war zone? These waters were cleaned by the Brits since Operation Valentine went into effect."

"A change of plans. Didn't need all of you...just you."

"What?" Kasper said. "Tell him to speak up, will you?"

"Seems I'll be going soon, so no use in keeping it from you any longer."

"What's that?"

"What happened here isn't important. Project Clockwork is."

"To hell with that," Mårten-Ludvig spat. "Who did this to you? Who killed these men?"

"Need you to listen, Brother."

"Just spill."

"Listen!"

It was the first time Vidal had ever looked human to either of them and it shook them rather deeply: the fear of impending death in his eye, the quiver of his bottom lip that was spotted with spittle that usually came around when the one quivering was close to, if not already, crying.

"You must listen," Vidal pleaded with a sense of sincerity that made them question whether they should believe this urban legend before them, this myth—a pathological liar for all they knew, and a murderer, one they all witnessed, and how he could change the levels and tones to his voice so radically, drastically, and quickly. "You must believe me when I tell you that these words are precious and need to be heard."

"Why?" Mårten-Ludvig asked sharply. "Why does Project Clockwork matter now? Here, at the fucking end of all things."

"If you make it out of this." Vidal paused and winced as if finally acknowledging the wound. "This information will ensure that you won't have to worry about dying for a long, long time."

"How's that?"

"You'll be protected. They'll finally give a fuck. Project

Clockwork is how you get home...I've already sent word out...though, it'll be too late for me."

"The same information that got you here?"

"I chose to be here, I calculated every risk—or thought I did at least. The world is a deck filled with more wild cards and jokers than I realized."

"Yes, yes, sure. But *how* does it protect us if it didn't protect you?"

Vidal gripped Mårten-Ludvig tightly by his jacket, a fierce seriousness—what some might call honesty—in his unblinking eyes, and said: "Everything dies...here. But not there. This is not a life either of you want now, but one you'll come to realize you're better off living. You won't die like me if that's what you're worried about." Vidal took a minute to focus through a belt of pain. "Listen, there was more: deeper than tunneling down *in* the ice. We found tunnels *already there*. These tunnels ran horizontally throughout the ice. Miles upon miles of tunnels. A frozen maze. The only way we could ever even hope to navigate a small portion of them was with a ship that was not yet created...technology invented by Nikola Tesla, inspired by Leonardo da Vinci, both of whom I introduced to the polyphasic sleep method which is twenty-minute naps every four hours—do yourselves a favor, Brothers, try it...it'll change your life. What we found in one section of the tunnels was an open space, and this is hundreds of miles below the surface...nothing there, just a giant hole in the ice that went down...deeper."

"To what?" Kasper croaked, deeply intrigued, forgetting about the hell breaking loose outside.

"To a world that has been 'lost'...since before time. We've all heard the tales when we were younger, never questioning where they *really* came from...I suppose, in a way, I relate to them..." Vidal smiled, eyes drifting, fascinated by the fact that he finally shared a genuine mythological-likeness to a legend he had deep admiration for. He turned back, remembering the importance of his words. "Plato talked of them...said it was an earthquake that destroyed them...but no, they understood the powers of the universe better than our species ever will..."

"You cannot mean—"

"Atlanteans. Yes...natives of lost Atlantis. Yes...it's all true. You realize now why I couldn't tell this to everyone back on the Island."

"But how could you—"

"They came up. At first, in all honesty, we thought they were Anunnaki, but that's a tale for the next life. Our ships, we quickly realized, could not sustain the intense pressure that far down...we lost good men who tried going bravely down into that dark unknown. Then one day I led a team to patrol other parts of the massive maze when I diverted back to the entrance, as we began calling it, like something was pulling me there...and there was a Light: a bright white light shooting straight up to the ice above. The light itself seemed to sway, moving with the concealed current that flowed throughout the maze, but to me, it looked...as if in a dance.

"It went out, the old darkness we've grown accustomed to exploring returned, the lights from my ship struggled as always to cut all the way through...that's when it appeared: a ship. Round, like a coin, not completely flat though...domed on the top...it flew right in front of me, I never learned how it was able to navigate, given that it bore no windows...next thing I knew, I was slipping out of the *reality of being in my ship* and was literally reassembled in the reality of being on their ship.

"They took me there, down the tunnel, to their underwater Eden. Never again will I experience such a paradise, such perfect harmony, such blissful peace, so clean...a glowing metropolis that was safely hidden under the ice, miles and miles below the surface of the water. And it's here that still to this day feels like a dream: we were breathing once we left the reality of being in their ship. Understand? I stood with them, breathing. Like we were standing on land. Fish swam around us, squid and sharks lingered overhead like a patrolling school of gargoyles. All peace all the time. If I had stayed...if they had let me...I would have lived forever...I would have finally understood peace...we meant to go back...

"They live on an elevated level of consciousness that allows them to understand more, all those little ancient secrets the universe holds...they became one with it. Plato was only half right: Atlantis did disappear after an earthquake, supposedly crumbling into the Atlantic...it did submerge, but it never crumbled. They likely have tunnels underneath all the waters of the world, even miles below this ship, I bet...they used the earthquake, though, as a *distraction* to physically create a new reality of Atlantis and of its people into a mutated and evolved species that lives in secret, underwater, miles below the ice of the world's largest desert, protected with secrets of the universe, ancient knowledge that our species is not yet ready to understand...don't you *see*? They left *because of us*. Athens declared war on them, a war that ended a week after it was declared when 'the great Athenian Earthquake declared Athens champions after it decimated Atlantis to the watery below.' A war we rarely talk about because of *what* it was fought over...the first and only war recorded that was fought over knowledge.

"It's just so human of them, isn't it? The Athenians declared war on people to learn of their ever-peaceful ways. That is how I came to meet them...for Atlantians desire to show humans their way, the way of elevated, god-like consciousness, but humans are a hard lot to trust...I'm sure if they knew who I was working for then they would have not taken me in, or...maybe that's why they took me and sent me back out, for they did know and wanted me to use the information to sway those capable of great evils...I hadn't thought of it...like that...till just now...did they ever intend to bring me back...?"

They could see the light fade from him, only a flicker of

fight remaining in him.

"Makes you wonder what else he knows," Kasper said. "What else was he involved in."

Vidal opened his eyes wider, looked at Kasper, and smiled, held one last secret for them—like throwing a dart at a wall of stories to tell while blindfolded, but he already had one in mind, always predetermined: "Everything."

"Eh?"

"I wish we had more time, Brothers."

"There, there,"Kasper said.

"I just wanted to shuffle the deck...wanted people to experience something new."

"Bullshit," Mårten-Ludvig hissed. "You're not a god."

"'Course not, wouldn't be busy dying right now if I was one."

"There, there."

"I think your whole life is a lie."

"You really want to debate this now, eh?"

"It's all *bull*shit."

"You believe what you want to believe, it's human of you to fear the truth...it's always more frightening than what you're choosing to believe."

"Shut it. We have the Project Clockwork information. We don't have to listen to this anymore."

"That is true, Brothers. They'll see you soon...words travel fast...I was always fond of you two the most. We would have worked well together."

"Really? Huh. Right then. I'm behind you, Kasp. It was...an experience."

"Wait. You're leaving me...to die alone?"

"To be fair, everyone dies alone."

"It's gone on long enough, hasn't it?"

Mårten-Ludvig and Kasper scurried away, Kasper remarking that he was by all rights fully impressed that Vidal was able to paint such a detailed picture for them with his dying breath, which both of them agreed had to be the longest dying breath ever. None of this reached Vidal's ear.

There was the door leading back to the dark outside, back down the slick and treacherous rain-drenched steps, and a door to the right of them which took them down an equally dark hallway, but there was moderate visibility—not the blinding white light of death, no—as all of the lights that usually glowed a soft yellow were somehow switched to a hellish red. Every ten steps or so Mårten-Ludvig would look back over his shoulder and find the hallway empty, the door to the room they had just left slightly ajar, enough to see Vidal's unmoving legs, still carrying worry that maybe all the stories were true and that devil would be up and after them any second now.

There was a scream. And another one. Both close by and of the same voice. They crept forward slowly, reaching the end of the hallway. Stairs ascended to their left, but they looked right; the face was hard to make out in the dark red light, this one especially as it was caked in blood. He was pulling at the bloody insides of Phillippe Lieberenz, who was positioned up against the wall, throat slit, guts spilled out on the ground, literally ripped out by—*my god,* sudden realization struck Mårten-Ludvig— "Asbjørn?"

Asbjørn Ruud turned quickly, flashed a big white smile through all the blood. "My Swedish Brothers. Hallå."

"What are you doing?"

"Found the spy." He pointed to Phillippe. "Got him to spill his guts."

"Jesus..." Kasper moaned.

"Get it? Spill. His. Guts."

"We see that," Mårten-Ludvig assured him.

"Think there's any more?"

"Any more?"

"Spies."

"Oh...well—"

"Say. Where've you two been?"

Oh fuck...

"We saw de la Fuente back that way," Kasper, the clever old goat, said.

"For true?"

"Yes. End of the hall. Believe he ducked into a room."

"Wait here." Asbjørn sprang up and began to run but slipped on Phillippe's slick blood and intestines, lost his balance, and tumbled headfirst into the steel wall, striking it with a loud BANG. They contemplated checking on him when he rose from the floor and shook his head, then got up and ran down the hall. They looked at each other, silently wondering if any of this was real, and shared a feeling that they were in the most violent circle of the inferno and didn't know where they'd be heading next. Kasper shrugged and they went up the stairs.

Back on the deck, the chaos was much louder. It was fully dark, spotlights illuminating only small parts of the black ocean, nothing particular at all. A few lights from electric torches danced in the distance. Rain stabbed their faces like cold knives and rushed over their feet like the river Styx had arrived early without a guide for them. Were they essentially— if they were, in fact, in hell—going *backward* then? A flash of lightning illuminated the world. The body of Werner Eriksen flashed before them, his eyes looking up, scaring the fucking shit out of them, but there was no life in them. Before he disappeared back into the black void, they saw that he was, surely, another victim at the hands of Asbjørn: throat slit, guts spilled out onto his pants and the watery deck, some chewed on, blood mixed with water soaking into their shoes, socks, skin.

Bravery struck Mårten-Ludvig that caused him to take the lead, almost slipping after blindly groping for the rail. Kasper followed his shouted instructions—still partially drowned out by the world—to hold on tight to the rail with his right hand

and with his left securely grasp the back collar of Mårten-Ludvig's jacket. They were ten steps along when they heard shots ring out, three of them, the first one almost unnoticed, lost in the storm, but the two that followed in such rapid succession that it was impossible not to identify the sound of man-made machinery in the night. How many were left? They started to creep along again, wondering who was on either end of the gun that fired...and how close were they? Even so, they kept on.

They came upon a soft light that flickered on and off like it was calling to them after what seemed like miles of walking blindly on the slippery dark. They reached the flickering light; it flashed warm, golden-amber energy from its core, which was attached to a wall on their left, and next to it was a door. The room was lit with the same weak light as outside, three of them attached to the ceiling, though these did not flicker. There were two tables bolted to the ground and chairs toppled over along with a mess of papers and maps. There was another door at the end of the room. Behind it, unmistakably, came the sound of a gunshot.

They kept still. "Tired of going in and out and in and back out," Kasper complained in a hushed voice. "Need to get off this—"

A scream followed, delayed. The lights went out and it was dark again...unnaturally dark. The kind of dark where even when you wait a few moments to let your eyes adjust you quickly realize it will do you no good as more and more darkness will smother your senses, but you don't have time to sit and hope you can adjust to the surroundings in which you're trapped, as another scream from the same voice echoed out—a soul-piercing, glass-shattering, banshee-like scream. Everything at that precise moment felt all too alien. Not of this world. They were so disoriented in all that dark that they could not distinguish where the doors to escape this void were anymore—for that's what it was: a void. How, in the light, it was so small and close to claustrophobic, but in the dark it expanded into an ocean of darkness where not even your shadow would be able to find you...a place so dark and depleted of light that no living thing would want to call it a home...a place so dark that you would be forced to wonder if the darkness was the end, if this was the eternal hell or purgatory-like waiting room they thought they were in before shit popped off, waiting to get into that hell that your soul was involuntarily coerced to float around idly like some forgotten ghost until, until...a place so dark it gave off the sensation of floating through the vacuum of space, though billions upon billions of years in the future to the point where all the stars had finally accepted their faiths and mortalities and went out, eternal slumber, to the point where every known galaxy had stretched far and thin and collided with one another leaving nothing behind but the dust of what once was, but in all that darkness you wouldn't be able to see it dance right there in front of you, their fading memory: that which was once life but is now all but gone and forgotten about completely, with no one, not one single soul capable of awareness around to remember to forget about it, the end of the collective consciousness...

The door opened suddenly. A smoke-wreathed Grease Holland stood there with a rifle of death in his hand. They suddenly thought they'd met their judge, jury, and executioner all in one moment.

"Come with me," Grease said as he puffed smoke from the cigarette sitting perfectly on his lips. "If you—"

Shots rang out behind him and a bullet struck Grease in the left shoulder. He merely glanced at the wound and swore as if it were a bee sting. He turned around and fired in retaliation. Another shot struck him in the left thigh. The firing stopped as quickly as it started. Grease still stood.

"C'mon," he said, limping forward.

Mårten-Ludvig and Kasper followed. They found the body

of Asbjørn Ruud—holding a rifle lifted from Anton Wade—
dead in the hallway. His eyes seemed to follow them as they
passed him as if he was, from the beyond, accusing them of
being the spies.

"Where're we going?" Mårten-Ludvig demanded.

"Trying to survive," Grease told him. "We have two
lifeboats. We won't be able to get all those who are left off."

"Why are you helping us?"

"New shit was brought to light."

"What's that?"

"No time. We gotta move."

"Have to get the others who stayed down below," Mårten-
Ludvig said.

"Was just down there. Empty. C'mon."

"Everyone at these boats then?"

"Not sure. If they are, we're out of luck, if they ain't, we're
in luck. The way shit goes. C'mon, hey."

They crept along, shadows on a dark planet. The two
Swedes stopped in front of an open door; Grease was right,
the others had come up. Everyone was scattered, but before
them, the scene was horrifically unbelievable: it was the voice
that made them stop first, and what it said, and who said it:
"I've had my eye on you." They watched Eugène St. Pierre
aggressively snarl at Lukas Lykke, whose face was pressed
down in a pool of his own blood, that leaked out from a crack
in the top of his skull, and against a metal desk bolted to the
floor. "Ever since we landed on that island." Eugène licked
Lukas's face which was wet with tears. He looked up and saw
Mårten-Ludvig and Kasper standing there, staring at
him...just watching.

"Help!" Lukas called out. "Please! Help me!"

"An audience?" Eugène noticed. "Alright then." He made a
moved to pulled out his pathetic cock.

The Danish lad cried out for help again. Grease Holland
was far up the hallway. Kasper began to walk away. Mårten-

Ludvig, the practicing pacifist, felt helpless and ashamed, and with bravery nowhere to be found he did nothing but look down at the ground and move forward. A shot rang out. Kasper, on the ground from the powerful kickback, held the rifle that Asbjørn had died with. Eugène St. Pierre was dead, a clean shot through the crown of the skull that painted the wall behind him with blood and brains. Mårten-Ludvig was stunned at how the old goat had moved so quickly to get the rifle and how ace of a shot he was. He went to help his old friend up.

"Jesus, Kasp, never knew—"

"Gotta move," Kasper said once on his feet.

"I am not turning back," Grease shouted from the end of the hallway.

"What about him?" Mårten-Ludvig asked Kasper.

"We'll leave him this," he said, setting the rifle down and starting into a weird sort of half-jog half-limp that could be attributed to age, of course, and with it the years of wear and tear of joints and ligaments and muscle tissue. Mårten-Ludvig was able to catch up with him at his normal walking pace, a sight which bewildered Grease Holland: one man trying his hardest, it seemed, to catch up, while the other walked almost leisurely, like everything was fine. It made him wonder why the hell he was waiting for them, but by the time he found a good reason they had caught up.

"You've wasted so much goddamn time," Grease told them. "S'go."

Away they went. It wasn't too long before they were out in the cold darkness again and felt the stinging wet of the ocean splashing at them. Pretty fucking used to it by now. Trent Gore stood on guard, smoking but not inhaling a tobacco cigarette. Sure enough, there were two lifeboats, one holding a few already: the Dutch—Bernard Jonker and Sylvester Klaasen—the Danish—Mikkel Skovgaard and Leif Dalgaard, oblivious to Lukas Lykke's suffering and Werner Eriksen's death, though they can't be faulted for that—and the lone Swissman, François Reuter, who knew and witnessed Philippe Lieberenz's grizzly death, had barely escaped with his own life, and was unaware of the horrors Eugène St. Pierre created, though maybe he was better off not knowing...

"Room for one more in this one," Trent Gore called out as he flicked a cigarette over the rail and into the blackness of the night which drifted away in the wind like a firefly until it disappeared completely, unable to tell where the water began for the darkness never ended. "Best if it takes off now. Get that next one filled."

Grease lit another cigarette, masking his face again, and nodded in agreement. "You two figure it out. Quick. One leaves now, the other waits."

"You go," Mårten-Ludvig said to Kasper.

"No, no—" Kasper tried to protest.

"Don't be a damn fool. Help me with him, will you?"

"C'mon, hey," Grease said as he ushered Kasper into the boat. "S'go."

"Here," Mårten-Ludvig said as Kasper slid down, reaching into his jacket pocket and pulling out a sealed note. "Just in case."

"Don't be foolish, M-L."

"Please. Take it. I meant to give it to you earlier. I've another copy. Please."

There was a slight hesitation, but Kasper couldn't deny his friend, whose eyes begged him to take the letter. The old goat took it, trying to see who it was addressed to before he put it in his pocket—alas, not enough light, eyes too old.

"They're family. They'll take care of you. Tell them everything."

"Let's say," Kasper suggested, "we meet there."

"It's a deal," Mårten-Ludvig agreed.

"C'mon, hey," Grease puffed. "In this one here. Others are coming up."

"Grease," Trent said. "You take this one, I'll hang back and load the next one."

"You sure?"

"I owe you. Remember?"

Grease Holland puffed, shrugged, then climbed into the boat as it was lowered to the watery, choppy blackness of the great Atlantic. He manned one oar, Bernard Jonker on the other. Above them, Mårten-Ludvig anxiously waited for others to join him so they could get lost in all that dark. Malcolm Levy-Willis came hauling up, paused to catch his breath when he saw the boat, hands on his knees, then joined. The others who followed were Eljas Takala with Valtteri Markkanen and the last of the Norwegians, Ingar Håkon.

"That all of you?" Trent Gorse asked.

"Mr. Lykke!" Mårten-Ludvig called out.

"Eh?"

BOOM.

The sky lit up again; round after round after round.

"No time!" Malcolm called out. "Get us the hell out of here!"

Trent hopped in. He went to hit the lever to lower them down, then saw the bloodied Lukas Lykke stagger out onto the deck. He cursed something under his breath. The others saw the poor bastard.

"There's no time!" Malcolm pleaded.

"I can get him!" Mårten-Ludvig yelled.

"Where's he from?" Trent asked no one in particular.

"Denmark!" Ingvar said.

Trent scratched his head. "We've got two of them down there already, don't necessarily need him."

"Yo," Grease Holland called from below. "What's the holdup?"

"Danish crawling out," Trent yelled down.

"Nix that."

Trent put a heavy hand on Mårten-Ludvig's shoulder and

forced him to sit down. The lifeboat began to descend to the water.

"You can't leave—"

In came the fatal blinding light that struck perfectly as if on a personal hellbound vendetta against him, completely obliterating the spot where Lukas Lykke had been, leaving a great smoking hole in the ship, missing the others by a minute.

They descended. The water below was now a bright and holy white. A vortex spun with intoxicating velocity. The other lifeboat looked on from a safe distance at their Brothers, who had narrowly missed death, as they descended, without choice...they watched the light surround them, as they faded out of this reality before the lifeboat touched the water and went down into the vortex, splintering into pieces, with no bodies on it...fading into a new reality on a new ship...far away from here.

The light went out.

They rowed away quietly in shock and thought: *what if I were a few minutes late?* They did not fully understand what they had seen. A few were convinced they died from the explosion, others unsure what the fuck to make of it. But old Kasper, who learned those secrets from Vidal, understood, as he had no choice but to believe that his friend was still alive and with gods down below. Still, tears flowed easily from his old eyes. They slipped unnoticed through the rocky water into the black abyss until the sky no longer lit up from the fake thunder and the war-loving echoes no longer threatened to blow out their hearing for good and the only sound left was the slapping of the water against the wood of their boat that they had no choice but to put all their trust and faith into. They rowed on. At one point the younger François Reuter wordlessly replaced Bernard Jonker at the oar. Grease Holland kept at his oar, only briefly pausing every now and then to either light a cigarette or to ash a bit of it into the water.

There was a real and paranoid sensation that something

was out there *watching* them. Whether it was German, British, American, or something else entirely, none of them would ever know. It was a ghostly sort of feeling. A haunting. Would that light from down below come back? The silence played a part in it. Something that, if not addressed, could turn them all mad. There was something about it, a piousness that lingered in the back of their minds that was directly associated with the light, like a deep part of them that they refused to acknowledge wanted it back, to see where it went. How do you even talk about it, with this lot, when you don't know what it is? Luckily for them, Kasper Lindquist—the only one who understood what the blessed horrors they witnessed could have meant—happened to be sitting next to Slyvester Klaasen and decided to ask him how he came to learn the art of sleeping standing up, casually, to make the conversation feel "normal," which led to a tale that they all listened to and which caused some to wonder if they should shut him up in fear of whatever might be out finding them or let him go on because as far as they were concerned the silence was the only real thing, of their earth, that they'd encountered so far and didn't well like being trapped in it. So on they rowed and listened— even Kasper's little mouse had come up from the safety of his jacket pocket—blindly through the unknown, a place where no map would find them, hoping to land where the sun shone through and where maps still held value, where the dark didn't linger for long.

21

"We can't stay here anymore," Ruth said, her voice firm and serious, with a strong belief in every word as if it were the only truth anymore.

"Where would we go, eh? Where could we go?"

"Karl!"

"Shhhh," he pleaded, puffing smoke. "Mustn't wake them."

"They're old enough now to be a part of this. This affects them."

"Yes yes, I know."

"We *have* to do something."

"We will."

"Now. Please, Karl—"

"Ruth, please—"

"—the more time we waste—"

"—don't get over your head—"

"—the more danger we put ourselves in."

"—we're safe."

"We need to talk to them, now."

"In the morning, my love. Let them rest tonight, I don't want them to worry. We need to talk this out rationally first.

This is...unprecedented."

The shock of the news had taken a massive toll on both of them. Karl looked as though he had aged ten years overnight and had not slept a wink since the radio broadcast, his consciousness tormenting itself with a thousand thoughts a second. They were both terrified, understandably so.

It was foolish of them to think that their children would not be able to hear them, that they were not listening, their doors cracked open just wide enough so the sound of their parent's voices could sneak into their dark rooms. They were old, no longer children, definitely too old to pretend to be sleeping while they listened from the safety of their beds, but this was, like father said, "unprecedented" and they quite frankly were unaware of how to act. It seemed as though life had begun to repeat itself—stuck in a loop, a valley of highs and lows—and they were near that dark time where poisoned thoughts clouded their minds and made them unsure what was the safest thing to do: stay in a place where you're almost—if not already—public enemy number one because of where you come from? Run again and start a new life somewhere else? But where? The whole world was close to falling off the edge.

THE ANNOUNCEMENT FROM KBDC RADIO WALLA WALLA ON FRIDAY 20 FEBRUARY, 1942, WITH YOUR HOST: ARETHA ROMA

FEATURING SPECIAL GUESTS: THEODORE B. FRANKLYN JR. IV & CY MCDONALD

"Good evening, Walla Walla, I'm Aretha Roma, thank you all for joining me, as always. These are dark days, and I fear they will only get darker before the dawn breaks through. Before we begin the recap of the President's address, let me welcome our guests tonight: political analysts Theodore B.

Franklyn Jr. IV, professor of logic and political philosophy at the University of Tasmania, and Cy McDonald, professor of law at Texas Technological College. Gentlemen, thank you for traveling all this way to be here."

"An honor," Theodore B. Franklyn Jr. IV said.

"Cheers," Cy McDonald agreed.

"Now," Aretha Roma began, "before we dive in, let's hear a little about yourselves, for our listeners. Us three have been writing to each other for a few months now, and this was supposed to happen sooner, but honestly sort of better now, anyway. *I* officially met you two before we started here and we got to chat a bit, and you two actually sort of grew up together and both graduated from the University of Tasmania. I found that rather fascinating."

"Yeah, well," Theodore B. Franklyn Jr. IV started, "I was born in Orange, that's down in New South Wales, Australia, for the listeners who are unaware, and this one's entire family was there, too, at around the same time. Never met then, think our fathers likely knew each other. Didn't really meet till Tasmania."

"Right, I always found it funny we ain't never met in Orange back then."

"Well, you are older than me."

"Hey now."

"You and your family," Aretha Roma stirred, "moved all the way to Australia from Texas?"

"That's correct, ma'am," Cy McDonald said. "O'Daniel, Texas."

"What for?"

"Same reason everyone was there during that time: Gold. Alls I remember we had in old O'Daniel was a dry copper mine. My old man heard about it from a friend who was heading down. Figured why not pack the family up and start over. Started livin' down under when I was ten, but been back teachin' in my home state for, oh, about twenty-eight years now, crazy to think about, and I'm sixty-six now, if you can believe it, so, actually, spent about the same amount of time down there as I have back here. Huh, ain't that somethin'.."

"And when you met at the University..."

"It was my second or third year there when we first met," Theodore said. "You were teaching my law class."

"Yes, that was the only class you had of mine. I only taught at UT for five years before I finally went back to Texas."

"How would you compare the two?"

"Impossibly similar and radically different."

"Hm, yes. Theodore, though you're an Australian by birth you have deep American roots."

"Right. I'm a second-generation Aussie. My grandfather, Theodore B. Franklyn Jr. II—I called him Papa Teddy—came to Orange with his father, Theodore B. Franklyn Sr., and his mother, my great-grandmother, Mable H. Franklyn, shortly after the American Civil War ended. Papa Teddy and my great-grandfather both served valiantly for the Union, and Papa Teddy met my grandmother there, in Orange, Viviette Franklyn—"

"Right, right, that is all nice," Aretha Roma admitted. "But more about where the particular roots originated from, rather than the whole origin."

"Of course, I apologize."

"No need."

"Right, so, T.B. Sr. was from Michigan, he and Papa Teddy were a part of *the* 1st Michigan Infantry. Papa Teddy's older brother, Theodore B. Franklyn Jr., foolishly left for the wrong side of history and fought for the South in Mississippi where I was told he died at the Battle of Iuka."

"Incredible. Such rich history, And, actually, a perfect transition to our main topic: President Franklin D. Roosevelt's Executive Order 9066. I have a copy of the transcript here that I'll read for those who have not heard it yet. Quote:

(THE TRANSCRIPT OF EXECUTIVE ORDER 9066)

"'Authorizing the Secretary of War to Prescribe Military Areas: Whereas the successful prosecution of the war requires every possible protection against espionage and against sabotage to national-defense material, national-defense premises, and national-defense utilities as defined in Section 4, Act of April 20, 1918, 40 Stat. 533, as amended by the Act of November 30, 1940, 54 Stat. 1220, and the Act of August 21, 1941, 55 Stat. 655 (U.S.C., Title 50, Sec. 104);

"'Now, therefore, by virtue of the authority vested in me as President of the United States, and Commander in Chief of the Army and Navy, I hereby authorize and direct the Secretary of War, and the Military Commanders whom he may from time to time designate, whenever he or any designated Commander deems such action necessary or desirable, to prescribe military areas in such places and of such extent as he or the appropriate Military Commander may determine, from which any or all persons may be excluded, and with respect to which, the right of any person to enter, remain in, or leave shall be subject to whatever restrictions the Secretary of War or the appropriate Military Commander may impose in his discretion. The Secretary of War is hereby authorized to provide for residents of any such area who are excluded therefrom, such transportation, food, shelter, and other accommodations as may be necessary, in the judgment of the Secretary of War or the said Military Commander, and until other arrangements are made, to accomplish the purpose of this order. The designation of military areas in any region or locality shall supersede designations of prohibited and restricted areas by the Attorney General under the Proclamations of 7 and 8 December, 1941, and shall supersede the responsibility and authority of the Attorney General under the said Proclamations in respect of such prohibited and restricted areas.

"'I hereby further authorize and direct the Secretary of War and the said Military Commanders to take such other steps as he or the appropriate Military Commander may deem advisable to enforce compliance with the restrictions applicable to each Military area herein above authorized to be designated, including the use of Federal troops and other Federal Agencies, with authority to accept assistance of state and local agencies. I hereby further authorize and direct all Executive Departments, independent establish-ments and other Federal Agencies, to assist the Secretary of War or the said Military Commanders in carrying out this Executive Order, including the furnishing of medical aid, hospitalization, food, clothing, transportation, use of land, shelter, and other supplies, equipment, utilities, facilities, and services.

"'This order shall not be construed as modifying or limiting in any way the authority heretofore granted under Executive Order No. 8972, dated 12 December 1941, nor shall it be construed as limiting or modifying the duty and responsibility of the Federal Bureau of Investigation, with respect to the investigation of alleged acts of sabotage or the duty and responsibility of the Attorney General and the Department of Justice under the Proclamations of 7 and 8 December, 1941, prescribing regulations for the conduct and control of alien enemies, except as such duty and responsibility is superseded by the designation of military areas hereunder.

"'Signed: Franklin D. Roosevelt. The White House, February 19, 1942.' End quote. Which, gentlemen I'm sure you'll agree with me when I say this, and please, forgive me for my language—this is fucking terrifying."

"Well said," Cy McDonald said. "They try to make it sound like they're helping..."

"It is baffling to me," Theodore B. Franklyn Jr. IV noted, "as an Aussie with American heritage, this doesn't seem like the place my ancestors fought for."

"You're right," Cy McDonald agreed.

"Locking your own citizens—nevermind citizens, *human beings, children*—locking them in cages? It's inhumane."

"The connection I was trying to make," Aretha Roma said. "Your family served and died in the bloodiest war on this soil, do you see a second civil war happening, maybe in our lifetime?"

"I think it's foolish not to think it's likely. Cy?"

"Completely agree. It seems like this country is always on the precipice of boiling over into anarchy again, like the wounds of the past never really healed."

"Makes you think that they'd be keen to find a reason to lock more folk if they could."

"Meaning what, Theodore?" Aretha Roma asked.

"Just given the history of this country—it's my first time here, but I've read and heard enough about it—it's got this problem, it always wants to be white."

"Australia doesn't have the brightest past."

"No, and there's a lot of work to do, a lot to make up for, but we're smart enough to not repeat it."

"It's true, it is horrific," Cy McDonald said. "This insane order, our history, the world, all of it."

"Do you think this will be acted on quickly?" Aretha Roma inquired. "Given the fact, of course, that FDR is set to sign another document, Public Law 503, in the coming weeks to provide extra enforcement to 9066."

"I don't think it will matter when that law is signed," Cy McDonald said. "Theodore made an excellent point earlier that his country has an affinity towards wanting to be white. It's sad. But it is true. You will see many Japanese and German and Italians rounded up and put into cages and camps."

"And no one," Theodore B. Franklyn Jr. IV chimed in, "will ask where those camps came from, how they were built and ready so quickly."

"Because they were planning on this."

"Long before Pearl Harbor happened."

"Whole damn world is a chessboard, pieces are always moving."

"It's their first step in creating their pure American race."

"Doesn't sound so different from old Adolf, now does it?"

"Gentlemen, gentlemen...let me understand you here. Are you seriously suggesting that Pearl Harbor was *an inside job*?"

"Oh, definitely."

"No doubt."

"They knew it was coming."

"Didn't say shit about it."

"You're saying—s-sorry gentlemen, listeners...my producer says we have to take a short commercial break. Terribly sorry. We'll be right back with Mr. Franklyn and Mr. McDonald after this."

22

"Pay attention!"

"Sorry, sir, it's just that, I, I—"

"You *what*, Private? Still thinking about Corporal Monday?"

"No, sir, I just don't quite understand why we're here, is all. Sir."

"And that gives you the right to fuck off into your simple imagination?"

"No, sir."

"We're here because those are our orders, Private."

"Yes, sir, I understand that, sir. It's just, with us entering the War and all..."

"What? You figured you were going to get drafted out of this unit? Kill some Nazis? Or were you fixing to burn some Japs?"

"I'll do whatever my country asks of me, sir."

"Your country is asking you to be here now, Private Reynolds."

"Yes, sir, I just didn't think this was a matter of pure urgency is all, sir."

"Take a better look at this scene, Private."

"Dead couple, sir. Been dead for a few months, I'd reckon. In their fifties, perhaps. Murder-suicide?"

"You'd think that, at first."

"Well, sir, I'd actually think, why does this couple, this crime scene, concern the U.S. Military?"

"Now you look here, Private, if it weren't just you and I in this room I'd smack you so hard you'd revert to calling me 'Mommy,' cause I don't just want to hurt you, Private, I want to humiliate you. By the time the others get back in, I will have gotten over your tone and comments because I *am* a forgiving man, Private. But so help me God if you speak to me like that again I will make you hear more than voices."

"What? Sorry, sir?"

"Did you hear any of what I said, Private?"

"Yes. But about that last part, sir?"

"What about it, Private? I said to check your tone! I may not be so forgiving of a man if you keep at it."

"Yes, sir."

"You are a member of the 422nd Military Police Brigade, Private. Your job is investigating matters that concern the U.S. Military."

"And this does, sir?"

"It does."

"If you say so, sir."

"Look here, get low now, feel that stench, that rotting death, sting your nose? Don't plug up now, Private, you thought you'd be doing some killing overseas, well, this is about all you'd smell during your duration, only fresher. Now look: the wounds, you really think this is murder-suicide? This your first case or something?"

"Yes, sir, it is, sir."

"Jesus fucking Christ. Looks like you're learning today. Okay, Mr. Vernon here: bullet in the shoulder, guts literally ripped out and throat cut. Mrs. Vernon: shot in the head, through the window there—"

"She disemboweled him then shot herself?"

"Sweet mother of god...no, Private. No. Listen. The bullet went through the window, others are out there looking in the garden for it now. You're going to see that the bullet will not match the one still lodged in his shoulder there."

"You think so, sir?"

"Let me hear what you think happened here, Private."

"Well, sir, if we're saying its murder-suicide—"

"We're not."

"Oh. I—"

"You don't seem all that bright to me, Private. You read too much Bill Shakespeare and not enough Sir Arthur Conan Doyle."

"..."

"Where are you from, Reynolds?"

"Wyoming, sir."

"Wyoming? Never met anyone from Wyoming."

"I've been getting that, sir. A lot."

"Whereabouts in Wyoming?"

"Small town called Ten Sleep. Me and about three-hundred some odd souls call it a home."

"Wow, that is small...were you planning on ever going back there, Private? Back
'home?'"

"I don't know, sir. Perhaps?"

"You've not thought of it?"

"I do sometimes, sir."

"Interesting."

"What that, sir?"

"Just that, well, you might not have a home to go back to, and you 'sometimes' think about it? A population that small, well, just think about it: how many men of Ten Sleep enlisted to join a branch of the Military Police? Just you? As I suspected. All able-bodied young men will be drafted to fight, even if it's, say, half of three hundred, Private, a hundred and fifty men in the U.S. Army will be lost in the full enormity of it all. And, as for the old souls that you left behind, well, you ought to know what'll happen sooner or later."

"It's possible some men could come home, sir."

"Yes, it is. All hundred and fifty could survive and go home to Ten Sleep and keep the town alive, forever telling the same tales amongst one another, all stories are the same, but unique only to themselves...but you won't be there, will you, Private?"

"I don't know...sir."

"Why is that?"

"..."

"Private?"

"..."

"Private!"

"Sir!"

"Lost you there. Again."

"Sorry, sir. I was thinking about—"

"I know, Private. My point being, you're from a *small* town, I get that now, but far as I'm concerned, Walla Walla is a small town, too. This area of town is where the farming is done, and this couple here, Wade and Macy Vernon, were sitting on a mighty fine piece of land here, but, as you could see when we arrived, they weren't taking much advantage of it."

"You think someone murdered them...for their land, sir?"

"I'm not ruling anything out, but it's my strongest feeling right now."

"Sir, what if it was just a random killing?"

"Random? What are you talking about, Private?"

"Well, sir, there's been talk about these brothers, The Devil's Twins of Yakima, folk call them, who've been going round and killing, for *fun*."

"Jesus Christ, Private, pull your head out of your ass. You've not been listening."

"But, sir—"

"Killing with no motive? First off, you heard that story and thought *murder-suicide* seemed more logical?"

"I'm new, sir. I'm sorry."

"You make me sick. Where'd you even hear that shit?"

"There was talk about another couple killed in town a week ago, sir. But they were in downtown Walla Walla."

"That has no concern to the U.S. Military! This case does! Now, if I may explain. There are many families in this area, but there are three families, each a mile from here, that we'll be interviewing today: The Poletti Family to the east, the Nyström Family to the west, and the Müller Family, southwest."

"Jesus...sorry, sir..."

"Yes, how shocking it must be for you."

"Surrounded by Swedes, Italianos, and fucking Nazis?! Truly, sir?"

"Now you understand? At long fucking last. This is why we're here, it's because of that Order old FDR signed yesterday."

"My god..."

"Calm down, Private. Know your surroundings."

"Sir."

"If my theory holds true, then this murder would've been carried out by enemies of the State."

"You think it was the Nazis, Sir?"

"My gut feeling, though we're paying all homes a visit today. The Polettis are an established name in the industry— they, of course, got a head start when they were making illegal wine during prohibition, and their family name comes with rumors of mafia ties. The Nyströms are simple farmers, mostly growing hops—"

"Reckon they're brewing up there, sir?"

"Matter of fact, they are...but that...isn't important. Where was I? Ah, the father, Mathias, is a cousin of some royal Swede, League of Nations members—"

"Spies, sir?"

"—interesting idea. It's not impossible."

"And the Nazis, sir?"

"The Müllers would be the only ones to gain anything, really. Smallest land owned between the three of them."

"W-we gotta go, sir! We gotta get 'em right now!"

"Calm down, Private. Breathe. Listen to me. I can only speculate as to the rapidly growing wine industry that not only this town is now striving to center itself around but the country as a whole. The art of fine winemaking is coming henceforth to America, only the timing of it appears poor."

"Sir...?"

"Upon doing further research of this area, I've come to the conclusion that Walla Walla is quite capable of growing varietals that are indigenous to Rhône and Châteauneuf-du-Pape."

"What's so special about that, sir?"

"One day you may learn the pleasures of drinking a Châteauneuf-du-Pape. Nevertheless, in this area here, a dedicated winemaker—artist, I should say—could make a version similar to that of a true Châteauneuf-du-Pape and, if capable of doing so, would be able to sell it to the consumer at an affordable cost, to start. Then, once they have a firm reputation in place, they can essentially dictate the prices on the industry. Now, sure, none of those three families are growing Rhône varietals right now, but who's to say they won't now that this land is available? And sure, there are others in Walla Walla who are already growing those varietals, but they are not a concern to us. Know why?"

"No, sir. Why?"

"Because of their damn lineage trace, Private. Keep up."

"So...sir, you think that the German family killed them to take their land...so they could make more wine?"

"So they could make *money*."

"And you're sure it's the Germans, sir?"

"Well, aren't you?"

"As you said, sir: they're the one with everything to gain."

"Exactly. Staff Sergeant! Get in here!"

"Sir?"

"Staff Sergeant, you and Sergeant Noah take Private Reynolds with you up to the Müller house. Inform Sergeant Underhill that he's to take Corporal Pope, and Privates Hume and Atwater and head to the Swedes' house. I'll check in on the Polettis."

"Alone, sir?"

"What?"

"You going at it alone, sir?"

"No, Private, if it's any of your business, which it isn't. Captain McPhail and Private-First-Class Castle will be with me."

"Good to know, sir. Joyce staying back then?"

"Someone has to."

"Sir, yes, sir."

"Private Reynolds, one more word."

"Yes, Major?"

"Come closer, Private."

"Sir?"

"You've got to kill them all, Jenson. You're the only one I can trust. No one is to be left breathing. Understand?"

"W-what? Sir?"

"Private?"

"Sir? Are you sure? Sir—"

"Am I sure? Private, I don't know what has gotten into you, but I need you to keep your head on your shoulders now. No one is to get hurt, understand?"

"But, sir, you said—"

"You continue to wear my patience thin, Private. Get out of here."

"Question before I go, sir?"

"What is it?"

"This is real, right?"

23

A fist pounded on the door. A harsh voice of authority shouted:

"Open the fucking door!"

"This is the U.S. Military! Open the door now!"

They were about ready to kick the damn thing down when a distraught voice called out: "Okay, okay!" and assured them that they would be there in a second, just please stop hurting that old wood.

The door barely creaked ajar when Pvt. Jenson Reynolds put his massive shoulder into it and it flew open. Karl Müller stumbled backward onto the floor and Ruth Müller, who had been seated at the table, let out a cry and ran to her husband. Before she was down at his side, Jenson was inside and had his gun pointed at one then the other, back and forth and back and forth, until SSG Booker LeDu entered and they each had a gun pointed at both suspects.

"On your fucking knees!" Jenson shouted. Karl and Ruth stayed still as stone. "NOW!" His voice nearly shook the whole house. Ruth helped her husband to his knees then knelt next to him, tears welling in her eyes and blurring her vision.

Sgt. Zachariah Noah was still outside, behind the house;

had this odd fucking hunch that he would catch the entire family just as he turned the corner, saw it like an oil painting in his mind's eye: they would be running, hand in hand, wearing lederhosen for some reason, into the vines, *escaping* he had to tell himself, for he would unload round after round after round till the gun would go *click*, the bullets would violently eat their way through the flesh of their unsuspecting backs, tearing through muscle and tissue and bone, if his aim was true enough, parts of the body he studied deeply, a thing he believed only God could have made. It wasn't until he turned the corner and found this fantasy was nothing more than that, that he wouldn't get to be a "hero" and gun down innocent lives. Darn. But there was a cellar door there. Oboy. He pulled, pulled, pulled—to no avail. It was locked. For the fourth time in his life, he almost took the Lord's name in vain. Someone had to be down there. He decided to go back inside and tell the commanding officer, SSG LeDu—his way of gloating and saying, "I'm better than you" —but quickly discovered that the information did not matter, as Jenson did not seem himself. There was something dark that lingered in his voice, and he was doing the "interview" himself.

WEEPING DAY

Meanwhile, over at the Nyström household, Sgt. Westley Underhill was doing his best as a Cat and leader to conduct a full investigation of the three frightened Swedes sitting together at their fine-looking dining table—polished mahogany, handcrafted by Mathias and Cade three summers ago, and six chairs, in case of guests but not guests like these men. Sgt. Underhill, so impressed with the craftsmanship—a big wood guy himself—had half a mind to halt the interview altogether if they would "sell" him this magnificent dining room set. He had a notebook and pencil in his lap in which he was writing notes of their responses and reading off questions he was required to ask them. He sat in a chair, which he felt was made for his structure and that he could sit there all damn day, but not at the table as they did not invite him to, which he understood—instead, the Nyströms sat in a row on the same side, facing him and his three men: Pvt. Atwater, who had his weapon aimed in their direction the entire time despite Sgt. Underhill's three feeble attempts to "command" him to lower his weapon, while Cpl. Pope and Pvt. Hume looked around for anything of interest when they stumbled upon some beers. He went through the questions: When did you arrive in this country? Are you now, or have you ever been anything less than a perfect American Patriot? Do you hate America? Do you have any contact or communications with one Mårten-Ludvig Stenberg? The last was a question that Mathis answered, explaining that Mårten-Ludvig Stenberg was, in fact, his cousin to whom he occasionally wrote, not as often as he would like, which caused Sgt. Underhill to scribble like a fucking paranoiac in his notebook three words that he held up for Pvt. Atwater to read—

THIS IS IT?

Pvt. Atwater read slowly and carefully, twice (he was never the best reader), then clicked the safety off, making Sgt. Underhill nearly piss his pants as if he had slid himself into the flesh of the family in front of him and could see the world from their point of view, and genuinely thought that his paranoia sent three people to their deaths, and that if they died he would, too, à la Cpl. Sonny Monday.

Breathe.

"When—" Sgt. Underhill put the notebook back down in his lap, fucking hoping his voice would not shake and break on him, "—did you last receive word from him?" He almost fell out of his chair when they said a week before Pearl Harbor. He was mentally, unconsciously preparing himself for the sound of gunfire extremely close to his leaf eardrum.

"Say the fucking word," Pvt. Atwater gritted through his teeth. Sgt. Underhill swore he heard "coward" at the end of the sentence.

"Do you have this letter?" Sgt. Underhill asked. The words spewed from his lips, fearing time was slipping away.

"Y-yes," Mathias said. "In the desk, over there—"

"Don't fucking move!" Pvt. Atwater, going full Red now, screamed at the man who merely pointed.

"Hey!" Pvt. Hume shouted from outside. "Think there's a fire! Hey!"

There were footsteps and Cpl. Pope yelled, "Holy shit!" with that certain voice filled with wonder and partial amusement that comes with the second beer which happened to be an Imperial Stout.

"Go check it out," Sgt. Underhill said.

"That's all you, Sarge."

"Private."

"Wouldn't want to leave these folks here alone, they might make a break for it."

"I'll make sure they won't."

"Will you now?"

"Hey!" Pvt. Hume shouted again.

Sgt. Underhill looked at Pvt. Atwater who looked right back at him. There was nothing there in the eyes of Sgt. Underhill that Pvt. Atwater could use against him, which was sort of Red's thing with the Cats as they would, at times of intense stress, carry a lot of emotions in their eyes—but somehow he didn't see anything in him then. He was surprisingly—and, he'd dare to say, impossibly—blank of all emotions as if he'd given up and accepted the situation for what it was, and goddamn if he didn't respect that.

"I'll be back," he said to the family in a way that sounded a lot like a threatening promise, then walked away.

Breathe. They finally did. With the weapon no longer pointed at them it was like the weight of the universe was lifted off their backs. They saw everything for the first time again: how unbelievably beautiful it was to be alive; how unimaginably perfect the table they sat at was; how it was the first time that they all realized and saw its perfectness and how remarkable it was that that realization came collectively to them; how god-like Mathias and Cade felt for creating something so perfect and how god-like Edith realized she was for creating Cade and passing her perfection onto him. If God was to ever willingly prove its existence to the universe and had to pick a human sex to be viewed and referred to as to please the simple minds that inhabited earth who couldn't fathom the idea of an omnipresent entity being anything but that—for it actually is nothing more than an idea, the same idea that they cannot or do not want to mentally perceive as it's all connected, is in fact what "it" (God) should be viewed as: an intangible entity that generally exists within you, that which is your consciousness and gives you the idea of "I" and perfection, which is all true—God would surely be a woman.

"It's coming from the German's place," Pvt. Atwater said. "The fire."

"Big smoke, Sarge," Pvt. Hume added. "What do you think we should—"

"Let's move out," Sgt. Underhill commanded, the perfect excuse to leave this place.

Pvt. Hume saluted and ran out. Sgt. Underhill rose to follow. Before he left and without turning back he suggested that they lock their doors. All four men piled into the truck, the G. Heads thinking, *Nevermind the Swedes, let's kill some Nazis.* And off they went. Sgt. Underhill was in the passenger seat. He never grabbed the letter that Mårten-Ludvig Stenberg wrote—still inside the desk—or even thought about it again.

GUTS AND GRAPES

Major George Wynne strolled merrily through the front door of the Poletti Family home—double-doors made out of old French oak wine barrels—completely ignoring the panicked cries from the father on his knees who switched from English to Italian (Mussolini's filthy pig Latin, as Major Wynne saw it), his four children around him holding each other. As they wept, two guns, one held by Captain Alan MacPhail and the other by PFC Jeremiah Castle, bounced their aim from head to head to head, ready to blow them all the fuck away and get drunk.

More senseless murder. It was as sure a thing as you could get, nine times out of ten: white, gun-loving, immigrant-hating Americans with clearly visible hard-ons for a taste of some good old-fashioned violence. When the universe aligned perfectly so that the one-time pulled through and forced them to lower their weapons and rush to the sound of a jubilant, singing Major Wynne, who, to his credit, belted his own lyrics like an operatic Bing Cosby gone pop:

> Welllllllll, I've got the key
> To the whole city,
> Whatever you want, baby pop,
> It's on me.
> Ooh ooh oohooh.
> Open up your heart to me,
> While we get drunk on this fineeeeeee
> Walla Walla Chianti.

He had reached the wine cellar. It was the alcoholics inside, the trespassing Americans, that awoke and caused them to join their Major, who had met them halfway, five bottles of wine cradled in his arms, at the family dinner table. He set the bottles down carefully. Captain MacPhail and PFC

Castle hurried down to the cellar not only to grab more but to get a view of it for themselves. It was below the basement, walls lined with stone, made to feel like an actual cave, small cubbies holding hundreds of bottles—it almost didn't seem possible. Some already had mushrooms and other fungus and molds making residence on the bodies of the bottles, signs of a good cellar, like on the neck of the 1923 Cabernet that PFC Castle grabbed.

By the time they got back up with an additional baker's dozen, Major Wynne was sitting down and already sipping on '34 Merlot. Had they arrived thirty seconds earlier they would have witnessed his first swirl, sniff, sip, and with it an instant, premature ejaculation that caused his right leg to shake violently under the table and visibly wet his pants followed by an almost religious awakening and a brief but intense and vivid out-of-body experience. A sensation, he was convinced, that only happened from the best bottles and to true wine lovers. The other bottles were placed on the table. Major Wynne, after they went to the cellar, had the courtesy to grab enough wine glasses for all of them. Captain MacPhail grabbed the Major's Victorinox Swiss Army knife, corkscrew smartly and respectively sticking out, and opened one of the youngest bottles in the house: a '40 Sangiovese, that, once Major Wynne saw the label, and Captain MacPhail drinking it straight out of the bottle, almost shit his pants. What a horrendous crime, he thought, a wine so young and abused like so. But he figured that there were likely more bottles of that stuff down there than he could take, so he tried to not let it eat away at him too much...but the fact that the bottle even existed still shocked him; thought he wouldn't see a Poletti Sangiovese for another three or four years, it was only a whisper of a rumor that they actually did harvest and bottle the Sangiovese from the '40 vintage, gossip that he paid little attention to, but now seeing it was true, thought they must have paid good money to keep the mouths who helped shut.

Michelangelo and his children used the opportunity to quickly flee. They piled into Michelangelo's truck—Teodoro, Vitro, and Ciro in the back and Noemi in the front—and sped to Pete's Last Stool. The entire ride all the children cried and Teodoro, the self-proclaimed Pope of the family, yelled prayers in Latin from the back.

While at their house they would lose forty or fifty bottles of wine, including all of the '26 Merlots, some would fight the good fight with gravity and die trying, shattering on the floor, while others would be consumed to the point where they were no longer enjoyable. Even Major Wynne's own palette was blown out and he could no longer make any coherent wine-snob comments on tasting notes—still tried, though, not that the drunk G. Heads he was with gave a fuck. He was so upset that neither of them were listening to his tasting notes that he climbed on the table to get their attention (they had been discussing the probability of life on another planet, which PFC Castle drunkenly dismissed as a downright sinful thought, his argument being Earth was God's only planetary creation, while Captain MacPhail found the idea fascinating and was drunk enough to sexualize alien beings), when he slipped on a bottle that rolled under his foot, his left leg folding the wrong way underneath his body, snapping in half, and piercing through his skin. He fell hard to the floor, screaming in pain. He screamed himself into shock and unconsciousness in a puddle of blood and wine while Captain MacPhail and PFC Castle laughed—all attention focused on the Major now—so hard that they both eventually passed out from exhaustion.

An Incoming Education On Fear

Jenson was practically foaming from the mouth. He was inches away from Karl and Ruth's faces: he accused her of fucking Hitler and accused him of being a cuckold and a Nazi spy who fucked little boys and girls. But most importantly, he accused them of killing Ward and Macy Vernon, a crime Ruth and Karl denied over and over again.

"This isn't right," Book more or less whispered to himself, thinking Sgt. Noah never really listened to him.

"We have to stop this," he agreed. "Follow the script."

Book, cool as ever and braver than all, stepped in—if he were to think back on it later he would find the memory altogether lost...like it wasn't at all important, then he would be forced to wonder why that didn't last for the entirety of the nightmare that would follow, why couldn't he stay strong and less human?—and put a hand on Jenson's shoulder which sort of froze him, like he had forgotten that there were others there.

"Take five, Private."

Jenson straightened, eyes fixed on the wall. "Yes, Staff Sergeant," he said mechanically. He stepped away and found a new spot of nothing to stare at.

"We are acting on Executive Order 9066," is all Jenson heard Book say before he tuned out the entire world for seven minutes—if it would go on his record that this would be the first incident in his short military career that Pvt. Jenson Reynold ever disobeyed a superior or any order at all, for that matter, but Book would always remember the time of the hour in which the horror was committed as he had a habit to check his wristwatch (0933h.), which he did before he took over the interview and immediately when the first round was fired; it was a reflex, nothing more than that, a thing he did all the time growing up when he got his first wristwatch ats thirteen, the same one he still wore, a black leather band and face to match and, underneath the face, pressed always against his wrist, the words "You Matter" etched there by some old watchmaker, a request from his parents, and he always thought of the likelihood of that watchmaker being white and if they were an ally and if they thought his or his parents' lives mattered at all while he was etching those words, words that were practically imprinted on his skin, and the habit of checking the time, this time after the gunshots, would haunt him for the rest of his life; that his first reaction to echoes of death was to make note of the construct of time—and became lost in the broken and poisoned fibers of his consciousness which, in this case, turned out to in the forms of a chaotic argument, which followed as:

THE PLAYBILL
For a Dialogue Between Egos of the Same Mind

The following scene is a brief inquiry into the thought process and decision-making that took place inside the consciousness of Pvt. Jenson Reynolds during the latter part of the Müller Family interrogation, recorded above, which led to the murders recorded in Episodes 1 & 23.

The characters featured are:
VOICE 1 (V1) referred to as John Rugby and/or Rugby
VOICE 2 (V2) referred to as Strafford
VOICE 3 (V3) referred to as Balthasar and/or Banquo
VOICE 4 (V4) referred to as Old Oberon
VOICE 5 (V5) referred to as Viola One-Two
VOICE 6 (V6) referred to as Pistol Paris

All characters played by Jenson Reynolds (JR) who is referred to as Jenson and/or Reynolds.

INT. THE CONSCIOUSNESS OF JENSON REYNOLDS

The tangible world, the construct of time itself, froze. Nearly every possible scenario came to life, but never really lived. Different futures, different histories; here, gone.

V1: "You need to breathe, Jenson. Breathe. There we go. See? Just stop a moment. We've time."

V2: "Thou art ov'rthinking."

JR: "At which hour am I not?"

V4: "Whatever the weather may be, it mocks you: the boring spring, the dull summer, the childing autumn...now this angry winter. How can change come to rest?"

V5: "Perhaps it cannot, isn't meant to."

V6: "Well fuck me. That's what Old Oberon is implying, no?"

V5: "Perhaps, perhaps not."

V6: "Oh? No? Well, Miss Viola One-Two, please, enlighten us, with whatever the fuck you're even thinking about speaking out loud now. I'm sure Strafford will make it sound pretty, intelligent."

V5: "Perhaps you piss off?"

V2: "P'rhaps thee piss off?"

V6: "Ha."

V1: "Need to focus on Jenson here."

V3: "Bah! Who are you to have ze stage, Rugby? Eh? Always out to make your intentions so pure. We see through you, boy. You can't always be ze lead."

V1: "Beg pardon? 'Be the lead?' Balthasar, are you—"

V3: "It's Banquo now, okay? Banquo."

V1: "Banquo? Since when?"

V2: "It hast been since the twenty-first. Wh're w're thee?"

V1: "Holiday."

V6: "Well fuck me. Lucky you."

V4: "An adventurer, seer of many lands, nontangible, nor on any plane of any true reality, though still, he goes to them all the same."

V5: "Perhaps it is the journey that is important, not the destination."

V6: "What the fuck."

V5: "Perhaps you check the language there, Pistol Paris."

V1: "I agree, no need for it."

V3: "Bah! It's free consciousness! You can't tell no one nothing, John Rugby. You hear me? You ain't ze lead."

JR: "Haven't f'rgotten about me?"

V2: "We couldst nev'r."

V1: "Literally."

V3: "There he goes again!"

V1: "No, you pompous ass, there *you* go again!"

V3: "You are a bastard man, John Rugby! No good for any stable mind."

JR: "Hey..."

V5: "Perhaps we get back on track? In one, two—"

V6: "One, a-two, a-threefourfivesixseven let's fucking gooooooo already. You all heard what the Major said."

V1: "Actually...maybe we need to talk about that."

JR: "I'm still here...I'm still here..."

V6: "What the fuck is there to talk about?"

V5: "Perhaps the Major didn't really say that."

V3: "You siding with that Rugby fuck now, Viola One-Two? I'd spit at both of ye, if I had the saliva."

V1: "We must entertain the fact that Jenson merely imagined the Major saying that he should kill them. Surely it's possible he did not say that."

V2: "Possible then yond the maj'r didst sayeth 't."

V5: "Perhaps the conversation didn't happen at all."

V3: "Bah! But of course! Anything is possible!"

JR: "Enough!"

V1–6: "..."

V4: "The path at hand appears to be fleeting, but only ends one way. Indeed, no matter the amount of time wasted here, the deed, out there, has been accepted as a reality soon to be. For, as we all know, these violent delights have violent ends."

V2: "...And in their triumph die, like fire and powd'r."

JR: "Differences aside for a moment...we've a decision?"

V1–6: "Kill them all."

24

It's a question as old as time: what happens after we die?

Your favorite philosopher's favorite philosopher will never agree on the same answer. Why would they? No living person has ever *really* died. You can't begin to describe death and the stage after if you're alive. You can only philosophize about it. Some people hope and pray for a certain outcome, not only for themselves, sometimes, either. It's possible: nothing happens. Well, perhaps not "*nothing*," for even to define "nothing" one must use words that mean *something*. So, maybe something does happen but on a much smaller scale...just warm, black darkness—so impressive is the dark that if you had eyes to see they would never fully adjust to it, but it holds a familiar feeling like you were always there, always a part of it—that your consciousness—you—will float around in, wrapped in that familiar feeling of love from your family, friends, and experiences, unspeakable but a blissful sense that they are always there, not necessarily beside you but within you. It's possible: there's something, another place. You break free of the cycle. Everything is pure, white, radiating, golden, sunshine, warm. You see yourself as you want, your family and friends, who you see as they want. You are always together, physically, without actually being alive. Like being in one of those motion pictures. Lovely dream. It's possible: you remain in the cycle. When you leave this current form you simply find another. Reborn. A fresh start. A blessing or a curse? Having to replay the game. Forgetting all the moves you made last time, the people you played with, how much better they made it. To relearn everything again. All the hardships, the loss, the ecstasy, the joys, the waves...an almost prison-like feel to it, trapped in one flat cycle, unable to break free and rest for a bit into that sweet deep nothing.

When the shots rang out—deafening sounds that would echo silently in the back of their minds forever—when the blood of their blood, the blood that created them, that flows within their own veins, started to warp within the old wooden floor, which their late father talked endlessly about replacing— like clockwork, really, nearly everyday, normally after breakfast, when the dishes were being washed and he sat down and lit up his pipe, a newspaper in his lap waiting to be read, and he'd hear that creak of deadwood crying after finally one too many steps, too much weight, it would say, too much now...and he'd, of course, comment: "Remind me to fix that," which they always did and he'd acknowledge with: "Right, right. I'll get after it tomorrow," which, as the evidence shows, did not happen—when the black-red droplets began to dripdripdrip onto the dirt they stood hiding on below, onto their shoes, their hands, when the initial shock subsided for the briefest of moments and reality wormed its way into their consciousness: they did not wonder, they did not pray for the souls of their parents or for their safe entry into heaven, the idea of "God" did not enter their minds at all. All they could comprehend was watching the true face of horror in which that is Man—which viewed itself as the epitome of righteous— and how something so vile and evil should be allowed to live with the insane power in deciding who continued to live, as you knew in your bones that this soul—if that's what you could call something so cold—that stood above had developed an obsession, if it hadn't already, whether born in that moment or histories previous, for killing...and would be doing it again.

So the question in question then was never really in question for the Müller children when they witnessed the traumatic event of their parents' murder, unbeknownst to their parents, though it would of course, naturally, come to them later down the road, when they had time to process such a question: the idea of the end.

It would be later, maybe within the hour, when they would seriously questioned—quite possibly for the first time—the existence of "God" and what purpose it served if it allowed something so horrible to happen. This supposedly perfect, omnipresent being, somehow there before the beginning and long after the end, built on love and virtue allowed evil to roam free? (We really should have created God in the image of a woman—it would have been more peaceful. Men, as God is sadly forever viewed, are trash, violent trash, like God.) People die all the time, sure. People are killed, too. War was war: always a crime. But then there was this; an evil that they did not know, before this day, existed. Was it due to the trusted community they lived in, once thought to be quiet and safe? Or the excellent job their parents did to keep them protected from God's bad side? Or was it in fact due to God's good grace, which had walked away for a good twenty minutes, possibly to check up on something else, that kept them safe until now? Moral compasses spinning off their axis. Everything was blood red. Ghostly. Red.

You could imagine this sort of thing having a detrimental impact on mental health.

For the rest of their lives they would subconsciously be looking over their shoulder, paranoid, like it was a natural thing, something their minds collectively came up with to protect them as a way to make them still think they were okay, almost erasing the words *paranoid* and *paranoia* from their vocabulary. Yet anyone who has ever seen a paranoid out in public before would be able to spot all the traits that the Müller children would come to inherit: the already-noted, constantly looking over their shoulders as if someone was listening or following them; the questioning of everything; the dramatic change in body language, arms wrapped around themselves, shielding, protecting, rarely showing skin; the occasional—if the paranoid belief was strong enough—writing of notes back and forth to each other, not speaking out loud, not even when the server was there to take their orders, read the note here, honey, (*but they're still watching*); the die-on-this-hill stand they would take when it came to what table they sat at in restaurants, closest to the exit or not at all.

It would seem then that the mind was doing them a disservice rather than any good, how cut off they could make themselves from the rest of the world, practically invisible, but never quite *fully* invisible. No. No, there was always *some*one watching, listening...

And this, in the minds of the Müller children, is what they forcibly accepted as rational thought. One, of course, could escape this cycle—for that's what it is, really, an endless loop that the new operator, that corrupted mind, will eventually stop when it feels it's had enough, when it finally overloads every cell with thoughts on top of thoughts, all crammed in, filled with paranoia, the point at which the body would take over as a defense mechanism and attempt to overthrow this new, corrupt operation which, with the body being slower than the mind, could lead one to believe that any strategy from the body was never well thought out, and would find itself successful in a coup d'état at the price of its sudden mortality.

But until then, it's biting your fingernails down to nubs, holding multiple conversations with yourself both internally and externally, sometimes not even realizing it; sleepless nights, unless you're able to find the proper medicine (the Brown Bottle Kind or The Old Seven-Fifty, as they call it), sometimes accompanied by something in the darkest corner of your room, some ominous, ghostly figure holding something you want to say you recognize from a lifelike nightmare, a bad memory—when you realize suddenly that you're not moving, frozen stiff, a statue on display solely for this ghost, this dark, and that's when you spy eyes on that shadow there and how sickly and poisoned they look and how they're *glued* to *you*, and how with every quick blink you take they get a little bit closer now, and how *you can't even fucking scream.*

Then there are always, of course, the ones closest to you. The neighbors, when they first hear about it—and in this particular case if they're even alive at all—will *actually pray* to the same God in question. What the actual fuck does this accomplish? Do they believe that their prayers are catalysts for the safe passage of these departed souls into heaven, like those who pray are so fucking high and mighty and important? Or is it just something that makes them feel better in a moral and personal way, like there was nothing else they can do, so might as well pray? As if it was part of some brainwashed list on what boxes they're conditioned to check off following some tragic event: offer up your sincere condolences, say something along the lines of "What a horrible tragedy," place them in your thoughts and prayers, bake them a casserole.

But if we're done speculating for now, back to the story at hand:

25

And so they went—on their own for the first time in their lives on a mission that did not seem totally rational nor plausible, just something to do, that needed doing. They couldn't be told any different.

They headed north, then east. Ahead of them stretched an open road to a part of the country with which they were completely unfamiliar, the same country they were no longer proud to call home. Bambi drove while Joseph rested his head against the window in the passenger seat. Neither of them spoke. She watched the road roll underneath them, and he watched the trees blur past, eventually becoming few and far between until there were none left and only empty land as far as the eye could see, land that to him appeared lifeless, vacant, bare and drained of its soul as if a fire recently swept through the area, like that's what it was known for: the part of the world that was constantly on fire, flames dying out long enough so those who happened past go by never knowing what this place really was, but never long enough for the vegetation there to be reborn and learn how to grow again, no...there they went, bereft flames that inched their way up out of the ground like grass and worked their way towards the

Nirvana they believed in above, allelu...to the life that he could not see, for he knew what they were in for came with the territory.

It wasn't until they had passed the border of Idaho when their first problem occurred: the engine suddenly stopped working as if it forgot how to work—forgot its only purpose. It was fine on petrol, strange...they wished they were farther along before they had to use the horses.

They sat in the car for a few minutes, each internally damning the world, silence raging between them. When they finally exited the car they noticed two trucks coming down the once-barren road, with beds of cages like theirs for the horses, but filled instead with heads and bodies. Joseph took to waving them down. To their surprise, they stopped. One person exited the passenger side of the lead truck. The cages in the beds of both trucks were filled with people: men, women, children. Mobile prisons whose prisoners sat and stared blankly at the two young people, who stared back with a melancholic wonderment, and someone somewhere was asking for forgiveness, necessary for the wrong reasons.

The man from the first truck wore army fatigues and Joseph almost screamed and had the beautiful and bloody thought of jumping on top of the man and clawing his eyes out but Bambi put her hand on his shoulder and it was like she momentarily—for it would always be momentary with him—transferred his burden onto herself so he was able to speak to the man and ask if he could take a look at their engine, please. Bambi wandered away, towards the prisons. She stood in front of one with her heart in her throat.

"Where're you from?" the soldier asked Joseph as they stood near the dead engine, not looking at it, hood unlifted.

"Washington," he said.

"No shit. Where're you heading?"

"Wyo-Monta-Minnesota?"

"Yeah? What's your name, kid?"

"Joe Mü-iller...Miller."

"Uh-huh."

"Can you fix the engine or not, man?"

"Looks like you have some horses here, should be able to get you to Wyo-Monta-Minnesota no problem." The soldier, Cpl. Waldron, according to his tag, turned to walk away with the full intention of going back to the truck and bitching out Pvt. Richardson, the driver, seeing as there was no real reason for them to get out of the truck in the first place, just wasting more fucking time.

"Wait—"

"You can either fuck off on your pony," Cpl. Waldron snapped, "or ride in back with those parasites there."

Joseph stood and stared at all those poor, trapped souls only a few dozen yards away from him. Seemed like the first time he really noticed them, really saw them, how their weary bodies struggled to hold their heads up but did anyway because there was pride still alive there, at the edges of their eyes, as Bambi could see vividly as she was so close to them, the outlines of their souls stood on the precipice of their being—one may interpret the scene as the spirit in a state of ready abandonment, to leap, to be free of that body and it's fate, to move onto the next big adventure whether that be the curse of being born again into another body, blank nothingness, or the ever-hopeful, dull Nirvana, their soul at the brink and holding on, on display, if you will, bearing itself naked and true before the world for all who have the wherewithal to find hidden beauties of life such as this to see and understand that it is there to tell you that it refuses to give up.

Through the watery filter that her eyes had created, blurring her vision ever so slightly, Bambi locked eyes with— though she did not realize it at the time—*the* Dr. Kyo Koite, and then Hiro Hachimura immediately after. The gentlemen of the undervalued Seattle Camera Club and the criminally-unappreciated Seattle Haiku Society, Rainier Ginsha (whose founder, Kyou Kawajiri, sat next to them), both looked at Bambi Müller and immediately knew her from the part of the being that exists outside the body, call it an aura, or more justly, the soul, that they identified with the same they presence that radiated from her parents, mixed with a heartbreaking shadow that she unknowingly wore like a mask and told them all they needed to know, like celestial ESP, that the light that created her had faded from this world.

"Back away," Cpl. Waldron said to Bambi as he climbed back into the truck.

"Where're you taking them?"

"Minidoka. Prison camp."

POPCORN, POPCORN

Rolling hills stretched and roamed freely before them, tobacco brown, alone, rarely explored, perfectly fine that way. It was unlike the lush green forests and grey mountains screaming towards the sky they had grown accustomed to calling a home. Yet still, what lay in and beyond the land before them still held some quiet wonder, that fantastic, quiet inspiration, that silent motivation. To the unappreciative eye, it was dull and boring: something that was there so you could lose focus of it and become trapped in your mind with thoughts of what will happen next, and soon you're filled to the brim with dread and anxiety and fear and paranoia to top it off. Instead of dreading the inevitable, Dr. Kyo Koike spent the time deeply admiring this part of the world he had never known existed before. The only thought that brought him and sort of ill-will was that sense of pining for his camera, a desperate want to capture this scene for those who would never come across it. How he longed to share the stillness of it all, literally capture the quiet, silent beauty...what you would call life.

The sinking twilight and the creeping dusk together painted the sky with a dark halo of golden-orange American light that lingered high enough like it needed to show you something before it left. There: surveying the scenery atop a hill a hundred or so years away: a herd of buffalo, more and more appearing with every blink of an eye, descending the slope to graze in the valley. None of them had ever witnessed such a mass gathering of any animal, aside from birds—Hiro Hachimura being the only one likely to have witnessed, and *captured*, the largest mass mammal gathering, that he knew of, on the planet: the phenomenon down in Texas at a sunken cave from which millions upon millions of *bats* emerged to cover the sky, usually around this same time, actually. The rare piece he titled *The Emergence* hung proudly, the only copy, of course, in the Detroit Institute of Arts, his first piece displayed in a museum outside of Washington. Hundreds of buffalo spilled into the valley. No one spoke. The stampede boomed like long, rolling thunder. They all sat silently, some heads forced to look over their respective shoulders, and stared through those cold metal bars at the beauty roaming free before them. Hiro offered Dr. Kyo a cigarette, which he accepted blindly with thanks. A flame from Hiro's silver Zippo kicked alive and attacked the cigarette then went and took the flame against his own cigarette. They inhaled and exhaled at the same time. The other eight men, two children, and six women crammed in there with them said nothing of the smoke. Four were already smoking, two whistling some tune they had just come up with—one high, the other fast and sharp—one was asleep but forced to wake up as the man next to him was kind enough to reckon that no soul should miss this phenomenon, and one had a book, now in her lap as the light became scarce and there were buffalo to be gawked at while they were still visible, and that's what they all did: stare at the buffalo before the light finally faded away and darkness wrapped them in its protective blanket, making them invisible to all eyes. Before Hiro put his Zippo away, Dr. Kyo caught the inscription etched on one side:

健在

True...they were still alive and well, for now. Dr. Kyo smiled, looked back at the disappearing buffalo, and thought that the picture laid out before him in the dying light, revealing itself right before the full dark arrived, must have been the heaven Laton Alton Huffman lived for. Hiro sat next to Dr. Kyo, caught in between an internal dialog of admiration for the scene before them and getting lost in his sudden and intense urge to pine and lament over some Nikka whiskey, wanting to dive into a bottle with every emotional door left unlocked on the inside—or some of that Shichirō stuff, real legendary.

All that made him focus on what lay ahead: when would be then next time he would be able to taste such fine whiskey, if ever again? Funny, how it's only after the thought of being denied alcohol—being deprived of your go-to drug, what you'd take for granted because it was always there—is born is when you realize the other freedoms you've lost and the hell that awaits you, and that's when your imagination runs wild on how gruesomely horrible the hell that awaits must be. Funnier, even, how your imagination, during times such as these, is damn near impossible to stop, especially when the lights go out, like it fucking feeds off of the negative energy you're inventing for it, thus leaving you with nothing else to do but listen to what it has to say, which, of course, is nothing nice.

The imagination can't help but wonder—practically romanticize—the idea of torture for you: how deeply they'll cut your flesh in places you wouldn't think of putting a blade anywhere near but they do it without hesitation and with knives that are stained wet with the blood of the poor bastard next to you who just gave you a sneak preview of the pain you're about to endure—how long they'll hold your head underwater, so cold it feels like your face is being stabbed with a thousand red-hot sewing needles, over and over and over and over again—how they'll deliver on threats of breaking multiple bones in your body, some more than once.

All this because of where someone happened to be born? As if they can help it. No one has ever asked permission to be alive, to be born into this world, let alone choose where they start their life. Why would they? It makes no sense to judge or hate someone for who they are by means of geography.

26

Never before had they lingered in a place so barren, so still, so quiet...not even the hooves of their horses made a sound; every step just a low, dull *thud*...an action they were aware was taking place but the sound from which could not escape from said action, like it was trapped in a different dimension, on the outside looking in. It was, in a way, like being underwater. On the moon. In a vacuum.

There was a silence between Bambi and Joseph that had existed and grown exponentially since they had crossed paths with Dr. Kyo and Hiro. It was a nasty silence, the kind that made you furious for existing because it was the only thing of relevance to acknowledge. They hadn't said anything about it yet, what had happened at home. Each of them carried, for some inexplicable and unexplainable reason, a cancerous thought of the other one *blaming* them for their parents' death. The make-believe accusation would lead to a violent and horrific exchange of words which would lead to the dissolution of the Müller bond altogether, with neither of them willing to speak to the other after it all. Neither could fathom being alone, without the other, so they each did their best to bury the thought entirely, which took a lot of mental effort, which was another contributor to the silence.

Their horses, siblings themselves—sisters, a pair of American paint horses, Laura's white with brown spots, Joseph's brown with white spots—never made a sound either. Not when they were tired or hungry or thirsty. They didn't even talk to each other which they were known to do, being sisters after all. Nothing. No banter or gossip about these two atop of them, no comment on the state of the place they were stuck in, no wonderment on where they were going or when they'd be going back. Nothing. They just went along, blinking now and then, silent step after silent step...their heads bobbed quietly up and down and up and down and up and down and up—

There was something in the air, something about this place...eerie and unco. How at all hours of the day the moon hung brightly overhead, close enough to touch, and over the soft peaks straight ahead, a view that looked like a G.G. Newell oil painting: the sun never quite breaking the horizon, its blood-orange rays stretching, really fucking trying, but never quite reaching the Twilight above, which left them with an image of a bloody-gold painted crown made of stone to follow. A couple of trees here and there on the side of the road. Thin, twisted branches bore nothing: no leaves, no fruit, no birds, no life. Dead spectators.

There was a time that not even thoughts ran through their minds. It was almost a tranquil, Zen-state of meditative consciousness that they had accidentally stumbled into without actually being aware of it. They weren't sure how long it lasted, or when it started—when they left Washington? After they helplessly ran into Dr. Kyo Koike and Hiro Hachimura? It was an encounter that felt set up, like "God" was having fun with them at this point: how it flaunted more pain in front of them (this applies to Dr. Kyo and Hiro, too), showing them how bad everything could get, memories brought back only to be suppressed again, for the time being, really rubbing their faces in it...the zone through which they were crossing had the ominous feeling of a place that was not really of this earth, as if they had passed through some portal and gone to another planet...but for what purpose? Was this place really any better? Some new experiment, perhaps, where if you take away everything, left with nothing, you can't really feel that pain anymore. But that's what makes you you, after all. Can someone live like that? A shell of themself. A living coma. You don't realize you're in it till you've woken up...but then, if you're awake now...when did you...now, wait a second...

Out of nowhere: sound. It started as a low chant, something they didn't notice, like something their mind conjured up to finally fill the void of silence. Then it grew louder and louder, coming from every direction as if—silence be damned—it was sound's turn to consume them. It was close to unbearable. Their horses could have easily bucked them, probably killed them, but instead they just shook their heads side to side like they did not approve of it, any of it, and kept the same pace until they were stopped by a group of gnomes, thirteen in total, each no more than three feet tall, dancing around them in rhythm to the chanting, which didn't come from their mouths—not a hallucination, in a circle, hand-in-hand:

ON FOOLS WHO FOOLISHLY FOLLOW THEIR HEARTS, OR: (WE REQUIRE BLOOD)

You finally understand what it's like to be utterly alone. Physically—when, for better or for worse (usually for worse), you become so aware of yourself that you start to notice things that, possibly, weren't there before. Maybe you're making them up to distract yourself from that great aloneness: a numb, tonal ring echoing in your ear, something living there, how heavy your bones feel, how dry your skin has become...this feeling, in extreme cases, can corrode your consciousness like acid: it can beat you down, mentally as well as physically if you don't adjust well to it. Most people are unable to. That sense, the feeling of crippling loneliness, is too much to bear. Death isn't an option then at that point, below rock bottom, for death doesn't really happen to you—it happens to those you surround yourself with. What's the point of dying if you're alone?

Keep up now.

There was a time. Back in the real, how open your heart was then—saying you were in love, knowing how to spell the word but never having one specific definition for it or one specific feeling. It comes in like the ocean: each wave entirely different, never the same. Each one still flows through you, changes you, even if forgotten mentally. There was a time. You were addicted to it, needed it at all times, wanted it from everyone...not realizing how difficult it was to reciprocate back the same affection to so many souls...no human is capable, can't give that much, we weren't built that way. There was a time. You thought you found the one you could really hold on to. That feeling. You felt it wouldn't hurt you, not this time. But journeys like that always lead down the same road: you tried to find it again attached to different faces...walking away before it had the opportunity to change, seeing the signs now...on to the next one. There was a time. You've convinced yourself to lose any and all hope in "happy endings." *How can the end be happy when so much bad has happened?* is always the first thought and not: *It can get better*...never learned to recognize and appreciate the highs and the lows. How high you felt when you were riding these highs with another one that broke through and stole a piece of your disappearing heart. Could it ever compare to how broken you felt when you dragged each other through the lows, never knowing who was at fault or for what, so you'd take turns blaming yourselves until you would take enough self-punishment and let it all out?

Thought this was all worth it. Why do the lows always seem to last longer, like they were always there even in the beginning, like you both mentally pre-selected a tiny imperfection you would one day bring up as leverage to use against them (i.e. "You never once pulled a chair out for me" or "I always ask *you* how your day went, you never ask me first"), and how, for the time being, you would mask that with verbal promises of loving physical "imperfections" that have been overlooked and underappreciated by everyone till now (i.e. "I've never met someone who didn't have cartilage in their ears," or "Toe thumbs? I don't see it, babe. Don't even know what that means, really. Every part of you is adorable, though"). There was a time. Over the years each door to your heart began to close, locks changed, keys thrown away; sometimes you noticed, other times were completely oblivious—easier that way, to be fair—until your heart shut completely, nothing foreign allowed in, and, sometimes, nothing domestic either, yes, you yourself—a lost love.

A MOST VIOLENT ATTACK ON PURE REASON
OR: (WE REQUIRE BLOOD PART II)

The monk-like chanting continued, perfectly, on a melancholic loop — highHighHIGHlowlowlowhighHighlow LowHighHIGHlow — while the thirteen dancers, still locked hand-in-hand in a cult-like circle, started to *sway* instead of dance: back and forth back and forth, slowly, like they were underwater—flowing with the current, the tide, the unknown, foregone exclusivity of the cold that lingers down there, waiting for the chosen few—and began to sing: the world's smallest and saddest choir, with voices surprisingly deep and rich and filled with that familiar dread no one ever wants to acknowledge or take ownership of, all entirely too human, with a bit of showmanship, too:

Where, o where do they
Think they can go-o-o-ooo?
Not here! Not here!
Hasn't been a word yet for the "All Clear."
Can't pass till the Big Boss says so-o-o-ooo.
But if we're being honest,
We have a feelin' that
This isn't the place
For the likes of yo-o-ooou.
We carry knives!
And we're pretty keen
On the sight of blood.
So who's it gonna be then:
Us, or yo-o-o-ooouuu?

As they sang it seemed like they were moving in closer... no, *definitely* moving closer...something sinister swirled in the wind around them...harder to breathe...probably a good time to panic...Bambi and Joseph though, at this time, were unfamiliar with the idea of hypnosis.

One by one, all those dancing, swaying, singing little fuckers broke away from the hand-holding bullshit and pulled out blades that were nearly longer than their forearms. True to their word, they carried knives. How many times did they practice this routine? Was it for every foolish traveler who had the misfortune of taking this godforsaken road, or, like everything else in this world, just for them?

Silence flushed in without warning. Deafening. Each knife-wielding gnome stopped moving, stood not more than five feet from Bambi and Joseph. Their horses were still as statues. The gnomes rolled up their left sleeves. The one directly in front of Bambi, eyes locked with hers, let a single tear fall free and roll down his left cheek, which made her wonder, naturally, if all of them did the same, followed suit, and cried. They placed the tips of their blades on their left wrists, began gouging through their flesh, horizontally, finishing that red line then bringing the knives down vertically, completing the capital *T*. Truth: they had never seen blood look so sickly before. It sprayed free like flesh and veins were prisons, black like oil, almost impossible to find a glimmer of red in this bright twilight. They collapsed to the dirt, unraveled from consciousness, not at the same time, but one by one again...

Bambi and Joseph were freed from the hypnosis like it was knocked out of them, and they got a rush of air back into their weak lungs. Joseph puked. Bambi, possibly still transfixed, looked around, then at the body in front of her, the one she could testify had some emotion, sadness for sure, melancholy if anything, or perhaps there was something else there—remorse?—such small bodies. Something left each body, at the same time, from a *physical place inside them*, where if the body and mind could meet, a ghostly aura hung around, above them, caught in between the idea of haunting or transcending to the cosmos.

There Are Ghosts Here

Three dodgy-looking men crept up the road toward them, practically crawling along—one in a poorly made wheelchair, missing both legs—old bones, skeletal, dragging along sorry sacks of wrinkled skin that looked as ancient as worn leather, as if they were attracted to the scent of blood and death that hung heavy in the air. They wore old—very old—super-annuated, navy blue military uniforms, practically falling apart from decades of wear. Veterans? Their beards were long and smoky white, stained yellow near their lips from tobacco juice. When they were close enough, Bambi and Joseph could finally see the age of the men upon their faces, deep within their eyes: all three of them centenarians, eyes themselves

sunken into their skulls, worn, and when one of them spoke—
the tallest, whose spine has not fully begun to hunch—slow
and with a voice rusted over, like old Father Time had broken
his hourglass in the man's throat, lodged it with sand and
shards of primeval memories: "What...year is...this?"

To say confusion was slapped upon the faces of Bambi and
Joseph would be an understatement. For Bambi, a vague
perplexity leaked from her mind and onto her face, and for
Joseph, he was caught in an upheaval of consternation and
bewildering ambiguity, with that sour taste of vomit still fresh
on his tongue. They looked at one another, then back to the
old soldiers. Their horses had nothing to offer.

"It's 1942," Bambi told them.

"My god..." the tall one quietly cried. "How...does time...fly
so...so..."

"Did...we win?" the second asked. He was clearly blind:
milky white eyes stared at nothing, skeletal hands wrapped
around a wooden walking stick, head bobbing to the left and
the right just like the horses that he likely didn't realize were
in front of him.

"Win what?" Joseph asked, his voice cracking but too
anxious to acknowledge the embarrassment.

"The war, of course," the blind one explained, his voice
rusty as well but holding onto a sliver of childlike joy.

"We just," Bambi started, "entered the war."

"No...no..." muttered the third one, the one in the
wheelchair, toothless and sorrowful. "No...no..."

Bambi couldn't help but wonder if the men were
brothers—triplets, perhaps, rare as it might be. She wondered
if they were from around here, wherever *here* was. She
wondered why these were the few thoughts she wondered at
all. She tried to distract herself from the scene around her: the
dead bodies, the blood, the awful stench of it all, all the gnarled
and twisted trees scattered about—not really of one family,
that held sickly branches, their roots flooded with rainwater,

yet the road they walked was dry, their own personal storms then, and, upon closer look, if they dared to examine something that decrepitated so closely, unsure which of these scarce trees were still alive and how long those that were dead were dead, knowing though that those trees looked as they both felt: not wanting to be here, needing to escape...

Then the sight of a sad, disgusting, embarrassing act caught her eye...she tried not to look, and saw Joseph staring: the blind one had pissed his pants. A huge, wet stain formed around his crotch and slithered down his leg onto the dirt, flowing like a small yellow river right into the hoof of Bambi's horse, who did not notice. They had never seen a grown man piss his pants before, and they had seen almost everything— they thought—imaginable in such a short amount of time. But this awkward act shook them. It was such a vulnerable thing...watching a human revert back to its infant instincts like he was aging in reverse. What was even stranger was how neither he nor anyone else acknowledged it. True, the stench of piss would be masked by the reeking horror of death around them. But couldn't he feel his now-soaking pants sticking to his weak legs? Or is that what it's like being that old: losing feeling in certain places day by day until you're a walking silhouette of lifeless cells that have lost all sense with the world, ready to take the final big sleep?

There was nothing left to do but push past them. They rode slowly away, in silence, leaving the trio alone with all that death and human waste and not knowing if they fought on the winning side of history. There was a change in the air the farther away they rose, with each step and every inhale and exhale noticeably better, easier.

They were unsure how much time had passed (half an hour? Three hours? Three days? A week? A month?)—as it always seemed to be night on this road—when they happened to cross another stranger, as if that was the purpose of this place—to meet fucking strangers. It was another old man, yet not nearly as old as the trio before. He had snow-white hair and was dressed in a crumbled, slightly torn suit of fine craftsmanship. He staggered, head down, only noticing Bambi and Joseph when he finally raised his head to drink from his small, silver flask. He seemed neither surprised nor pleased to see them—more off-put, leery.

"What do you want?" he asked apprehensively, a heavy, worn accent weighing his voice, pressing the flask close to his chest.

"We're just passing by," Bambi reassured him.

"By where?"

A heavy, awkward silence lingered all around them.

"Where'd you come from?" Bambi asked.

"Someplace far away."

"You know where you're going?"

"Washington." He reached into the breast pocket of his jacket and pulled out a note. "Walla Walla. A note...for my friend's family."

"What's the family's name?" Bambi asked, voice on the brink of shattering into a shaky spasm.

"N—"

"We just came from there," Joseph cut in. "It's a pretty far walk."

"That way?" The man pointed behind them, towards where they had come from.

"Yes."

The man staggered past them, mumbling something in an eerily familiar language—on they were unable to speak themselves, their minds, with so much to deal with, unable to place it...he was talking to a small mouse that poked its small head and large ears out of the same jacket pocket from which he had produced the note.

"What's your name?" Bambi asked unconsciously.

"Kasper," he said, not stopping or turning around. "I'm a friendly—"

27

When you combine the histories of souls whose lives have not directly touched yours with an unnatural amount of unearthly spirits, then the realm of truth becomes more blurred than the self-abuser's vision.

— One Who Lives in the Clouds,
Pend d'Oreille Dialog

The No Meaning Saloon in Missoula, Montana was full. All fifteen seats at the bar were occupied and the three small tables each held a trio. It was always just busy enough for those working to not be bored and to make some honest money, and comfortable and lively enough for those losing themselves to their drink (many of whom, that night, indulged in beer, whiskey, some wine [one table split between the three of them—three depressed, rebellious, anarchist alcoholics with expensive taste who happened to be talking about just how it's in the fucking constitution that these so-called "patriots" loved to misquote and have probably never even read that it's our fucking right to overthrow the government, and with the way the world is right now we the people should do something, can't let the bigots win, revolt and change, make history, instead of sitting around and talking about it, which is what they were doing—four bottles of '37 Poletti Cellars Merlot {the first legal vintage Poletti sold after Prohibition had ended}, which caused Bambi to do a double-take and wonder how far their own name would've spread if they followed steps like the Polettis. The wine caused them to get louder and more of an annoyance for the other patrons as the night progressed, their faces becoming more flushed with every sip, their lips stained with the fine wine that sloshed around in their bellies and made them feel, for the first time in a great number of years, happy, with a rush of ecstasy that they never knew existed], and one gin drinker who sat at the end of the bar by himself staring sadly, with young eyes, into his clear poison, as he chased his wild and anxiety-ridden thoughts, like a dog after a squirrel, wondering if this next drink would do the trick and ease him into that eternal slumber or if he ought to steal his father's shotgun finally be done with it), and falling further away from their consciousnesses—allowed the drug to flood them, to flow through their thinning bloodstreams, to warm them as the dark had brought upon a haunting cold that chilled their bones, a cold that found its way to everyone's soul, slowly draining them, like a well running dry and, quite literally, freezing them. It was something no one ever got used to, and the only way to stave it off was to drink up and forget about it—to have a good time.

They rode for another hour after running into all that strangeness on the road before finding this glimmer of civilization, if one could call it that. Bambi sat in the middle of the bar with perfect posture, looking taller than everyone else, more held together than the rest, all hunched over whispering sweet nothings into their drinks or whispering among one another about the foreign-looking couple. Though she looked the proper part, her mind was still wrapped around what had happened on the road: the old man with the note heading towards their home, and how if Joseph had not cut him off he most surely would have said "Nyström," which made her think of Cade and wondered if thoughts of happiness with the likes of him—or anyone really—could be really on the table anymore or if it was a waste of time dreaming on about it. She circled back to wonder about the old man and the note, what it may have contained, where he could have come from, if he made it there...too much now. She looked at her brother and saw how even he was hunched over his drink, either ignoring or oblivious to the unfriendly glares that were shot their way every now and then, which she had really begun to notice and took to heart. Joseph gripped his glass tightly like he feared it would grow fragile little legs and attempt to flee if he took his hand away from it for even a second. He never drank this much and had only had a beer one other time in his life (his eighteenth birthday last year, a Nyström Stout), but this stuff was making him feel good, better than he felt before it hit his lips. Sure, the room was spinning a little more than usual and he had to piss like a racehorse every ten minutes, but none of that mattered to him. He finally felt good.

A tall, slender man silently took a seat next to Bambi. The seat wasn't there before; it was as if they brought an extra chair out of storage just for him. He wore a blank expression along with a long, black leather trench coat and an ox-blood three-piece suit. The bartender came along and placed a drink in front of him before he asked for it: a mojito, perfectly muddled, in a nine-inch tall Collins glass...with sweaty palms, the bartender then pulled out a stack of American currency— if it was his tips for the night there'd have to be some sort of investigation done on whether this lad was, in fact, stealing from his customers or if he was simply the greatest goddamn bartender alive—and nervously placed it next to the man's mojito before quickly peeking down the bar to see if anyone was watching—seemed all normal to the left, but to the right...Bambi's eyes were casually locked on the man's hands— and how quickly the bartender scooted away like he was never there and started making drinks that didn't need making at that time. The man's left hand went around the cold glass and his right hand rested over the cash, covered it—she was more interested in *his hands* in general...how soft they looked, yet weathered by labor and time; how perfectly manicured his fingernails were; how the tattoo sat atop his right hand: a black rose with a long stem, bearing thirteen thorns from top to bottom. It had just started to bloom. She wondered where he had got it done—would he even tell her if she asked? Was it even worth it? Cause then you're *stuck* in a conversation with some strange man for God knows how long, Bambi. Always have to weigh those options.

He finally acknowledged her presence, maybe had waited until this exact moment, giving her enough time to play out a few scenarios in her head. "What's your name, girl?" He was still looking straight ahead, eyes glued to the wall of the bar that bore nothing of importance, just old oak panels. His accent was some sort of nasally American posh, and when she looked up she finally noticed his silver-white hair and pencil-thin—yet somehow curled—mustache, which made him, in her mind, look like some rich creature whose morals didn't aline with those of regular humans and who probably hunted poor people for sport.

She caught his eyes as he glanced at her, his head and body still at attention to the wall—eyes as white as they could possibly be like there was no color to them at all, just two black dots in separate, twin seas of unusual white with tiny rivers of red flowing through them here and there—and immediately turned away...felt like she was choking on air for a second, hard to breathe...like she was back in no-man's-land..."Laura," suddenly spilled out, for some reason. Not Bambi.

"Nice to meet you, Laura. I'm Robin. Robin Montréal. Some people call me Ralph, others call me Gideon."

"...what? Why? What's wrong with Robin?"

"Ralph comes from the English origin for 'wolf

counselor.'"

"And you...counsel wolves."

"Some people may refer to them as wolves but I like to think of them as pups: my loving little pups."

"And Gideon?"

Robin ("Ralph"/"Gideon") Montréal suppressed a smile. "Have you ever heard of a place called The Garden, Laura?"

"No."

"Ever been to Fargo, Laura?"

"No. I don't know where that is."

"It's in North Dakota, Laura. That's where The Garden is, just outside Fargo."

"And that's, what, where you're from?"

"In a way, I suppose I do like to think that my soul has always been connected to that place. But, to answer your question, yes, I do reside there. I take care of it."

"'Take care of it?'"

"Yes, as, say, a mayor would."

"Ah."

"People come from all over to visit."

"Really?"

"Oh yes."

"Why's that? What do you have to offer just outside Fargo, North Dakota?"

Another suppressed smile, again gone unnoticed. "How old are you, Laura? Clearly old enough to drink. But, tell me, are you north of eighteen?"

Creepy, Bambi thought. "Yes..."

"Shame. But still, you do look young enough."

Jesusfuckingchrist. "What?"

"I could take you there, Laura, to The Garden. You'd be one of the older girls, but it would be nice for you, they would look to you for guidance."

What the fuck are you talking about? "What the fuck are you talking about?"

"Most of the clientele who come to visit us prefer them no older than fifteen. Now that's *most*, but not *all*. There's still a market for you, for now...as long as you keep this form."

Please stop talking. "Please stop talking."

"If you ever change your mind—" he fished into his jacket pocket, "—my card." He placed it down next to her. "But remember: the clock is ticking for you."

There was a shift in the air; she looked to where he sat and found the chair, thankfully, empty. The card was ox-blood in color, firm. In gold ink, a drawing of Eve: she stood naked under a tree, alone save for a snake that crawled up her leg, tongue out, so close to licking cunt. On the flip-side, also in gold, the initials *R.M.*, which could stand for Robin or Ralph, she wasn't sure which, and below that, at the bottom, in smaller gold print:

(GIVE THIS TO YOUR BARTENDER. WAIT 7 MINS.)

The grandfather clock—which stood against the wall, facing the bar, past the three tables, sort of watching over the place, but never enforcing anything, just observing the human way of being—struck 10:38. The bartender looked over his patron's heads, saw the old face. He looked down at his wristwatch to confirm and then rang a silver bell with a small hammer. Four lonely men, all dressed in dirty ragged clothes, with stringy beards and eyes and cheeks that claimed they'd not had a proper meal in a long while, for the only proper meal they preferred—aside from beans over a small fire out of the can, or whatever scraps of meat or cheese or bread the patrons at the bar threw their way at the end of the night, or, when desperate, whatever they found in trash cans after successfully fighting off the local raccoon or possum—was alcohol, how their livers hadn't shut down yet was a mystery and a goddamn miracle, all sat side by side towards the end of the bar, looking up from their drinks, taking, a deep breath, and beginning to sing deeply in unison:

> Solitude! Solitude!
> O! what we owe to Solitude!
> For she is always there,
> When none dare to come near!
> Solitude! Solitude!
> O! what we owe to Solitude!
> We cannot refute, nor dispute,
> The elementary facts:
> We owe our life to Solitude!

The four men, dubbed last summer by an awestricken audience member as The Loneliest Quartet in Missoula, fell back into silence, the echoes of their impossibly lovely voices, deep with melancholy, ringing heaven-like in all the patron's ears, leaving everyone to wonder, per usual, who held the last note, their eyes glued once again to their drinks. You never knew how long they would perform, what you got that night was what you got. There was not much known about The LQiM, bits and pieces glued together to create an American Mythology: there was a rumor that the one who went by Bagsy—the shortest and youngest of the group, by a least a decade—had faked his own death once upon a time a week before his wedding to his high school sweetheart, reason being—theorized and claimed to be heard straight from the lips of Bagsy himself, but if you were to ask him straight he'd never give you a yes or no answer, not even after buying him a drink, which someone always did—he faked his death to be regarded in a higher light in the eyes of his family and friends and, more importantly, in the eyes of his wife-to-be and her family as he—it was said—was a firm believer in the stresses and pressures that come with marriage and he understood and respected the fact that the financial burden would only bring out the worst in each other, resentment, and eventually divorce, something he never wanted to experience; loved her too much to hurt her like that, so in a way he was doing it for her, so she would always think on the good times they had together before the bad times had a chance to bloom and grow and destroy. Another member of The LQiM went by Gob, though it was unsure why—surprise surprise—he once convinced a young lad that his name was actually the proper way to spell "God," though there was a time where it was once thought by some that he went by "Sport," as he would always refer to other people as Sport ("Buy me a round, sport?" along with "Need my pipes wet, sport, spot me a drink?"), but Gob pulled a knife on a man when he said to Gob, "Here's that drink for you, Sport," and that was the end of that, calling Gob Sport, it was like he had obtained the rights to the word Sport and no one could use it against him. He was easily recognizable as the one with yellow eyes from years and years of heavy drinking. The third was referred to as The One Formerly Known As Jon Dirty who appeared to be the oldest— though it was never confirmed nor asked—and was the most talkative, though most of what he said was drunken gibberish, shit-talking, and conning his way into free drinks (as they all did), which he really enjoyed doing even though he was missing all but seven of his teeth, and also made it a fucking point to be referred to as The One Formerly Known As Jon Dirty and would not acknowledge any other name. Gotta respect the folks who stand firm with their identities. The last one was known as Zero because, outside of belting lyrics, he would only respond to natural human interactions by saying: "I am divided by zero," or "I allow myself," both statements which no one ever understood. Many attempted to decipher it as if it were of a greater importance, looking for hidden clues in those eight words, and would sit nearby watching old Zero mumble sweet nothings to himself and match him drink for drink as with each one more confidence grew faux-organically inside them and they conducted mental operations on that man's consciousness, for reasons never questioned as this was all there was, and it cured them of having to acknowledge their real lives, the lives that they've only grown to despise, as we all do when we grow to understand, in one way or another, that old Buddah was right in saying that all life is suffering, but we lack the patiences and will-power needed to find a way to learn to adapt on how we can better ourselves for accepting the suffering, so instead we bury it and lie to ourselves and claim that there is no way, that this is how it is now, so the only real cure we're brave enough to try is in other human distractions, in falsely placing higher purposes in ideals that are mundane and meaningless, in forever longing for that special child-like feeling of believing in something bigger than yourself, something really worth while, but looking for it in all the wrong places, like the confabulated lives of lonely drunks across the bar whom you don't know and never will. The bartender, a hard-looking man—the usual mask when not handing money over to some ox-blood-suit-wearing pedophile—with soot-black hair, a thick beard, and a grisly scar across his neck from some wild animal attack, named Patches Chauncey, placed four small shot glasses in front of each man and filled them with Old Forester. The bottle was special, from the Prohibition days; the liquid inside was that they distilled legally for medicinal purposes, and for The Loneliest Quartet in Missoula it was the strongest stuff they could get ahold of anywhere, for which they just had to work.

Bambi looked at her brother and thought about cutting him off—he didn't look well at all. A little green, even. She was so lost in her thoughts that she wasn't paying attention to him, had no idea how many pints he had downed. All she wanted was to find a warm room for them and finally get some sleep out of this never-ending cold. When she heard his voice suddenly it caused great fear to stab through her mind like a knife. She grabbed his left forearm.

"There's nothing to worry about, Bam," he said, seeing the

anxiety that crawled over her face like ants. He turned back to the man next to him. "Like I was trying to say, my sister and I, we were born here. Okay? Well, I was. We're Americans. I am. We all are. Our parents left the German Empire in 1919, after the War. We're not Nazi."

"Look, son—" the man said.

"Not to be rude," Joseph barked. "But I'm not your fucking son."

"Now, look. I am a reasonable man. And, aside from that comment that you just made, you seem like a nice enough young man, and I'm sure your sister is a fine person as well. But, come closer here, not everyone here is as reasonable or as understanding as I am, you understand? If you want to talk about your family to me, kid, go right ahead. But do yourself a favor and keep your voice down, okay? I'll have the bartender get you some water."

"What are you doing?" Bambi asked harshly, turning Joseph to face her, her hands grasping his shoulders.

"I'm talking to someone who will actually listen."

The tension in her fingertips slowly faded into a relaxed state of sadness and fell away to her lap, eyes swelling dumbly with tears, wondering: *what good will crying do now?* Joseph could not hold her gaze for long and looked down at the dirty floor before turning back to the stranger, whose company he preferred over that of his own blood.

They Were Never Really There

It went something like this:

It was a brisk spring night in Berlin, Deutsches Reich on 21 May 1909. The sun had just set, not a cloud in the sky, stars illuminated, twinkling on and off happily for the people below as their light had finally reached them, and they were already gone by now. There wasn't a cloud in the sky. A bottle of 1883

Château Lafite Rothschild stood on the small, circular table, half-empty, most of its perfect contents in their wine glasses, the rest flowing merrily through their bloodstream.

Tobias Wickham sat leisurely and at peace with his wife, Louise, who he stared at with great lust, and she returned the favor. Both of their eyes danced on the edge of intoxication, drunk not only from the rare wine but also from one another's beauty. The fiery passion that they felt between them was constant energy that never left since the day they met ten years ago and it continually grew stronger and fuller, richer, a gold rush. It was an ecstasy not many people ever felt, no matter how long they travel about this universe: pure love.

"Tell me again, Tobias," she said, her accent English, posh. "How did you acquire this bottle? It's fourteen years *younger* than I am."

He flashed her a cheeky smile and revealed his enormous, grotesque teeth beneath his great, bushy mustache. "Well, my dear, best not to date yourself. You may be older than this wine, sure, but is it not nearly as delicious as you." Her laughter warmed his young heart. "I, of course, spoke with the ghost of late Jakob Mayer Rothschild when we were in Paris. The old boy was able to get this bottle for us, no questions asked."

She laughed. "Oh, really now? Must be the fastest ghost to travel to Pauillac and back. We were only in Paris for one night."

"Yes, it is remarkable indeed. I do suppose that phantoms travel quicker than us living mortals, quicker than trains, too, perhaps even faster than time itself. He must be able to move through walls, too. Unless he revealed himself to the current winemaker, the magician himself, and as Jakob bought the property in his last days he must still own all that is made, whether he be able to have the luxury of enjoying it or not."

"Young, handsome, wealthy, and can communicate with souls that no longer inhabited flesh...how did I ever get so lucky? What a rare man you are."

"War hero, too." He tapped the medals on his chest. "Lest we forget."

"Oh, but of course."

A smartly-dressed family walked up to their table. Three of them: mother and father—who both stood four-foot-four, the father sporting a metal hook in place of his left hand, which he lost in '94 during the Dutch intervention in Lombok and Karangasem, which he told every stranger, whether they asked or not, and the mother—whose eyebrows were painted on, black as motor oil, and whose hair was black as her faux eyebrows and layered with short, tight curls on the border of natural and painfully forced—wearing a smile well on that same border of forced—and their daughter, who was only thirteen but stood towering over them at five-foot-five, with strawberry blonde hair, looking nothing like either of her parents.

"My God!" Tobias yelled joyously. "Willem Van Sneijder, my good sir, how are you? Please, please pull up some chairs; sit down for a minute, won't you? Willem, this is my wife, Louise."

"A pleasure. This is my family: my wife Alma, our daughter, Ruth. I spied you from over there, I hope you don't mind, I had to approach to say hello."

"Very pleased to meet you both, very pleased indeed. My friend. Please, sit, sit."

They finally did.

"Tell me, Tobias, how do you know our new friends here?"

"Ah, yes, my dear, of course. 'Twas during the summer, nine years ago now, at the Siege of the International Legations in Peking, where we were fighting those damned Boxers."

"*You* were fighting," Willem corrected politely, his English still choppy with a heavy Dutch accent. "Still a boy then, what were you, twenty?" Tobias nodded. "My how time flies...I was only commanding then." He held up his hook and explained to

Louise how he lost it '94 during the Dutch intervention in Lombok and Karangasem. "Infection had set in, they had to take the hand. No other way."

"Yes...tragic...you know, dear. Dear? You know, without this man's tactical mind, the fighting in Peking may have gone on a bit longer."

"Perhaps," he laughed, loving the attention.

"May I ask what you lovely people are doing in Berlin tonight?" Louise asked.

"Well," Alma began, "we—"

"Lord above!" Tobias interrupted. "Is that Jakob Müller there?"

"What? Dear, I thought you said that Jakob fella was a ghost..."

"Jakob *Rothschild*. This fine man —" he clasped Jakob Müller's arm in an embrace, "—is another friend I fought alongside. Good to see you again, sir."

"And you," Jakob said warmly, struggling, like most, with his English, this one with heavy German, but happy to try it out nonetheless. "What are the odds?"

"Nonexistent until this moment."

Jakob Müller stood proudly with his family, another family of three, the tallest amongst them at six-foot-three, with a clean baby face and sandy blonde hair, his wife, Oda, a striking beauty, only a few inches shorter than Jakob and a member of the illustrious Großherzogtum Baden Ballet with high and realistic hopes of one day soon making the world-renown Deutsches Reich Ballet. Their son, Karl, stood like the awkward and lanky lad he was, with that first growth of peach fuzz that finally sprouted from his chin—more than his father had—and stared at Ruth Van Sneijder with butterflies whirling in his gut.

"What a fine soldier, this man was," Tobias Wickham continued. "No finer soldier, I'll tell you what."

"No, no," Jakob pleaded, humbly. "Please. I'm not proud of

that time of my life, truth be told."

"For true?" Tobias gasped.

"All that killing...and for what? We shouldn't have been there in the first place."

"By God, man! You sound like a bloody Boxer! If they could even speak the King's, that is. Willem, do you hear this man?"

Willem shrugged awkwardly. "Eh?"

"By the way, have you two met?"

"N-no?"

"Willem Van Sneijder, Jakob Müller. Jakob Müller, Willem Van Sneijder."

They shook hands.

"A pleasure."

"Likewise."

They introduced their families. Karl and Ruth finally met. Real awkward at first but, hey, call it love at first sight—

"—and what? Guess fucking what? Here we fucking are because Tobias fucking Wickham was more interested in the past than his own current life, his own wife even. It had to be that night that all his pasts somehow lined up in Berlin and families that had no right crossing paths did just that because this guy was such a fucking gentleman he had to go and fucking introduce our fucking grandparents to each other so then our parents met and fucked a few times and had us. God-fucking-damn—"

Joseph was so animated at this point in telling the story that he had begun to unintentionally lean back in his chair. Patrons who might have been watching him from nearby (surely there were a few, he was not only loudly cursing but talking with his hands, pointing a lot and clapping to emphasize certain words) would be able to tell how drunk he was and comment on it by whispering to their friends, "Boy, that kid sure is fucked up," which if said at the precise moment would coincide perfectly with Joseph leaning too far back in his chair: he tried to fight gravity, hands groping in front of him but only grasping air before he crashed to the ground. Everyone looked on but no one went to help him, and he laid there with a drunken grin on his face, passed out. Bambi didn't even notice right away—blame it on the alcohol, it had finally hit—and had been so engrossed in the story Joseph was (poorly) telling before he went off the rails. *Fuck it then*, she thought, *I can take it from here*:

That's pretty much how they met, same date and location, at least. Tobias Wickham's name may have actually been Terry and Louise may have actually been Lois, but that is not of any real importance. Really, though, he sort of focused too much on Tobias and not enough on what everyone was doing there. Right?

Willem and Alma and Ruth Van Sneijder had moved to Berlin *permanently* for a job that Willem had all but no choice to take as he was able to speak German as well as a little English. He was—shit you not—a royal spy sent there by Queen Wilhelmina herself. His mission was to monitor a high-ranking military official who may or may not have helped design—or at the very least knew someone involved in designing weapons of mass destruction that were devilishly Tesla-like. The high-ranking military official was, of course, Jakob Müller, who was given a heads-up about a possible confrontation with espionage and was always on his toes because of this. Soon enough the two families would find each other living oddly close to one another. Jakob watched Willem; Willem watched Jakob. A mundane game of cat and mouse. Oda and Alma both dying of boredom. Karl grew courageous enough, finally, to secretly find ways to see Ruth and they became something like a Dutch and Germanic *Romeo and Juliet*, never telling their parents, of course, until years later when, by some divine miracle, the two families had grown quite fond of one another. Jakob and Willem bonded over their respect for the other's work ethic, Oda and Alma shared similar dreams of living in places far away as people who were strangers even to them now...so when Karl proposed, no one was all that surprised. But when they eloped that very same week people did find it a bit odd, a bit rushed.

"If you thought about it even half deeply, you'd understand," Bambi hiccupped. "They announced that Ruth was pregnant with yours truly two weeks after their wedding, leaving out the bit that she was actually a month or two along already and they probably used the excuse that she was just showing early, that the bun that was cooking must've been a big one. Passed it onto yours truly. A scapegoat before I was born."

"Eh," the stranger said. "That true?"

"Calling me a liar?"

"C'mon now, girl."

"Huh?"

"Settle down."

"'Settle down?'"

"For crying out loud..."

"Who are you telling to settle down? You pig fuck—"

"Reckon," the bartender, Patches Chauncey, said, "your brother has laid there long enough."

Bambi looked to the floor and saw him there, and immediately felt embarrassed, not really for him, but for herself. Her cheeks flushed hot and crimson red. For some reason, her eyes filled with tears. Fucking alcohol. She felt drunk and alone.

"Reckon," Patches said again, "time you two head out."

"You say something now," Bambi said. "But not when that Gideon fuck was harassing me."

Was it just her or did it...no, it definitely got quieter in there.

"Please," Patches pleaded in a whisper, unable to meet her eyes. He appeared to be shaking a bit and had somehow accumulated, rather instantly, an intense sweat on his brow. "Just go."

A full minute passed before she got up, and most if not all of the misogynistic fucks in there thought she was stone-cold dumbfounded, for some reason, by being told to go...when in reality she was trying to regain her composure. If she was center stage, as she felt, she had to face the crowd of strangers while inebriated and collect her even more inebriated brother. All she had to do was stand, push her chair in, help Joseph up, maybe a few smacks on the cheek, pick *his* chair up and push it in—manners—then walk out. Simple. Easy.

Well then, she thought. *Showtime.*

28

The wind howled madly, tundra-like, thundering in their ears, blowing through them like a phantom forcing its way through and rattling their bones like thin sticks loosely wrapped in a bundle desperately trying to hold itself together, kicking up the fresh snow and swirling it around, ruffling their hair, falling wild and free back down to earth, melting upon their faces—not like when they were younger, back when they didn't mind the cold, when they would stick their tongues out and let the unique flakes subtly quench the thirsts they didn't know they had. Echoes of voices escaped as the door to the Saloon closed and rang out to the void, then quickly died. A fresh snowfall had started suddenly, more violently. It was so dark, only the great white blanket that seemed to stretch out forever into that vast infinite blackness was visible and the cold dark of the night seemed to be consuming that, too, in an alarming and unnatural way. Bambi's cheeks burned angrily from the harsh gusts, her eyes watered, ears on the verge of numbness, lips chapped and bleeding. And there was Joseph: throwing up in the snow and feeling melancholy for memories that did not belong to him. The sounds he made suddenly reminded her of Shirley Nivek, her old best friend, who, the very last time she saw her, was making the same grotesque noises: puking her guts out onto a dirty floor, her dark, chestnut-brown hair getting caught in her mouth, a belt tied tightly around her skinny right arm just above the elbow, her veins below the belt bleeding with her pulse, collapsing before Bambi's eyes, a syringe and dirty spoon idle between them, the drug melting on the spoon and floor, cut with petrol and who knows what else, the dark all around them, covering every inch of the universe. She could barely make out Shirley's corpse at that point, reached her hand out and it fell upon the window ledge; she stared out the window on the second story of the run-down barn—she remembered it leaned slightly to the left as if the earth had been tilted in that very spot, its old red paint chipping away to reveal its nakedness underneath, the bare, dead wood, the rusted nails that looked to eagerly snag at your flesh and have a drink of your iron—the dark drank up all the light and left them alone in its void, and Bambi finally noticed that Shirley had stopped breathing, still couldn't see her, but was able to hear her until she no longer did. She blindly found the matchbox that housed those wooden soldiers Shirley used to heat up the underbelly of the spoon and lit one, barely illuminating the world but enough to find her with a thick stream of vomit that spilled out of her agape mouth and onto her blouse, and Bambi stood there, sixteen years old, not knowing what to do, realizing how cold it was, and wishing—oddly, and later feeling bad about—that she had brought a jacket. How strange to forget to take into consideration the cold summer nights in Walla Walla that she had known all her life, thinking about all this while she stared at her best friend, whose form was becoming more and more visible—even after the match had gone out, her eyes adjusted to the dark, like the dark wanted her to see it—and more and more real, still dead, fading and reappearing before her eyes, as if her soul was happy there for the time being or waiting for her to join so she wouldn't have to go into the unknown alone, all because they wanted to get high and heard nice things about the wonderful feeling you get from opium, which they heard from someone who heard from someone who knew someone that did it regularly. They had procured the drug—secretly and for what they thought was a fair price, not that they knew anything about pricing—from Shirley's boyfriend's cousin's boyfriend, a man with a forgettable name, who lingered longer than he should've at the barn, who poked his head in a not-so-subtle and quite creepy kind of way, who spoke with an ominous and eerie curiosity and looked at them for longer than anyone should look at a person, let alone girls that young, who wanted to shoot up with them because he, as he told them, was tired of shooting up alone, and maybe to see what they wore under those loose blouses of theirs...no—and now this scene was burned into the intangible files of her mind, locked away only to be reopened on occasions like this: in the darkest nights that carried harsh into their lungs, stung their nostrils, and reeked of vomit and hopelessness.

Laura stood her little brother up and brushed away some of the snow entrapped in his hair. Everything was numb. He was drunk, the kind where you can't really see straight anymore and have to really concentrate on what's in front of you, which for him was darkness and an erection as his drunken consciousness was thinking about Shirley Nivek, oddly enough, and how she died during a dark night like this, unaware that he and his sister shared thoughts of the same soul who was no longer there, and how he longed to fuck her before she left this world, an urge that he had forgotten about until just now when his blood was rushing towards his penis instead of working to keep him warm, an urge he didn't know he wanted back then—a bit too young—but older and drunker remembered her not only dead but in a different, sexualized light. Everything was numb and the drunken, devilish voice in his mind lied and told him it was the first day of the rest of his life and his heart was beating as fast as his mind was racing.

It could have been a euphoric moment, pure, genuine, orgasmic ecstasy, but he was not aware and could not feel like you and I feel—but if you had to throw a word to describe what someone in his position was feeling, if he *could* feel it, would be far from that giddy sort of jubilation but more on the side of a dreamlike realm where manic melancholy—that was as close as he would ever get to a natural psychedelic high but the kind where you feel trapped in the trip and you just noticed your skin melting off of your bones and there isn't a damn thing you can do about except just stand there hope it will all sort itself out, all end soon—ruled so naturally, which is what poor Joseph did: just stand in the cold and wait, not sure what for, for God knows how long, completely oblivious to everything around him. The last light from the Saloon faded into the black behind them along with a voice that was slightly drowned out by drunk roars, seeming to get further and further away from them, a strong feminine voice belting lines that could still reach them but just barely, that belonged to some stranger in there—a local legend known as Olivia Christmas, known for her solo performances of old plays which usually took place about an hour after The LQiM sung their one and only song. That night she was in the midst of *King Lear* and *shouted* every single line—which is how Bambi and Joseph were still able to make out some lines—and gave each character a different voice to make it more authentic for the audience of rowdy and horny drunks. Olivia would strip throughout her performance and add some never-before-seen sexual act (last month when she performed Sophocles' *Oedipus Rex* she grabbed an empty wine bottle off a nearby table and fucked herself with it [it was unknown if she did this because she believed that her sexual nature added to the story, if she was just as horny as her audience if not more, or if it was the only way to get them to pay attention to her art]), that night using, for the first time, an audience member as a sort of prop—she took off his pants and started to jerk off his micro-penis, pouring hot wax from a candle onto his thighs, him so drunk he could barely get hard and it burned so much but felt so good that he was laughing, screaming, and crying all at once—during Act V, Scene III. She wailed Lear's lines like a banshee: "Howl, howl, howl, howl! O! you are men of stones: Had I your tongues and eyes, I'd use them so that heaven's vaults should crack!"

Which they did. The geometrical patterns of the universe that silently congregated above them were made of massive grey clouds that took away the last of the natural light, the stars and the moon, which weren't doing them much good to begin with, and if they could see through all that dark they would see those patterns as the faces that they would recognize vaguely from some half-remembered dreams that were all convoluted and torn apart and sloppily glued back together inside their consciousness, all consisted of the universal language that was, unbeknownst to them, embedded in their DNA and the DNA of all things living, which made the formulae—

$$V = \left(2 + \frac{4\sqrt{2}}{3}\right) a^3 \approx 3.88562...a^3$$

$$A = 2(5 + \sqrt{3})a^2 \approx 13.4641...a^2$$

—that, to even be considered possible, was more based upon volume and surface area and those faces up there were more concerned with faces of plane surfaces but there they were *real* faces from their past and present and possible futures that were actually mouthed incoming premonitions, before they cracked and shattered completely, down to them which of course they did not see...but suddenly felt the terrifying, blind rush of an ungodly amount of dead birds that began to litter the the earth around them in the dark; how, if they could see, they fell from the sky and crashed into the earth with a sickening crunch even in all that soft snow, the impact so great it still made an audibly haunting noise that caused Bambi to blindly grab Joseph's hand and run, in what direction she did not know, until they huddled together at the base of a great protective pine tree, and wondered if all these birds died mid-flight or had collectively decided to become nature's kamikazes at that exact moment like they all held on to something holy when it came to that hour of the day (midnight? why the fuck were these things even airborne?) when the sun was still on the rise on the other side of the planet and reflected brightly against the face of the moon who was sadly still hidden from view, like the moon knew what was coming and wanted no part in it so it summoned the clouds to hide its already shy crescent face, and, far away from Bambi and Joseph, one bird actually struck a member of Oliva Christmas's audience—who would be identified later as one Washington Mo-Peers—who had stepped outside to have a smoke and breath of fresh air, as the air inside was thick with sweat and smoke and the stench of semen and shame, and penetrated straight through his skull, beak-first, and laid in a soupy pool of brains and blood and was dead before he hit the snow and before he understood that he was alone out there and that it would be a few hours before anyone would find him, right outside the door.

They sat huddled together under that great tree while Bambi yelled into the dark for help until her throat was raw and voice was all but gone. Joseph was so drunk that he was close to passing out. He mumbled through stoned tears, things like: "I want to go. I want to go," along with, "Life never loved me at ease," as his mind swam through the deep, choppy waters of his heavily-poisoned consciousness, where it painted a mental image of actually treading through a dark, vast, and seemingly endless ocean, which was the only thing in nature that he was willing to admit scared him shitless, and he continued to think about it, this mental ocean, and it made him depressed and then thought that "depressed," as you would call it, was not the preferred nomenclature he wished to go by, if he had to go by anything at all, and realized that he didn't feel any sort of feeling that could be antiquated with the nostalgic sense of fear and could actually bring himself to think about any unnamed body of water for longer than five seconds (his maximum before this) and felt that he could sit there all damn night just thinking about any great and terribly powerful beast of nature until his eyes fell out of his head and finally learned all the secrets it, the water, held and understood for the first time in his life why people, normal ones, admired this scene so much (water, beaches, swimming) and how he wanted to be more a part of it, wanted to breathe it in deep and let it fill his lungs until he and the water were one and the same because he remembered reading one time, somewhere, back when things were normal, that drowning was the most euphoric way to die, damn near orgasmic if it was done via suicide, or maybe he just made that up which he was likely to do and not realize it—but that was Joseph Müller for you: Walla Walla's own maniac insomniac who would stay awake and cry and get to know all the ungodly hours of the day when no living thing should be awake—of which many weren't aware existed—and when blessed enough to find a few hours of sleep would dream strictly of different ways to die and would not understand why his mind would torture him this way and would be forced to lie to his family if they ever asked about the dreams he had at night and would instead confess the *day*dreams he had...and in this daydream, under the pine tree, he felt, for the first time in what seemed like a lifetime, the strangest sensation of what you would call "happiness" for having found solace in the water, even if there was no tangible body of water around, and he pictured himself white-knuckling a rail at the end of some pier and he was suddenly airborne over it—and even though it was all a dream it seemed so real that he could not begin to see the defiance in the definition of gravity, and how close he would be to fully-granted psychotic immunity along with the longing to finally feel free, and how he could not begin to see the pre-divulged internal mystery of what was hidden deep in his premeditated mental psychosis—and headed towards a cold plunge into that darkness that was a lot like the darkness they were currently trapped in, and down there he hoped to find a deeper darkness to follow and if he could choose what his final thoughts would be he might consider the idea that he might actually give it a try whenever this was all over, whatever this was, and by the time he mentally hit the water, he would find a new, silent go-to saying that he would only whisper to himself, that would ring true internally: it was ethically immoral to be alive.

And as fast as it all started the kamikaze birds suddenly stopped falling and all that was left was the dark and blood-stained snow and a litter of bird corpses...Bambi still screamed for help, but there was no one around to return the call, and they got so turned around in that Stygian void looking for shelter during that biblical mass animal suicide that there was no way to navigate back to the warmth of the Saloon—all her eyes could see was black and all she could hear, aside from her voice, was the harsh whipping of the wind that forced her to shut her eyes—until they both passed out from drunken exhaustion, cold and alone in the dark.

29

All of a sudden it was warm and Bambi was awake. She was on her back, blankets to her chin, and laid next to the purest fire she'd ever seen, made with love. It burned her throat when she tried to call out for her brother. A woman approached, knelt beside her—*shhh shhh*—held a cup to her lips, and encouraged her to drink. It was hot and slightly bitter, but soothing. Something magical.

"My brother," she finally managed to say. "Where is my brother?"

The woman said something in a language she did not understand, could not even begin to guess the origin of. *Perhaps*, she thought, *I am dreaming.* The woman motioned to a spot across the fire. Through the flames, Bambi was able to make out the slender frame of her brother. He was sitting upright and looked to be half-conscious, lips blistered, face red and wind-burnt. Bambi watched him for eons like time lost its purpose—if it had any to begin with—like watching a river flow, always moving and always staying the same, separated by a spiritual dance of flames. He was unmoving, at peace. The only indicator of something happening, of time, was the logs turning to ash—a few more eons and lifetimes had come to pass when she turned her attention back to the fire itself, watched the smoke rise and exit through a small gap at the top of the tent and out into the still night sky. A flap nearby opened and a rush of frozen wind hit her, causing her to realize how warm it was inside and how appreciative of it she was.

The man who entered had a powerful aura about him, felt as well as seen. She never really experienced anything like it when it came to casting unintentional, unconscious judgment upon a stranger. He first looked at Joseph, then asked the men who were taking care of him something in that language that fascinated her, one she could not place. Each word flew from his lips like a feather, soft and low, but held a weight comparable to the boulder that Sisyphus was surely happy to push up the side of a mountain for all of eternity. His words were to be respected.

Attention was then turned to Bambi; he knelt to her eye level. She could see in his eyes that he began searching for words she would understand.

"Will you...eat?" He motioned hand to mouth as if consuming food, his English rusty as if he had not practiced it in a while but still better than she expected.

"Yes."

He reached into his pouch, pulling out and unwrapping a small chunk of red meat, still bloody, filled with rich nutrients, iron, and protein.

"Slowly," he advised her.

"Thank you," she said with honest sincerity as she nibbled on the lifesaving meal. She paused occasionally to force it down, her mind pleading with her body to throw it up, to get rid of this dead thing it was so unused to. There was something else, too. A natural occurrence that told her she must accept this, being as though all evidence pointed that these people saved her and Joseph, that they wanted to keep them alive, that it would be an insult to not accept this meal or, even worse, throw up in front of them. All credit to mother and father, she reckoned, who raised me right and polite.

The man sat down and began packing tobacco—the sweet smell instantly found its way over to Bambi and reminded her of her father packing his own pipe with similar-smelling tobacco, or maybe all tobacco smelled so lovely—and another herb she did not recognize into an incredible pipe; it was long and thin, carved and hollowed out from—she would learn—a buffalo's rib, indeed pale as bone with a few faint stripes of red along the length of it, blood most likely, but to them, she was sure, a work of art.

"They call me...Quiet Owl," he said to Bambi, still focused on the pipe. "What is it we may call you?"

"Bambi, I mean L-Laura...Laura Müller. That's my brother, Joseph, there."

"Hmmm..." he contemplated, and finished packing the pipe. "Which one?"

"What?"

"Bambi or Laura?"

"Doesn't matter. Either one is fine."

"M-m..."

"Müller."

"Müller..." He looked at her. "It is very fortunate that we found you...many can die quickly when the wind bites as it is now."

"We're very grateful. I'm not even sure how we got lost, we were looking for our horses, following their tracks, we must've not tied them up tight enough...next thing I know I couldn't see a foot in front of me...and we were so stupid to be at that saloon, drinking as much as we did."

"It is a dangerous and vile place. We rarely travel so near anymore...your voice carried so far. It would have been a shame upon us to ignore a call for help."

The pipe was lit. Quiet Owl inhaled the smoke deeply, filling his lungs, and, upon exhaling he felt, though Bambi could not tell, both lighter than a feather and heavy as a boulder, like his voice, a warm, blissful calm wash over him like radiating lights encompassing his consciousness, as though now he was living as all should be: outside this form of mortal flesh, formless, floating above himself, bound by an invisible cosmic string, what you might call the soul, only to be broken once death finally enters the picture, or when the high ends. It was natural. A warm smile that matched the light that flowed through his blood melted across his face. He offered the pipe to Bambi. This was traditional with guests: to show them, the honored guest, that what they are being offered was not only safe but also a spiritual experience. Bambi, of course, wasn't aware that if she were to deny this peace pipe that it would be a direct insult and they would be asked to leave, to brave the cold and the dark on their own, alone. Yet, that was never a thought that danced across her mind, and she accepted it with grace, inhaled as deep as Quiet Owl did, held the smoke in her lungs as long as he did, and, upon the exhale, coughed and coughed and coughed to the point she thought she might throw up. Thankfully it passed. Eyes filled with tears, she regained her composure and felt that same euphoria that he was happily drowning in.

High as an eagle, she held the pipe in her hands as though it was an ancient relic—which, to be fair, it was—unsure what to do with it. She looked to Quiet Owl who smiled and pointed to a woman who sat next to her. Had she been there this entire time? How was it possible to experience the loss of other presences right beside you so quickly? It was deeper than numbness. Better, too. A state of consciousness you never knew possible to reach until now. The pipe levitated from her palms and floated over to the woman's. And how Quiet Owl stared at this woman, eyes filled with a certain kind of lust that would only occur between two lovers born from the same star, those who are halves of a whole soul. A look that reminded you of how your parents once shared a similar longing. How his eyes admired every aspect of her comely face, the way her cheeks moved when she inhaled then collapsed into twin craters of flawless dimples, and how her eyes met his, and she saw them for the first time: warm oceans of amber that reflected the silent flames, quickly hidden by the smoke she exhaled for no longer than a second only to reappear again. What beautiful constellations did he find there? What wondrous galaxies was she fond of getting lost in? And how long must Bambi travel to find and understand a love like this? Was it possible, after all that had happened, to ever feel that way? Would it be worth it? Or would it just be another hopeless experiment bound on a course that would only end and fill her with more pain, different from the pain she was filled with now, but fucking pain nonetheless? My, my, my, my, my! Didn't realize thoughts like these were possible during *times like this*. Sure, they've occurred in the bar, maybe on the road—but after almost freezing to death? It caught her off guard. Oh! So *this* is what it's *like*: a strange mixture of instant euphoria followed by unrelenting paranoia. A perfect concoction. When can we properly abuse it?

30

The land, older than memory, was endless: covered completely white with snow, an arctic desert, untouched save for the harsh gusts of wind that blew to and fro and rattled the weak bough of the bare trees—naked, only frozen daggers clinging to the dead branches, not knowing why, clear as glass, gently knocking together with the breeze like a glacial wind chime—that stood tall, not quite touching the pale blue sky, which was vast and empty of any life this time of year, the sun shining brightly down on them but providing no warmth...the trees were all scattered around the ancient field with an unusual amount of space in between them as if the trees themselves were consciously, constantly, slowly moving away from each other, inch by inch, day by day, like they wanted, in the end, to be alone...never asked to grow here.

Fresh tracks in the snow—five distinct paw prints, spread out, together—wolves. There were four of them hunting the creatures who had been stalking their tribe's territory for weeks now: killed a horse last night, an older one, left them with no other choice but to hunt and eradicate the beasts before they did any more harm. The snow had fallen heavily throughout the night and covered most of the tracks. They were close to giving up when the tracks appeared before them, out of nowhere—a gift from the great invisible who worked behind the scenes, off-stage—it was Speaks to the Rain who noticed them. They quickened their horses to a trot. They were close.

Quiet Owl called them to a halt, all eyes on the pack huddled under a tree that had no earthly business being amongst the others—it was not Douglas fir, nor ponderosa pine, not Western larch or Engelmann spruce, just a great dead tree, black as night like it had been set on fire, twisted and gnarled branches sagging almost to the ground as if to conceal the wolves.

They dismounted and drew their bows, moved with grace through the snow, Quiet Owl leading the small party until they were thirty yards out. Nothing stirred, not even the wind. The wolves were asleep. The earth around them was dark, not from the shadows of the sickening tree but from the dirt that clung to their fur, and the blood that stained the snow like wine on a carpet—where did that come from? There: a small pile of something unnatural, concealed heavily by shadows, away from the pack...torn up, dead, still fresh, wet, not yet rank, at least that's what the air told them when it decided to move again. It blew right into their faces and carried their own scents away from those sleeping predators. All grey, save for one whose fur was black as midnight, like the tree, the leader, with four white socks, eyes shut in peace but everyone there knowing that what lay under was a horrible sea of yellow with pupils dark as its fur. A beast long talked about in legend, a great warrior their tribe respected and feared, now real and before them, as they had whispered; how it would come to this one day. Now it must be cast from their minds. The sight of the great beast made a couple of hearts drop in agony.

Quiet Owl shook his head, longing to see a different enemy before them. No one had ever killed a wolf, few had ever even dreamed of it. It was not something they did. It was a known thing, in their blood. Though, there is always a chance to alter our DNA slightly, to rewrite history, if only for a brief moment. But to ask him of this now...this rare one that, yes, has caused so much chaos in such a short while, but one he's known all his life...

The youngest of the group, Laughing Coyote, looked at the holy man and said in their language, "They killed our horse. Who knows what they will take next? They are only wolves."

Speaks to the Rain placed a firm hand on him, motioned him to lower his voice. The creatures up ahead remained still as stone. An eerie, cold wind blew through their hair. All were dressed for the elements in their buffalo skins.

The fourth one, the only woman in the company, Walks With Fire, one of the bravest warriors in the tribe, spoke in a low voice that had certain teeth to it: "You are a young fool, Laughing Coyote. One day I hope you will be learned." She slowly moved forward, kept her body close to the snow, leading. It was only a few yards before she stopped suddenly, saw one of them lift their heads.

The sound of Laughing Coyote shifting to one knee for leverage was an avalanche to them, yet surprisingly nonexistent to the wolves. Like they were frozen from the cold or awaiting their sentencing, aware of their crimes. The leader, the midnight wolf, looked at them, at first as a group and then individually, eye to eye, four times. Those horrible seas of yellow they heard so much about were not toxic at all, rather soft and filled with deep, tragic mourning to which two of them could relate and felt like they'd seen before. The wolf turned and looked at the mangled, shadowy pile, then back at the hunters, and began to walk away. Alone.

The hunters looked at one another, hearts in their throats, and moved in closer. Quiet Owl fired first, a silent arrow ending one life. Four more quickly followed into the sleeping beasts, Walks With Fire claiming two, not entirely proud of it. The leader never looked back, and they let him go.

They skinned the wolves, they wasted nothing. The sun broke through the grey clouds then, casting a blinding blanket of light over reflective snow that drove away the shadows from under the dark tree, warming their backs like it was spring...someone's voiceless wish for that great star to stay like this forever had finally come true, at least for the moment. No one spoke. Laughing Coyote brought the horses over and they began to store the pelts and meat and bones. Quiet Owl walked over to the dark pile that they all had forgotten about— or, more accurately, did not want to notice—a thing so mournful that not even the light from that magical ball of fire in the sky wanted to touch it. He bent down low to it and had to cover his mouth and nose with his gloved hand. He had never encountered such a vile, sinister foulness in death before. How did the wind not warn them of this? It was acrid, erosive to the atmosphere around it. It burned his eyes. The idea of it. Such gruesome, unholy brutality burned into his memory forever. Such small hands, torn up, bloody, nigh to the bones...such small coats—tatonka leather, from a neighboring tribe—shredded to strips, unfit for anyone now.

He rose to his feet, fighting off vertigo that tried to flood his brain, and then rejoined his companions. Walks With Fire went to him as he was mounting his horse.

"What was it?"

He looked at his wife, the light of his life. "We must go now. Leave the game."

The skins, the bones, the meat, was dropped. It was all tainted. Wasted.

A haunting chill blew through them, took the light of the sun with it—the clouds that moved swiftly in were dark as the nightmares that lay dead behind them and stretched beyond sight, leaving no trace of any golden eternity to come—and with that, the knowledge that the next light they would see would be the light from the moon, which they knew would be full and would guide them safely home, for there were no more enemies who hunted by that cold, reflective light near them now. They moved on, away from that place of horrors which no words from their language or any language could make sense of. Perched high above them in a tree they rode past was a large, old raven; it cawed at them, over and over and over again. The ominous calls echoed through the great open space, cutting through the cold air like a jagged arrow through bone. It flew away and landed on the sickening tree they longed to forget about. It stayed there and looked down at the awful carnage that sat, bloody and freezing, its black eyes studying the deaths carefully before understanding and taking the situation for what it was: nature being as it were. It made no more sound for the hunters to hear.

They returned to their tribe to no warm reception, no one waiting for them to ensure their safety, only the solitary dance of the ceremonial flames that with each mad gust fought off the surrounding darkness wildly, with bereft brevity. The could smell smoke rising from the tents, different, unique scents from home to home blending together, invisible against the backdrop of the night sky's blackness, revealed when the clouds moved on and the grand audience of all the stars in the great plains of the heavens looked down, and the smoke tried to reach them, wanting to console the moon.

From out of the blackness of the night, moments before all were ready to gather their tired bodies off to their respective homes and fall peacefully asleep, the wind carried to the tribe the sound of soft, pain-filled cries, a voice that recognized that it was truly lost, not only physically, but in mind and spirit. Without words, without questioning what actions to take amongst one another, Quiet Owl, Walks With Fire, and Speaks to the Rain, led by one torch, made their way towards the voice. It was the way of the tribe to offer help to those in need, even with the knowledge that many of the people that surrounded their depleting land would never do the same for them. It mattered not; they would show what the true nature of a human being ought to be, the best of us, simple acts of kindness, walking bravely into that unknown darkness towards those who give humanity an ill-mannered name, all of us who are living on stolen land, their home. The winds were picking up, blistering snow whipping around them, the voice becoming fainter—but it was still there, in all that darkness, so they pressed on. They were familiar with the land even in these conditions, the stars still visible above all that swirling snow. The clouds would part for them and the moon would smile its light down to guide them; they weren't far from the white man's watering hole. To their trained ears, they heard more voices: fainter singing, laughing, almost inaudible glasses clinking together, a drunkard throwing up the poison. A mile or two away from the No Meaning Saloon— a forbidden place full of toxic energy, unblessed tobacco, addicts, ghosts unaware of what they've become or when— they crossed paths with a young girl and boy who had no business being there, or being as intoxicated as they were. Never noticed the suicided birds. The girl was still calling for help, though her voice was hoarse, barely audible. Help had arrived just in time. Quiet Owl's heart broke for them...to see these, in his eyes, children, he knew this was not a place for them to die...enough children died alone in the cold for one day. They covered their freezing bodies with spare furs, placed them atop a horse, and led them back to warmth and safety.

A blood-red sun rose the next morning and filled the sky with a milky, dreamlike image: mesmerizing shades of ruby, indigo, and scarlet, all aflame with those hidden stars, hypnotic, and those looking up at that floating river had the sudden, silent, yet connected, realization that every inch of the sky above was the veins of the universe, the Earth the body we were assigned to, and all of us down here the tiny cells swimming through the bloodstream of life.

31

The sun went from blood-red and dreamy to blinding white, all-powerful—or so it wished to be—in a cloudless sky as if to say, "Don't dare look at me, or if ye do, ye Mighty, do despair." It was the first peaceful sleep Bambi had had since...well, you know. She looked about the tent; at the low burning coals, the ghostly wisp of smoke that floated up and away, still providing a needed warmth; at all the resting bodies: the slow movements of their breathing, Quiet Owl and Walks With Fire intertwined together under thick furs, as one body, and Joseph, still asleep, feet still wrapped. And miraculously, it had just occurred to her, no sickening headache! No deathly hangover. No withdrawals. Her brain was, somehow, not sticking to her skull, not dehydrated and weak. Was it...? No, no couldn't be...a plant *that* powerful? It was the only thing that would make sense. She figured she would test her hypothesis when Joseph woke up, as he was the only one in the tent that did not smoke. What an experience he missed out on.

The wind from outside slapped against the tent, like it wanted to break in and nestle up by the dying fire, maybe give it some air, bring it back to life, and, who knows, share in some of the smoke if they still had some. Bambi wrapped some furs around her shoulders, clenched them tightly with her hands, and stepped outside. Everything was alive. Always has been, always will be...until...the wind burned her cheeks almost instantly, yet she wanted to stay out there, told herself she would find comfort basking in the light of the sun. She did. And how foreign that feeling was to her: comfort. She watched members of the community exit their homes and immediately begin to toil at what needed doing to keep alive: water to be fetched from the creek nearby, hunters gearing up to bring in more food, what food they already had being prepared for the day's meals, and the children—so young and full of life and love and laughter—ran around with sticks, pretended to be grown soldiers, shooting each other down or sword fighting, and for a split second she was dumbfounded: how—or, better yet, *why*—do children so young know how to practice violence? Is it something we're born with, embedded in our DNA, in the very fibers of our being, coursing through our cursed bloodstream? One child stared at her, warm, dark eyes trying to make sense of this person who did not look like them, smiled, missing a few baby teeth, and waved. Bambi returned the kind gesture. This place, vibing back to reality, must be something holy, a place untouched by outside evils, and perhaps, on their side here, only understand violence as a way to *survive*, to not only bring in food when out for a hunt but to protect themselves from those who want what they have, to steal their peace of mind, their very way of life...

When Joseph woke up, it turned out that he did, in fact, have a hangover—and a crippling one at that, the poor boy could hardly keep water down. *Is there anything we can do?* Bambi asked Quiet Owl as they watched him lay in agony. She did not want to hear or see or smell her brother vomit anymore, and she knew they couldn't stay much longer, perfect as it was. Quiet Owl suggested a technique where they would get Joseph to do labors around the camp, get a workout in, build up a sweat then *drink* his own sweat, swish it around, and spit it all out. *Works every time,* he assured her. Alas, woe is he, it would never work, as she explained to the kind man that her brother was stubborn as they came and in no way would he do any physical activities in this shape. If he was clear of mind, sure, out of kindness and respect, no problem, was raised right and all, but like this? Not a chance. To which Quiet Owl told her that he understood, which he likely did not, and left them alone for around twenty minutes. When he returned he had with him a small pouch and began to brew tea, steeping what looked like tiny pellets of dirt from the pouch.

"Have him drink this," Quiet Owl told Bambi when the tea was ready.

"All of it?"

"Yes. It will take effect instantly."

"What is it?"

"Rabbit shit," he said, and left again.

Bambi smelled it, nose hovering over the steaming cup. She found that it smelled quite nice, like lilacs and juniper and warm earth on a perfect mid-summer day. She was tempted to have a taste...but then remembered Quiet Owl said "rabbit shit" and decided that Joseph could use that right away, come to think of it. She didn't force him to drink it but nursed him, holding his head and bringing the beverage to his chapped lips like he was some big baby. *It's just a fucking hangover,* was the only thought that ran through her mind, and it was all she could do to keep from slapping him across the face and telling him to grow up and get the fuck over it.

To the Buffalo Who Roamed Free
To the Wolves Who Never Said Die

On top of the hill in front of the sun stood the lone wolf,

midnight-black with white socks, a picture that was clear and richly detailed like it was captured and placed before you by Joseph Wright of Derby. In fact, from that distance, the wolf looked like a sort of animal version of the alchemist who was depicted in an ever-lasting image as the discoverer of phosphorus in J.W. of Derby's *The Alchymist, in Search of the Philosopher's Stone*, as the wolf bore an oddly similar look of pious, tormented wonderment. Bambi stared at him and felt an uneasy numbness in her bones. There was something ancient happening, she knew. She had found herself in the middle of some kind of ritual, the village around her coming to life, all eyes on the wolf.

Next to her, Walks With Fire stood rigid and still with Quiet Owl. Their stone expressions were unreadable, eyes squinted hard against the slow rise of the sun. Though their facial expressions were masked, their body language told a different story: worn down, deflated in a way, clearly something they did not want to deal with, something personal...

"What should we do?" Walks With Fire asked in their native tongue.

"I trust your judgment," Quiet Owl said after a sigh. "I'm lost now."

"You know this wolf," Bambi said.

Walks With Fire looked her way, the first unfriendly look Bambi had received there, then walked away, leaving a burning trail of melancholy in her wake. Quiet Owl stayed, let out another heavy sigh that was thick with sorrow, and waited for Bambi to ask the question he knew she would eventually ask:

"What is he to you?"

He never looked at her.

"He is our son."

"He's wha—"

"He is around the age of your brother. Some time ago he

was cursed by a high elder, One Who Lives in the Clouds, for abusing alcohol, another comparison to your brother...but worse, he was abusing that poison and killing buffalo for the sake of killing...letting the animal go to waste. He was cursed for the rest of his days to spend half the year among the wild as a wolf...every time he comes back he is less of himself. I am afraid we will lose him to that life."

"You mean he'll stay as a wolf?"

"If only it were so simple." Quiet Owl finally looked at her, tears staining his face. "No. They want us to kill him now...he has become too chaotic, leading violent packs. He has shamed us...but we cannot stop loving him."

"I'm sorry."

"People are always sorry for the wrong reasons."

She didn't know what to say. She tried to distract herself, momentarily, but finding a color that would be fitting for the wind that blew through them. Couldn't be done.

"We are not so different," Quiet Owl noted.

"How's that?"

"Aside from...the obvious: they don't want us here—"

"'They?'" she asked, then with quick realization: "Oh."

"—the ones who caused you the pain, it radiates off of you...what They would give, now, to see you, your brother, my people...gone...eradicated...the same people who preach the idea of fearing their creator. Have ever heard of such an idea? Fearing that which is love and perfection, what made you?"

"Does sound a bit odd, now that you mention it."

"We will always welcome your people with open arms if they'll have us...but I fear we will never understand one another fully...you're the first people I have found a common ground with."

"The fact that we're not wanted here."

"Yes."

"Even though we live here, have lived here for years."

"Yes...don't take this the wrong way, but to us, you are all intruders."

"We didn't know..."

"Your people were looking for a better opportunity...that's what they all say...but you were young, yes, so who can blame you? But...even if your people had known of our situation here would that have stopped you?"

Remorse quietly filled her. He noticed:

"Forgive me...it's impolite to attack you like this...it's overwhelming sometimes..."

"It's not easy being alive."

"That is the other thing that makes us so...so...alike?"

"Similar?"

"Hmmm." Quiet Owl nodded in agreement. "Yes. The pain we both share is not...entirely the same, but they are branches of the same tree. Understand."

"I do."

"You cannot kill the pain, the tree...you can only hope to nurture it, yourself, into a better state than what it is."

A hangover-free Joseph moseyed his way over to them and stood taciturnly next to his sister, looking now and then from the snow-covered ground to the ridge were the wolf-son still stood—looking to Bambi like a little kid again, near tears, as if he had just been yelled at by mom and dad for throwing rocks in the direction of the house, as kids do, and accidentally breaking a window, a real thing that happened when she was nine and he a dumb five-year-old. He did not comment on it or even feel any particular way. The wolf was just there. Big whoop.

"I must go speak with One Who Lives in the Clouds," Quiet Owl said.

"What about?" Bambi asked.

Quiet Owl looked over at Joseph. Their eyes met for a second, maybe half of that, before Joseph cast his gaze again towards the ground.

"About...my son. He has a few moons left till he is allowed

to return to us," Quiet Owl said, then he left them.

Bambi looked again at his wolf-son. Joseph continued to stare at the ground: "I'm leaving," he mumbled.

"We don't have to go yet."

"You're going on, but I have to go back."

"What?" Bambi finally looked at her brother, who somehow looked tragically smaller than he had last night. "What are you talking about? You expect me to just find this guy by myself?"

"I'm holding you back."

"We're in this together."

"Look. I had a dream, alright? One worth remembering. One I don't have to lie about."

She didn't entirely follow, didn't realize that he made up *every* dream he'd ever talked about—if that's what he was saying, which it was. If she were to think of it later she would be able to connect the dots: all those sleepless and tearful nights, when would he have the time to dream of such pleasant things?

"It felt real, you know? Like I thought it was real life? I was talking to who he's going to see, Clouds-whatever, he was telling me something that I had to do, that I'm not supposed to go with you."

"And you think, what, because of a dream you can just bail?"

"No. I—"

A beautiful woman with soft, bronze skin and long, dark hair approached them, her eyes like the morning of a perfect autumn day. She went by the name Flower Gatherer. She touched Joseph's arm and smiled at him, leading him silently to the hut of One Who Lives in the Clouds. They didn't realize it was their chance to say goodbye before they went their separate ways, not that it likely would have turned out any differently.

Flower Gatherer had him wait outside while she walked

in, then walked out in less than five seconds. She walked away and never looked back...never to see him or him to see her again...and if he was capable of comprehending such emotions during that time he might have felt a real bitter tragedy in the spot of his heart solely reserved for those mysterious beauties with whom you never speak and are better left to the imagination, where you two can be happy and in love and never learn of each other's faults and live in between the fear of facing the anxiety to open up completely and the chance of not being accepted for who you are on the inside, all those imperfections that you hope someone will love one day but fear it's a fleeting dream because you are so used to being alone...instead, for now, it's best to fall in love from afar...with the eyes you locked with from the other side of the bar, or with that figure that walked right past you on a busy sidewalk, or, in this case, the hand that led you to the Chief of the tribe...all pieces of a person you can put together mentally but never have physically, a person who you're not sure you'd be good for anyway...better off alone, kid.

He was actually all packed up—was the first thing he did when he woke up—and ready to *walk* away, had one of those feelings that sit fat and heavy in the depths of your guts, one you can't ignore, that half-convinced him that a long walk in the fresh country air would make him forget that he drank rabbit shit because dear old sis just *had* to tell him about that. But they did end up sparing another horse for him, another obviously reserved for Bambi. A few—Laughing Coyote especially—were vocally reluctant to the idea of giving that— as he said— "soul-poisoned drunk" one of their horses as he was likely to—again, his words— "fuck her or cut her open for warmth before he figured out to feed her." To which Quiet Owl was close to erring on the side of supporting, which surprised himself until he spoke with his Chief on the matter, and One Who Lives in the Clouds said to him, after they passed the pipe back and forth a few times, "I don't think he has the strength to will her into some sort of perverted intercourse..."

"What?"

"Give him the horse," One Who Lives in the Clouds went on. "He needs it and she is not being used. Our minds should be pressed by more important issues."

"But the life of the horse, her safety, is important. Precious. Right?"

"All things in life are. Yes."

"Then we should protect her."

"Ah, but if we do that then we are revoking her right to experience life, the world, all the beauty it has to offer."

"You trust this boy to guide her well?"

"He is troubled, you can feel that in his energy...but I didn't get the sense of outward violence, did you?"

"No. These foolish young ones...they cause my thoughts to betray themselves."

"And here I thought I was finally getting old. Ignore them. Always trust yourself. And I know you feel the same as I do."

"What about the horse?"

"Her life is no longer in our hands. She will be okay, I have a sense. But whether or not she returns to us is unknown to me. There is a lot of world for her to see after he leaves her."

"Should we tell Laura what we see in him?"

"She already knows but now is not the time to bring it into the light. It will only distract her. And what lies ahead needs all of her in the moment."

"I'll let Laughing Coyote know to ready the horse."

"He may not listen."

"He'll learn."

"Now, care to discuss a more personal matter?"

"The moons will pass quickly and he will be back home."

"But those moons will pass quickly as well, will they not?"

"He is my son...what would you have me do?"

"This is not a question I can answer for you."

"You know what they say about us, what they whisper

behind our backs."

"I do."

"I fear a few of them may soon take matters into their own hands."

"I have grown to recognize this as fear as well."

"Walks With Fire and I must take time to think on this matter deeply."

"Yes. Think well, my friend. Come back when you are ready."

"I will. Thank you."

"The Moon may not wait."

"I understand."

"Send the boy in on your way out."

"Of course."

"Quiet Owl."

"Hm?"

"Pass the pipe."

32

Joseph, plagued with déjà vu for the first time in his life, was pulled inside by Quiet Owl to have a private conversation with One Who Lives in the Clouds. He noted how both men smelled the same, sweetly dank, and how this One Who Lives in the Clouds fellow, who sat across from him, a small fire between then, possessed a powerful, comforting aura and could sense that he knew about his dream as if he had conjured it for him. And yet, Joseph still found it childishly funny—it looked like the old man was falling asleep before him: eyes barely open but a friendly smile never fading from his face, reminding him of a time when he was younger and his father would stay up late to tell him stories. He would always beg Karl for one more and the old man was unable to say no back then, told a little fib that the reason his eyes were getting heavier was not because he was tired of reading these stories to his one and only son but because der sandmann was sneaking about and throwing that magical sand into his eyes that would whisk him away to an eventual sleep, and that really freaked Joseph out, especially when his father told him that the same sand was going into his eyes and he couldn't feel it because it was "magic," but not to fear because anytime der sandmann visits he also gifts you with pleasant and peaceful dreams, and if he really thought about it, as he did, he would identify that precise moment as the first and only time that his father ever lied to him as he grew up with horrific insomnia and terrifying nightmares that at times made it difficult to distinguish dream from reality, and not a single fucking visit from der sandmann.

One Who Lives in the Clouds spoke soft and low, each word carefully chosen and delivered with care and sympathy. "You will find your way back...there is a new path that has been brought to us, to deliver to you...if you wish to have it?"

"'A new path?'"

"You will still make it back...but this new path will take you somewhere else first...to another soul responsible for the grief you carry...though, of course, it won't cure the pain that you were born with."

Joseph fought off a wave of tears. "What—" his voice cracked, "are you talking about?"

"You understand..."

"How could you know *any* of this?"

"I speak regularly to the Great Eagle in the Sky, the one who knows all."

"And what? Tells you where I can find someone responsible for...for..."

"Yes."

"And do what, exactly?"

"What you do is your decision, it is between you and the one above us...I am only here to deliver the information...if you wish to have it."

He told him to take the route of the Coeur d'Alene, six-hundred miles, if not more, to Bend, Oregon, Mirror Pond, where, in false belief of undeserved peace, lived one (former) Major George Wynne of the 422nd Military Police Brigade, commander of Pvt. Jenson Reynolds, the murderer of Karl and Ruth Müller.

On the trail, he first passed through Idaho—thought instantly how satisfied to be given a horse, and how foolishly he was for thinking he could walk it, and then of dissatisfaction at the look that Laughing Coyote gave him while he suited up the ride and how reluctant he was to do so; was all but forced, possibly threatened, and it made Joseph feel like Laughing Coyote didn't trust him and felt a strange sort of cosmic mental vibration between the two of them that made him feel like the guy would accuse him of sodomizing this poor horse—and normally this sort of place was strictly forbidden by any outside member of any tribe and punishable by nothing less than death, a fact he was warned about but ensured not to worry as Quiet Owl had sent two riders ahead to speak to the Coeur d'Alene people and grant him safe passage, something along the lines of each tribe is allowed one "guest pass" every year or something, Joseph didn't really follow. But there he was: trotting along on old Beula (the name he'd given the horse) pretending like he hadn't already let his mind roam free and wonder if those riders Quiet Owl had sworn by delivered the message, or if they held some resentment against Joseph for taking their horse and didn't just go for a ride with no intention of ever letting him pass, or if they were, in fact, good guys but the Coeur d'Alenes had all of a sudden turned bloodthirsty and had killed those poor souls and were now waiting for the cover of darkness to make their attack...wouldn't hurt to pick up the pace a little bit there, Beula.

He had not realized how close the trail had taken him back to Walla Walla, and that was for the best. There were no signs welcoming him into the states whenever he crossed those invisible lines. He had a sense that he had crossed into Washington at some point, or wished, but he had come to a point in his journey where everything started to look the same, a copy of a copy, like it was under the same filter, similar in theory to wearing jade-colored glasses. Picture Charles-

François Daubigny at his darkest, or Théodore Rousseau if it's easier, but instead of all those unnamed French fields they grew up with they would have their canvas set up against the background of some random location in the Pacific Northwest where they found some beauty there, among all that grey pessimism, that needed to be captured. It all seemed to be the same painting, just slight, minimal variations here and there, all more or less like a staged backdrop, and if he were to reach out he would feel the brushstrokes themselves and be forced to wonder who else was watching him.

He eventually rode long enough and felt a change in the air, in gravity itself like it was trying to weigh him down and prevent him from going any further, and knew he was getting close. He remembered seeing the water before something scared Beula bad enough for her to buck widely and throw him completely off of her, toss him in the air, and gallop away, back the way they came...back home.

It felt like he was in the air for a long time, and thought maybe this was his chance to really escape and to fly away. He managed to attempt one midair swim stroke before he came crashing back down to earth, where he landed hard and knocked himself unconscious, rolling downhill onto the cold, wet shore of Mirror Pond. A few hours later—could have been days, in all honesty, he had no way to tell (the sun, or some bright star, maybe its reflection, hung behind the clouds all the time...that's winter for you, the season he wasn't born into but related heavily to, they were one and the same: grey, unable to shine, not well-liked by the masses, in their minds that is)— Joseph awoke on the shores of that body of water he saw briefly before unconsciousness. The water lapped his cheek like a playful smack. His face rested on the frigid, stony shore, eyes stuck together with frost; he forced them open, adjusted to the light that was hardly there. Joseph lifted himself to his feet, icicles breaking free from his body, and looked at the winter wonderland around him: a hidden reservoir surrounded by green, still soldiers of pine, larch, and fir patched here and there with unbearably white snow acting as their armor, and in the distance behind them the tall, steel-blue stone Cascades that they guarded for all of time...this little paradise created some eons ago...Eden, once upon a time, for all he knew. The water of the lake was not yet frozen, or was maybe thawing out, and reflected the sky like a mirror. He knew he had made it then—was close, at least.

There was no use in calling out for Beula, he thought. He took it personally, felt like she didn't want to be here to see it through with him. It forced him to recognize his aloneness and blamed that on her, too. He stumbled forward with nothing to focus on but the burning numbness on the outside stabbing every inch of him like knives, as well as the cold opening pit of despair, of acceptance that sank deeper and deeper and burned his soul. An intense, cold burn. With each heavy step, his mind raced further with the anxious possibility that his hunt was, at long last, coming to an end...he recognized that he referred to it, even mentally, as a "hunt." It made him stop, but he pushed himself forward, knowing himself well enough that if he spent any amount of time now dwelling on that thought then he would have come all this way for nothing.

No more than seven minutes of walking until he saw signs of human creation. Spaced out were a few small log cabins, seven in total, like a little community of Henry David Thoreau fanatics who viewed *Walden* as scripture and a way of life rather than a simple memoir. He continued to press on with full intentions of knocking on every door when, as he got closer, he noticed that grapevines grew near every house, all dormant, younger than the ones he grew up with. It sent a chill through his bones; he was experiencing different levels of cold throughout each layer of his body—another first for him, not like he was keeping count.

A man wearing nothing but boots stood, in front of a house chopping wood into kindling with a large ax. He was in his forties, tall, thin, hair as black as oil and a thick beard that went down to his chest. His eyes, Joseph noted—after the man felt his presence three minutes later and finally stopped chopping—were different colors: the left eye a warm amber-brown, the right a permanently-dilated icy blue.

"Yes?" the naked man said, steam rising from his sweaty body like a ghost.

"I'm looking for someone."

"Who might that be?"

"George Wynne."

"Nobody of that name here."

"That so?"

"Far as I'm aware, lad."

"Any former military men?"

"You're looking for the Major...?"

"Think so. You know his real name?"

"He never told us. He's been here for about a month now. Real swell man. Really knowledgeable with the vines here which will bode well for this coming season. His philosophies on wine are really something. That's why we grow it here, you know, it's a holy drink. Perfect soil, too. You should stick around, he's giving a lecture on Pinot Noir tonight."

"Which house is his? I just have to see him before then."

"Over yonder." The man pointed to a cabin a few hundred yards away, close to another part of the Pond's shoreline. "You know him well?"

"Sorta..."

"Eh?"

"He, um, is a fan of my family's Riesling?" He wasn't sure why it came out as a question, but somehow it went unnoticed.

"Your family makes Riesling?"

"Müller Estate," he said, choking back tears—it never got easier. "Out in Walla Walla."

"For true? I've heard of that juice, legendary stuff. You won't happen to have a bottle on you?"

Joseph wanted to clock him but remembered he had an ax, and instead turned out his empty, water-soaked pockets.

"Hell. Maybe one day...listen, you can go see the Major but try not to bother him, he doesn't like to be thrown off his routine and I'm not saying this necessarily *will* throw him off his routine, but just don't be offended if he doesn't want to chat too long. He takes these lecture nights seriously. Real educational."

"Thanks," Joseph said, and marched as fast as his body could manage which was not fast at all. He reached the door and knocked with a shaky fist that was hardly audible even to him. Somehow, almost too suddenly, as if he was expected, the door opened. In front of him was the Major: he sat in a wheelchair, eyes heavy with dark bags underneath, likely due to sleepless, paranoid nights, and his left leg was amputated at the knee. He wore a white nightgown made of thin material—one that would look better on someone more feminine instead of his wine-bloated body, the seams pushing to their near-final strain—and nothing else.

"Best come in," the Major said. "You look cold."

Joseph followed him inside and closed the door behind him. It was instantly warmer. They sat in his den next to a fire. He had four glasses on a small table, two into which he was pouring, from an unlabeled bottle, something red and light, then into the other two poured from a bottle with a white label, something French, of a similar red color. Joseph had no intention of being there longer than he was already, let alone drink with the man, but something pulled him in, call it a spell or some bullshit like that, to him it was the warmth of the fire...just wanted to get a little warm by the fire, before...

"Pinot Noir," the Major announced, his nose halfway submerged in one of his glasses, "is, by all means, the pinnacle of Vitis vinifera. There's a saying, so it goes, that all roads lead back to Burgundy." He took a sip of the first one, from the unlabeled bottle, and did a loud and obnoxious rendition of the inhale of air through the mouth, aerating the wine. "But, my latest discovery, thanks in part to my early retirement, was the discovery of the potential that the Willamette Valley here holds in the wine industry. It's a perfect climate from here to Eugene and up to Salme and Portland even. But here, well you saw it. How could you top this? Incredible, right?"

Joseph hadn't taken a sip.

The Major grabbed the other glass. "Now this —" he went on, swirling the fuck out it, "—is some of the best stuff on the planet. Please, do try, it's just wine. Domaine de la Romanée-Conti, 1929, no need to thank me, it's meant to be enjoyed, right? Now this is good stuff, right? Of course it is, who am I kidding. But let's go back to the first one. Mhhhmmm. Good stuff, right? Dare I sin and say, *just as good*? And for nearly eighty-percent less than the DRC. This stuff here is liquid gold, mark my words. This industry is going to boom."

A sinsister awakening was rising inside of young Joseph from the back of his brain.

"Are you following? Son?"

There it was again: that violent motivation...felt natural this time.

"You like wine, lad?"

He valiantly fought back tears.

"What's your name, boy?"

"Joseph," he said through clenched teeth. "Müller."

"Müller..." The Major searched his alcohol-flooded brain for the name. "Müller...Müller...not the family that makes such exceptional Rieslings out in Walla Walla?"

Joseph was, to be perfectly frank, fucking stunned. "We—they—I—"

"Pleasure to meet you, Joseph." The major had the audacity to extend his hand and expect a shake in return. "How are the folks?"

"You—what?—you...you're the Major...right? Major George Wynne?"

He noticeably swallowed. "No one here could have told you that."

"Have you really forgotten? Is this what happens if you drown yourself in this stuff day after day, you actually *do* forget?"

"Forget—"

"Walla Walla. February twentieth. I know you fucking remember." Joseph grabbed the man by the neck of his gown, had him balancing on one leg, tears running down his face. "You gave the order," he cried. "And your man, Jenson fucking Reynolds, *killed* my parents."

The Major turned ghostly white, haunted that the demons from his past found him like he truly believed he could go on living without it coming back to him, like he could bring himself to actually believe the lie...like he could actually forget.

"I d-didn't, I had no idea. I would never! He was unstable!"

"And still you allowed him to break into my family's home and accuse us of being enemies of the state. You allowed this to happen, yes?"

Tears filled the Major's eyes, maybe genuine with regret, maybe out of fear or remorse, maybe just mirroring Joseph's emotions. "Please! Forgive me! I had no idea. L-look at me, have I not suffered enough?"

Joseph released him and sat him back down in his wheelchair, wiped his eyes dry, and took a deep breath. Oxygen flowed to his brain. He looked at the Major's stump: wrapped in white gauze, spotted here and there with red spots of blood ringed by sickly yellow, likely suffering from the phantom limb syndrome where the victim has an intense mental belief that the missing limb is still there and that they can *feel* it, like the need to scratch the ankle that is no longer there—though that, of course, is all mental, like if they close their eyes they can still picture themselves with the limb, but when they go scratch that itch they swear they feel, made up, they'll find nothing but air. He bent to eye level with the Major and presented his hands like one does when prepared to say a prayer. George Wynne (fuck his title) was scared and reluctant, but piousness got the better of him and he submitted his hands to the young man. Joseph examined them closely—how oddly soft they were, how short and chewed his nails. With both hands, he took one, the left, and quickly snapped his wrist. Before George Wynne was done screaming, he snapped the other wrist.

It was like an out-of-body experience because he wasn't sure what or how it happened; all Joseph was aware of, suddenly, was George Wynne sitting in front of him with two freshly-broken wrists just *hanging* limp and lifeless, and he was screaming in pain like a creature that didn't sound human at all. The screams came out like radio silence, like electricity running through trees forcibly rubbed together. It was loud but not in a sharp way, more like blunt static. It was almost enough to make Joseph leave right then. He drowned out the world in front of him as best he could and pushed G. Wynne outside. His chair caught in the grass a bit, but settled close enough to the shore. Joseph forcefully spilled him from the chair and watched him crawl on the ground like a worm. He cried out as loud as he could, that painful static, when Joseph grabbed him by the back of his shirt and dragged him to the water. Everyone in the small village was out of their tiny cabins and silently watched as the most violent baptism took place before them—which, as practicers of transcendentalism and Unitarianism believed that everything was as it should be and all things that happened were supposed to happen and saw no sense in interfering, even if it was lecture night and he was as great as they believed he was—they believed that even if he didn't come up breathing, he was awaited on the other side. And they were privileged to witness.

This, truth be told, was a belief of faith at which Joseph, had he known, would have shamelessly laughed, all while drowning and damning George Wynne to hell, instead of silently fighting back tears, again, and pressing the piece-of-shit's face down in water so shallow he could see the mud and sand sink into the man's mouth.

Which is what he did, and is how the man died.

33

A strange, deformed shadow lingered over her every move, it seemed, ever since she crossed the border into Wyoming. The sun hung high and hot in the sky—yet still, the shadow, wherever it was cast from, covered her like a blanket that provided no warmth nor comfort. Time didn't seem to exist out here; the nearly unnoticeable rotation of the earth was the only indication of any real change. The landscape was barren and beautiful: golden-brown hills that rolled on for miles and looked like a family of giant sleeping bears. She imagined, during the proper season, how alive they must look, luscious with vibrant green and herds of beasts that grazed for miles upon miles of open freedoms. Farther in the distance, beyond the great grizzlies, stood great frozen peaks that climbed into the sky, the tops of which disappeared into the great white Kingdoms of Cumulus.

Buck had to stop. The poor old horse had been riding all day and night. Bambi, honestly, did not realize it. Time had completely lost meaning. She couldn't remember how long it had been since they left Walla Walla, or when she left the Tribe, no point in keeping track of dates anymore. But the more she thought about it...the weather was getting warmer, though snow still stuck around...was it possible that it was a few weeks into April? And if it was...*goddamnit*. Meaning: *Happy Birthday, little brother.* It's the thought that counts, right? A part of her felt bad for what she had said—or didn't say—but the other part, the side she tried to listen to the most, told her that it was for the best...he never should have come in the first place. It felt like they had both aged rapidly during the short journey, and yet she still felt like a babysitter around him. She hoped he would be alright to the point where she forced herself to create a mental picture of him back in Walla Walla with everyone else: silently speaking it into existence...all she had to do was make it back home.

"Howdy there," a voice called out from behind.

Bambi turned quickly. A young cowboy sat atop a great, pale white horse, an Appaloosa, that looked like the death that festered on her ever racing mind. She was sure hell was close by. The cowboy didn't look sinister—though any strange would come off as untrustworthy to a woman—with a comely face only a few years older than her, fresh five o'clock shadow that would never leave his jaw, and a voice that didn't match him at all, it was too rough, too dark and brooding for a face like his, young and innocent. His eyes squinted hard into the vast distance, but when connected with hers, were soft and welcoming; he wore black from head to toe, as if on the way to a funeral, or ready to send someone to theirs, the only things of color the red bandana around his neck and the great eagle feather that stuck out of his hat.

"Who are you?"

"Billy. Billy Utah. Who might you be, Miss?"

She hesitated. "Your horse is very quiet."

"Beg pardon?"

"Your horse didn't make a sound...hasn't. How'd you sneak up on me? Where did you come from?"

"Big Blue, here? Yeah, reckon he don't talk much. But I was just on the road, over yonder." He pointed over yonder, behind him. "Saw a stranger, you, reckoned I come over and see what's what."

"Is that your job? Seeing 'what's what' around here?"

"Might be it is, Miss."

"That so?"

"Yes, ma'am. You're lookin' at the fastest gunslinger in all of Wyoming. Not sure what the price is on my head nowadays, but nobody's shot me dead and collected yet, so I reckon it'll continue to go up. But the reason nobody's collecting that old bounty is 'cause I keep my head up and see what's what. Understand?"

"Not really..."

"No?"

"What year is this?"

Billy snorted. Spat.

"You never told me your name."

"Laura."

He waited for her last name, realized he wasn't getting one. Nodded. "Where you heading, Laura?"

"Ten Sleep."

His great beast of a horse stirred then, but he calmed it quickly. "Ten Sleep? Man, about a week ago, took the same path you're on to that town. Didn't want my help, said he didn't need it. First time anyone ever turned down Billy Utah's gun..."

Bambi was quite unsure of what to say but knew in the sad pit of her gut that this was the man she was looking for. Sure of that.

"This man...he didn't look all there," he tapped the side of his temple with his right index finger, "...unstable-like. Made Big Blue here uneasy. Can't trust a man that an animal don't trust."

"Well, that's where I'm heading. For better or for worse."

Billy nodded, admired the spirit she carried. "I can take you there."

His spurs dug into the horse, which started slowly in the direction that Bambi was already heading. A slow trot, hooves knocking along the dirt, kicking up dust that danced that invisible dance we all do with the wind when no one's looking while thunder in the distance rolled along through the great hills like it's always been there, had to be.

"Oh, I know how to get there—"

"I don't doubt that at all, Miss Laura. But you're gonna want the fastest gun in Wyoming by your side further in you go. This—" *spit*, "—is an unforgiving land."

Ultimately she saw no sense in arguing with the strange cowboy, so she followed, first at a distance, like the sun above, then, not really realizing it, side by side. Billy never acknowledged it either, like all he wanted to do was protect her, keep her safe from whatever lay beyond those gloomy hills, like it was his only purpose...and if it was, at least he found one—a purpose, a reason to stay alive, to endure through the suffering that is life.

SCARY MONSTERS LIKE TO HUNT AT NIGHT
OR: (WE REQUIRE BLOOD PART III)

It was silent. Wind blew from time to time but never made a sound—no trees to wrestle with, no leaves to kick up, just a silent breeze that was neither cool nor warm, just there. Billy pressed his lips together and began to whistle a beautiful and sad tune, one Bambi had never heard before; there was a strange familiarity, a sad calmness, she would never learn it herself, never even learn how to whistle, but the tune would linger in her consciousness, play on repeat in her soul, until her last days. She marveled at the amount of air in his lungs: how he could make a song that held no words, just sound, evoke so much emotion, and, when you really listened, the melancholy that hid behind every face, every phrase, every moment in the world, came to life in that tune he created, blue and filled with loss, tormented with a pain that she understood, not necessarily to the degree of the tune's creator, but in her own personal way of course. Perhaps, she figured, that was the purpose of it: to allow the listener, however many he came across in his lonely travels, to realize that they were not alone in carrying their pain, that maybe no one could really understand what they were going through, but that others, too, were suffering. Here she thought her world had ended—parents murdered, brother gone away, now off on a mission of revenge, forgetting who she was, and yet some strange cowboy who rode next to her, who whistled along, a song he's played more times than lives lived, could cause all those worries to melt away. It was like a drug. Muzak to him; music to her; art to both. It felt like it was going to last forever, she wasn't even aware of how long he'd been at it. And then, suddenly, it was silent again.

Billy was looking behind. Bambi went to turn her head. "Don't," he said quickly. Oddly enough, she listened. Even with curiosity gnawing at her brain, she turned her head back around and stared at the empty road ahead. "Don't look behind, Miss Laura. Hear me? You keep on going forward." He pulled out two shiny revolvers from their respective holsters and kept hold of the reins with his left hand, still looking back.

"What is it?"

"Goddamn bloodsuckers—" (If you were to see these "bloodsuckers," as Billy Utah referred to them, it would likely be the last thing you'd ever see. That or the ghastly image of your own blood spilling, still warm, from a mortal wound located you're-not-entirely-sure-where on your body, everything's numb by that point. But if you were to somehow survive that [and there have been at least three proven cases throughout the centuries—all three written recordings detailing similar descriptions and situations when passing through this area known as The Badlands or No Man's Land—

the first case recorded 8 September 1885 outside of Cheyenne, Wyoming, from the eyewitness account of a Mr. Nix ("Bull") McCool, twenty-nine at the time, who worked as a Deputy for the county and claimed to have witnessed three brightly pale men devouring the corpse of Mr. Damien Rooney, a respected banker in Cheyenne. His report featured claims that their eyes were "bright blood-red and wild with a desperate hunger," and "had bright teeth sharp as fucking knives," but "scared them off after firing a few shots at them," but still hightailed it out of there with the body of Mr. Damien Rooney which would never be found, and Bull McCool swore, till his dying day {which came six years later—cancer}, to the location where he brought a posse of three other lawmen at the first light of daybreak. Case #2 reported on 20 and 26 March 1910 in Deadwood, South Dakota, surrounded by the Black Hills, witnesses on the 20th being one Tolliver Moon and his wife-to-be Victoria Ioli {T. Moon being noted first, before V. Ioli, because in the written report it was detailed with "Mr. Tolliver Moon getting the attention of Ms. Victoria Ioli by, as he said, 'tapping her on the shoulder, two or three times,' then motioning over to where the claim of these, again as Mr. Moon said, 'demons' stood."} occurring after they had closed their store for the evening {living and sharing ownership of a business before marriage was unheard of, the business, *Over the Moon Services*, stood as the town of Deadwood's repair shop: V. Ioli mending to fabrics, dresses, some interior design for the right price, while T. Moon was the cobbler, made any worn-down boot reborn again, both took great pride in it, and in his spare time he also liked to draw—a damn fine artist he was—bold concept shoe designs, for men and women, a fashion he knew the people of Deadwood were sadly not ready for.} when they saw a group {number never recorded} of pale figures that "seemed to be wearing some torn, ragged clothes," and were "dripping with blood...covered their mouths and hands," and stated that their "blood-red eyes were hypnotizing," only managed to escape when T. Moon "heroically" threw a "big rock" at them and fled with V. Ioli to safety. In Deadwood on the 26th the witnesses were one Tolliver Moon, his "mistress," Velvet Sharp, and "some dumb fucking drunk who was just passing through town...wouldn't leave us alone," in a Mr. Jett Eco...T. Moon and V. Sharp claim to have left an {unnamed} saloon late at night, with J. Eco following them out, after having been lurking around them all night {true, learned later after fact-checking interviews with patrons who were there that night such as Fran Upton, customer, Asher Gallagher, customer, and Howard ("Howie") Vang, bartender, all attested that T. Moon and V. Sharp were not only there together but verbally harassed by one Jett Eco and was "asked him to leave them alone at least four times," until "good old Howie Vang got the drunk bastard out of there," but "didn't think he'd actually linger around till they left," which J. Eco did: followed T. Moon and V. Sharp until he was "swept away by some pale, flying animal" and though they didn't see the violence occur they could hear J. Eco's "blood-curdling" screams as they "were real close {and} wanted us to hear it...sounded like a Banshee." T. Moon never found the poor drunk's body but, after he reported it, was caught as a red-handed "cheating bastard" and essentially spiraled down into a deep depression that turned into compulsive madness that made him obsessed with "catching monsters." Reports on his further findings are still withheld.

Case #3 was reported on 13 October 1927 in Westby, Montana, right on the border of North Dakota, the sole witness being one Minnie Griffin who noted to have said that she was out with her sister, Nova Griffin, her boyfriend, Cal Morris, and Nova's boyfriend Seymour ("Buddy") Cooper on the night of the 13th "just driving around in Buddy Copper's truck, drinking whiskey...nothing unusual," when they pulled over near the outlook of Biff's Bluff Hill "around ten, I think," where they consumed their whiskey in the parked truck and engaged in sexual intercourse: "we'd always have to go to the hill or someplace like that to have sex cause all our mamas stay home and believe that God doesn't want us to get fucked till after we said our vows...that's just no fun...me and Nova would flip a coin to see who gets the bed of the truck and who gets the back seat, you can imagine which is better...when I felt Cal's head slide in is when I heard Nova and Buddy scream {note: M. Griffin and C. Morris were in the backseat of the truck}...then blood on the windows...Cal got out, I begged him not to...something lifted him up off the ground...he screamed, first time I ever heard him do that...dropped him to the ground...deep bite marks in his neck," and though C. Morris was the only body recovered that day, M. Griffin, when she exited the car in hysteria to examine C. Morris, saw a pack of pale beings lugging two bodies away from the scene with ease. The pack "was screaming like a bunch of sick, happy coyotes...damned by the devil," and headed in the direction of the cave at the base of Biff's Bluff Hill, which is home to hundreds of miles of underground tunnels still unexplored to this day {search parties would find the scattered remains, bones, of what they believe still to be N. Griffin and B. Cooper but not enough remains to be confident and conclusive, six months later.}] you would be the fourth to do so, among rarity. Seeing those creatures—products of the devil some would say, which would be a product of God then, right?— with pale, corpse-like flesh, eyes as red as the blood they so desperately craved, fangs as sharp as the hunger that crawled at the edge of their eyes, voices as violent as their desires...you would struggle to believe it, which is why it's likely there are only three "official" reports of the—as Billy Utah called them— bloodsuckers...how many were unreported out of fear or disbelief, or dismissed entirely, understandably, for sounding downright unbelievable?) "—are back again..."

"What?" Curiosity, the strong beast, took over; Laura only managed to look at Billy. The sun was completely gone now, colder than it was before they met. How was it night already?

"Don't look, please, Miss Laura," he commanded, kindly as he could. "This kinda business ain't meant for those pretty eyes to see."

"I've seen some pretty horrible things."

Billy looked at her. "I know, I can tell, and I'm sorry you have. But this is my job and mine alone. I gotta take care of it now. Don't you worry, no harm will come to you. Got about another five miles before you get to Ten Sleep. So ride hard, Miss Laura."

"Is someone following us?"

"You could say that."

"What do we do?" She couldn't hide the panic in her voice and felt embarrassed.

"Well...it's my duty to deal with it now. This ain't your business, your business is in Ten Sleep. Now listen: when you get there, and you come back, take this same road. Don't detour. Don't take shortcuts. Same road you took, same one we're on right now. It'll be safe. Promise."

"You'll be here?"

"Not likely we'll meet again, Miss Laura, but I can promise that you'll be safe. Everyone who meets Billy Utah always makes it out. That's a given. Here." He handed her his red bandana. "The air there is...different. That boy, he did some bad things there, I reckon, had a look of evil on him."

"I—"

"Ride hard. Now."

Billy fired a shot in the air which startled young Buck so much so that he galloped away into a mad frenzy. Bambi hung on to the reins, white-knuckled. Billy whipped Big Blue around and darted off heroically to face some evil that Bambi couldn't fathom. She wanted to look back, but this time couldn't bring her head to move to the left or right at all, like she was frozen solid, eyes glued to the fast-moving world in front of her, with wind that silently whipped at her face and tears that streaked down her cheeks.

The air was pierced by another Billy Utah whistle—this one more high-pitched, another sad, familiar tune that she never heard of before, that rushed through her mind—and then gunfire, too many shots to count. A blood-curdling shriek—two, three, four. Echoes. Quick as it all came, it left. Silence flooded the world again.

34

The moon illuminated the darkness of the road where their headlights could not reach. They sat in silence and watched the snow softly crash into the windshield and melt immediately: each one different, each one unique, each one alive, each one gone with not so much as a trace, save for the water they become that evaporated back into the heavens where they all began to repeat the cycle.

Brody was behind the wheel, his twin brother Brooks seated next to him, struggling to stay awake. The Deering Brothers—better known by their folklore name, The Devil's Twins of Yakima—looked thinner than they did three months ago, when their campaign started, not sickly, yet, but like they had forgotten the importance of a good meal. It didn't concern them. Neither of them minded the stench of the other at this point, either, having foregone bathing since their first victims back home, in Yakima, for no good reason in particular, just forgetting about hygiene. But now, having finished off their latest victims in Walla Walla, their thirteenth in total and fifth in the city, they were on the road again—the number of mutilated corpses slowly decomposing around the city had caused them to choose a new destination (which they still hadn't decided on: Brody elected to head north for Spokane, or backtrack and make for Olympia, while Brooks wanted to get out of the state, suggested they head down to Oregon), best not to linger too long where blood is fresh. They realized that their horrible odor, if not eradicated, would cause further obstacles as it did with their last kills: the owners of the home, Lyric and Frank Nass, smelled them before they broke in, caused a near fifteen-minute cat-and-mouse chase about the large, ranch-style house. It was, they realized after the fact, the hardest they ever had to work. Though at the time, their terror-filled screams that bounced off the walls were music to the Brothers' ears as they ran after their victims from room to room, dodging chairs that were thrown in the way, adrenaline pumping violently and rapidly through their veins. Considerable and rather unnecessary damage was done to the house, the pictures on the wall smashed, the tables broken, the lights exploded as if an act of suicide—as if they no longer wanted to bear witness to such gross horror—all because the homeowners had a will to live, all because the Devil's Twins felt terribly inconvenienced. So when they were finally trapped, cornered, the Brothers' pinned the sacred souls down with impossible, herculean strength, a gruesome red rage painted over their faces, the panicked couple trembling violently, a dreadful fear filling their hearts and pooling out of their eyes. So the delirium was finally acknowledged that they should wash up some or find a way to really build up that cardio because if the wind was just right one night they might smell them from a mile away, adding to the list of what the Devil's Twins were known for.

There was no consistency to their routine: sometimes Brooks would interview the victims before they would kill them—they would usually, at first, be unwilling to share anything, terrified to speak, but somehow Brooks would get them to open up and spill all those little secrets they kept buried for so long...Brody always marvelled at that, how his brother could convince these people to tell him, a stranger and their soon-to-be murderer, all the things they intended to die with—he would write down their life story in a little black notebook, never saying what he was going to do with all the personal information; other times they broke right in and did their business, no questions asked, no words spoken (like their second and third victims in Walla Walla, that fucking old couple who *shot* at them which after they had a lengthy and paranoid discussion on the possibility that people were *expecting* them now, that every home in Washington was prepared for them, which of course wasn't entirely true); and a few times they would go about their methods nice and slow: torturing the poor souls, Brody's personally favorite way of going about it—they hadn't planned on torturing the most recent couple, but after the exhausting pursuit Brody was able to convince Brooks that they deserved it, and involved Brody using a blood-stained hunting knife to peel the clean, white flesh off the man and woman's cheek. "They've gotta match," he told his brother, "for better or for worse," then proceeded to slowly remove other strips of flesh from different parts of their bodies as he admired their screams: their left thighs, their abdomen, the back of their hands—until he got tired and cut out their tongues and watched them choke on their own blood...their grips always simultaneously released from the fresh corpses after the final heartbeat...was something they had to feel themselves.

Brody kicked the radio on: "The effects of this horrific attack on our nati—" began a thick, melancholy voice before it was switched to the start of "I Don't Want to Set the World On Fire" by The Ink Spots:

> I don't want to set the world on fire,
> I just want to start a flame in your heart.
> In my heart I have but one desire
> And that one is you.

No other will do,
I've lost all ambition for worldly acclaim
I just want to be the one you love.
And with your admission
That you feel the same,
I'll have reached the goal I'm dreaming of.
Believe me.

The lyrics, the music, which woke Brooks up and held his attention, washed over them like some half-remembered dream they both shared once, long ago, when they still had the morals to dream dreams worth remembering—or half-remembering—of love they once desired and pined for, of days filled with golden sunshine and clear blue skies...but now, with their hearts unable to feel the natural ecstasies of love, the world itself was foreign to them, their minds always drifting into nightmarish landscapes whenever they attempted to get a good night's sleep, which was never often anymore.

"Good tune." Brody nodded along.

Brooks looked at his brother then opened the glove compartment—which held two pairs of black leather gloves, at least a dozen matchbooks, far too many empty cigarette boxes, frayed rope, and maps. He grabbed a map and scowled at it, tossed it back then grabbed another, the correct one. Brody turned the radio down a touch.

"We should head south. Milton-Freewater ain't too far. Get us out of Washington, get a motel for the night, shower up, scope out the city in the morning."

"You really want to take this over state lines?"

"We've been in this city for too long, Brody."

"Yeah, yeah. Mean, we could head up to Dixie Crossing, then maybe make for Kennewick in the morning, do what we do." He said it casually, like they were going to catch a play while in town. "Then head back—"

"No," Brooks said. "Not trying to head back home just yet."

"Kavanksch echk mal geezk?" Brody's grip tightened around the wheel, knuckles white. Anxious. Ready.

"No one is lookin' for us in Oregon."

"Ghanwk gall vundundun."

"People are talking too much here...hell, Brody, we've got a nickname now, only a matter of time before they find out how many twins are from Yakima."

"Zout," Brody swore as he scratched at his unkempt beard. "Buher me naddada zoinked o chyle."

"No shit."

The song had ended. A cool, carefree voice quietly filled the silence between them.

"Alright, that was The Ink Spots. Next up we have 'I'll Be With You In Apple Blossom Time' by The Andrews Sisters. Hope you all enjoy, and remember: as long as the songs are a-singing then the worries will always be a-fading." They listened to the instruments build up, the volume still low, until Brody turned it off completely. Brooks looked over with a curious eye, saw his brother's eye well up with a tear.

"You alright?"

"It was our birthday today, you know," Brody told him.

"Ah hell..."

"You ain't even said anythin' all day."

"Shit—"

"Can't even talk in *our* fuckin' language."

"Hell, Brody, I understood you, didn't I? It's hard talkin' like that all the time, you know? Takes lotta jaw muscle."

"Yeah, yeah."

"And hell, you ain't said nothin' about our birthday neither."

"Hell I didn't."

"What. Was talkin' like that supposed to be a hint to remind me, or somethin' like that? Hell. We ain't talked it in a month, have we? Zout foullyer chzch—aw hell, now you got me goin', happy now?"

"Like hell I didn't say anythin' all day."

"Name it."

"This mornin', round nine."

"Was asleep."

"And that's another thing there, Brooks."

"What now?"

"Been drivin' us all day."

"Figured you liked drivin'."

"Ain't the point."

"What is it then?"

"You ain't even care. Hell."

"What the—"

"You ain't."

"Ain't true, Brody. Hell, we'll celebrate tomorrow. Alright?"

"Yeah?"

"Sure."

"Oregon then," Brody said after a long silence. He pressed his foot a bit harder to the pedal, turned the radio back on, and stopped himself from finding another senseless argument to have with his brother just for the fuck of it. Didn't matter where—he was able to tell himself—as long as he was able to see some blood flow out of a body.

Dirty, twisted yellow grins inched their way across both of their faces, seen only by the private, sunken eyes of the old man on the moon; by the owls perched, it seemed, on every other tree branch, who observed with wide, watchful eyes their uninvited passage through this stretch of land which must have been the owl's kingdom; by the silent ghosts of forgotten pioneers who died nameless and without a trace, forever trapped in those dark woods hugging either side of the road, not understanding what their dead eyes perceived—that which passed by so quickly...as if the devil chased it, or gave it speed.

35

North.

This was the only thought in Joseph's mind as he stood on the shoulder of the empty two-lane highway—home was north, he had to go north.

He stole a car, an all-black 1939 Plymouth Coupe, and made it from Bend to John Day just before the sun began to set—the sky morphed into a vast but finite canvas, an oil painting by some anonymous artist (must be your God, working overtime on aesthetics), the color of dead lilacs and fool's gold. The great Strawberry and Blue Mountains surrounding the small town stood jagged and sharp in the distance against the dark. What secrets they held together, those mountains, connected by the tributary of the Columbia River, the John Day River, a source of life that gave this town its name, all came from the Virginian tapper and explorer, John Day—who, as a member of the Pacific Fur Company, was stripped naked and robbed by (what he never called) Native Americans at the mouth of the river which would later bear his name, yes, he whose mind was lost some years later in those very waters, only to perish, in 1820, at age fifty, in the foreign waters of the Little Lost River...how cold it must have been in that snowy February unknown.

As weariness set in deeper and deeper, Joseph's eyelids became heavier and heavier. He was twenty miles outside of town when he veered far to the left, crossed lanes, and crashed into a tree twenty yards off the road. The sudden crunching sound of the impact jolted him awake, but just as quickly his head slammed against the steering wheel; it honked once and knocked him unconscious.

It was fully dark when he awoke sometime later in a milky haze. His forehead was burning and throbbing, wet with blood. He looked in the mirror and saw his bloody, fuzzy reflection. Even concussed he could tell the wound was bad and deep. The blood flowed at a steady pace. The windshield was cracked, spider-webbed, yet somehow not shattered. The engine coughed out a cloud of thick black smoke. The cold crept its way through the cracks and found him. He sat in the car for five more minutes that felt like hours with a foolish hope that someone would come and save him. He wasn't sure he had enough left to save himself this time.

It was then that a bright hallucination appeared before him in the form of his mother, older than he remembered her ever being, but not by much, her voice remaining the same as it always had, right up until the very end. "Joseph," she said, calm but firm. "You cannot die here."

"I'm tired." He barely spoke, his chapped, bloody lips hardly parting.

"You have to get home first. You have to see your sister again. After that...you can sleep as long as you want."

"You'd want that?"

"I have no wants, Joseph...these are *your* wants."

"Huh? What is—"

The engine of the car suddenly caught fire; hot, roaring light illuminated the uncertain night. Joseph shielded his eyes and turned back to his mother, only to find her gone. He sat dumbfounded until the wind blew a harsh whisper: "*Go!*"

He stumbled out of the inferno and crawled away until he no longer felt the radiating heat, and watched the fire devour the car until it had its fill. He wandered towards the road and realized that it was too dark and too cold to wait around for someone, that he needed to cover what little ground he could by walking and pray—though not literally—that he could make it to the next town, Fox, within the hour, which was unlikely. As he slowly trekked north he came across no cars going that way, only one that was southbound, didn't bother to slow when his headlights lit him up, not that it mattered anyway, he told himself...there was nothing he could do to block out the sharp, stabbing pain that came with each step. He didn't know the world could get this cold; he was sure his bones would shatter soon, like glass, frozen to the touch and no longer able to bear the weight of living. The raw idea of death wormed its way into his consciousness and feasted on him and brought him, literally, to his knees. It was there, lying flat on his stomach, head cradled by a frozen snowbank, that his mind tricked him into believing that if he stayed like that, perfectly still, he'd get warm soon. The blood would find a way to flow.

The low hum of an engine filled the void of silence, though to him it felt as though it were miles away. Joseph opened his eyes. The car *did* look like it was far away—it was at the very end of a narrow tunnel, black walls slowly closing in around it.

"He's still breathin'," he heard, though the speech was rough, almost muted, like some invisible force blocked him from their world and whichever worlds he was in between.

"Get 'em in then, Brooks," another syrupy voice said. Rough hands immediately grabbed him and forced him to his blistered feet, dirty, broken fingernails digging into his shoulders through the wet and heavy fabric of his coat, too numb to complain but not numb enough to ignore it completely. "I'm gettin' hungry."

Hungry? The word nearly snapped him out of his lucid

323

dream. *I could eat, too,* his mind began to wonder—*yes, I could eat. What was it we had for Laura's birthday? Smoked chicken breasts, yes, I'd like to finally try chicken, I reckon...with mushrooms, chopped onions, and lemon juice. Yes...*the thought made him wonder, for half a heartbeat, just how dear old Sis, good old Bambi, was doing...

Dreams of happiness in the form of a warm meal took over and filled him with unconscious joy as he lay in the backseat of the Deering Brother's truck, held alive by the genuine warmth that the owners of the old automobile never noticed...took it as a sign that his journey wasn't done yet.

"Walla Walla," Joseph croaked suddenly. "Need to get to Walla Walla..."

The Devil's Twins of Yakima looked at the wounded boy and laughed maniacally, shocking Joseph, who perceived them as sharp hyena—or, more appropriately in terms of geography to where he grew up, wolf-like—howls, like sandpaper rubbing against his mind, crimson red, a violent, sporadic flash of the color, like blood, filling his eyes until it was all he could see and forced him to concentrate on keeping his eyes shut for the time...how the dark was finally wanted, needed, how it had won.

"Reckon we could stop up in Fox, get it done then," Brody said.

"No," Brooks argued, shaking his head. "Don't stop till Pilot Rock, hell, I'd say Athena if you'd think you could make it."

"Athena? Goddamn, brother, I don't wanna drive all night."

"I'd rather be closer to the border."

"Washington and Oregon are one and the same. We ever get caught, which we won't, we'd be fucked in either state. Dead."

"Chuckcua zut skal!"

"Moiny huzfe lousch bbhyr!"

"Zjasher, *zjasher*, mcmcdzrky foolooch."

This unintelligible gibberish bickering went on for—Joseph felt—an unnecessarily long time with seemingly no end as they could likely make up anything to be upset about in this made-up language of theirs, which he was sure they did. It went on for so long that he began to believe he was able to decipher some words and had pinpointed their meanings, though highly unlikely, it really felt true to him though, like he had accomplished something while trapped there.

"Pilot Rock," Brooks said suddenly in their rustic-style English.

"Fine," Brody agreed after a long silence.

The drive to Pilot Rock took longer than it should have given the poor road conditions, the snow still held on to a bit of life. It was silent for the most part: the brothers only fought two other times for ten minutes each, both arguments weighing the topic of how and where they would kill and consume Joseph, how it was only their third time eating a victim and they were still learning the proper way to prepare the meal; do they skin him first or roast him as is? Alive, of course—the fresher the better. Or, as Brody suggested, perhaps they should drain his blood first and drink it, warm and rich.

Joseph heard the conversations—not knowing who they were or who would prefer skinning him to roasting him first as their voices sounded all too alike—and was fully aware of things now. A dull haziness still lingered, but he knew he was not hallucinating this time; he assured himself of that. He listened to them argue and breathe disgustingly heavy in silence, all while he pretended to be unconscious. He listened and thought of hundreds and hundreds of scenarios on what he should do, how he could get away. He had no sense at all for time, but for some reason—thankfully is what he thought of it later—a phenomenon occurred that allowed him to perceive everything around him in slow motion, how all his small movements—like his hand raised to touch his wet, bloody forehead—now took a lifetime and gave him the illusion that he could come up with a plan on how not to die at the hands of cannibals. What luck. What dumb luck. What act of God. *Right*. At long last, after all this, the universe was finally on his side. In his favor. How do you like that, Joseph? Remember what mother said, Joseph? Remember what mother said: can't die here.

A Meditation On Being a Nightmare

Every thought he processed was all for naught as sometime later Brooks shook him with a dirty hand: "Wake up, boy." The words were rough and sludgy as the Twins' accents carried a sort of guttural slur. This was something that Joseph was unprepared for. What could he possibly want? An opinion on how he would like to be consumed?

Joseph sat up and looked at Brooks, dirty and twitchy, eyes bright and curious and holding an almost childlike enthusiasm within. He was holding a little black notebook and a pencil.

"What's your story, boy?"

"Nothing to tell," Joseph assured him, didn't believe the words himself, and knew this man could somehow see that in him, the disbelief painted across his face; could sense the tragedy that radiated off of his body, like a shark smelling blood in the water. It enthralled these two—they needed it, that fear, to know where it came from originally, to understand their meal more intimately, personally, to have them understand that whatever fear they once held onto was nothing compared to what they were about to experience.

This new exercise of theirs, it's all they have now. Their fucked-up design.

"Bullshit. Everyone's got one. You'll tell us yours."

"Why? What difference does it make? You're still gonna

kill me. Why give you satisfaction?"

"You probably think you're the first person to say that to us. You ain't."

"It won't be fun for you," Brody said as he looked at Joseph in the rearview mirror. "Once Brooks got hooked on this thing, it's been impossible to pry him away from it. He'll get them words out of you before we're full."

"What's it matter, anyway?"

"What?" they asked in unison.

"My story, my words. It's all the same in the end, really. Just said a different way, maybe."

Silence briefly reigned supreme as they contemplated his words, which hung in the dank car like an ugly weight above their heads threatening to compress and crush them at any moment. Brooks took his time to examine Joseph, who looked as though he had seen better days.

"You look like you could use some more oatmeal."

"How's that?"

"Bit thin, aren't ya? Not too much meat on them bones."

"I don't care."

"Don't 'care?'" Brody asked, perplexed, revolted.

"Why's it matter? Not like you've any oatmeal—"

"No, no we do not. Brody ate it back 'fore we picked you up."

"Apologies."

"—and you're planning on killing me anyway, right? Why would I bulk up for you or do anything for you? Not even like I have the time anymore."

"That is a good point."

"And," Brooks pointed out, with hope in his voice, like what he was about to speak philosophically would come off as pure fact with little to no argument, for it was the only truth there was, "if we don't kill you, reckon you'd do the job for us."

"How's that?"

"Everyone dies, kid."

"I don't plan on dying soon."

"No one does. But they do. This planet itself is dying, everything is always dying, and we're just helpin' em along. Shit, well, this was never really planned, see? Just one just led to another led to another led to another till we plum lost count...but it felt like we was doin' the right thing. Papers said—"

"Papers?"

"—that what we do are, what was it? 'Crimes of passion,' yeah. Ain't know much about that, like I said, was just something to do, at first, and it felt good, see? Like it made sense, if that makes sense...hell, you can throw that fancy word on us now if you want to, 'passion,' hell, we don't give a damn—"

"Hell, I might."

"Alls I know, kid, is this: This planet is filled, over-populated, with a dominant, powerful species that is two things: suicidal, and in denial."

Brody smiled grossly to himself as he listened to his brother speak their truth as if he were speaking the gospel, which in a sense he was—*their* gospel. The words crashed over Joseph like the foundations of a building crumbling down, piece by piece, after decades and decades of wear and tear, too much life. He tried to ignore it at first; the Brothers let silence fill the car so the boy could lament over these facts of life, which he eventually did. As he watched the world pass by, he couldn't get those thoughts out of his head—it infected his mind like a disease, spread rapidly...oh, hey there, old Nihilism, see you found another victim...

"He's in deep thought now," Brody observed.

"That he is," Brooks concurred.

"Let's hear your thoughts, boy."

"Why? Do you think they matter?"

"Maybe not entirely," Brooks told him honestly. "Just want to pass the time and get some writing in, is all."

"Hell," Brody said with what seemed to be an attempt at

innocence. "Realized we never introduced ourselves, I'm Brody Deering, and this my brother Brooks. People been callin' us The Devil's Twins of Yakima, as of late."

Brooks let out a howl of laughter. "Tell us, now that you know us a little better," he said, like fucking names all of a sudden fall under the class of knowing someone better. "Where were you 'fore we picked you up? Start there."

Joseph looked at the psychotic brothers: Brody with his eyes on the road and Brooks staring directly at him in the rearview mirror, unmoving, unblinking. He turned his head and looked out the window. It was hard to look at their demonic faces— sickening yellow eyes, greasy, stringy hair— for longer than five seconds, and if he thought about their stench for too long, he was afraid he might throw up completely.

"I killed a man," Joseph told them. "Back in Bend."

Brooks began writing frantically. Joseph imagined his handwriting was likely unreadable chicken scratch, a written language that only the Deering Brothers—the Devil's own Twins—could understand.

"How?" Brooks asked.

"I drowned him in Mirror Pond."

"Why?"

"He—" a brief pause, as if he'd actually forgotten what George Wynne did to him, or considered the possibility for the first time that he took a human life and how that did not fill the void within him, "—deserved it."

"Who're you to say who deserves to die and who doesn't?" Brody asked.

"What'd he do?" Brooks wondered.

"He was in charge of the man that killed my parents."

"Why didn't you kill him?"

"Who says I won't?"

"But still," Brody pressed, "who are you to say who lives and who dies? God?"

"Sure, I don't see why not. You kill people, too. Did they all deserve it? Honestly. Do I?"

"Now boy," Brooks started. "You just compare yourself to the Almighty."

"Funny how you believe in 'God' when you go around butchering and eating people. Fucking hilarious. I think we all should have a bit of a god-complex in us, at least entertain the idea of it. The idea of perfection, enlightenment, what everyone strives for, or should, at least, think of it...how impossible it is to obtain. At least for blind Christians who haven't even read the damn book they bash people with, who think they have it all figured out cause they attend a money-hungry church every fucking Sunday morning. When you pray at night or in the morning, you're only talking to yourself, no one is listening to you up there. Heaven isn't a real, tangible place, and you two slimy fucks sure as shit wouldn't get in if it was, it's only here on earth, or, it was. It was perfect for a time. Now look: you two are running around killing *for fucking fun*, the entire world is at war with each other, the planet is dying, this country is putting people in cages if they don't have pure white American blood, which no one fucking does. We're treating free people like animals, and for what? To feel safe? Bullshit. You think your crusade, the Nazis' crusade or any crusade since the dawn of time and consciousness would or could prove God, or any god in any fucking religion, exists? Not a chance. Fuck God. We try to make our own paradise. Though, that dream was taken from me...so I figured I might as well take someone else's. That's what you two do, right? Take away people's dreams, ruin their paradises? Figured I'd give that life a shot since it's all fallen apart anyway. And no, I don't feel any better, I still feel the same."

He wasn't aware that those words were always inside of him, was so filled with adrenaline that he lost control of himself, but knew he meant every word.

Brooks looked over his notes and studied each line, each

word, carefully before he looked at Joseph. "You think you're better than us then?"

"No. No one is better or worse than anyone. We're all the same in the end."

"We're all the same?" Brody shirked madly, almost running them off the road. "You comparing us to some dirty fucking degenerate ass—"

"Shut the fuck up," Joseph cut him off. "Shut your stupid, racist ass up. You're the lowest of the low, if you want me to be honest. That's why you're doing what you're doing. You feel like society has shunned you away and made you feel obsolete, like you can't compete. But the truth is: you did it to yourself. The innocent lives you continue to take from this world did not go out of their way to make you feel insufficient, did they?"

"What would you know about it?" Brooks barked. "You weren't there."

"Does it make you feel better? Killing them? Torturing them? Consuming them? Does that make you feel better about who you are? When you look in a mirror now, are you finally satisfied with who you see?" The silence from the Brothers was deafening. "I bet it makes you feel powerful for a split second, that's how it felt for me. But then it was gone, forever. Is that why you continue this spree of yours? To try and capture that feeling of power, physically, to have it constantly flow through your bloodstream until it's really a part of you? It will never happen. You're better off taking your own advice: stop living in denial and kill yourself."

There was a moment of primal remembrance that rushed through Joseph's consciousness, as if reincarnation, the idea of it, was allowed during this passage of time and gifted him with the ability to prepare for the bloody violence that was sure to ensue in a matter of seconds. He saw the way Brooks held his pencil now, how he gripped it like he had half a mind to try and sink it into his eye. *Any second now.* He wasn't afraid anymore, like he already saw it all play out.

36

The air was near toxic: burning flesh and singed hair mixed with death, shit, rotting cedar, piss, black smoke, and a tinge of something metallic, like twisted metal. Bambi tied the bandana that Billy had given her around her face, concealing her mouth and nose. The fabric faintly held his scent and she was surprised she was even aware of it given how little time they spent together, but, even so, it was her only comfort. Buck froze; she hopped off, remembered her legs that then felt like two pieces of dead wood. She saw him suddenly—his shadow: illuminated by some phantom light, standing tall, a blood-red skull that still held onto bits of hair and flesh firmly gripped in his left hand... he saw himself immortalized forever in a priceless work by Jules Lion. She froze. Clear, manic eyes cut through the smoke, lit up his dirty face streaked with tears. His consciousness had chosen the final character. The stage— *his* stage—was now set.

PURSUED BY BEAR
OR: (ODE TO KING LEAR)

"Who dare stand befˊre me. *Me*: the mad nave whom

wished to draw all those tiny ghosts to my own land. Heavy and honest w're their soulless eyes, bethinking me vile, as I balk'd with my own consciousness on how to alloweth those folk the choice of rapture, and within the confines of my own heart I hath felt a zany want, telling me to retire...a thing I nev'r thought I couldst bare to fancy, still...

"'Twas a case of a spiritual revolution," he said as he moved closer towards her, and with this, she saw finally the long revolver in his right hand. "Almost sexual in nature: all the souls dying with their last wishes being of me, making them quake, which quickens their blood and induces them to their des'rving sleep, and they catcheth but a wink of that et'rnal darkness much clos'r than anticipated, each one of them w're so eag'rly willing to inh'rit this judicial blade into their beating hearts. The men, the brave and the cunning lot those gents, w're wanting desp'rately to beest the st'rybook hero...but we shall f'rget thy songs! Thy tales shan't be whisper'd in any halls, wheth'r 't be in this w'rld 'r the oth'r, f'r those lads w're the ones with a fear in their bones: a want to hold on, to be alive in this w'rld, still...what outrageous fools...that feeling ought to be 'radicat'd.

"I wast in isolation f'r god knoweth how long...high-lone with nay one saveth f'r mine own thoughts, all of whom bareth voices of their own and in turn hath tried to rule ov'r me...hath tried to becometh me to the point wh're I nay long'r knoweth who is't I am...O! what a noble mind is here o'erthrown! I has't become my own w'rst foe!...'t is the same f'r all of thee...thee who be unwilling to admit yond thou art as hath lost as I."

This Is Not An Exit

He gripped that .38 Special tightly and pressed it firmly against his skull. Bambi's voice caught in her throat. She saw how rusty the damn thing was and wondered, for half a moment, if it even worked, if this all was just an act—the corpses merely props and extras, a marvelous makeup team hiding off set somewhere, and what must be the world's finest actor standing humbly before her, performing a private monologue:

"Don't thee und'rstand?" Jenson shirked madly, snapping her back to this horrific reality. "I've the sickness—we all has't the sickness!—I knoweth not what else to do! I thought their blood wouldst cleanse me, but now I believe mine shall be spill'd as well.

"How longeth the nights has't been in the confines of mine own mind, which I know now is m'rely a cell, mine own corpse the prison, and I am t's lonesome prison'r. Thoughts pull as if 't be true t w're a ball of yarn, pulling me furth'r and furth'r hence from what thee call 'reality.' Doth thee und'rstand? What is't thee desire from me? Can't thee see yond I've nothing hath left to off'r?"

The tears were hot and blurred her vision. "An apology," she said.

"Pardon?" Jenson lowered the gun, felt the full force of this angel before him even with that soft voice of hers.

"You murdered my parents."

"I've murd'r'd many parents," he finally said, then gestured around at the massacre that surrounded them. "I wast freeing those folk, spoke to them with daggers."

"Stop..."

"We'll free ourselves one day; t's the way of life: f'rev'r ending in death. Has't desire to joineth already?"

HAMLET V. MACBETH V. JENSON
OR: (PURSUED BY BEAR PART II)

The silence boomed. Blood rushed vigorously throughout her body, tidal waves in her ears, the only sound she minded.

"I am," Jenson began, putting an end to the tidal waves, "to be..." The words fluttered soft as a butterfly off of his lips but rang like a metallic echo in her mind. "You...who come most carefully upon thy hour...most foul...how strange and unnatural...I reckon'd we e're sure of our roles...now they're all talking at the same time...telling me: to die, to sleep...the bell invites me..." He pressed the pistol against his temple again. The world stood at attention, silent and still and awaiting the performer's final line: "O, full of scorpions is my mind," he whispered, an unoriginal man of broken mind and soul—lost to the system in which the country he thought so proud to defend had created, a country which, if he were to live, would shun and shame him, rightfully so, still—with a voice soft and proud, hardly audible at all, but loud enough to echo in Bambi's consciousness forever.

He pulled the trigger and crumpled to the ground like a sad sack of bones.

Bambi took a half step forward then stopped.

All this way...

LONG LIVE THE BRUCE

It transfixed her, vexed her entirely: how she had come all this way...for this...never really knew what to expect...what was a proper reaction, then? She had dreamed of killing the man, but seeing so much death in such a small amount of time broke her soul...she didn't want to add to it, even with that most powerful word known as hate that lashed out against the walls of her heart. So to see him do it himself, to relieve her of the vengeful duty, started to feel like a weight lifted off of her tired shoulders. She buried her face in her palms, collapsed to her knees in the bloody mud, and began to sob violently. She cried, her chest rising and falling rapidly, like a leaf in a storm...she cried so hard she threw up...she clutched her chest, for she swore she felt her heart shatter into pieces—and now it was time to go home...?

"Oi!" a hoarse voice cried out. "God bless ya." Which Bambi didn't make out too well, as it sounded like "Gawdblezzyah," for it was spat out in less than a second, like his words were stuck together, covered in some thick, guttural Irish-Cockney-Gypsy accent. The owner of the voice revealed himself when he walked out from a ruined stone hut: a cheeky smile across a bearded, dirty face, a front tooth missing, clothed in a grizzly bear fur robe—the bear's head atop of his, teeth hanging down just to his eyebrows—and some tattered pants. "Oi," he said again as he walked towards her. "Thank ya so much for dealing with him. Really, honestly, thank ya," which sounded like "Tankyasomochfahdealinwithiim. Reely-honest-tankya."

Bambi stood, her tired eyes locked on him—wished now and forever that all strange men of the world would leave her alone. Forever. Her and every woman on the planet. Amen. She longed to be home—whatever that was anymore, really—for the first time since this journey began. It was all too much. She started to cry again, and didn't give a damn who saw.

The man stopped short. "Yaalright?"

A few more disheveled-looking humans left their ruined huts, got a good look at what was left of Ten Sleep.

"MenamesDigby-da-Bruce," the man in the grizzly bear robe told her. "Justwanttathank-ya—" he slowed his speech some as if finally fucking realizing that she may not fully understand him, "—tank ya-fah-dealin-wit-iim."

She wiped her eyes, looked up at Digby the Bruce, and then noticed all the people standing around them (them being Bambi, Digby, and the late Jenson), fifty if not more, who had evaded slaughter and were waiting to see what would happen in the next scene, the final act in living progress. She scanned the crowd: it was hard to get a read on them, what they wanted...they were mostly older, with a few young children, one newborn held by someone who was likely the grandmother which left the fate of mother unknown or to your optimistic or pessimistic imagination. They all looked tired and rail-thin—like skeletons, as if their meals, whenever they could find or afford one, consisted of stale bread, luke-warm and watery porridge (which they would eat with their eyes closed and imagine it as oatmeal), and raw leeks for their vegetables—fruit was rare, as were sweets, though there was an old legend of long-remembered Blake Jenson, an actual great-great-second-aunt of the late Jenson Reynolds who he was named after, who years ago found the only apple ever in Ten Sleep, Wyoming. They simply did not exist there—no one was sure why or even questioned it—until Blake Jenson found one after a walk around town one day: it lay in the mud, skin bright and golden-yellow, edible treasure. Unsure where it could have come from, she picked it up, cleaned it off as best she could—it proved to be a bit soft, rotten, a hole in it where a worm lived, though she took care of him—then took a bite; she had never tasted something so juicy and sweet before, she was near orgasm, and to think what a fully ripe apple would have done...

Half of the crowd showed emotion on their faces—that spelled out depression and anxiety—and half were still as stone—controlled undoubtedly by dear old Nihilism that rewired the brain entirely—and always a dead giveaway in the eyes, but truth be told, all the eyes in Ten Sleep looked the same: dark, chestnut brown or cold, cobalt blue, filled to the brim with a joylessness ennui as if the haunting idea of being alive was always on their minds in the worst kind of way. It looked like they weren't fully there; like they were fading in and out of time and reality, with the sun at long last breaking through just in time to seep into a warm twilight. Bambi could *see* the last of the light's rays dance *through them*, all these ghosts who stood with the same nervous apprehensiveness that she could finally relate to...all alone in the gloaming, as if

H. Golden Dearth was the director on set. But it took her mind off all that hopeless despair she *was* focused on, she realized... focusing on their pain distracted her from her own.

"How did you know him?"

"Hebe-from ere."

"It's always been like this. Here."

"Eh?"

"Who was he to you?"

"Ah! Daboih-Jenson-dere-wahs-mecouzin. Shamed-ta-say."

"Was he always evil?"

The question struck a chord. Everyone felt it. Digby could only nod his head.

"Why'd he come back?"

"Wanted-me-trone."

"What?"

"Yee-be-speakintada King-o-Ten Sleep dere!" a voice from the crowd called out, faceless, could have been anyone.

"You're the 'King?'"

"Aye. Iiz."

"Where's your crown?"

Everyone laughed—it must have been some great inside joke from long ago, a part of the history of Ten Sleep. All the laughs sounded the same as if recorded on a record and played on a loop.

"What? No crown?"

"Neva."

"What then?"

Digby the Bruce pulled out a dagger, hidden in a holster behind his back, and showed it to Bambi. The handle was made out of bone from the grizzly bear he wore as a robe, another sign of Kingship. The blade was a mirror but in the center was a milky black spot, an inkblot *swimming* within the blade, like there was something *alive* in it.

"What the—"

"Alchemy."

"So—"

"Hee-comedbackta-killme. Dats-how-one-goesaboot-ruli-nere." He tapped the blade to his bare chest, his heart. "Plundge-disbastard-intomefookin-heart."

"Is that why you hid?"

He was taken aback.

"Well?"

"I-wasn't-fookin-hidin."

"You weren't out here, though."

"Coz-I-wahs-waitinfaiim-ta-fight-witout-a-fookin-*hand-cannon*."

"Weak."

"Ain't-dyinframsum-aun*fair*-fioght."

"Fair enough."

"But-tankgoodneess-youzwahsere."

"Right."

Bambi had enough of the conversation then, not just because she could barely understand him, but to be around other humans right now, to interact with them like everything, all of this, was good and normal—no. She couldn't do it anymore. She walked quietly to Buck and they rode away. No longer felt or cared about the eyes of those from Ten Sleep that were upon her...she left them behind, in this past that would always haunt her—like a real ghost: like the one from the first house you grew up in, the one you stopped believing in at seventeen but found fear in again at twenty-three when you were living on your own for the first time, and you felt it there, too, and again, not too long after, when you and and "the love of your life" bought a house together, a real old one, feeling it again like you did when you were young, that same intense fear of a ghost you catch out of the corner of your eye, how they watch you from afar in the corner of your bedroom, how you're never sure who it is because for some reason you believe that multiple people want to haunt you, and how you'll realize that the ghost will follow you to wherever you sleep and haunt you a little more...slowly you'll learn how to live with—then how to love—the fear, how not to mind it there, to damn-near depend on it, to the point where you can never imagine your life without it, that fucking ghost—it was always there, right? Though maybe it was you who was doing the haunting—always taking over places lived in long before your arrival, living in a world reserved for those who know their role, you clearly don't belong, and now, while both schools of thought are plenty agreeable, you're likely to err on the side of the former rather than the latter, for the former sees you as the haunted rather than the haunter, the ghost, meaning you're important enough that someone chose to stick around a little while longer, just for you, but being haunted by something is directly inspired by the reasoning for believing in God: finding a reason to fill that empty longing to feel special... and at long last, before the end, the real understanding that believing in God is believing in a ghost.

37

The world was tinted in a murky, bluish-green haze, a thin layer of fog painted over, the rush of a river roaring nearby...everything fell perfectly into place, like an unframed American answer to T.S. Dabo's *The River Seine*, which would be *The River Willamette* in this case. Joseph stumbled blindly towards the sound of water, parted trees with his right arm extended in front of him, his left arm pinned tight to his chest, hand wrapped in a layer of a torn shirt, dark with blood that occasionally dripped to the earth or on some dead leaf of a hibernating tree. He began to notice that he was numb all over again, a tingly-prickly sensation that crawled over both feet, like being stabbed with thousands of little hot knives.

The next thing he realized about his feet was that they suddenly stepped into water. He stopped and crouched low, right hand extended so it would be the first to touch the water. The cold stabbed violently at his fingers which he forced himself to ignore; he cupped the water and brought it up to his eyes which he repeated ten times until he could finally see a bit of the world out of his left eye, his right was shut: burned, leaked. He felt the cold numbness burn bright pink all over his face and felt the jagged piece of wood and graphite stuck in the socket. He walked out of the river, sat down, and cried.

It had all happened so fast.

The last thing Joseph had said to the Brothers was to take their own advice and kill themselves. Then he saw that wild look in Brooks's eye. He wasn't afraid, remembered that, was proud of that. The first move he made was to grab Brody by the neck, a chokehold, and try to force him into a crash. The car swerved twice before Brooks moved in and sunk the pencil into Joseph's right eye. The pencil snapped in half in Joseph's eye socket, causing him to release Brody and let out a soul-piercing scream of pain. He cursed them. Brooks reached into the glove box and pulled out a long, sharp knife, dirtied with blood, and squirmed into the backseat. His movements gave Joseph enough time to remember the promise he made: he can't die here. Won't. Can't. A rush of adrenaline shot through his body, shock nearly setting in, his brain temporarily blacking out the parts that felt pain. He twisted and grabbed the right wrist, which caused Brooks to try and switch the blade to his left hand, during which Joseph was able to punch Brooks in the fucking jaw with his right hand. The knife dropped near Joseph's feet and Brooks tumbled into the backseat, practically onto Joseph, where a wrestling match of sorts occurred, Brody all the while yelling back at them, one hand on the wheel and the other holding a gun in the air. Blood everywhere. Attempts at chokeholds. Brooks came up with the knife, on his stomach on the floor, but was not quick enough as Joseph fell on his back and sunk his teeth into the side of Brooks' neck, chaotically close to the jugular. He sank his teeth as deep as he could into the tough flesh, his teeth entirely unused to the texture, tasting blood, rich and warm, almost puked. He finally felt his hand around the knife handle, could hardly hear a thing with so much close-quarter screaming. He rose up quickly and slid the blade into Brooks' rib cage then pulled it out again. The car had stopped. Joseph made a hasty exit, Brody turning around and firing a shot right as he opened the door, then opening his own door, left leg out when Joseph slammed the door shut on it, thrusting all his weight right into the door, snapping Brody's shin in half. More screams of agonizing pain that never really left him. Joseph, maybe overplaying his hand, opened the door and reached for the gun. In a blind fury, a shot was fired and a bullet went straight through Joseph's left hand. Tough skin and bone and blood and veins. He drove the knife straight through Brody's right forearm, then stumbled away. The car had stopped on the shoulder of an empty highway surrounded by tall, snow-covered trees. Joseph ran. He disappeared into the trees, the screams from The Devil's Twins of Yakima fading into ghostly echoes behind him.

And so he found himself here: half-blind and crying near a partially frozen river that still flowed freely. He heard them first, their voices. It took him a minute to locate the source. His left eye blinked fast through tears, and with every blink the world went completely dark. It took time to adjust. Not far down the river were two men... *fishing* as if it were a fine midsummer day. They bickered loudly back and forth like an old married couple alone in their home, one holding a long fishing pole and the other a net. The one with the net complained that they should have come out yesterday when it was *colder*. The one with the pole disagreed and claimed that the temperature of twenty-eight degrees—which he claimed it was then—was the perfect temperature to catch the beast they were fishing for as it was the recorded temperature when his grandfather and his grandfather's brother caught it sixty-nine years ago today. This went back and forth for longer than it probably should have, until there was a sudden sharp pull on the line of the fishing pole (which was a nothing more than a long, firm tree branch that was finely smoothed down and bound tightly with a thick line) so the men began to pull and pull at it. The one with the net immediately dropped it and wrapped his arms around the other man's waist, lowering his hips into his back, centering his gravity, and fucking pulled. They grunted like animals. There was a dreaded wonderment that filled Joseph almost instantly as he watched, with one eye, these men who were so unaware of him and the traumas he carried and how they might have been lucky enough to be so unaware that such pain existed, leaving him longing for an answer to a question—one he knew he would never have the courage to satisfy himself with realizing any of the possibilities of what should be considered the correct answer to—would he ever be able to enjoy a life such as that? A life so simple? So completely oblivious to the torment and turmoil that stood only a few dozen yards away, and able to live carefree, where the only real worry—if you want to call it that—that pressed them currently was what they were going to do now that they actually caught this monstrous fish, a beast worthy of lore in respects to the likeness of Nessie?

Eventually the men went away, carrying the great fish in the net, one at each end like a harness. Joseph sat under a tree; part of him wanted to move, the other part wanted to stay still. All of him wanted to die. But sure enough there it was again, that voice of his mother in the back of his mind that told him that this place, too, was not a place for the likes of him to die in, that he still had a ways to go yet...but it would be over soon, before he knew it.

38

By some incalculable and astronomical miracle, Bambi and
Joseph arrived at what was once the front porch of their home
at the same exact moment, though it was unknown to Bambi,
who assumed her brother had been home for a few days and
was just walking around until she saw his face: covered with
blood and dirt and dried tears, a broken pencil sticking out of
his right eye and surely more wounds hidden under his
tattered clothes...a complete shell of himself. And to him, the
idea of seeing his sister again was an unfathomable thought,
as his mind was attached to dark and terrible memories that
would haunt him forever, repeating infinitely, and who felt
like he was more or less swimming through the moments in
what was left of his life in a sort of dim purgatory—but Dante
had got it wrong and his divine tragedy was told in reverse:
he started out in paradise, was currently stuck in a hellish
purgatory and would have to wait for only he knew how long
for that first gate of limbo to open, halfway between the
memories of the life behind him and the hell he believed
awaited him ahead...never even considered if others felt this
way about the world, being alive, too. There was no exchange
of greetings, only a build-up of tears in their eyes that

eventually flooded and flowed free like tiny waterfalls down the smooth, pale mountains of their faces.

"I'm sorry," they said tragically at the same time. They paused together and, again, cruelly spoke in unison: "You are?" and painfully ended the duet with: "For what?"

They stood impossibly still, mirrors of one another, before they turned their heads at the scorched pile of wood and ash piled high like black and grey dunes that became smaller and smaller with every eroding gust of wind. It had been more than just a shelter when it still stood, more than walls and a roof, bigger than what the floor design looked like under the rubble; it was something that lived on, inside of them, buried away under a pain that would linger long after the cells died off and were replaced by new cells, reborn, but carried on the pain as if it were the same old cell, like it was fully embedded in them now and as much a part of them as they are of it, as they, them and their pain, can no longer live without one another and if that day was to come sooner or later then that pain that lived within them will be passed on to someone else and they will then harbor the pain until they pass it onto someone else and they pass it onto someone else and so on and so forth. As you see, the pain never really dies—it's a parasite and we're its favorite hosts, human beings, and the parasitic pain will adapt and change into new forms when it enters a new host and will feast and feast, never fulfilled, always lingering like that ghost in the corner of the room that you might be able to block out for one minute but then become haunted by the next...it's been here for long as we have, with us, and it won't leave anytime soon.

A strong, Zephyr-blessed (or cursed?) rush of wind blew through them and rattled their bones, shaking them enough to where they noticed that the rubble was sorted out into piles, like someone thought some things were still salvageable, wasn't much—upon closer examination later they would find a few pictures with minimal burn marks, one Hiro Hachimura original: a black and white picture of an unlabeled bottle of wine, a red, half-empty, a partially empty glass, a person, one young-and-new-to-Washington Karl Müller, face down asleep—drunkenly passed out on the table—titled *Dionysus Prevails,* signed and dedicated to Karl and Ruth on the back, locked in a lockbox along with one photo of them together, when they were both young and still in their homeland, and another of the four of them when they were still new to the whole family thing, a smile on the young parents' faces, the baby boy with his tongue sticking out and drooling and the young girl all smiles but looked like it is a pain to smile at this point as if she felt like she had been doing it for far too long...the photos, all of them, were something that didn't seem real at first, memories so distant they'd for a second believe it was a different family entirely, until they looked closer; the eyes, their windows, told the story of the memory and they swore they could stare at it all day, each face hovering so close to the other and staring at a memory captured by Dr. Kyo Koike; by Hiro Hachimura; by the Seattle Camera Club; by names history allowed you to forget—and crates of wine, untouched by flames, brought up from the cellar and gently placed on the ground by Ruggles Thibodeaux and 'Flip Peoples, who let out joyous cries that gave the illusion of ghosts escaping their bodies from their mouths as if they had suddenly grown tired of haunting them, and evaporated into the world—unknown if they somehow found peace or if they're still here, all around us, haunting from afar—and upon further inspection, you would see that all of them let out tiny ghosts from deep inside, little by little, breath by breath, calling to wonder how many have stayed to haunt us a little more and how many are still inside of us, completely invisible to our eyes, except for that brief moment in the right cold, blended with the world we thought we knew...they look like rain, they look like sunshine, they look like you, they look like me...all these little ghosts.

"Jesus," Ruggles gasped when he and 'Flip were close enough to clearly see Joseph's face. "What—"

"Good lord!" 'Flip yelled.

"—happened?"

Bambi opened her mouth to speak but quickly stopped herself, knew the question was understandably directed towards Joseph, her little brother who looked almost unrecognizable, as he bore gruesome wounds that all could see. What people couldn't see, though, were the wounds that would eventually turn into scars that each of them carried on the inside. Scars so terrible that, now that she thought about it, she likely wouldn't be able to talk about it right away. So why did she instantly feel like she should be the one to respond, like they deserved an answer right fucking now? She had no idea what to say, and the silence made her more and more uncomfortable. Just as she had that conscious slip and noticed that deafening silence that loves to lurk around you and was going to allow it to creep in and break her down, was just so tired, Joseph suddenly spoke:

"It..." He tried a few times to swallow, his voice was dry and hoarse, powering through it somehow, "...did not go, exactly, as we planned."

"You were gone longer than we thought," Ruggles confessed meekly, like he assumed the date upon which they agreed was the part that did not go exactly as planned. "It's April twenty-third."

Gone...for over two months. They suspected it had been that long, or longer, but to hear it as fact...it seemed like it had gone by in a lifetime and in the blink of an eye all at once. Reality had somehow distorted itself in a paradoxical copy of the former reality, or maybe it had been this way all along and they were finally waking up to the true realization, like they had reached a level beyond shock and denial that acted as a key into crossing this portal which was nothing more than floating around in a sea of empty.

"I was with the...the ones who killed Ward and Macy Vernon," Joseph said.

"What?" 'Flip Peoples yelled. "For true?! Where? Who are they!?"

"Why don't we get them inside," Ruggles interjected, grabbing Joseph by the arm as the poor lad was about to collapse. "Out of the cold, some food and water, eh?"

"But of course! Come along! We've had accommodations made after you left! They are ready for you! Come along!"

They managed to pile into 'Flip's spacious Cadillac and drove hastily to the Nyström residence where, inside, at Cade's insistence, was a second bed made up in Cade's room; he had been sleeping on the couch. His old bed and the new one matched with fresh sheets and blankets, and at the foot of each bed, clothes for them, not much but enough, something. All Bambi and Joseph could manage were a few pieces of warm bread each, some cool water, and a small thank-you before they passed out and slept for thirteen hours, during which time 'Flip Peoples had offered a Walla Walla surgeon an undisclosed amount of money to come, quickly, and perform some sort of miracle work on Joseph. The surgeon, Dr. Driscoll Langlais—admittedly a bit past his prime in regards to his profession, so they say, 1942 being his sixty-sixth trip around the sun, officially next month in May, and honestly lacked in proper experience when it came to situations such as this, involving a horrific bodily wound—had served as a medic during the first great war thirty years ago and many of those memories from that time—if not all of them—he'd like very much to forget, if they hadn't already faded away (the words "trench" and "foot" were ghosts that still haunted him; even so, he's never really seen anything that gruesome until Joseph, as anytime a soldier came into the med-tent [he never saw the front lines] he would hide or complain that his liver hurt and let the other surgeons take care of it), so no, when he first heard about the job and the injury he was not enthusiastic at all because he'd become so accustomed to treating the same sort of injuries (hand wounds that ranged from minor cuts all the way to full-blown accidental amputation—that he didn't always stomach, would usually recommend the worst injuries head up to Seattle to see a specialtist—from farmers out in the vineyards, always during harvest season, his busiest time of the year), and because it was April, almost May (and he was the type of person who, nearing sixty-six, would celebrate his birthday for the entire month, even though it fell on the 30th, would tell people the day May began, anytime he'd go out, even at his fucking age: "It's my Birthday Month!" and he'd actually expect anyone who heard to buy him things [drinks] and treat him as though it was his special day, a possible case of Peter Pan syndrome or just goddamn annoyance). How the hell would something that gruesome happen to someone in April? (The month held a certain romantic grip on his heart, not because of the old saying that its showers would bring with it beautiful flowers, though this month, for the most part, lacked rain and was heavier with snow, but because he admired the unpredictability of it, hopeful—as nature does not always cooperate as expected—of the transition of the last of the winter snow melting away and the first bloom coming through with casual grace when the month he was so fond of would bleed into that hopeful, blooming May that were always sure to follow, and with that the end of his leisure months and back to business.) Just didn't make sense to him. And finally, because when he learned it was a procedure on that Joseph Müller kid he spat and said no amount of money could make him help those Nazis. A statement that, upon hearing, lit 'Flip motherfucking Peoples up with a fiery rage that he had not felt since his violent and angsty adolescence, a past he was better off without, as anger like this was so unnatural, yet so human...so for the only time in his life he justified it. He walked out of Dr. Langlais's office and thought that was the end of that, that he would harbor this anger and unleash it on himself later through violent masturbation when, just as that thought occurred, Ruggles Thibodeaux, Cade Nyström, *and* Michelangelo Poletti walked into the office with a real affliction for violence that predominantly protruded from the edges of their eyes, far more intense than anything 'Flip ever felt, thankfully, as it were a tangible, chaotic energy that actually leaped from the windows of their souls and was dying to get a hold of that xenophobe. They knew, of course, that they couldn't fuck him up too bad, he had an operation to perform after all, so as long as he could see and still use his hands...it, the operation, took him longer than it should have. Dr. Langlais blamed it firstly on the gun that Ruggles pointed at him, his trusty .22, the entire time he toiled away at Joseph's eye—saving him from an infection that was about to set in, stitching him up with a bandage, a sort of eye patch—which did cause him to piss himself twice—being forcibly dragged from his office, held at gunpoint and sat (could no longer stand, they fucked up his legs a bit, let's say) in a puddle of piss while he helped—in his dumb fucking mind—the enemy. In the end, Dr. Laglais received no money, 'Flip made sure they got it back and reminded him that he, Dr. Laglais, had said that no amount of money would ever please him, and was practically forced into retirement after Ruggles, Cade, and Michelangelo broke both his arms and hands—post-surgery— in more places than they were aware. They felt it was the right thing to do. You should have heard the shit he talked while performing the surgery with a gun pointed at him—the guy had balls then, piss-stained and all, knew he could say whatever he wanted and they wouldn't kill him. He meant every hateful word. So fuck his xenophobic bones and break them.

The next day, Bambi and Joseph sat silently, alone together, for the better part of an hour before anyone knew that they were awake. Bambi was lost in her thoughts and unable to distinguish what was a dream and what was real, but unwilling to admit that, and Joseph still getting used to half the world being totally black now. It wasn't until after eleven when Cade came to check on them, and, seeing as how they were awake, maybe they'd like some breakfast. They sat at the Nyström family table and stared blankly at blood sausage, fried bacon, perfectly burnt sourdough toast with fresh butter and raspberry jam, two eggs each, sunny-side up, all going cold by the second and everyone gathered around like they were some sort of exhibit. It was Cade who finally broke the silence, unable to contain his concern any longer:

"You've got to eat something, Laura." It was like speaking to a statue. "Laura?" Still, she stared at her food, not even blinking. "Laura? Laura."

"Bambi," Joseph said, breaking whatever spell was temporarily cast over her. She looked up at him. "Bambi."

Was this the first time they spoke at a dinner table?

It was hard to look at her brother, so Bambi looked at Cade. Tears clouded her eyes and those same words she could not remember stuck in her throat and she wanted to claw them out but was blocked because ghosts never really leave, remember?

"Just eat a little bit, here—" Cade stopped, betrayed by the sudden presence of his own tears and the feeling that he was babying her and making her feel small which is the last thing he would ever want to do. Suddenly she took a small bite of toast, like a bird, and there was a silent sigh of relief from everyone in the room. Cade leaned back in his chair like a great weight had been lifted from his shoulders. His eyes went to her, admiring the side of her face. She felt them, but didn't look, was too tired, even after all that sleep. It was deeper than exhaustion.

"I just need time," Bambi was able to whisper.

No one said anything.

"I just need time," she said again. "I...don't know how to say...what it is I..." It was there she paused, unable to determine what to say next: what it is I *want* to say, what it is I *should* say, what it is I *have* to say, what it is I *need* to say.

Cade gently placed his hand on top of hers—she surprised herself by not flinching—and silently let her know that she did not have to say anything to anybody until she felt completely ready. There was a warmness in that touch that sparked or at least made her recognize her appetite more. She took a few more bites and looked over at Joseph, who was chewing but had no look of satisfaction, no look at all really, his face a blank mask, like he was just going through the motions of eating to appease everyone. But it didn't slip by Bambi, who saw in his one good eye a look of despair so deep that it nearly broke her heart and would have totally shattered it had she known that there was nothing she could do to stop him—she may have secretly known it all along, deep in her blood, but hid it from herself, as a way of protection, to make her believe that he still had a chance, something else to fight for now—he was already gone and no matter how much of a fight she put up to save him from himself...

Their final conversation would come later that night, and looking back on it as a memory it was only valuable because it was, in fact, their last conversation, other than that it would have been easily forgotten as not much at all occurred and that was the saddest part of all. Joseph was so broken that he had nothing left to offer in the form of conversations and goodbyes, though he still managed to slip in an apology. Classic.

Bambi had been staring at the ceiling and wishing she was reading a book, but knew that her mind would get too distracted by her thoughts to be able to pay attention, a fact that made her more miserable because all she wanted—needed—was to escape into another world, but she couldn't even if she tried. Joseph got out of his bed and stood by the door for a while.

"Sorry," he said, prompting Bambi to notice him. "If I ever

woke you. I never meant to...I never learned how to control myself."

"Where are you going?"

His back still faced her. "It won't be long."

"What?"

"The time in between."

He left—gently closed the door behind him, a gesture that would eternally echo, soft as a whisper in the depths of her soul—out into the cold April night only to be found the next morning on an ashy pile of rubble in what would have been the floor of his room a few short months ago. It was a macabre sight that—when the tragic news spread like the parasitic gossip everyone would view it as—added more fuel to the Müller fire, forced everyone who knew him to philosophize deeply on how a boy—for that's what they still thought and would always think of him as, a boy, barely over twenty with endless possibilities once at the edges of his fingertips, now forced into a collective imagination of "what could have been"—got dealt such a poor hand that you can't help but understand and sympathize with the decision he made and wonder why he didn't do it sooner? Before he endured all that pain and heartbreak and loss? It seemed a shame. Always too late. To live in denial all that time, hidden under a mask he hardly knew he wore, as it had become such an intricate part of him that it was as if the mask *had* become his face, only to be unveiled before the last of his kind and showered with tears that lacked both shock and surprise, filled instead with obvious anguish and heavy bits of relief and empathy... because he was home now.

39

Frost covered the last remaining Riesling grapes that clung fervently to their twisted, frozen, vines, masking their dark, sugary colors. A great white blanket of snow spread itself over the vineyard and all neighboring vineyards, over every inch of earth until it met the shoreline of the Grand Traverse Bay that bled out into Lake Michigan, which rolled in and out heavily with melancholy onto the sandy, snow-drenched beaches, as if the Great Lake itself wished to be like them: unmoving, at rest.

The end of October, prime harvest season, brought an unannounced snowfall—but hey, that's Northern Michigan for you—which provided a slight detrimental worry to the growers who left grapes like Pinot Noir hanging on the vines which likely would be destroyed by this weather, along with Merlot and Cabernet Franc, which may have been left on to get to that ripeness the grower was after, but now losing sugar, and with that, alcohol, body, life.

Thankfully though, for us, we live on fifty-five acres on Old Mission Peninsula and have forty-five dedicated to growing eight different grapes (nine acres of Blaufränkisch, seven acres of Cabernet Franc, two acres of Merlot, twelve acres of Pinot

Noir, and one acre of Syrah [Shiraz, actually, brought from McLaren Vale, Australia] that grew under a greenhouse-like tent, a canopy, to ensure that the precious fruit could survive, and only three white varietals: four acres of Gewürztraminer, three acres of Pinot Blanc, and seven acres of Riesling) and our harvest team had worked tirelessly to bring everything in *last* week, as our vineyards face East Bay and receive the first day's light and are exposed to it longer, thus accelerating the growth and ripening process by a few weeks.

We had come to Traverse City in the mid-seventies—1975, to be exact—when we were both nearing sixty and ready to settle down to a new view. Always close to the water. The land we purchased was, at that time, pretty damn cheap, and we had done much research into the land itself, the soil, the climate, all that, noting that it sat perfectly on the forty-fifth parallel, an invisible line on the map halfway between the equator and the north pole—the same invisible line travels not just through the Old Mission and Leelanau Peninsula of Michigan but also through Willamette Valley, Oregon/Bordeaux, France/Rhône, France/Piedmont, Italy, to name a few, some of the most prestigious growing regions on the planets, so, even though Michigan's winters may be a little harsher, growing season sometimes shorter for the weather in general chaotic and random (the unofficial state slogan, we would come to learn, was: "Experiencing four seasons in one day, that's Pure Michigan."), but this spot in particular was surrounded by two bays of fresh lake water, and the view was too hard to pass up.

A year after the war ended, we officially married. We thought it best if both names lived on and became Mr. and Mrs. Müller-Nyström. Laura still goes by Bambi now and then but after the wedding she felt sort of officially "grown-up" and wanted to shed the nickname and go more by her real name, had lived in my parent's house till the war ended, always being respectful and grateful for taking her in, as if they could ever turn her away. We would sneak away from time to time to make private memories which we look back on sometimes, together, alone, all the same, thankful they're still there, real. About a year after we eloped we decided to move, and no one stood up in protest against it. Not my parents, none of our friends. They all knew it had to be done. We would have been gone years ago had they not promised my parents to at least wait out the end of the war—which back then would have been foolish as they would have just run off in search of a fresh start somewhere without telling anyone like they could make it happen that quick on their own; instead we played it smart, saved money, and considered a dozen options—which allowed them to give us a proper wedding. Everyone was there: Michelangelo and Emilia Poletti with their happy children Noemi, Teodoro, Vito, and Ciro; Alfonso and Agnese Rossini (the wedding was actually held at the Poletti Villa, the ceremony right in front of the Pinot Grigio vines); Ruggles Thibodeaux and Victoria VanVleet—a true warrior who still harbors pain inside her, like Laura, but two pains, losses, are never the same, and no one copes the same, but the strength she always wears is her own, potent and palpable—who wore a ring given to her by that man who had grown into a that, a man, and learned what it meant when they said it was all finite so hold on tight; 'Flip Peoples and his new wife, Daria, fresh love radiating, the dear friend and colleague of my uncle Mårten-Ludvig Stenberg, who's safe with You, Kasper Lindquist—he who told us about You, those ancient secrets, that I can't let go of, because it's all for her, finding You—with his mouse, Viggo; and somehow, almost impossibly, Hiro Hachimura, who wore a warm smile on a face that said he wouldn't miss this for the world, a smile that tried its best to mask the horrors he witnessed, unaware that everyone there wore the similar masks...all welcomed all the same. It was my father, Mathias Nyström, who walked Laura down the aisle and gave her away to me, an act of kindness that gently pulled at the strings of her heart...mine too...both her and I stood there, all smiles, happy tears, and wondered: if it feels this good, then how good would it have felt had everybody been there instead of just their ghosts?

The first place we moved to, in 1947, was the coastal city of Florence, Oregon, the place Laura and her family went to when she was young, the place where she first saw the natural, neutral connection between river and ocean. Always close to the water. We stayed there for two years. Next stop was Geelong in Victoria, Australia where we stayed peacefully for twenty-six years. Always close to the water. We were both still young and made an honest, quiet living: Laura was a stay-at-home anonymous columnist for the *Geelong Gazette* who wrote under the alias P.H. Dunagan and was a sort of professional advice-giver; people would send letters to the *Gazette*, all their troubles, and the *Gazette* would then send them to her and she would pick a few and answer them to appear in the next day's paper. The idea came about when Laura kept writing to the paper as P.H. Dunagan with complaints on how her neighbors kept asking her things such as: what's the weather was looking like today and tomorrow? Did the lads win the match last night?—like she hadn't just fucking moved here. Sure, it was nice to talk to people and get to know thy neighbor, but when all one side offers is mundane questions that could be easily answered without having to ask out loud, then yeah, it does get a little bit annoying. The *Gazette*, though, explained to her, as if she didn't already know, that all the answers to those questions were in the was paper that they surely received, and sure, she wrote back, that was true, but no one is reading it because it doesn't have anything, really, to do with *them*. The idea was simple, sort of like a community bulletin board that would be updated every day and delivered right to them about their problems and their troubles, and while they're searching for that particular piece (they put purposely put her column near the end), they would pause here and there and find the answers they were looking for: clear skies today, likely that tomorrow, lads took a gutted loss on the pitch last night, 28-14, but they're looking to bounce back next week against the lads from Bendigo. I worked as a postman and one of my routes was to deliver letters to and from our own house, and thus no one at the *Gazette* ever knew the true identity of P.H. Dunagan but kept writing them checks, as their columns started making people who didn't receive a copy go out and buy it themself, the inception of a subscription service—people stopped sharing the *Gazette* with their neighbors as once your question was answered it was like a trophy of sorts and they would hang it on the wall and say: this is when and how the town learned of my bullshit.

In our spare time, Laura and I grew three acres of Pinot Noir and two acres of Chardonnay, enough to harvest a few barrels worth and try our hand at the whole viticulture thing, and found that it must run in Laura's blood as a few vintages ('51 and '52 especially) turned out beyond exceptional to the point where most of the town was buzzing about the stuff, the Pinot Noir mainly, reminiscent to the times back in Walla Walla where people clamored for some of that Müller Riesling or those Nyström Stouts (some of those Müller Riesling that Ruggles and 'Flip had rescued from the cellar were still with us, the others generously shared among those back "home"). Though we found that our Pinot Noir did well, it seemed that Shiraz was going to be the grape of the continent as it thrived in those hotter summers in the regions further from us and the cool coastline. And that was fine with us; we didn't want any of the attention anymore and tried to keep the buzz as minimal as possible, but there was that old saying: wine is meant to be shared.

Back in TC at the end of October 1995, Laura and I are comfortable at home watching the snow fall over their freshly-picked vineyards while they enjoy some warm glögg that I made using a bottle of Blaufränkisch from '92. We sell our harvests to other winemakers at a handsome cost. In return, aside from money, we get cases of the wine made for half-off—we insist on paying for something as we view winemakers as artists, what they are, and want to support some local business, as you should.

Our favorite customer is the winemaker for the third-oldest winery on OMP, out of six, Château de OM, one Shooter Parsons, a kind-eyed brute of a man from Adelaide, Australia who studied viticulture and winemaking at the University of Adelaide and came to Traverse City in 1988 to work in and get a jump on a cool, old-world style climate, could have been the Aussie bit that sold it, though. His Pinot Noirs, truth be told, were outstanding and makes us wonder what a man of his talent would do with the stuff we had down in Geelong back in the day, but he is actually known for his méthode ancestrale, pét-nat sparkling wines, most noticeably the sparkling Riesling, another grape he buys from us, and the classic blanc de blanc style made only from single vintage Chardonnay grapes. Shooter was not only the winemaker at Château de OM—which looked nothing like a château and was actually a giant old barn built back in the late 1880s, redone and painted a fresh white, installed with tall windows to let the sun in and allow a beautiful look of West Bay—but also part-owner. The other owner, Stanford Irving, is more of the business and operation side, though still has a decent knowledge of the art of winemaking. The two met on the local Traverse City men's rugby squad, the TC Blues (Stanford was the scrum-half and Shooter was the fly-half), and formed a sort of brotherly bond (they are actually, unbeknownst to them until only three weeks ago, half-brothers who share the same father neither of them ever met). Over the years they worked at other wineries together, Shooter the assistant winemaker, Stanford just a cellar rat, when they began drawing up a serious business plan on opening their own spot which would become Château de OM. They would plant twenty-eight acres of grapes for their estate wines—fifteen of Cab Franc, eight of Chardonnay, three of Merlot, two of and Pinot Meunier (used solely for blending). Shooter put up just about every dollar he had to his name, got him forty-nine-percent ownership, title of head winemaker, and final say on winemaking decisions as the fifty-one-percent was owned by Stanford Irving and his wife, Blair, who comes from a long line of deep pockets and ties to TC and OMP—her parents, Lorne and Poppy Quincey, claim to be the first to plant vines in the area (Riesling, of course), and say that their blood stood along with the founding father of TC himself, Perry Hannah.

Another favorite of ours, who uses the Blaufränkisch, is Jean-Claude Dejardins, owner and winemaker of Domaine de Jardins, an estate that looks more like a proper French château than Château de OM, like it was actually air-lifted from France and carefully placed just south of Suttons Bay, twenty acres total, the only estate-grown wines being the Pinot Noir, Chardonnay, and Gamay Noir he grows. A Kiwi by birth with some French and African on his father's side, who had moved to TC—technically Suttons Bay—only five years ago and had already established a successful winery and a rugby team—the Leelanau Peninsula All Noirs, a tribute to the All Blacks of his native New Zealand, to rival the Traverse City Blues, and the Old Mission Crushers, established by Shooter and Stanford once Château de OM was up and running and most of their time was spent on OM and not in town, and the newer clubs such as the Petoskey Stones, the Elk Rapids Rouge, and the Northport Wickies whose shielded-badge logo looked nothing like the lighthouse at the end of the Peninsula and more like the Pharos of Alexandria—all before he was thirty-five years old, where his biggest worry was about a dipshit tasting room manager who he should not have to worry about as he, you know, is busy trying to make the fucking wine that the manager he hired is supposed to sell. But that was J.C.'s life, he would tell us when he would stop by for visits—checking on the crops. It could always be worse, he would say. Then we'd get a story that meant something.

We're older now, tired, but we maintain our manners and are always polite and smile and nod in agreement, listening to those who come to us, usually young winemakers who tell us their troubles as if we were their therapists, like she was still writing those anonymous columns, only this time she just had to listen: to the dilemma that is keeping Shooter up at night which was whether or not to capitalize this vintage of Cab Franc, a thing he'd never done before, since Stanford had elected to leave their CF on the vines, thus getting hit by that early snow and them having no estate CF left to sell; or to Jean-Claude, who talks of wanting to fire his tasting room manager, at long fucking last, because of reports of sexual harassment against him from other employees, which is the right decision...but we've more pressing matters on our minds...really don't want to be bothered by problems such as these. Sorry to say.

As we sit together now and stare out our window at the cold waters of the Great Lake and watch at how it chops at itself and rushes onto the gloomy beach only to retreat back out from whence it came and repeat again, waiting for that light, I can sense deep in my bones, in the voice in my head, like she is speaking to me and only me, without words; that she feels, not for the first time, as if she were balancing in between two worlds, as You are, in a way: in the painless present whose days grow shorter with each tick on the metaphorical clock, this present which in itself is a sort of new reality where everything is simple and easy-going and the worst pains we endure are those of minor annoyances from work-related ventures we are quite frankly getting too old to still be in, which sometimes, such as a time like this, cause her (and I, for her) to remember what real problems were: that of the pain-filled past, the second world, the world that will always haunt and feast on her memories and live inside of her like a parasitic, termitic ghost that she tried to bury long ago with all those ashes but forgot that ghosts don't haunt houses, they haunt homes—what we all aim to be, one day, for somebody else, but ultimately and unselfishly for ourself...and yet, still, home is where you feel most haunted because home is inside you—and this feeling, this ghost, flows consistently through her memories and her veins, heavy like the waves before our eyes: constantly crashing and flowing to and fro, trapped in a state of not knowing what side you belong on...who you are...all there is...our last page filling...

A reassuring hand on the shoulder.

We always stayed close to the water...for if and when—

(We don't want to pass our pains onto others. We know what home means now.)

—the ever-waiting Light, a vortex below, rises, for us, from the water. Consuming.

At long last.

"You're home."

"I'm no longer sure which of all the words, images, dreams or ghosts are 'yours' and which are 'mine.' It's past sorting out. We're both being someone new now, someone incredible..."

— Thomas Pynchon, *Gravity's Rainbow*

About Atmosphere Press

Atmosphere Press is an independent, full-service publisher for excellent books in all genres and for all audiences. Learn more about what we do at atmospherepress.com.

We encourage you to check out some of Atmosphere's latest releases, which are available at Amazon.com and via order from your local bookstore:

House of Clocks, a novel by Fred Caron

Comfrey, Wyoming, a novel by Daphne Birkmeyer

The Size of the Moon, a novel by EJ Michaels

Nate's New Age, a novel by Michael Hanson

Relatively Painless, short stories by Dylan Brody

The Tattered Black Book, a novel by Lexi Duck

All Things In Time, a novel by Sue Byers

American Genes, a novel by Kirby Nelson

Newer Testaments, a novel by Philip Brunetti

Hobson's Mischief, a novel by Caitlin Decatur

The Red Castle, a novel by Noah Verhoeff

The Farthing Quest, a novel by Casey Bruce

The Black Marketer's Daughter, a novel by Suman Mallick

This Side of Babylon, a novel by James Stoia

Within the Gray, a novel by Jennifer Ash

Where No Man Pursueth, a novel by Michael E. Jimerson

About the Author

When he's not pouring wine at a vineyard on Old Mission Peninsula, Brian Nisun is working on his next novel while also studying for his Certified Sommelier exam. He grew up in Metro-Detroit and has been living in Traverse City, Michigan since 2019.